MEDEA
AND HER
CHILDREN

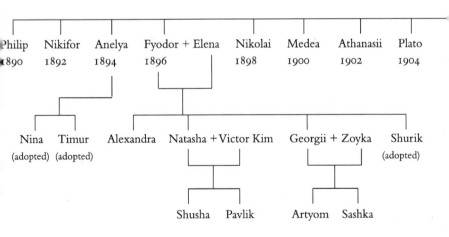

Philip · Nikifor · Anelya · Fyodor + Elena · Nikolai · Medea · Athanasii · Plato
1890 · 1892 · 1894 · 1896 · 1898 · 1900 · 1902 · 1904

Nina (adopted) · Timur (adopted) · Alexandra · Natasha + Victor Kim · Georgii + Zoyka · Shurik (adopted)

Shusha · Pavlik · Artyom · Sashka

THE SINOPLY FAMILY

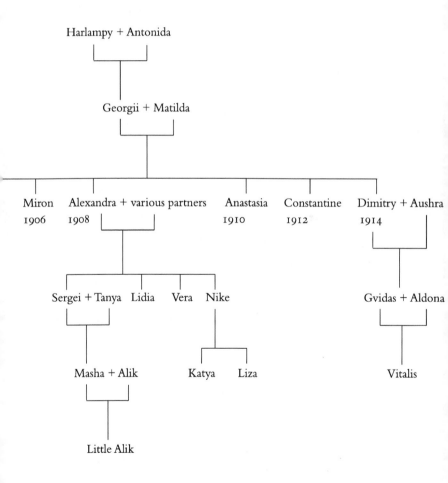

Harlampy + Antonida

Georgii + Matilda

Miron 1906

Alexandra + various partners 1908

Anastasia 1910

Constantine 1912

Dimitry + Aushra 1914

Sergei + Tanya   Lidia   Vera   Nike

Gvidas + Aldona

Masha + Alik

Katya   Liza

Vitalis

Little Alik

MEDEA
AND HER
CHILDREN

LUDMILA ULITSKAYA

Translated from the Russian by Arch Tait

Schocken Books
New York

Originally published in Russia as *Medea I Ee Deti* by Vagrius
Publishing House, Moscow, in 1998. Copyright © 1998 by
Vagrius Publishing House. Copyright © 1996 by L. Ulitskaya.

This translation originally published in hardcover by
Schocken Books, a division of Random House, Inc.,
New York, in 2002.

A Cataloging-in-Publication record has been established
for *Medea and Her Children* by the Library of Congress.
ISBN: 978-0-8052-1144-3

www.schocken.com

Book design by Anthea Lingeman

First Paperback Edition

MEDEA
AND HER
CHILDREN

Medea Mendez had the maiden name of Sinoply and was, if we disqualify her younger sister Alexandra who moved to Moscow in the late 1920s, the last remaining pure-blooded Greek of a family settled since time immemorial on the Tauride coast, a land still mindful of its ties with Ancient Greece. She was also the last member of the family who could speak passably the medieval Pontic Greek which survived only in the Tauride colonies and lagged one thousand years behind modern Greek, the same length of time it was separated from the language of antiquity.

There had long been no one for her to talk to in this worn-out, resonant language from which the majority of philosophical and religious terms had sprung and which retained to this day a pristine literalness in words like *metaphorisis*, which meant "transportation." The other Tauride Greeks of Medea's generation had either died or been deported, but she had lived on in the Crimea by the grace of God, as she supposed, but partly no doubt also because of the Spanish surname bequeathed by her late husband, a jolly Jewish dentist with vices which were minor but not insignificant, and virtues which were great but meticulously concealed.

She was a widow for many years but didn't remarry, ever the stereotypical figure in black, and the color suited her very well. For the first ten years she wore *only* black, then relented and allowed a scattering of white spots or small polka dots, but still on black. She wound a black shawl around her head in a way that was neither Russian nor rustic and fastened it with two knots, one of which hung to the right of her forehead. The long end of the shawl fell away in small classical folds to her shoulders and covered her wrinkled neck. Her eyes were brown, clear, and dry, and the dark skin of her face also fell in small dry folds. When she sat framed in the painted registration window of the Village's little hospital wearing her back-fastening medical white coat, she looked like a portrait Goya had omitted to paint.

She entered notes in the hospital records in large, sweeping handwriting, and she stalked the land in these parts no less sweepingly. She thought nothing of rising before daybreak on a Sunday, putting the twenty kilometers to Theodosia behind her, standing through the liturgy, and walking back home toward evening.

For local people Medea Mendez had long been a part of the landscape. When she was not sitting on her stool in the white frame of the registration window, her dark figure was to be seen out on the eastern hills or on the rocky slopes to the west of the Village. She was not strolling idly but gathering sage, thyme, mountain mint, barberry, mushrooms, and rose hips, and she did not neglect the carnelian, the layered and structured rock crystal, or the dark antique coins with which the dull soil of this minor arena of world history was brimming.

She knew the region near and far like the inside of her own buffet, and not only remembered when and where a useful plant could be picked, but also noted to herself how the green mantle was gradually changing over the decades: the runners of mountain mint advancing down the spring flood channels on the eastern slope of Mount Kiyan; the barberry being killed by a canker which ate away its lower branches; the chicory attacking underground, its rhizomes stifling the delicate spring flowers.

The Crimea had always been generous in yielding up its treasures to Medea, and in return she appreciatively remembered every detail about every one of her finds: the time, the place, and all the nuances of feeling she had experienced, beginning with July 1, 1906, when as a little girl she had discovered, in the middle of the abandoned road to Ak-Mechet, a magic circle of nineteen identical-sized little mushrooms with pale green caps, the local variant of the white boletus. The most wonderful of all her nonedible finds was a flat gold ring with a lackluster aquamarine, cast at her feet by the sea as it was subsiding after a storm, on a little beach near Koktebel on August 20, 1916, her sixteenth birthday. She was still wearing that ring, which had become deeply embedded in her finger and hadn't been taken off for some thirty years now.

She could feel the goodness of this land through the soles of her feet. It was in a poor state now, but she wouldn't have changed it for anywhere else and had been outside the Crimea only twice in her life, for a total of six weeks.

Medea was born in Theodosia, or more precisely in a great rambling house, once well proportioned, in the Greek colony which had long ago been swallowed up by the outskirts of Theodosia. By the time of her birth the house had lost its original elegance, sprouting annexes, terraces, and verandahs to accommodate the rapid expansion of the family in the first decade of a century which had such a cheerful beginning.

The fast growth of the family was accompanied by the slow bankruptcy of her grandfather, Harlampy Sinoply, a wealthy merchant who owned four cargo ships registered to what was then the new port of Theodosia. In old age Harlampy lost his earlier driving and insatiable avarice, and looked on in wonder as fate, which had sorely tried him with many years of waiting for an heir, and visited on him six stillborn babies and innumerable miscarriages from both his wives, prodigally endowed his only son, Georgii (whom he had managed to produce only after thirty years of tribulation), with progeny. Georgii's fruitfulness might, however, have been the merit of Harlampy's second wife, Antonida, who walked in pilgrimage to Kiev in fulfilment of a vow and, having given birth to and weaned her son, fasted in thanksgiving for the rest of her life. Or perhaps his son's fecundity came from the scrawny redheaded bride, Matilda, whom he had brought from Batumi and who entered the house already scandalously with child and thereafter gave birth to a round-headed baby once every two years, in late summer, with unfathomable but cosmic regularity.

As the number of his grandchildren increased, old Harlampy declined, growing kindlier until by the end of his life he had lost along with his wealth even the appearance of a hard, authoritarian, and shrewd merchant. His blood proved strong, however, not yielding to other lines, and those of his posterity who were not winnowed by the bloodthirsty times inherited robustness of spirit and talent from him, while his renowned avarice manifested itself in his male issue in great energy and a passion for building. In the women, as in Medea, it turned into thrift, a heightened interest in material things, and a practical resourcefulness.

Harlampy's family was blessed with so many members it might have provided an admirable subject for a research project into the distribution of hereditary characteristics. No suitably motivated geneticist appeared, but Medea with her characteristic urge to bring system and order to everything, from the teacups on the table to the clouds in the sky, did more than once in her life, for fun, rank her brothers and sisters in order of the gingerishness of their hair—in her mind's eye, necessarily, since she could not remember the entire family gathered together in one place at any one time. One or another of the elder brothers was invariably absent. Their mother's coppery hair was passed on to some extent to all of them, but only Medea herself and the youngest of her brothers, Dimitry, were radically redheaded.

Alexandra's hair was a complex mahogany hue, and even had the highlights of mahogany.

Other family traits were passed on: the stunted little finger of their grandfather was occasionally inherited but, for some reason, only by the boys; their grandmother's earlobe had been attached to her cheek, and she had had exceptional night vision. These features Medea inherited. All these family peculiarities and a few less obvious ones were at play among Harlampy's descendants.

Even the family's fertility split clearly along two lines. Some, like Harlampy, struggled for years to bring forth even the tiniest child. Others, in contrast, scattered copper small change about the world without giving the matter a second thought. From 1910, Harlampy lay in the Greek cemetery of Theodosia, at its highest point, with a view of the bay where right up until the Second World War the last two of his steamers plied the waves, registered as in earlier times to the port of Theodosia.

Many years later the childless Medea would gather her numerous nephews and nieces, grandnephews and grandnieces together in her Crimean home and subject them to quiet, unscientific observation. It was assumed that she loved them all dearly, although what kind of love a childless woman has for other people's children is uncertain. At all events, she took a lively interest in them, and this even grew stronger when she was old.

The seasonal influxes of her extended family were not burdensome to Medea, but neither was her solitude in autumn and winter. The first relatives usually arrived in late April when, after the rains of February and the gales of March, the Crimean spring sprouted from the earth with the lilac blooming of wisteria, the pink of tamarisks, and the Chinese yellow of the broom.

The first group visit was usually brief: a few days around the First of May holiday, with one or two people staying on until the ninth. Then there would be a short break, and in the last ten days of May the girls would congregate: the young mothers with preschool-age children. There were around thirty younger members of the family, so a roster would be drawn up the preceding winter: there was no way the four-room house could accommodate more than twenty people at one time.

The taxi-drivers of Theodosia and Simferopol who transported vacationers for a living were very familiar with Medea's house. Sometimes they gave her family members a modest discount, but specified that they would not take them up the hill if it was raining but set them down in the Lower Village.

Medea did not believe in chance, and her life had been full of portentous meetings, strange coincidences, and surprises which came together in a quite incredible manner. Someone she had once met would return many years later and change the whole direction of her life; threads would be drawn tighter, joined together, would form stitches and make a pattern which became ever clearer as the years passed.

In mid-April the weather seemed to have settled when there was suddenly an extremely dull day. It turned colder and a dreary rain set in which looked as though it might turn to snow.

Medea drew the curtains and turned the light on rather early. She threw a handful of firewood and two logs into her small, clever stove, which used little fuel and gave out a lot of heat, spread out a worn sheet on the table and was in the process of deciding whether to cut it up for kitchen towels or discard the torn middle part and make it into a cot sheet.

At just this moment there came a loud knock at the door. She opened it. Outside stood a young man in a wet coat and a fur hat. Medea took him for one of her less frequently visiting relatives and let him in.

"Are you Medea Georgievna Sinoply?" the young man asked, and Medea realized he was not a relative.

"Yes, I am, although I've borne a different surname these last forty years," Medea smiled.

The young man was pleasant looking, with light-colored eyes and a thin, drooping black mustache.

"Do take your coat off."

"Forgive me, I've landed in on you quite without warning." He shook a dusting of snow from his wet hat. "I am Ravil Yusupov, from Karaganda."

Everything that transpired that evening and night Medea described in a letter to her sister Elena probably written the following day but never sent. Many years later it was to come into the hands of her nephew Georgii and explain to him the riddle of a completely unexpected will which he had found in the same bundle of papers and which was dated April 11, 1976. The letter read:

Dear Elena,

Although I wrote to you only a week ago, something really quite extraordinary has happened, and that is what I would like to tell you about. It is one of those stories which begin a long, long time ago. Of course you will remember Yusim, the carter who drove you and Armik Tigranovna to Theodosia in December 1918. Imagine, his grandson has managed to find me through friends in Theodosia. Isn't it amazing to think that to this day you can find a person in a big city entirely without address books! It is a fairly common story for these parts. They were deported from Alushta after the war, when Yusim had already passed away. Ravil's mother was sent to Karaganda, despite the fact that the father of her little children had died fighting at the front. My young man had known since he was a child what happened (I mean your evacuation), and even remembers the sapphire ring you gave Yusim then in gratitude. Ravil's mother wore it for many years and exchanged it for a sack of flour when the famine was at its worst. But this was only the introduction to a conversation which, I will say frankly, touched me deeply. It brought back memories of things we aren't that keen to remember, the ordeals of those years. Then Ravil revealed that he is a member of a movement for the Tatars to return to the Crimea, and that they long ago began to take official and unofficial measures.

He eagerly asked me in great detail about the old Tatar Crimea. He even produced a tape recorder and recorded me so that his Uzbek and Kazakh Tatars could hear what I had to relate. I told him what I could remember about my old neighbors in the Village, Galya and Mustapha, and Grandfather Akhmet the ditcher who cleaned the irrigation aryks here from dawn to dusk, pulling out every speck of rubbish like a mote from someone's eye. I told him of how the Tatars were deported from here at two in the morning, without being given time to gather their belongings, and how Shura Gorodovikova the Party boss came herself when they were being sent away, and helped them pack their things, and cried buckets, and the very next day had a stroke and had to stop being a boss and hobbled around her land for another ten years with her face twisted and couldn't speak so anyone would understand her. In our region there was nothing like it even under the Germans, although it wasn't Germans but Romanians we had here. I know, of course, they took the Jews, but not in our region.

I told him too about how in 1947, in the middle of August, the order came to cut down the nut groves here which the Tatars had planted. No matter how we begged them, the dimwits came and cut down those wonderful trees, not even waiting for us to gather the harvest. So there the murdered trees lay all along the road, their branches laden with unripened nuts, and then the order came to burn them. Tasha Lavinskaya from Kerch was staying with me at the time, and we sat and cried as we watched that barbaric bonfire.

Thank God, my memory is still good. It retains everything, and we talked beyond midnight and even drank some wine. The old Tatars, you'll remember, wouldn't touch wine. We agreed that the next day I would take him around and show him all there is to see. And then he asked me a secret favor: to buy him a house in the Crimea, but in my name, because apparently houses can't be sold to Tatars. There is a special government decree on the matter which dates back to Stalin's time.

Do you remember, Elena, what the Eastern Crimea used to be like when the Tatars were here? And Central Crimea? What orchards there were in Bakhchisarai! And now as you travel the road to Bakhchisarai, there's not a tree to be seen: they've flattened them all, destroyed the lot. I had just made up a bed for Ravil in Samuel's room when I heard a car drive up to the house. A minute later there was a knock at the door. He looked at me so sadly: "They'll have come for me, Medea Georgievna."

He suddenly seemed terribly tired, and I realized that he wasn't in fact all that young—past thirty probably. He pulled the tape out of the tape recorder and threw it in the stove. "You'll be in trouble, forgive me. I'll tell them I just came in to find a room for the night, no more than that." That tape, with all my long narrative, was gone in an instant.

I went to open the door. There were two men there. One was Petka Shevchuk, the son of Ivan Gavrilovich, a local fisherman. He says to me as brazen as can be it's a passport check to make sure I'm not renting out rooms illegally.

Well, I gave him a piece of my mind. "How dare you come bursting into my house at night! No, I'm not letting out rooms, but just now I do have a guest in the house," and they can take themselves off wherever they like, but not disturb me till morning. That swine dared to come to my house. You may remember I kept our little hospital going all through the war. Apart from me, there were absolutely no medical personnel here. How many furuncles I treated him for, and one was in his ear. I had to lance it. I was scared to death. It was no joking matter, a five-year-old child with all the symptoms of a cerebral lesion, and what was I? A nursing assistant. Think of the responsibility . . . They turned and left, but the car did not drive off. They parked it by the house up the hill.

Ravil, my Tatar boy, smiles serenely: "Thank you, Medea Georgievna, you are unusually courageous. I haven't come across that very often. It's a shame you won't be able to show me the valley or the eastern hills tomorrow. But I will come back here. Times will change, I am sure of that."

I got out another bottle of wine and we decided to forget sleep and talk instead. Then we drank some coffee, and when dawn broke, he had a wash. I baked him a cake and wanted to give him some tinned food from Moscow which I still had from last summer, but he wouldn't take it. He said they would only confiscate it. I saw him to the gate, right to the top. The rain had stopped, the day was so lovely. Petka was standing by his car with the other one next to him. I said goodbye to Ravil. They had the door open already. So there we are, Elena, that's my adventure. Oh yes, and he forgot his fur hat. Well, I thought, fine. Perhaps that means he'll retrace his steps. The Tatars will come back, and I'll be able to return his hat. It would be no more than simple justice. Well, God's will be done. But the reason I am writing to you in such haste is just that, although I have never in my life got drawn into any political shenanigans—

Samuel was the specialist in that—just imagine, perhaps at the end of my life, just when things are getting a bit more relaxed, they might start giving an old woman a hard time. I'd like you to know where to look for me. Oh yes, in the last letter I forgot to ask how you're finding the new hearing aid, although, to tell the truth I'm not sure that most of what people around you say is worth listening to, so you may not have been missing much.

Much love from
Medea

It was the end of April. Medea's vineyard had been pruned, all the neat borders in her vegetable garden were sprouting vigorously, and for the last two days a gigantic flounder some fishermen she knew had brought her had been lying dissected in the fridge.

First to appear were her nephew Georgii and his thirteen-year-old son Artyom. Georgii threw off his rucksack and stood in the middle of the little yard, frowning in the powerful direct sunlight and breathing in the sweet, heavy aroma.

"You could slice it and eat it," he said to his son, but Artyom didn't understand.

"Medea's hanging the washing out over there," Artyom said, pointing.

Medea's house stood in the highest part of the village, but her land was stepped in terraces and had a well at the very bottom of it. There was a rope stretched there between a large nut tree and an old vinegar tree, and Medea, who usually spent her lunch break on household chores, was hanging out the heavily blued laundry. Dark blue shadows played over the light blue line of mended sheets, and they slowly billowed like sails, threatening to slew round and float away into the deeper blue of the sky.

"I should just pack it all in and buy a house here," Georgii thought, climbing down toward his aunt, who hadn't yet noticed them. "Zoyka can do as she pleases. I could keep Artyom and Sashka."

For the last ten years this had been the thought which invariably came into his mind during the first minutes at Medea's home in the Crimea. Medea finally noticed Georgii and his son, threw the last sheet, which she had wrung out tightly, into the empty basin, and straightened up.

"Ah, you're here. I've been expecting you these last two days. Just a minute, just a minute, I'll be up directly, Georgiou."

Only Medea called him that, in the Greek way. He kissed the old woman. She ran her hand over the familiar black hair with its copper tinge, and stroked his son's too.

"He's grown."

"Can I have a look how much, on the door?" the boy asked.

Both sides of the doorframe were scarred with innumerable notches where the children had marked off their height as they grew.

Medea pegged the last sheet and it flew up, half covering a baby cloud which had strayed into the bare sky. Georgii lifted the empty basins and they went back up: Medea in black, Georgii in a crumpled white shirt, and Artyom in his red T-shirt. They were being watched from the neighboring homestead through the stunted, twisted vines of the Soviet farm by Ada Kravchuk, along with her husband Mikhail and their lodger from Leningrad, the white-mouse-like Nora.

"We get dozens of them coming down here! All Mendez's nephews and nieces and what have you. That's Georgii arrived. He's always first," Ada enlightened her paying guest, although whether approvingly or with irritation it was hard to tell.

Georgii was only a few years younger than Ada. They had run around together as children, and now Ada couldn't forgive him for the fact that she had grown old and lost her looks, while he was still young and had only just started going grey.

Nora gazed over enchanted to where the gorge met a hill and there seemed to be a long, meandering fold in the earth, and a house with a tiled roof nestled there in its groin, its clean windows sparkling to welcome three graceful figures, one black, one white, and one red. She gazed appreciatively at the composition and thought with a sublime sense of regret, "If only I could paint that; but no, it's beyond me." She had graduated less than brilliantly from art college, but some of the things she painted came out well: watercolors of ethereal flowers, phloxes, lilacs, or artless bouquets of wildflowers.

Even now, barely arrived for a holiday, she had had her eye caught by the wisteria and was looking forward to putting just the racemes, quite without leaves, into a glass jar on the pink tablecloth, and when her daughter was having her daytime nap, she would sit down to draw them in the rear courtyard. However, this curve of space with its primeval bend stirred her, urging her to paint it even though she thought it more than she could convey. Meanwhile the three figures had climbed up to the house and disappeared from view.

In the little square halfway between the verandah and the summer kitchen, Georgii was unpacking two boxes he had brought and Medea was deciding what should be put where. It was a ritual moment. Every new arrival brought presents, and Medea received them as if not for herself but on behalf of the house.

Four pillow slips, two plastic bottles of imported washing-up liquid, some household soap which had been unobtainable last year but had reappeared this year, some tins, coffee—the old lady was pleasantly excited by it all. She put it away in the cupboards and dressers, told Georgii not to open the second box before she returned, and hurried off back to work. The lunch break was over and she didn't usually allow herself to be late.

Georgii ascended to the highest point of his aunt's domains, where the wooden hut of the toilet erected by the late Mendez rose like a watchtower. He went inside and sat down without the least need on the smoothly planed wooden seat. He looked around. There was a bucket of ash with a broken scoop beside it, while a faded cardboard notice on the wall gave instructions for use of the toilet written with his characteristic wry humor by Mendez himself. It concluded with the words, "When departing, look back to ensure that your conscience is clean."

In a contemplative mood Georgii looked over the short door, which shut off only the lower part of the toilet, into the rectangular window formed above it and saw the twin mountain ranges falling quite steeply away to a distant scrap of sea and the ruins of an ancient fortress visible only to a keen eye and even then only on a clear day. He loved looking at this land, with its weathered mountains and its rounded foothills. It had been Scythian, Greek, Tatar, and although now it was part of the Soviet farming system and had long been languishing, unloved and slowly dying from the ineptitude of its masters, history had not forsaken it but was hovering in this blissful springtime, every stone, every tree reminding him of its presence. Medea's relatives had long ago reached consensus that the best view in the world was to be seen from her lavatory.

Just outside the door Artyom was dancing from one foot to the other, waiting to ask his father a question which he knew would get him nowhere right now but which, when his father did finally emerge, he asked nevertheless, "Dad, when can we go to the sea?"

The sea was a fair distance from here, which was why no tourists stayed in the Lower Village, let alone the Upper Village. You had either to take the bus to the municipal beach at Sudak or walk to the coves twelve kilometers or more away, a major expedition which could last for several days and involve camping.

"Just grow up!" Georgii snapped back. "This is no time to be thinking about the seaside. Go and get yourself ready, we're going to the graveyard."

Artyom didn't want to go to the graveyard, but now he had no choice and went to put on his sneakers. For his part, Georgii took a canvas bag and put a German sapper's spade in it. Then he hesitated over whether or not to take a tin of silver paint and decided to leave this time-consuming chore for the next occasion. He took down a faded hat from a hook in the shed, part of a Central Asian soldier's uniform which he had brought here once himself, banged it on his knee, releasing a cloud of fine dust, and, after locking the door of the house, popped the key in its special place, his heart warming in passing to the triangular stone with its double point, which he remembered from his childhood.

Georgii had been a geologist and loped along with an easy professional gait. Artyom scurried behind him. Georgii didn't look around. He could see Artyom rushing along, breaking into a run, with eyes in the back of his head.

"He isn't growing. He's going to be like Zoyka," Georgii thought with a familiar pang of regret.

His younger son, three-year-old Sashka, was much more to his liking, with a scowling fearlessness and indeflectable stubbornness which suggested he would develop into someone much more unambiguously masculine than his firstborn, with his diffidence and girlish chatter. Artyom for his part worshiped his father, was proud of his so evident manliness, and was already coming to realize that he would never be as strong, steady, and confident; and the sweetness of his love for his father had an aftertaste of bitterness.

But right now Artyom was feeling as good as if he had succeeded in persuading his father to take him to the sea. He himself didn't fully understand that what mattered to him was not going to the sea but stepping out together with his father on this road, which had not yet become dry and dusty but was fresh and young, and just walking along with him whatever the destination, even to the graveyard.

The graveyard sloped up from the road. Above was the ruined Tatar section with what remained of the mosque. The eastern slope was Christian, but after the deportation of the Tatars, Christian burials had begun to creep over onto Tatar territory, as if even the dead were involved in depriving them of their land.

All the Sinoply forebears had been laid to rest in the old Theodosia cemetery, but by this time it was closed and in part even demolished, and Medea had buried her Jewish husband here with an easy mind, a good distance from her mother. Redheaded Matilda, a good Christian in every respect, was zealously Orthodox, had no time for Muslims, feared the Jews, and had an aversion for Catholics. Her views on sundry Buddhists, Taoists, and the like are not known, if indeed she had ever heard of them.

Over the grave of Medea's husband stood an obelisk with a star on its point and an inscription in flattened letters on the pedestal: "Samuel Mendez, Soldier of the ChON Special Detachments, Party Member from 1914. 1890–1952." The inscription was in accordance with the wishes of the deceased, expressed long before his death, soon after the war. Medea had amended the symbolism of the five-pointed Soviet star, silvering not only it but also the point of the obelisk to which it was attached, with the result that it acquired a sixth, inverted ray and looked more like the Christmas star as depicted on pre-Soviet greeting cards and also hinted at more ancient associations.

To the left of the obelisk stood a small stele with the oval photograph of round-faced little Pavlik Kim, with his clever, narrow, smiling eyes, Georgii's nephew who had drowned in 1954 on the beach at Sudak in front of his mother, father, and grandfather, Medea's older brother, Fyodor.

Georgii's critical scrutiny failed to find anything out of order. As usual, Medea had beaten him to it. The railing was painted and the flower border dug over and planted with wild crocuses taken from the eastern hills.

For the sake of something to do, Georgii firmed the edge of the border, then wiped the blade of the spade, folded it, and threw it in the bag. Father and son sat for a time on the low bench, and Georgii smoked a cigarette. Artyom did not interrupt his father's silence, and Georgii placed a hand on the boy's shoulder in gratitude.

The sun was declining toward the western ridge, aiming at a gully between the rounded Twin Hills like a billiard ball heading into a pocket. In April the sun set between the Twins: the September sun disappeared behind the horizon, slitting its belly on the pointed hat of Mount Kiyan.

Year by year the springs were running dry, the vineyards dying, the land falling into decay, a land he had hiked over as a boy, and only the outlines of the hills maintained the familiar structure of the region. Georgii loved them as one can love a mother's face or the body of a wife: by heart, with your eyes closed, for all time.

"Let's go," he said abruptly to his son, and began the descent to the road, striding in a straight line, oblivious of the broken slabs with their Arabic script.

It seemed to Artyom as he looked down that the grey road below was moving, like an escalator in the underground, and he stopped short for a moment in astonishment. "Dad!" Then he laughed out loud: it was the sheep coming up, blocking the road with their brown mass and spilling over onto the shoulder. "I thought the road was moving." Georgii smiled indulgently.

They watched the flowing of the leisurely river of sheep and were not the only people observing the road. Some fifty meters away two girls were sitting on a knoll, a teenager and one who was only little.

"Let's walk around the side of the flock," Artyom suggested.

Georgii nodded agreement. As they passed close to the girls, they saw that it was not the sheep they were staring at but something they had found on the ground. Artyom craned his neck: between two dry runners of a caper bush a snake skin was standing straight up. It was the color of an old man's nail, half transparent, twisted in places, here and there it had split, and the little girl, afraid to touch it, was prodding it apprehensively with a twig. The teenager proved to be a grown woman. It was Nora. Both of them were fair-haired, both were wearing light head scarves, long colorful skirts, and identical blouses with pockets.

Artyom squatted down beside the snake skin too. "Dad, was it poisonous?"

"A racer," Georgii said, taking a close look at it. "Constrictor. Lots of them around here."

"We've never seen anything like it," Nora said with a smile. She recognized him as the man from this morning, the figure in the white shirt.

"I once found a snake pit here when I was a child," Georgii said, picking the rustling skin up and spreading it out. "This one is still fresh."

"It's thoroughly nasty," Nora said, shuddering.

"I'm scared of it," the girl said in a whisper, and Georgii noticed that, with their round eyes and little pointed chins, mother and daughter bore a comical resemblance to a pair of kittens.

"What sweethearts," Georgii thought, and put their scary skin down on the ground. Then he asked, "Who are you staying with?"

"Aunt Ada," the woman answered without taking her eyes off the snake skin.

"Ah," he nodded, "we'll be seeing you then. Come and visit us. We live over there." He gestured in the direction of Medea's farm and, without looking around, ran on down. Artyom bounded after him.

The flock of sheep had meanwhile passed by, and only an *arrière-garde* sheepdog, totally uninterested in the passersby, trotted along the road covered in sheep droppings.

"He's got big legs, like an elephant," the girl said damningly.

"He's nothing like an elephant," Nora protested.

"I didn't say he is, just his legs are," the girl insisted.

"If you really want to know, he's like a Roman legionary." Nora trod resolutely on the snake skin.

"Like what?"

Nora laughed at her silly habit of talking to her five-year-old daughter as if she were a grown-up, and corrected herself. "He doesn't really look like a Roman legionary either, because they shaved and he has a beard."

"And legs like an elephant."

Late in the evening of that day, when Nora and Tanya were sound asleep in the little cottage they had been allotted and Artyom was curled up like a cat in Mendez's room, Medea was sitting with Georgii in the summer kitchen. She usually started using it from the beginning of May, but spring had come early this year. The weather had become really quite warm in late April, and she had opened up the kitchen and cleaned it thoroughly even before her first visitors arrived. It got colder toward evening, however, and Medea put on a worn sleeveless velvet jacket with a fur lining. Georgii donned a Tatar robe which had been serving all Medea's family members for many years now.

The kitchen was constructed of natural stone after the manner of a clay saklya. One wall was built into the hill where the slope had been dug out, and low, irregularly shaped windows had been made in the side walls. A hanging oil lamp cast a dim light over the table, and in its circle stood one last bottle of homemade wine which Medea had been keeping for just this occasion and an already opened bottle of her favorite apple vodka.

A slightly odd routine had long ago been established in the house: they usually had supper with the children between seven and eight, put them to bed early, and then came together again in the night for a late meal which was as bad for the digestion as it was good for the soul. Now, at a late hour, having finished numerous chores around the house, Medea and Georgii were sitting in the light of the oil lamp and enjoying each other's company. They had a lot in common: both were agile, quick on their feet, appreciated small pleasures, and brooked no interference in their private lives.

Medea set a plate of the fried flounder on the table. Her generous nature was amusingly combined with parsimony: her helpings were invariably slightly smaller than one might wish, and she was fully capable of refusing a child a second helping with a dismissive "That's quite sufficient. If you aren't full, take another piece of bread."

The children soon got used to this strange leveling down of all who ate at her table, and relatives who didn't like the way she ran her house didn't come back.

Propping her head up with her hand, she observed Georgii adding a small log to the open hearth, a primitive approximation to a fireplace.

A car drove along the upper road, stopped, and gave two hoarse honks. It was the night post. A telegram then. Georgii went up. He knew the postwoman, but the driver was new. They exchanged greetings and she gave him the telegram.

"Your family coming?"

"Yes, it's that time already. How is your Kostya?"

"Well, how would he be? Half the time he's drunk and the rest he's ill. He really knows how to live."

Georgii read the telegram by the light of the headlamps: "ARRIVING THIRTIETH NIKE MASHA CHILDREN."

He placed the telegram before Medea. She read it and nodded.

"Well, Auntie, how about that drink?" He unscrewed the vodka bottle and poured them both a glass.

"What a pity," he thought, "that they're coming quite so soon. It would have been good to have Medea to myself for a bit longer."

All her relatives liked having Medea to themselves.

"Tomorrow morning I'll run an overhead cable through," Georgii said.

"Come again?" Medea asked, puzzled.

"I'll run the main electricity through to the kitchen," Georgii elaborated.

"Yes, yes, you've been meaning to do that for a while," Medea recalled.

"Mother asked me to have a word with you," Georgii began, but Medea wanted nothing of this long-familiar topic.

"Here's to your stay, Georgiou," she said, taking up her glass.

"This is the only place I really feel at home," he said, as if complaining.

"And that's why every year you bother me with this foolish talk," Medea grunted.

"Mother asked—"

"Yes, I got her letter. It's all nonsense, of course. The winter is over, there's the summer to look forward to. I've no intention of living in Tashkent either in the winter or in the summer. I don't invite Elena to come and stay here. At our age you don't go to live in a new place."

"I was there in February. Mother's grown older. It's impossible to speak to her on the telephone now. She can't hear. She's reading a lot, even the newspapers, watching television."

"Your great-grandfather read all the newspapers too. Mind you, there weren't so many of them in those days." They were silent for a long time.

Georgii threw a few more sticks on the fire, and they crackled and lit up the kitchen.

What a good life he could have here in the Crimea, if he could just make up his mind to write off these ten lost years, the discovery he had never made, the dissertation he had never finished and which sucked him into itself like an evil quagmire if he went anywhere near it. And yet, no sooner were Akademgorodok and that moldering pile of papers out of sight than his dissertation contracted into a dark little lump which he tended to forget. He should build a house here. He knew the top officials in Theodosia—they were all the children of friends of Medea's. He could build it at Atuzy or on the road to Novy Svet. He'd seen someone's gaunt, half-ruined dacha there. He should find out whose it was.

Medea was thinking along the same lines. It was him, Georgii, she would like to see come back here, so that the Sinoply family should again be living in these parts.

They drank the vodka slowly, the old woman dozing off and Georgii mulling over how to make an artesian well: it would be good if he could get hold of an industrial drill.

CHAPTER 2

Elena Stepanyan, Georgii's mother, belonged to a highly cultured Armenian family and had had no expectation at all of becoming the wife of a rather simple Greek from a suburb of Theodosia, the elder brother of her bosom schoolmate.

Medea Sinoply was the star in the firmament of the girls' grammar school: her exemplary exercise books were to be shown to future generations of school students. The girls' friendship began with covert but intense rivalry. That year, 1912, the Stepanyan family had not left to spend the winter in St. Petersburg as they usually did, because Elena's younger sister, Anait, was suffering from a chest complaint. The family stayed behind to winter in their dacha at Sudak, and Elena and her governess spent the whole year in Theodosia, living in a hotel. She attended the girls' school and provided a formidable challenge to Medea's reputation as its cleverest pupil.

Plumpish and affable, Elena didn't seem flummoxed in the least and indeed appeared not to be competing with anyone. It was behavior explicable as angelic magnanimity, or satanic pride. Elena didn't care two hoots about her successes: the Stepanyan sisters had received a good education at home and had been taught French and German by governesses. They had, moreover, spent their early childhood in Switzerland, where their father had held a post in the diplomatic service.

Both Medea and Elena finished the third grade with top marks in all subjects, but there was nevertheless a difference between their marks. Elena's were effortless, with plenty in reserve:

Medea's were the hard-won product of sweat and toil. For all the unequal weight of their marks, they received identical awards at the prize-giving at the end of the year: dark green volumes of the selected works of Nekrasov, with gold lettering on the cover and a calligraphic inscription on the flyleaf.

The day after school ended, at about five in the evening, the entire complement of the Stepanyan family drove up unannounced to the Sinoply mansion. All the women of the house, with Matilda at their head, her by now somewhat faded hair tidied under a white head scarf, were drawing out the dough for baklava beside a large table in the shade of two old mulberry trees. The easier part of the procedure, performed on the table itself, had been completed and now they were teasing out the edges of the dough on the backs of their hands. Medea was taking a full part in this, together with her sisters.

Madame Stepanyan threw up her hands. When she was a child in Tiflis, they had made baklava in exactly this way.

"My grandmother could do it better than anyone else!" she exclaimed, asking for an apron.

Stepanyan *père*, smoothing his greying mustache with one hand, observed the women enjoying their work with a benevolent smile, admiring the quick movements of their buttered hands in the dappled shade, and the light and delicate way they tugged the leaf of dough.

Afterward, Matilda invited them up to the terrace, and they drank coffee with candied fruits, and Armik Tigranovna again melted at a childhood memory of this dry allotrope of jam. Their shared culinary preferences, which had Turkish roots, disposed the illustrious lady even more in favor of this hardworking and united family, and the project which had initially struck her as dubious, of inviting a little-known girl from the family of a port mechanic to be the young companion of her daughter, seemed now to be eminently sensible.

The proposal came as a surprise to Matilda but was flattering, and she promised to consult her husband that very day. This evidence of proper matrimonial respect in such a simple family won Armik Tigranovna over even more.

Four days later Medea and Elena were packed off to Sudak, to a splendid villa on the coast which stands to this day, refurbished now as a sanatorium, not too far from the Upper Village to which many years later the common descendants of Armik Tigranovna and red-haired Matilda, who had teased out the baklava dough so deftly, would come to stay.

Each of the girls found perfection in the other. Medea appreciated the aristocratic directness and radiant kindness of Elena, and Elena greatly admired Medea's fearlessness, her self-reliance, and a particular womanly giftedness of her hands, partly inherited, partly learned from her mother.

At night, lying on their firm, medically approved German folding beds, they engaged in long, deeply meaningful conversations and retained from that time for the whole of the rest of their lives a deep emotional bond, although in later years they were barely able to recall what it was that they had talked about so confidentially until dawn.

However, Medea distinctly remembered Elena telling the story of how one night when she was ill she had seen a vision of an angel against the background of a wall which suddenly became transparent, and beyond which she could see a young, brightly lit forest; and what impressed themselves on Elena's memory were Medea's tales of the numerous finds in which her life was so rich. She went on to amply demonstrate her talent that summer by assembling a whole collection of Crimean gemstones.

One further incident they remembered was a fit of laughter which overcame them one night when they imagined their singing teacher, an affected young man with a limp, marrying the headmistress, a stern, enormous woman before whom even the flowers in the window boxes trembled.

When autumn came, Elena was moved to St. Petersburg, and that was the beginning of a correspondence which, with a few breaks, had already lasted more than sixty years. For the first few years they wrote to each other exclusively in French, which in those years Elena wrote considerably better than Russian. Medea made no small effort to achieve the same degree of fluency her friend had acquired strolling along the shores of Lake Geneva with her governess. The girls, following the intellectual fashion of those years, confessed their willful thoughts and intentions to each other (". . . and I suddenly felt a strong desire to hit her on the head! . . . I knew the story of the inkwell, but said nothing, and I think that was a real deception on my part . . . and Mama to this day is convinced that Fyodor took the money, and I could hardly keep myself from saying that Galya had done it . . ."). And all this in French.

This touching baring of souls was abruptly interrupted by Medea's letter of October 10, 1916. The letter was written in Russian and was short and to the point. It communicated the information that on October 7, 1916, the ship *The Empress Maria* had been blown up in the vicinity of the Bay of Sebastopol and that among the casualties was Georgii Sinoply, ship's mechanic. Sabotage was suspected. The circumstances of a war which passed smoothly over into revolution and a chaotic civil war in the Crimea made it impossible to raise the ship at the time of its sinking, and only three years later, already in Soviet times, did further investigation show that an explosive device had indeed been placed in the ship's engine. One of Georgii's sons, Nikolai, was a member of the team of divers working to raise the sunken vessel.

That October, Matilda was about to give birth to her fourteenth child, who had decided to be born not in August like all her other children but in mid-October. Ten days after the loss of Georgii both of them, Matilda and her little pink-headed girl, followed him in death.

Medea was the first to learn of her mother's death. She went to the hospital in the morning to be met by Fatima the nurse, who stopped her on the stairs and said in the Crimean Tatar language which many inhabitants of the Crimea knew in those days, "Don't go in there, my dear, go and see the doctor. He is expecting you."

Dr. Lesnichevskii came out to see her, his face wet with tears. He was a plump little old man; Medea was taller than him by a head. He said, "My dear, dear child!" and reached up to pat her head. He and Matilda had begun their complementary labors in the same year, she giving birth to babies and he running the obstetrics department, and he had delivered all her babies himself.

That left thirteen of them, thirteen children who had just lost their father and not yet come to terms with the reality of that death. The symbolic funeral for sailors who died at sea, with an orchestra and volleys of gunfire, had seemed to the younger children to be some kind of military entertainment, like a parade. In 1916 death had not yet become as cheapened as in 1918 when the dead were buried in pits, barely clothed and without coffins. Although the war had been going on for a long time, it was far away, while here, in the Crimea, death was still an individual matter.

Matilda was dressed in her finest, her strident hair covered in black lace and her unbaptized little girl laid beside her. Her older sons bore the coffin first to the Greek church and then on to the old graveyard, to rest beside Harlampy.

Even the youngest child, two-year-old Dimitry, remembered his mother's funeral. Four years later he told Medea about two things which had made an impression on him that day. The funeral was held on a Sunday, and a wedding had been scheduled in the church for an earlier hour. On the narrow road leading from the church, the wedding party encountered the funeral procession. There was an awkward moment before those carrying the coffin had to step aside onto the shoulder in order to let the car through, on the back seat of which there sat in glory, like a fly in sour cream, a frightened dark-haired bride in a white cloud of wedding dress with a bald bridegroom beside her. This was almost the first car in the town and belonged to the wealthy Muruzi family, and it was green. Dimitry described the car to Medea. "It really was green," she recalled. The second incident was puzzling. The boy asked her what those white birds were called which were sitting beside mother's head.

"Seagulls?" Medea asked in surprise.

"No, one was big and one was little, and they had different faces, not like seagulls have," Dimitry explained.

Beyond that he could remember nothing. That year Medea was sixteen. There were five children older than her and seven younger. Two were missing that day, Philip and Nikifor. They were both away at the war. Both were later killed, one by the Reds, the other by the Whites, and throughout her life Medea wrote their names on the same line on the requiem slip.

Sophia, Matilda's younger widowed sister, came from Batumi for the funeral and thought it would make sense for her to take the two older boys back with her. Since her husband's death she had had a large farm to cope with, and she and her three daughters were barely managing. In the not-too-distant future, fourteen-year-old Athanasii and twelve-year-old Plato would be growing into the men she so much needed in her household.

They were not, however, destined to revive the fortunes of their aunt's farm, because two years later Sophia wisely sold what remained of her property and took all the children first to Bulgaria and later to Yugoslavia. In Yugoslavia, Athanasii, still a callow young man, became a novice in an Orthodox monastery and moved from there to Greece where all trace of him was lost. The last anyone heard was that he was living in the mountains of Meteora, which nobody knew anything about. Sophia, her daughters, and Plato finally put down roots in Marseilles, and the summit of her achievement was a little Greek restaurant built up from retail sales of oriental sweetmeats, in particular baklava, the dough for which her busy, ugly daughters were adept at drawing out. Plato, the only man in the house, really was its main support. He saw his sisters married, saw his aunt buried just before the Second World War, and only after the war, when already by no means a young man, married a Frenchwoman and fathered two Frenchmen with the jolly surname of Sinoply.

Ten-year-old Miron was taken by a relative from the Sinoply side, the very charming Alexander Grigorievich, who owned the Diamonds café in Koktebel. He had come to Matilda's funeral with no intention of taking new children into his home, but his heart softened and he did. The boy died a few years later after a short, incomprehensible illness.

A month later Anelya, Matilda's older sister, whom people considered the most fortunate of them all, took Nastya to her home in Tbilisi where she lived with her husband, a musician of some renown at that time. She had intended to take the youngest boys as well, but they howled the house down, and it was decided to leave them with Medea for the time being. Eight-year-old Alexandra also stayed with Medea. Alexandra had always been very attached to her, and of late hadn't strayed from her side.

Anelya was perplexed: how could she leave three small children in the hands of a sixteen-year-old girl? At this point old

Pelagea, their one-eyed nurse, intervened. All her life she had worked in their house, and she had been a distant relative of Harlampy.

"For as long as I am alive, let the littlest ones grow up in this house."

And that was how everything was decided.

Some time later Medea received three letters simultaneously from St. Petersburg: from Elena, Armik Tigranovna, and Alexander Ashotovich. His letter was the shortest: "Our whole family deeply condoles with you in the great sorrow that has befallen and asks you to accept the little help we can offer in this hour of need."

The "little help" proved to be a very considerable sum of money for those times, half of which Medea spent on a cross of brittle black marble into which were incised the names of her mother and of her father, whose body had dissolved in the pure and potent waters of the Pontus Euxinus, which had received so many of the Sinoply family's seafaring men.

It was there, in the shadow of the wild olive tree planted on Harlampy's grave, during the revolutionary holidays of early November 1926, that Medea nodded off on a bench and saw all three of them: Matilda in a halo of red hair, not gathered in a bun as when she was alive but magnificently standing up full length on her head; with a little, naked girl with a pink head in her arms, not newborn but for some reason three years old; and her father, grey haired, with a completely grey beard and looking much older than Medea remembered him, to say nothing of the fact that he had never had a beard while alive.

They radiated love toward her but said nothing, and when they disappeared, Medea knew that she had not been dozing. At all events, she was not conscious of any transition from sleeping to wakefulness, and she sensed a wonderful resinous aroma in the air, dark and ancient. Inhaling the fragrance, she guessed that their appearance, so ethereal yet so solemn, was to thank her for having kept the little ones from harm, and as it were to release her from the authority she had voluntarily assumed so long ago.

Some time passed before she could describe this extraordinary occurrence in a letter to Elena. "Several weeks have passed already, Elena, during which I have been quite unable to sit down to write you a letter describing a very unusual mystical experience."

After that she slipped into French. All the Russian words she could have used, like "vision," "apparition," or "miracle," seemed completely unsuitable, and it was easier to resort to a foreign language which didn't carry the same plethora of overtones.

While she was writing the letter, there floated in through the window the same resinous aroma which she had breathed in at the graveyard.

"*Qu'en penses-tu?*" she concluded in her calligraphic handwriting, whose French variant was more angular and decisive.

Their letters spent a long time being shaken around in tarpaulin mail sacks in postal carriages, and the correspondence lagged two or three months behind life. Three months later Medea received a reply. It was one of the longest letters Elena wrote, and it was written in the schoolgirl handwriting so similar to Medea's own.

She thanked her for the letter and wrote that she had shed many tears recollecting those terrible years when it had seemed that everything was lost. Further, Elena confessed that she herself had experienced a similar mystical encounter on the eve of the family's hasty evacuation on the night of November 17, 1918.

Three days before that, Mama suffered a stroke. She looked terrible, much worse than when you saw her three weeks later when we reached Theodosia. Her face was blue, one eye was staring up behind the eyelid, we were expecting her to die at any minute. There was shooting throughout the city, and at the port the military-headquarters staff and the civilian population were embarking at a furious pace. As you know, Papa was a member of the Crimean government, and it was quite impossible for him to remain behind. Arsik was suffering one of his endless angina attacks and Anait, who had always been so full of joy and happiness, just couldn't stop crying. Father was spending all his time in the town, returning for just a few minutes, laying his hand on Mama's head and going off again. I told you all this before except, perhaps, for the most important thing.

That evening I put Arsik and Anait to bed, lay down next to Mama, and immediately drifted off. The rooms were all connecting, in enfilade, and I mention this advisedly because it is relevant. Suddenly, in my sleep, I heard someone coming in. "Father," I thought, and didn't realize straight away that whoever it was had come in through the right-hand door, from inside the apartment, whereas the entrance from the street was to the left. I meant to get up, to get tea for Father, but I felt fettered, I couldn't move at all. Father, as you will remember, was not tall, yet the person standing by the door was a big man and, as it seemed to me, wearing a dressing gown. I could only vaguely make out an old man whose face was very white and seemed to be shining. I was scared but also, can you believe it, very curious. I realized this was someone close, a relative, and immediately someone seemed to say aloud to me, "Shinararyan." Mama had told me about one amazing branch of her ancestors who built Armenian churches. He somehow glided over to me and said quite clearly, in a singsong voice, "Let them all leave, but you, maid, stay behind. You will go to Theodosia. You have nothing to fear."

And then I noticed that he wasn't a complete person but only the upper part, and below was just mist, as if the specter hadn't had time to form completely.

And that is how everything turned out. We parted in early morning, weeping absolute buckets. They left on the last steamer, and Mama and I stayed behind. Twenty-four hours later the city was taken by the Reds. In those dreadful days, when people were being murdered and shot by firing squads, nobody touched us. Yusim, the carter of the late princess in whose palace we were living all that time, first took Mama and me away to a suburb to his relatives, and a week later he put us in a phaeton and took us away from there. We were two weeks on the road to Theodosia, and you know everything about that journey. I had the feeling as I was traveling back to you that I was coming home, but my heart stopped when we saw that the gates of your house were boarded up. I didn't guess at first that you had started using the side entrance.

Neither Mama nor Papa have ever appeared to me even in a dream—probably because I sleep too soundly: you simply wouldn't get through to me. What a joy you have been given, Medea, receiving such a live greeting from your parents. Don't be disturbed, don't trouble yourself with questions of why or wherefore. We'll never guess the answer ourselves anyway. Do you remember reading me your favorite passage from St. Paul about seeing through a glass darkly? Everything will become clear with time, or outside of time. In my childhood, in Tbilisi, the Lord lived in our house alongside us, the angels walked in our rooms, but here in Asia everything is different. He is far away from me, and the church here feels empty. But it is a sin to complain. All is well. Natasha has been ill but is almost completely recovered now; she's just coughing a bit still. Fyodor has gone off on an expedition for a week. I have some exciting news: I'm going to have another baby, very soon now. There is nothing I so dream of as your coming to see us. Perhaps you could just pack the boys' things and come in the spring?

CHAPTER 3

Medea always got up early, but this morning it was Artyom who was first out of bed. The sun was not yet bright, the morning rather pale with patches of shining mist, and cool. A few minutes later, roused by the noise of his son washing under the tap, Georgii emerged. This time Medea was the last to rise.

Taciturn by nature, Medea was particularly short on conversation in the mornings. Everyone knew this and saved up their questions for her until evening. This morning too she gave only a nod and went off to the toilet, and from there to the kitchen to light the Primus stove. There was no water left, so she brought out an empty bucket and put it at Georgii's feet. It was one of the customs of the house that nobody could go to the well after sundown. Out of respect for Medea this and other inexplicable laws were strictly observed by all visitors, and the more inexplicable the law, the more force it had.

Georgii went off down to the well. It was a deep stone reservoir constructed by the Tatars at the end of the last century. Precious water brought from elsewhere was kept in it, and it had constantly to be refilled. Just now the level was low, and Georgii, pulling up the bucket, took a long, close look at it. The water was murky and the hardness in it could even be seen. For him, born in Central Asia, the water shortage in the Crimea was nothing out of the ordinary.

"I'll need to put down an artesian borehole," he thought for the second time in two days, climbing back to the house up an awkwardly stepped path which seemed to have been designed to suit the gait of a woman carrying a pitcher on her head.

Medea put the kettle on and went outside, the hem of her faded black skirt sweeping the clay floor of the kitchen. Georgii sat down on the bench and looked at the neat bundles of herbs hanging from a beam in the ceiling. Tatar copper pots and pans stood on the high shelves, and in the corners enormous cauldrons were piled on top of each other. A copper *kungan* pitcher crowned the pyramid. All these items were cruder and simpler than the familiar Uzbek ones sold in the Tashkent bazaar, but Georgii, who had a keen and slightly ascetic eye, preferred these poor relations to the others with all their lavish craftwork and garrulous Asiatic ornamentation.

"Dad, how about the seaside?" Artyom butted in.

"Hardly," he retorted, concealing his irritation. His son was well versed in the nuances of his father's speech and understood that there was no prospect of going to the sea.

His natural inclination was to whine and keep pestering his father, but the sensitivity of his nature took in the wonder of the morning stillness and he kept quiet.

While the water was heating on the stove, Medea made her bed, putting away the pillows and blankets in a chest at the foot of the bed, and murmured a short morning injunction to herself in the long-familiar words of a prayer which, however worn-out it might be, did in some unfathomable way help her in what she was asking for: to accept the new day with its toil, its disappointments, other people's empty talk, and her own weariness toward evening; to live through to the evening joyfully, without losing her temper with anyone and without taking umbrage. She had known since childhood that she had a bad habit of taking offense, and had been fighting it for so long she failed to notice that it was already many years since she had last taken offense at anyone. Only one old hurt from many years back still rankled, hanging over her like a dark shadow. "Am I really going to take it to my grave?" she wondered before moving on.

Having murmured this last, she meticulously braided her hair with movements practiced over many years, tied it in a knot, and wrapped the black silk shawl around her head. She freed the long tail of hair from beneath the bun down onto her neck, and suddenly, in the oval mirror encrusted with seashells, saw her own face. Of course, she tied her shawl in front of the mirror every morning but saw only a fold of cloth, a cheek, the collar of her dress. Today, however—and this was somehow connected with Georgii's arrival—she suddenly saw her own face and was surprised by it. With the years, it had come to look even longer, probably as a result of the hollowed cheeks with two deep wrinkles etched into them. Her nose was the Sinoply nose, and the years had not detracted from it. It was fairly long but not in the least protruding, quite flat at the end and with rounded nostrils.

She had a face like a rather handsome horse. This had been especially true in the years immediately after her marriage, when she unexpectedly cut her fringe and for a short time had her hair styled instead of wearing it in the invariable bun which hung heavily and irksomely on her neck.

Medea examined her face with some surprise, not glancing at it sideways but viewing it attentively and severely, and suddenly realized that she liked it. As a young girl, she had been distressed by her appearance: she had red hair, she was too tall, her mouth was too big. She was embarrassed by her large hands and the man-sized shoes she wore.

"I've turned into a fine-looking old woman." She smiled and shook her head. To the left of the mirror, among the clutch of photographs, a young couple looked out at her from a black rectangular frame, a woman with a low fringe and a man with a grand head of hair; a thin, patrician, Levantine face; and a mustache that was too large for it.

Medea shook her head once more: what had she been so upset about in her youth? She had been given a good face, a good height, she was strong and had a beautiful body, as Samuel, her dear husband Samuel, had assured her. She shifted her gaze to the portrait, enlarged from the last photograph of him, with the black mourning ribbon in the corner. In it he still had his splendid hair but with two bald spots encroaching on it and raising his low forehead; his mustache had faded and become less dashing, and there was a gentleness in his eyes and an overall kindliness in his face.

"All's well. It's all in the past," Medea told herself, driving away the shadow of old pain. She came out of the room and closed the door behind her. For all visitors her room was an inner sanctum which nobody entered without special invitation.

Georgii had already made the coffee. He did it in exactly the same way that Medea and his mother Elena did, the Turkish way. The little copper coffeepot was standing in the middle of the table on an unpolished tray. For all her pedantic tidiness, Medea did not enjoy polishing copper. Perhaps she preferred it with a patina. Medea poured the coffee into a crude china cup she had been drinking out of for the past fifteen years. It was a heavy, clumsy cup, a present from her niece Nike, one of her first ventures into ceramics, the fruit of a short-lived enthusiasm for modeling in clay. It was painted dark blue and red and had runs of dried glaze; its surface was rough and it was too ornate for everyday use, but for some reason Medea had taken to it and to this day Nike was proud to have pleased her aunt so much.

As she started drinking the coffee, Medea thought about Nike, and that she would be coming today with her children and Masha. Masha was an early grandniece and Nike a belated daughter of her sister Alexandra, and there was little difference in their ages.

"I expect they'll come on the morning flight, so they'll be

here in time for lunch," Medea said, addressing herself to no-body in particular.

Georgii made no reply, although he himself was thinking of going down to the market for some wine and some little seasonal treat like spring greens or medlars.

"Not, it's too early for medlars," he calculated, and shortly afterward asked his aunt whether she would be coming back home for lunch.

She nodded and finished drinking her coffee in silence.

When she had left, Artyom launched a further halfhearted attack on his father, but Georgii told him to get ready to go to the bazaar.

"It's always the same, first the graveyard, then the bazaar," Artyom grumbled.

"You can stay here if you'd rather," his father proposed mollifyingly, but Artyom had already decided that actually going to the bazaar wasn't that bad either.

Half an hour later they were walking down the road. Both were carrying rucksacks, and Artyom was wearing a canvas panama, while Georgii had a tarpaulin soldier's cap which gave him a jaunty, military air. At almost the exact same spot as yesterday, they saw the mother and daughter, and they were again dressed identically, except that this time the woman was sitting on a small folding stool and drawing at a child's easel.

Spotting them from the road, Georgii called to ask whether he could get them anything from the bazaar, but the light breeze carried his words away and the woman signaled with her hand that she could not hear him.

"Run up and ask whether they need anything," he told his son, and Artyom ran up the hillside in a flurry of small stones.

Georgii looked up with pleasure. The grass was still young and fresh, and on the brow of the hill a tamarisk with never a leaf to be seen was dusted with lilac-pink flowers.

The woman said something to Artyom, but then gave up and came running downhill herself. "Could you buy us some potatoes? Two kilos, please. I haven't got anyone to leave Tanya with, and it's too far for her to walk, she'd be worn-out. Oh, and a bunch of dill. Only I haven't got any money on me." She spoke rapidly, with a slight lisp, and blushing more deeply by the minute.

She climbed back up to her daughter who was standing next to the easel. Her heart was racing and affecting her throat. "What's happened? What's happened?" she blurted. "Nothing's happened. Two kilos of potatoes and a bunch of dill."

She saw how much everything had changed in the few minutes she had run down to the road: The sun had finally burned through the shining mist, and the tamarisks which she was trying to draw were no longer rising like a pink cloud but lay solidly, like cranberry mousse, on the skyline. All the delicate indefiniteness of the scene had gone, and the spot where she was standing suddenly seemed to her to be that fixed center around which everything revolves: worlds, the stars, the clouds, and flocks of sheep.

This fancy did not, however, calm her pounding heart. It was still galloping somewhere, unable to keep up with itself, and, independently of her mind, her eye was taking in the surroundings, eager to miss nothing, to forget not one feature of this world. Oh, if she could only have picked and pressed this moment with all its different aspects, like a flower she had taken a fancy to, as she had when she was a child with a passion for botany: her daughter standing beside the easel set crookedly in the center of God's creation; the flowering tamarisk; the road along which two travelers were proceeding with never a backward glance; the distant patch of sea; the folded valley with the furrow of a long-departed river; everything that was behind her back and everything that did not fit into her field of vision: the table mountains neat behind the hump-backed hills which had aged in this place, the table mountains with their lopped-off summits, stretched out in line one behind the other like obedient animals.

The bus from Simferopol to Medea's house took about five hours, and until the beginning of the holiday season the service was only once a day; but in any case Nike and Masha usually came by taxi despite the expense. (The two-hour journey by taxi was almost more than the price of a plane ticket from Moscow to Simferopol.)

As soon as Artyom got back from the bazaar, he went up to the roof armed with an old pair of binoculars and did not take his seeing eye from the gap between the hills where every car coming to the Village was briefly to be glimpsed. Georgii was sorting out his purchases in the kitchen. It had turned out not to be a market day, and there had been few traders and little going on. He had bought a pack of homemade plum pastilla scrolls which had been left to dry in the sun for rather too long, a favorite treat of the children; some spring greens; and a large packet of cheburek meat pastries.

It was the hardware shop where Georgii had scored his greatest success. Tourists were always surprised how well stocked it was. This time Georgii had bought a newly fashionable whistling kettle, two dozen glass tumblers, and half a kilo of *akhnali*, horseshoe nails which his friend Tarasov, the chairman of a collective farm near Novosibirsk, was desperate for. He also bought some Czech glue, which was in short supply in those days, and a fairly hideous oilcloth for the table. He laid all his purchases out and gloated over them. He enjoyed shopping. He liked the sport of choosing, haggling, and bringing home the booty. His wife Zoyka got angry each time he came back from a trip bringing a whole pile of completely unnecessary acquisitions which only cluttered up their house and dacha. She was an economist working in the municipal trading inspectorate and took the view that purchases should be judicious, thought through, and that you shouldn't just scoop up all sorts of junk.

He uncorked a bottle of Tauride fortified wine and regretted not having bought more, although it was readily available and he could always get some later in the little store in the Village. Having sorted everything out, he sat down in the doorway with a glass of wine and a cheburek in his hand, only to see the artist and her daughter coming down from the hill.

"Damn, I forgot the potatoes," he remembered. "Well, there can't have been any. If I'd seen them, it would have reminded me."

He had, however, bought plenty of dill and so, as a conscientious person, he called to Artyom to come down from the roof and take the vacationer some dill. The inhabitants of Medea's house never considered themselves to be vacationers, and the local people also treated them as belonging.

Artyom refused point-blank to take her the dill. The moment when the car would appear was too important and he was afraid of missing it. Indeed, before they had finished arguing over the dill, a yellow Volga did appear in the gap where it was expected.

"They're coming!" Artyom yelled in a voice breaking with happiness, and rushed down from the roof and out to the gate.

Only a few minutes later a taxi drove up to the house, stopped, its four doors burst open simultaneously and six people bundled out, two of them quite small. While the taxi-driver was retrieving suitcases and cardboard boxes from the boot, a scrum of relatives began kissing and hugging. The taxi had not left by the time Medea returned unnoticed with a bulging bag, smiling with her mouth firmly closed and her eyes narrowed.

"Auntie! My sunshine! How I've missed you! How pretty you

look! And you smell of sage!" Tall, redheaded Nike kissed her, but she pushed her away slightly and muttered,

"What nonsense! I'm reeking of gloss paint. They've been re-decorating the hospital these past two months and still haven't finished."

Thirteen-year-old Katya, Nike's elder daughter, was standing beside Medea waiting her turn to be kissed. Wherever Nike was, she had some inalienable right always to be first, and few there were who could dispute it. Masha too was waiting her turn, with her boyish haircut and her adolescent figure, as if she wasn't a grown woman but a scrawny runt on wobbly legs. But her face was pretty, with a beauty not yet fully revealed, like an unused transfer. Georgii caught her and kissed the top of her head.

"Shame on you, I'm not talking to you," Masha said, pushing him away. "You were in Moscow and didn't even call."

Masha's son, five-year-old Alik, and Nike's younger daughter Liza also embraced, acting out a passionate reunion although they hadn't been parted since yesterday, as they had all stayed overnight at Nike's apartment on Zubovskoy Street. The children were almost the same age and it was no exaggeration to say they had loved each other from birth. They amused everyone by constantly replicating adult relationships: feminine flirtatiousness, jealousy, and dashing acts of courtship.

"*Cousinage, dangereux voisinage,*" Medea said for the umpteenth time, looking at the cousins.

"I'll kiss you as if you were already here," Alik said, drawing Liza toward himself, but she decided to play hard-to-get, only she couldn't think of a condition for agreeing to be kissed and so prevaricated,

"No, first, um, you've got to, you've got to, um, show me the little doggie!"

Two of those present exchanged curt nods: Artyom and

Katya. There had been a time when they, like Liza and Alik now, had also loved each other passionately, but a couple of years ago everything had fallen apart. Katya had grown up markedly, sprouting hair in various places, which she promptly shaved off, and acquiring a pair of small but indisputably real breasts, and between the cousins there had opened up the abyss of puberty.

Artyom, his heart deeply wounded by last year's dismissiveness, which he had done nothing to deserve, although he had been desperately looking forward to seeing Katya again, now turned defensively away and meditatively dug the toe of his shoe into the pale brown earth.

Katya had been thrown out of the Bolshoi Ballet School last year for being totally without prospects but retained all the mannerisms of a professional ballerina, for which Nike, although secretly admiring of her wonderful deportment, was constantly ribbing her: "Chin up, shoulders down, chest forward, stomach back, and toes pointing outward." In just this *placement* Katya now stood immobile, giving all present the opportunity of delighting in the beauty of ballet, of which she firmly remained the representative.

"Medea, take a look at our little ones!" Masha said, touching Medea's shoulder.

Alik had been to the kennel of Medea's immensely long, but short-legged, bitch Nyukta and brought back an equally long puppy. Liza was holding it in her arms, and Alik, moving the puppy to one side, was proceeding toward Liza's promised cheek.

Everybody laughed. Georgii took two suitcases; Artyom, turning away from Katya, lifted a cardboard box with provisions; and Katya, tripping lightly like a prima ballerina taking her curtain call, ran down to take up her position in the sunlit patch of land between the house and the kitchen and posed there, exquisite and unattainable, like a princess, and Artyom perceived all this with an anguish in his heart the like of which he had never known before, the first victim of this early spring.

Nora, meanwhile, had again found herself in the role of snooper. Little Tanya was asleep after lunch. Neither potatoes nor dill had that handsome man brought her who looked, she now realized, not in the least like a Roman legionary, but like Odysseus. And then, while she was washing the dishes in Aunt Ada's kitchen yard, she had seen a taxi drive up and a tall, red-headed woman in a vulgar red dress embrace an old woman while a whole horde of children jumped around; and her breath was taken away by a sudden access of jealousy for people who could be so pleased to see each other and who could make such an occasion out of their meeting up again.

Another taxi drove into the Village a couple of hours later, but this one stopped at the Kravchuks' house. Nora, pulling back a corner of the embroidered curtain, saw how, in response to a voice calling for the owners, first Ada and shortly afterward her husband, wiping his greasy mouth with his oily driver's hand, leapt out of the summer kitchen.

In the wide-open gate stood a strapping young man with long hair held like a girl's ponytail by a rubber band, wearing tight-fitting white jeans and a pink T-shirt. Ada was quite flabber-gasted by the sheer brazenness of his appearance. The new arrival smiled, however, waved a white envelope, and asked, without moving from the garden gate, "The Kravchuks? A letter from your son with new greetings. Saw him yesterday."

Ada snatched the envelope, and, without saying a word, the Kravchuks disappeared into the kitchen to read the letter from their only son, Vitka, who since graduating from army college had been living in Moscow province for three years now, and as it seemed from the perspective of the Village was making a great career for himself. The new arrival, showing not the least concern for the taxi-driver who was still waiting by the outside gate, sat himself down on a bench. The Kravchuks had meanwhile read that their son was sending them a very useful contact whom they should under no circumstances charge for accommodation, whose every whim they should indulge, and that the commandant of the entire military district himself queued up for massage at the hands of this same Valerii Butonov.

Before they had finished reading the letter, the Kravchuks rushed out to the new arrival. "But please come in, do. Where is your luggage?"

The new arrival brought in his luggage, a leather suitcase with a thick layered handle, covered in foreign stickers. Nora wearied of holding up in the air the old-fashioned smoothing iron with which she was ironing Tanya's skirt and put it back on its holder. Her landlord and landlady were running in circles around the new arrival: the suitcase had impressed them too.

He was probably an actor, or a jazz musician, or something of that kind, Nora supposed. The iron had cooled, but she did not want to leave her little cottage to heat it up again in the kitchen. She put the half-ironed skirt aside.

CHAPTER 4

Medea had grown up in a house where meals were cooked in cauldrons, eggplants pickled by the barrel, and fruit dried many kilograms at a time on the roof, yielding up its sweet fragrances to the salty sea breeze. While this was going on, brothers and sisters were being born and filling up the house. By midseason Medea's present dwelling, lonely and silent in the winter, was reminding her of that childhood home, so crowded and full of children had it become. Laundry was endlessly boiling in great vessels standing on iron tripods; in the kitchen there was always someone drinking coffee or wine; guests were arriving from Koktebel or Sudak. Sometimes free-spirited young people—unshaven students and unkempt girls—would pitch a tent nearby, loudly playing their new music and surprising everyone with their politically daring new songs. And Medea, introverted, childless Medea, although long accustomed to this free-for-all in the summer, did sometimes wonder why it should be her house, baked by the sun and blown by the winds from the sea, that should draw all these tribes from Lithuania, Georgia, Siberia, and Central Asia.

A new season was beginning. Last night she had been alone with Georgii and this evening eight people sat down to the early supper.

The younger children, tired from their journey, were put to bed early. Artyom went off too in order to avoid the humiliation of being sent to bed. His voluntary departure went some way toward making him the equal of Katya, whom nobody had packed off to bed for a long time now.

The early supper developed imperceptibly into the late supper. They drank the wine Georgii had bought. Georgii had lived in Moscow for five years while studying in the Geographical Faculty of Moscow State University. He hadn't taken to the city, but news of the capital always interested him, and now he was trying to extract it out of his cousins. Nike's narrative, however, was constantly going off at a tangent, either about herself or moving on to family gossip, and Masha's tended to politics. Such were the times. No matter where a conversation started, it invariably ended with a conspiratorial lowering of voices and a raising of the temperature by politics.

This time they were discussing Gvidas the Hun, Medea's Vilnius nephew, the son of her late brother Dimitry. He had built himself a very extensive house indeed.

"What about the authorities? Have they allowed it?" Georgii asked, his whole being quivering with interest in just this matter.

"In the first place, in Lithuania things just are a bit more liberal. In addition to that, he is an architect. And don't forget, his father-in-law is a top bastard in the Party."

"Gvidas doesn't play those games, does he?" Georgii asked in surprise.

"Well, how can I put it? On the whole, Soviet power is a bit of a pantomime there. Lithuanians have always taken their smoked sausage, eels, and beer more seriously than meetings of the Communist Party, that's for sure. Cannibalism is less widespread there," Nike explained.

Masha flared up: "You're talking complete rubbish, Nike. After the war half of Lithuania was put in prison, almost half a million young men. More than they lost in the war. Some pantomime!"

Medea got up. She had been wanting to get to bed for a

while. She knew she had missed her usual time when she slipped easily and smoothly into sleep, and now she would be tossing and turning till morning on her mattress stuffed with marine eel-grass. "Good night," she said, and went out.

"Look at that," Masha said, chagrined. "No one can deny what a great personality our Medea is, hard as flint, yet even she is downtrodden. She didn't say a word and just left."

That made Georgii angry.

"You're a half-wit, Masha. You think all the evil in the world comes down to Soviet power. She had one of her brothers killed by the Reds, another by the Whites; in the war one was killed by the Fascists, and another by the Communists. For her all govern-ments are the same. My grandfather Stepanyan was an aristocrat and a monarchist, and he sent her money when she was or-phaned as a young girl. He sent her everything they had in the house at that time. And my mother was married by my father, who was, forgive my mentioning it, a red-hot revolutionary, just because Medea told him, 'We've got to save Elena.' What does it matter to her who's in power? She's a Christian, her allegiance is to a higher authority. And never say again that she's afraid of any-thing."

"Oh, for heaven's sake!" Masha shouted. "That's not what I meant at all! I only meant she left as soon as we started talking politics."

"Well, why should she want to talk to a half-wit like you, anyway?" Georgii retorted.

"That's enough now," Nike intervened lazily. "Have we got anything tucked away in the reserve?"

"Need you ask?" Georgii said, cheering up immediately. He rummaged behind his back and pulled out the bottle he had started earlier in the day.

Masha's mouth was trembling and she was just waiting to rush into battle, but Nike, who hated quarrels, moved a glass in her direction and began singing. "The river is flowing over the sand, washing the shore, a handsome young fellow, a dashing young rascal, is begging his foreman . . ."

Her voice was quiet and moist at first. Georgii and Masha relaxed, leaning against each other as members of one family, and all the disputation ended of its own accord. Nike's voice poured like light out through the chink of the partly open door, through the small, irregular windows, and the simple, semioutlaw song lit up the whole of Medea's realm.

Valerii Butonov came out into the night to relieve himself and, rather than bothering to walk all the way to the little planked house, disconcerted the tomato seedlings by giving them an unexpected warm watering. Now he gazed up into the star-studded southern sky dissected by lascivious searchlights probing the coastal strip in search of cinematographic spies in black frogmen's suits. At this time of the year, however, not even the buttocks of lovers on the beach were to be seen gleaming in the moonlight.

The earth was shrouded in darkness and a single window shone with a pure yellow light from a valley in the hills; he even seemed to hear the sound of a woman's singing coming from there. Valerii listened. Occasionally a dog barked.

The night truly was a sleepless one, but Medea had been used to sleeping little since she was young and, now that she was old, one sleepless night did not unsettle her. She lay in her narrow maidenly bed in her nightgown with its worn embroidery on the front, and her loosely braided nighttime plait rested alongside her, grown sparser with the years but still extending down to her hip.

The house was soon filled with little recognizable sounds: Nike shuffling past barefoot, Masha clinking the lid of the chamber pot, whispering "Piss-piss" to a sleeping child, and the little stream flowing audibly and musically. A light switch clicked, followed by muffled giggling.

Neither her hearing nor her eyesight were yet letting Medea down, and being naturally observant, she picked out many things in her young relatives' lives which they themselves were quite unaware of. The young mothers with babies or toddlers usually arrived at the beginning of the season; their working husbands didn't stay long, a couple of weeks, rarely a month. Friends of some sort would come, rent a bed in the Lower Village, and at night they would come secretly to the house, moaning and crying out on the other side of Medea's wall. Then those mothers separated from one husband and married another. The new husbands brought up the old children and fathered new ones; the stepbrothers and stepsisters visited each other, and then the ex-husbands came back with their new wives and new children to spend the holidays together with the older ones.

When Nike married Katya's father, a promising young film producer who never did fulfill his promise, for years she brought with her Misha, the producer's ungainly and uncouth son from his first marriage. Katya did all she could to make his life a misery, but Nike was kind to him and looked after him, and when she swapped the producer for a physicist, she continued dragging the boy around with her for many years. Medea was witness to a change of partners between two married couples, an ardent romance between a brother- and sister-in-law with an age difference of thirty years, and several youthful flings between cousins which fully validated the French proverb.

The life of the postwar generation, especially of those who were now around twenty, seemed to her to be not quite serious. She could not detect in either their marriages or their parenting the sense of responsibility which from an early age had defined her own life. She was never judgmental but had immense respect for those who, like her mother, her grandmother, and her friend Elena, performed the least significant and the most important acts in the only way that was possible for Medea herself: seriously and definitively.

Medea had lived her life as the wife of one husband and continued to live as his widow. Her life as a widow was good, not a whit worse than her marriage. Over the long years, almost thirty of them, since he died, the past itself had changed radically, and the only bitter hurt her husband had caused her, strangely enough when he was already dead, had dissolved away and in her memory he had become a man of monumental importance, something of which there had been not the slightest evidence while he was alive.

She had been a widow considerably longer than she had been a wife, and her relationship with her departed husband was as good as ever and was even improving with the years.

Although experiencing her semiwakefulness as insomnia, Medea was actually in a subtle drowsy sleep which did not inhibit her usual thinking processes: half-prayer, half-conversation, half-reminiscence, it sometimes even casually strayed beyond the limits of what she personally knew or had seen.

Recalling almost word for word all her husband had told her about his childhood, she could remember him now as a boy, even though she hadn't met him until he was approaching forty. Samuel Yakovlevich was the son of a widow who prized the affronts and misfortunes she suffered above any property. With inexplicable pride she would point out her weakling son's defects to her sisters: "Just look how skinny he is, he looks like a chicken, in the whole of our street there is not another child so puny. And look at his scabs! He's completely scrofulous. And he's got red blotches on his hands."

Little Sam grew bigger nevertheless, together with his spots and pimples and boils, and was in truth both skinny and pale but in that differed little from other children of his age. At thirteen he began to experience a certain special perturbation associated with a tenting of his trousers, raised from within by a rapidly sprouting shoot which inconvenienced him extremely.

The boy regarded his new condition as one of his numerous illnesses which his mother took such pride in talking about, and he adapted a drawstring from her underskirt to constrain the wayward organ and stop it troubling him. Meanwhile two more visible parts of his body, his ears and nose, entered a phase of irrepressible growth. Out of the good-looking boy there hatched a ridiculous creature with rounded, overhanging eyebrows and a long and motile nose. His skinniness acquired a new quality at this time: no matter where he sat down he felt he was sitting on two sharp stones. His late father's striped grey trousers hung on him as if he were a scarecrow in the kitchen garden, and it was now he received the hurtful nickname of "Sammy Empty-Pants."

At the age of fourteen, soon after the celebration of his bar mitzvah, which for Sam was remarkable only for his having made five times as many mistakes in the reading of the prescribed texts as the five other boys from poor families who had completed their synagogal studies at public expense, and after an exasperatingly evasive correspondence between his mother and an elder brother of his late father, he was finally sent to Odessa, where he began his career in the style and dignity of office boy with a round of interminable and ill-defined duties.

The post of office boy left him almost no free time, but he nevertheless managed to fit in an acquaintance with the Jewish Enlightenment, which even then was outdated, at the hands of Ephraim, the eldest of his father's brothers. Ephraim was a self-taught Jewish intellectual who hoped, despite all evidence to the contrary, that well-founded education would resolve all the world's thorny problems, including such misunderstandings as anti-Semitism.

Sam did not stand for long beneath the noble but seriously faded banners of the Jewish Enlightenment and defected, to his uncle's great distress, to the contiguous camp of Zionism, which turned its face away from the Jew trying to raise his educational level to that of other civilized peoples and instead backed the Natural Jew, who had taken the straightforward but two-edged decision to plant his orchard once more in Canaan.

Sam's cousin had already managed to emigrate to Palestine, was now living in a place no one had ever heard of called Ein Gedi, working as a farm laborer, and was sending infrequent but enthusiastic letters urging Sam to follow. To the displeasure of his office uncle, Sam enrolled in the Jewish agricultural courses for settlers. His studies took up an inordinate amount of working time; his uncle was displeased and halved Sam's wages, which he had in any case never once got around to paying; his wife, however, Aunt Genichka, was a real Jewish woman with designs to marry Sam to her no-longer-young niece who had, moreover, a slight congenital dislocation of the hip joint.

Sam attended the courses diligently for two months, delving into the arts of vaccination and inoculation, but his fickle heart couldn't wait for the laid eggs of intention to hatch into accomplished actions, and even as the other students were being drawn ever more deeply into the world of horticulture and viticulture, he transferred to another class: a clandestine Marxist study circle organized for workers in the engineering workshops and port services. The enticements of small-scale Jewish socialism in provincial Palestine stood no chance against the world-girdling perspectives of the proletariat.

His office uncle, whose interests did not extend beyond the market price of wheat, had reacted with considerable disinterest to all his nephew's previous hobbyhorses, but Marxism was too much and he told him to find another place to stay. To be fair, he did seem to have grasped from Sam's account what surplus value was, but displayed an unexpected hostility to the young economic genius and shouted in a rage, "You think he knows better than I do what to do with surplus value? Let him first try getting it!"

Sam suspected that his uncle was confusing surplus value with pure profit, but wasn't given an opportunity to explain this to him properly. His uncle assured him that he would land himself in jail in the very near future, words which proved to be prophetic, although almost two years were to pass before they were fulfilled. During this time Sam learned the metalworker's trade, acquired a great deal of varied book-learning, and himself conducted a study circle to bring light into the benighted consciousness of the People.

At the end of 1912 he was subjected to administrative exile in Vologda province, where he spent two years, afterward traveling from town to town, carrying raw propaganda literature of his own devising in a doctor's bag, meeting in conspiratorial apartments with unknown but clearly very important personages, and engaging in agitation and more agitation. For the rest of his life he styled himself a professional revolutionary and was in Moscow for the Revolution, where he became a middle-ranking leader since he was good at working with the proletarian masses; and then he was outfitted in ChON Special Detachment leather and sent to Tambov province, at which point his glorious biography mysteriously breaks off. Part of the story is glaringly missing, and then he reappears as someone entirely run-of-the-mill, devoid of any higher interests in life, a dental prosthetist enthused only by the sight of ample ladies.

The meeting between Medea, already withering after having inconspicuously spent the golden years of maidenhood in the daily caring for her younger brothers Constantine and Dimitry and her sister Alexandra (whom she had accompanied with her firstborn baby, Sergei, to her new husband in Moscow not long before), and the jolly dentist, whose smile revealed large short teeth along with a strip of pale raspberry-colored gum, took place in a sanatorium. The therapeutic Crimean mud was believed to stimulate fertility, and Nurse Medea Georgievna facilitated the process by applying mud compresses to barren loins.

There hadn't been a dentist in the sanatorium before, but the chief consultant had managed to get the post established by the Commissariat of Health. The dentist duly appeared and created in this tranquil and slightly mysterious place a quite unholy hullabaloo. He was loud, he joked, he waved his nickel-plated instruments around, he flirted with all his patients at the same time, he offered unscheduled services for the promotion of childbirth, and Medea Georgievna, the best nurse in the sanatorium, was allocated to him as his assistant in these stomatological tours de force. She mixed the amalgam for fillings with a spatula on a specimen glass slide, passed him the instruments, and was quietly amazed at the dentist's unparalleled impudence, and even more by the mind-boggling wantonness of most of the women suffering from infertility, who would consent to a rendezvous with him before they were even out of the dentist's chair.

With a curiosity which grew by the day, she observed this thin Jew whose baggy trousers were inelegantly gathered around his thin waist by a Caucasian belt and who wore an old blue shirt. After donning his white coat he assumed a marginally more prepossessing appearance.

"He is a doctor, I suppose," Medea reflected in explanation of his manifest success with the ladies. "And witty in his way."

While Medea was filling in the patient's record card, even before the patient had trustingly opened her mouth, his keen eye would have completed a benevolent and professional masculine examination from the crown of her head down to her ankle. Nothing escaped the connoisseur's gaze, and the first compliment, Medea deduced, related exclusively to the upper story: hair, complexion, eyes. Receiving a favorable reaction, and in this respect the dentist showed great delicacy, he would throw himself into a purposeful outpouring of eloquence.

Medea observed the doctor surreptitiously, and was amazed how he came to life at the sight of each woman entering and how his face fell when he was alone with himself, that is, with stern Medea. He had subjected her to his critical analysis on the first day of their acquaintance, had praised her wonderful copper hair but, receiving no encouragement, had not returned to the subject of her physical merits.

After a time Medea recognized, to her surprise, that he really did have a keen eye and could pick out a woman's most elusive merits in an instant; indeed, he was the more sincerely pleased to discover these the less obvious they were.

To one improbably fat woman manifestly suffering from obesity, he said admiringly as she was squeezing her soft backside into the seat of his dentist's chair, "If we lived in Istanbul, you would be considered the most beautiful woman in the city!"

The bloated woman blushed, her eyes filled with tears, and she squeaked in a hurt voice, "What do you mean by that?"

"My God," Samuel said in great concern. "Of course, I mean it as a great compliment. Everybody wants lots of something good."

It even seemed to Medea that by the end of his reception hours he was tired less by the work itself than by his superhuman efforts to find a compliment for each woman based on their actual, if sometimes well hidden, virtues.

With the few members of the male sex who chanced to come his way (the basic specialization of the sanatorium was after all the treatment of infertility, although it also had a small orthopedics department), he was stiff, even, perhaps, timid. Medea smiled at her observation. It occurred to her that the merry dentist was afraid of men. She was later to discover how painful the reality behind that casual observation was.

Medea was nearing thirty at this time. Dimitry was preparing to enter the military academy at Taganrog. Constantine was fifteen and hoping to become a geologist.

Her sister Anelya, who had taken Anastasia, the youngest of the children, to Tbilisi, had long been urging Medea to come and visit her. Anelya had her eye on a certain charming and still-young widower who was one of her husband's relatives, and had it in mind to introduce them. Medea, who had no inkling of these plans, was also intending to visit her sisters, only not in the spring but in the autumn after she had laid in her supplies for the winter. If Anelya's plans had come to fruition, this house, possibly the last Greek house in the Crimea, would not have survived, and the next generation of the Sinoply family, Greeks in Tashkent, Tbilisi, and Vilnius, would have forgotten its seafaring heritage. But things turned out differently.

In the middle of March 1929 all the sanatorium staff were called to an urgent meeting; absolutely all, including even feebleminded Rais with the asymmetrical smile on half his face. If Rais had been told to come, it was an indication that the meeting was on a matter of national importance.

The municipal Party boss, enormous Vyalov, was ranting at a table covered with glossy red material. He had already read out the Party directive and was now improvising on the subject of everyone's wonderful tomorrow and the grandeur of the idea of collective farms. The mainly female staff of the sanatorium were listening obediently. These were mostly women who lived in the suburbs, owned half a house, a kitchen garden extending to a few hundredths of a hectare, a couple of small trees, half a dozen hens, and received a wage from working for the state. They were disinclined to heckle. Firkovich, the sanatorium's chief consultant, was a native Crimean from a scholarly Karaim family and had been kicked about quite a bit in his time. He had been drafted into the Red Army in 1918 and worked in hospitals but had never joined the Communist Party. He still feared for his family so was always willing to keep his head down and make available the time and place for anyone else who wanted to speechify.

"Who's got something to say?" Vyalov inquired, and immediately up jumped stout Filozov, the secretary of the Party cell.

Samuel Yakovlevich was sitting in the back row twitching, even bouncing up and down on his chair slightly and looking all around. Medea was sitting next to him and covertly observing his inexplicable agitation. Catching her eye, he seized her hand and whispered in her ear, "I have to speak. It's imperative that I should speak."

"Well, why are you getting so excited, Samuel Yakovlevich? Get up and speak if you want to." She gently extricated her hand from his grasp.

"I've been a member of the Party, do you see, since 1912. It's my duty." His paleness was not a noble pallor, but an ashen, frightened greyness.

A new doctor, a curly-headed woman with a flat lock of hair to the left of her part and a German surname, spoke at length about collectivization, and kept repeating, "From the standpoint of the present moment in time . . ."

Clutching Medea's hand, Samuel calmed down and sat that way through to the end of the meeting, his face twitching, mouthing something. When the meeting had thundered to an end, people started going out, but he was still holding her hand.

"This is a terrible day, believe me, a terrible day. Don't leave me alone," he begged her, and his eyes, light hazel, imploring, were completely feminine.

"All right." Medea unexpectedly found herself readily agreeing, and they walked together out of the sanatorium's limewashed gate, past the bus station, and turned into a quiet street inhabited by railway workers ever since the railway had been brought to the town.

Samuel Yakovlevich rented a room with its own front door and a front garden in which there were two old vines growing and a table so gnarled and mossy it might have grown here at the same time as the trees. The vine had already twined itself around wires stretched above the table. The tiny courtyard was contained on one side by a rickety fence, and on the other by the clay wall of the neighboring house.

Sitting at the table, Medea watched Samuel Yakovlevich hopping around by the Primus stove in the entrance hall, taking down some goat's cheese wrapped in a napkin from behind the door lintel, pouring vegetable oil into the frying pan, and managing to do everything rather fussily but nonetheless expeditiously. Medea looked at her watch. Her brothers would not be back today because both of them were in Koktebel at the gliding center and would stay there, most likely with Medea's old friend who owned a dacha well known in those parts.

"I'm not in any hurry to go anywhere," Medea noted to herself in surprise. "I am visiting."

Samuel Yakovlevich didn't stop chattering, and was so quick and at ease that you would have thought quite another person had just been clutching Medea's hand.

"What an odd and changeable man," Medea thought, and offered to help him prepare the tea.

But he asked her to sit still and enjoy the wonderful sky through the little leaves of the vine. "Let me tell you a secret, Medea Georgievna. I've done many things in my life. I even completed a course in farming for Jewish settlers, and now as I look at that vine," he gestured sweepingly toward the two gnarled bushes, "I think to myself what a splendid job that is. Much better than fitting false teeth, eh? What do you think?"

Then he served supper at the table, and they ate potatoes which smelled of paraffin, and goat's cheese, and she kept thinking it was time to get up and leave, but for some reason didn't.

Later he escorted Medea right across town, telling her about himself, the minor and major upsets in his life, the times he'd been out of luck and the times he'd fallen on his nose. Yet he seemed not to be complaining, but laughing about it and wondering at it all. Then he respectfully took his leave of her and left her quite perplexed as to what it was about him that was so touching. Perhaps it was that he didn't take himself very seriously.

They met again the next morning as usual, in the stomatology department. He seemed to have been replaced by a quite different dentist who didn't talk much, was very correct with his lady patients, and didn't joke at all. By lunchtime Medea had the impression there was something he wanted to tell her, and sure enough, when the last patient before lunch left, he spread out his doorstep sandwiches next to Medea's slim, flat scones sandwiched around the first spring onions, shook his head, clicked his tongue, and asked, "How would it be, Medea Georgievna, if I were to invite you to dinner at the Caucasus restaurant?"

Medea smiled. He had invited not a few of his chosen lady patients to the Caucasus restaurant. She also found his grammar amusing: "How would it be if . . ."

"I would think about it," Medea replied wryly.

"Well, what is there for you to think about?" he asked heatedly. "We'll finish work and just go there."

Medea understood that he really was very keen to take her to this restaurant of his. "Well, at the least I shall have to go home first to change," Medea resisted weakly.

"Stuff and nonsense! Do you think all the ladies are wearing sables?" the dentist pressed home his attack.

That day Medea was wearing a grey serge dress with a round white collar and cuffs which made her look like a chambermaid or an old-age pensioner; one of the probably one hundred dresses of exactly the same style which she had worn all her life since she was a schoolgirl and which she could have sewn with her eyes shut: one of those widow's dresses which she was wearing to this day.

The evening at the Caucasus restaurant was a delight. Samuel Yakovlevich was trying to cut a bit of a dash. He knew the waiter and was pleased about that. Bending at the waist and lifting his sharp little mustache with a smile, the waiter cast hors d'oeuvres in little transparent dishes down on the table in a casual but symmetrical cross. Among the plush and the palm trees of the restaurant, Medea Georgievna seemed more attractive to the dentist than yesterday when she had been sitting in his little garden with her classical Greek profile silhouetted against the whitewashed wall.

Breaking off a piece of lavash bread, she dipped it in the chakhokhbili stew and ate it so delicately that she didn't get the slightest orange outline around her mouth. Watching the relaxed and amiably absentminded look on her face as she was eating, hardly looking down at the plate, he supposed that she had good manners and it struck him that he himself had never been taught good table manners. He quite lost his appetite for a minute. The chakhokhbili suddenly seemed bitter.

He moved the metal bowl and plate to one side. He refilled his wineglass with dark, heavy Khvanchkara from the round decanter, gulped it down, put the glass back on the table, and said emphatically, "You keep eating, Medea Georgievna, and pay no attention to what I am about to say."

She looked at him expectantly. It was cosy in the niche where they were sitting, if a bit on the dark side.

"I need to explain my behavior yesterday to you. I mean at the meeting. Bear in mind that I am a professional revolutionary. I was known throughout Odessa and spent three years in political exile. I tried to organize the escape from prison of someone so important that it would be simply improper to mention his name now. And I am no coward, believe me."

He was very agitated now, moved the plate of chakhokhbili back, impaled a large piece of meat, and chewed at it, smacking his lips like a gourmet. His appetite had evidently returned.

"You see, I simply have a nervous i-illness." He moved the plate away again. "I am thirty-nine years old: no longer young, but not yet old. I have no contact with my family. I am as good as orphaned," he joked.

He leaned forward, and some of his thick hair, which he combed back, tumbled onto his forehead. His hair really was very attractive.

"He's going to propose," Medea surmised.

"I have never been married and, just between ourselves, had no intention of changing that. Only, you see, I had a slight attack yesterday, when we were sitting in that meeting, and purely because you were there it passed off quite without any consequences. Then you came home with me and we sat together all evening and I didn't feel a thing."

"He's so daft it's comical," Medea thought, smiling to herself.

"You see," the dentist battled on, "you really aren't my type at all . . ."

Such frankness seemed, even to someone as devoid of flirtatiousness as Medea, to be going too far, but by now she was completely at sea and had no idea where this conversation was leading. Then the dentist made an abrupt turn, as if twisting his molar forceps: "In general I like smaller women, solid, firmly planted, you know, on the ground in the Russian style. No, don't think I'm a simpleton, I realize that you are something of a princess, but since I was a young man I haven't been accustomed to looking in the direction of princesses. Laundresses, cafeteria assistants, forgive me, nurses . . ."

"He is a scream, but I have a pile of laundry at home waiting to be ironed," she thought. Samuel Yakovlevich speared a piece of the by now cold meat with his fork, hastily chewed and swallowed it, and now Medea could see how nervous he was.

"When you took my hand, Medea Georgievna . . . No, forgive me, it was I who took your hand, I felt that by your side I feared nothing. The whole evening I felt nothing for you, only that by your side I feared nothing. I escorted you back, then I came back home, lay down, and decided immediately that I must marry you."

The information left Medea completely unmoved. She was an old maid of twenty-nine and for many years had contemptuously rejected propositions of various kinds made to her by a rather small number of men.

"And then I dreamed of my mother!" he exclaimed dramatically. "If you only knew what a dreadful personality she had, but that's beside the point. I have never in my life dreamt of her before, but last night I did. She came very close to me, and I could even smell her hair, you know, her old grey hair, and she said to me sternly, 'Yes, Sam, yes.' And that was it. I can only think myself that it's 'yes.' "

Medea was sitting bolt upright. She always did carry herself very upright. Her collar was slightly crumpled on the left, but she did not notice it. She was wondering how to turn this eccentric down gently, so as not to offend him. It didn't seem to have occurred to him that she might say no.

"Yes, Medea Georgievna, and there is one more thing I should tell you about myself as your future husband. The point is, I am a certified psychiatric patient. That is, I am perfectly all right. It is an old story, but I should nevertheless tell it to you. In 1920, I was drafted into a subdivision of the ChON Special Detachments and sent out to requisition grain. It was a matter of the highest priority, I always understood that. And grain, of course, we duly found in the village of Vasilishchevo in Tambov province. I am quite sure there was grain hidden in every homestead, but we found it in two, which didn't at all look to be among the richest. We had our orders: anyone found concealing grain was to be shot as an example to others. The Red Army soldiers arrested three peasants and took them outside the village boundary. As they were taking them away, all the people of the village followed. Two of the men were brothers with a shared farm, and the other was an older peasant. Their wives were running after us, and their children. An old paralyzed woman, the mother of the older man, was crawling after us. We took away a hundredweight and a half of grain from them in total, and from the brothers a measly half a hundredweight. There was I, Medea Georgievna, the commanding officer of the grain squad. We lined the three of them up, the Red Army soldiers facing them with their rifles. Well, then the women and the little children raised such a shriek that something struck me in the head and I fell down. I'd had something like an epileptic seizure. After that, of course, I remember nothing. They put me in the cart, right there on top of the grain, and took me back to the city. I was told I turned black, and my arms and legs were like sticks, completely rigid. Three months I was in the hospital, and then they sent me to a sanatorium and then set up a commission and decided that I had weak nerves. After the commission they wanted to transfer me to work for the Party administering the economy, but I had second thoughts and asked them to let me be a dentist. They took my weak nerves into account and released me. You may perhaps have noticed that I am a good dentist. I know the prophylactic side, and all about dentures. I have not changed my Party views, only physically I really am weak. Whenever I need to support a Party decision, my spirit is all for it, but my flesh relapses into weakness and fear that I might be about to have another fit, a nervous fever . . . like at yesterday's meeting. I am telling you all this as a very big personal secret, although actually it's all written down in my medical record. I had an opportunity to have it removed, but I thought, 'No, I'm not going to. What if the Party were to call me again to do my duty in operational work. I just can't do it. Shoot me like a dog, but I still can't do it.' But I have no other failings, Medea Georgievna."

Medea then reflected, "God help us, my brother Philip was shot by the Reds; my brother Nikifor was hanged by the Whites, but before that both of them had become murderers themselves. This one couldn't do it, and he's lamenting his weakness. Truly, the wind of the Spirit blows where it wills."

Samuel saw her back to her house. The road glistened dimly beneath their feet. That part of the suburbs was a desolate place then, not built up, and strewn with rubbish. It was about four kilometers to Medea's house. Samuel, who talked ceaselessly, suddenly fell silent when they were halfway there. He had actually said everything there was to say about himself. In the years of their marriage he only added minor details to what he had told her that evening.

Medea too was silent. He was holding her arm with his thin, strong hand, but she nevertheless had the feeling that it was she who was leading him.

When they reached Harlampy's old estate, the moon came out, silvering the trees in the orchard; the gates had long ago been barricaded and the house's residents used two gates at the side and back. They stopped by the side gate. He coughed and asked brusquely, "So, when shall we go to the Registry Office?"

"We shan't," she said, shaking her head. "I need to think about it."

"What is there to think about?" he asked in surprise. "Today we have collectivization of agriculture, tomorrow there will be something else. Of course, life is just getting better all the time, but I think we shall find it easier to get through this wonderful life together, if you see what I mean."

It was quiet in the house. She took off the grey dress and put on another very similar one for wearing at home. Then she sat down to write a letter to Elena. It was a long, sad letter. She wrote not a word about the comical dentist and his ridiculous courtship but told Elena only about how the boys had grown up and were leaving her; and about how it was night now and she was alone at home, and that her youth had passed, and she was feeling tired.

A wind blew up toward morning, and Medea developed a severe headache. She wrapped an old scarf around her head and lay down in her cold bed. The following day her temperature rose and her joints ached. The influenza was severe and lasted a long time. Samuel Yakovlevich nursed her zealously. By the time she recovered, he was head over heels in love with her, and she felt immeasurably and undeservedly happy: she could never remember anybody bringing her tea in bed before, boiling broth for her, and tucking her blankets in at the sides. After the illness they got married, and their marriage was happy from its first day to its last.

Medea knew his main weakness: after a few vodkas he would start furiously boasting about his revolutionary past and looking victoriously at the women present. Then she would quietly get up from the table and say, "Home, Sam!" and he would hurry guiltily after her. It was a small thing, and she forgave him for it.

On the other side of the wall a child started crying—Alik or Liza, Medea couldn't tell which. A new day was beginning and Medea was unsure whether she had slept that night or not. She had been having ill-defined nights of this sort ever more frequently of late.

The child, and now it was clearly Liza, was demanding to be taken to the seaside right away.

Nike scolded her: "I'm sure I don't know what all this crying is about! Get up, get washed, have breakfast, and then we'll decide where we're going."

CHAPTER 5

There were two ways to the sea. There was the main road, which had been laid before the war. It wound in a great semi-circle past the creek and from there rushed headlong downhill, turning into a difficult path. The main branch of the road climbed uphill to disappear through a barrier, beyond which military installations led an underground life of their own. Another branch of the road went to Theodosia, from where it was often possible to hitch a lift.

The second, old road was a much shorter route, but steeper and more difficult. The roads came together twice: at the creek and at a round meadow between the Upper and Lower Villages. Here a view opened out which was almost more than the eye could bear. The hill on which the Tatars had once built a little village was not all that high, but, as if subordinating itself to some kind of Chinese brainteaser, the scenery here refused necessarily to follow the laws of optics and spread over a broad convex surface, clinging perilously to the point of transition where a plane surface becomes three dimensional, and miraculously uniting one-point with reverse perspective. In one smooth sweep everything was fitted in: the terraced hills once covered with vineyards but retaining them now only at their very tops; the faded table mountains beyond them dotted with the lichen patches of grazing flocks; and higher and farther still, a tremendously ancient mountain massif with leafy forests at its foot, the bald spots of old landslips, and bare, fantastical cliff figures and capricious natural features which seemed like the dwellings of dead boulders at its very summits; and there was no telling whether the stony crust of the mountains was floating in the blue chalice of a sea which encompassed half the horizon, or whether an enormous ring of mountains too large for the eye to see was the vast container of the elongated drop of the Black Sea.

Medea and Samuel found themselves here in the autumn of 1931. Sitting in this meadow covered in capers and grey wormwood, they both had a sense of being at the exact center of the world; that the smooth sweep of the mountains, the rhythmical sighing of the sea, the passing overhead of the clouds, scudding, half-transparent, and the slower ones, more substantial, the vast palpable flow of warm air from the hills, circulating, all in concert engendered a perfect tranquility.

"It's the hub of the universe," was all the astounded Samuel could say at the time, although Medea knew several such hubs in the region.

There and then, they decided to move here, exchanging Medea's Theodosia residence, the two rooms in Harlampy's house which she had been allotted, for an old Tatar homestead on the very edge of the Village, out on its own. This was the place from which the family's expeditions to the sea usually set out, often joined by friends living in the Village who had children, and local children too. Preparations were made in advance for these expeditions to the coves, with food, tent poles, and all the other paraphernalia of tourism. Occasionally they spent only one day at the sea, but more often two or three, and would strike camp before sundown in order to negotiate the difficult precipitous path in daylight. They would get home late, carrying the youngest children, already sleepy, on their shoulders. Sometimes they managed to hitch a lift from the creek, but that was only if they were in luck.

Like most of the local people, Medea went to the sea rarely;

but unlike the new, recently imported residents, the postwar settlers from the Ukraine, the North Caucasus, and as far away as Siberia, who couldn't even swim, Medea was born on the seacoast and knew the sea here the way a country dweller knows his own woodlands: all the ways of the water, its fickleness and its constancies, the changing of its colors from morning to evening, from autumn to spring, all the winds and currents together with their calendar periods. When Medea was planning to visit the sea, she preferred to go alone. This time, however, Georgii persuaded her to come along with the rest of them.

It was the holiday period, the hospital was closed, and she couldn't get out of it. She wrapped a scarf which had once been black but now was bleached almost white around her head and slung an old Tatar bag over her shoulder with her supplies for the trip and her swimming costume.

They locked the house and put the key in a place agreed on many years ago, since unexpected guests were always expected. Nora and Tanya were already sitting at the Hub, both dressed in white from top to toe, and from under Nora's spectacles a narrow little poplar leaf protruded, just the right size for her nose. Georgii inspected their footwear.

"Right, we're off!"

The caravan moved off. Artyom walked in front, behind him the beaming Alik with Liza, and behind them the girls in a riot of color, while Georgii and Medea brought up the rear.

On this stretch the road went smoothly downhill and after the first steep descent led them out to Fox Canyon. There had been a stream here once, but like most of the local streams it was long since gone. No one could even remember what it had been called, and it reappeared only for a few days in the year, when the snows were melting, as a trickle of murky meltwater. They walked in semidarkness along the stony bed of the shallow canyon. In its walls, which were clay lower down and rocky farther up, there were numerous fox lairs, a whole ancient city. These lairs were empty now, or had been reoccupied by rather unprepossessing little corsac foxes with pale fur and morose little snouts. Georgii kept looking higher up: his hunter's eye had never yet failed to spot some kind of small game here.

They came out through Fox Canyon to an old defunct waterfall and turned onto a path which eventually crossed the main road and brought them out to the creek. By now the longer, and easier, part of the journey was behind them, and they called a halt here at a small grassy clearing overgrown with dwarf juniper before beginning the dangerous descent along the precipitous path on the coastal cliffs. This enclosed space, bounded by the cliffs and on one side by the slope of a steep little hill, always had its own pungent and individual smell, a mingling of the scent of juniper with the smells of seaweed, salt, and fish.

They always kept the break here short, in order not to let the heat of the day get to them and make them too relaxed, but just long enough for them to gather their strength before the last leg of the journey. Georgii, without the least pedagogical intention, year after year gave all the family's children incomparable lessons in the art of survival. He versed the boys and girls in a pagan's exact and subtle knowledge of how to treat water, fire, and wood. Thus even now Artyom, not the best of his pupils, had squatted down without taking his rucksack off, while Katya was giving the little ones a drink of the boiled water they had brought from home, a small tumblerful to each.

Medea sat with her old legs stretched out. She picked at the soil between the roots of a juniper bush and called to Nike. A tarnished ring with a small pink coral lay in her hand.

"Another find?" Nike asked in delight.

Everybody knew about Medea's unusual talent. She shook her head. "How shall I put it? A loss, more like. Your mother lost this ring. She thought the sea had washed it away, but here it is."

She put the simple little ring in Nike's hand and thought, "Does it still hurt? It seems it does."

"When?" Nike asked tersely. She guessed she was skirting a forbidden topic, the long-standing quarrel between the sisters.

"The summer of 1946," Medea replied quickly.

Nike held the ring in her hand, the coral still gleaming pink, but dead. Everybody crowded around, looking into her hand, as if it really was a living creature that was lying there.

Georgii glanced down over the women's heads: "Tatar. My mother has one almost exactly the same."

Katya cast a covetous eye at it. "Mum, can I try it on."

Masha too held out her hand to take a closer look. It was not a big miracle, but a miracle nevertheless.

Suddenly little Tanya shouted, "Look! Look who it is!"

Someone was hurtling down the steep slope of the hill toward them. He was flying with the speed of a skier, jumping over the occasional bushes, skating over the scree, squatting down, swerving from side to side, braking with one foot then with the other. Before him rushed a cascade of small stones, and behind him rose a plume of dust. His face was invisible beneath the peak of his baseball cap, but Nora immediately recognized him by his white jeans: it was her new neighbor.

Georgii glowered at him. The man was agile, but a poser. Butonov flew, just ahead of a minor avalanche of stones, into the middle of the clearing, jumped up on the spot, and froze like a statue. Then he dusted himself down and, addressing himself to Nora, said, "I saw you from the Village when you were approaching the road, and now I've caught up."

Everyone, including Medea, looked at him with interest, but that was nothing new for Butonov. He took off his cap, ran his hands over his face, and shook them as if they were wet.

"You approached Karatash from the left, then?" Georgii asked briskly.

"Where?" Butonov asked in return.

"This hill," Georgii said, indicating it with a nod.

"Yes, from the left," Butonov confirmed.

Georgii knew this inconspicuous path but did not take the children along it, considering the descent with its loose scree too dangerous.

"Who is he? Who is he?" Masha nagged Nike.

Nike shrugged. "A vacationer. He's staying with Aunt Ada. He looked in yesterday with Nora."

"Oh yes, of course, I heard someone come in. I put the children to bed and fell asleep myself."

"And see what a dreamboat you missed. Some hunk!" Nike whispered in Masha's ear.

"Right, on your feet now, everyone!" Georgii commanded.

Liza started whining and clinging to her mother's legs. "Mummy, carry me, I'm tired."

"Walk, walk yourself, you're a big girl," Nike said, fending her daughter off absentmindedly.

"Masha, carry me for a bit, eh, Masha?" she said, latching on to Masha.

"Who is he, then?" Masha asked.

"Half-athlete, half-masseur," Nike grunted. "Don't get too excited, he's not your cup of tea. He's completely thick." She promptly called over to Butonov, who was standing some way off: "So what's this, Valerii? Changed your mind at the last minute and decided to catch up with us?"

"Yes, I looked down and saw this nice bunch of people. I thought I must be completely thick to be the only person left behind in the Village."

Masha and Nike burst out laughing: the man was a mind-reader.

"Have your landlord and landlady gone out?" Nike enquired.

"This is their second day hitting the bottle. They've got visitors, and that's not my favorite occupation," Butonov replied, unexpectedly primly, having probably sensed something uncomplimentary in the women's laughter.

Georgii turned to Butonov: "I'll go first, you bring up the rear."

Valerii nodded. Georgii jumped down, following the path. Butonov let everyone go in front of him. Masha with Liza on her shoulders went immediately ahead of him. He caught up with her and touched her forearm: "Let me carry your daughter."

Masha shook her head.

"No, she won't let you. Take Alik if you like."

But Alik didn't want him to either.

Masha felt the spot this athlete or whatever he was had just touched. The skin was burning. She automatically felt her other arm—no, it was only the spot he had touched that was burning. She stopped, took Liza off her shoulders, and said quietly to her: "Liza, walk yourself, I'm not feeling well just at the moment."

Liza looked at her with her clever eyes. "Shall I carry your bag?"

"Oh, how sweet you are," Masha said, delighted by such unexpected goodheartedness in the spoiled child. "When I get tired, I'll ask you, all right?"

It was the start of the section of the path with a sheer drop on one side. Once upon a time, a hundred years ago, there had been a road here which the local smugglers had used to ferry their precious goods out through the coves, and in those days you could drive a bullock cart along it. Year by year the path had crumbled away. The smugglers who had once looked after the road, shoring it up, reinforcing the slopes, had long since died out, some of old age, some more violently, and their descendants had either been deported or become bureaucrats, first in the old tsarist council, then in the district soviet, exchanging one form of criminality for another. Now it was only Medea who remembered the illicit romantic past of these parts, and perhaps a few old Crimeans who had long since moved on, to the Central Crimea if they were lucky.

"In a hundred years or so it will have crumbled away completely," Georgii remarked.

Medea nodded fairly indifferently. Katya and Artyom seemed not to hear what he had said—for the old and the very young a hundred years, for different reasons, is too long a period of time to be taken very seriously.

Nora, trying not to look to the right, into the ravine, was leading Tanya with hands damp with fear. Tanya had refused a ride on Georgii's shoulders. Nora was upbraiding herself for dragging the child on such a hazardous outing. It was very, very unwise, but she could hardly be the only one to turn back halfway. Tanya, incredibly enough, was not complaining but, lost in some fantasy of her own, asked periodically, "Mummy, are we going to see a castle?" She couldn't be persuaded that there wasn't going to be a castle, only sea.

On the last stretch of the sheer path, however, a castle duly materialized. It was an eroded limestone feature raising gothic spires of different heights toward heaven. The underlying granite of the Karadag spur, igneous tufas, and tertiary deposits combined, as Georgii told them, in a formation of geological strata the like of which was to be found nowhere else in the world. It was as if icicles many meters long were growing upward, in some places vertically, while in others, revealing the prevalence of a wind blowing from one direction, they all inclined the same way, like the tentacles of some gigantic subterranean creature.

"Mummy, look, there's the castle!" Tanya shouted, and everyone laughed.

This spectacle was so strange that it soon became unbearable. You wanted to move on; it was just too unearthly.

Every time Medea found herself in this spot, she was reminded of the late artist Bogaevsky, whom she had known from her days in the grammar school, one of Theodosia's many artists and perhaps, after Aivazovsky, the best known. His strange pictures were inspired by these rock caprices, the black and green precipices and pink fractures of Karadag. She did not like the pictures for their falsity and improbableness, yet each time she came back here, she would say to herself, this too was all impossible, completely improbable, and yet here it was, existing in the world, changing shape, dropping large light-colored grains of sand, and down there a small sandy beach had already been formed out of them quite unlike anything else in the neighborhood.

After another thirty meters or so the path gingerly broke away from the cliff and split up into several little winding paths running down to the sea. Here the small children were let down from shoulders, the hands of those who were older were let go of, and through the clefts and past the great uneven boulders they descended and received their reward: in this inaccessible spot the sea was at its purest and most precious, and each time they felt as if they had conquered it anew.

There were two little twin coves, with a thin rocky bridge dividing them. They cut back quite deeply into the coastline, and a number of large rocks jutted out of the sea directly opposite them. Both these coves and the rocks in the sea had had their names changed on many occasions, but in recent decades it had become increasingly common to refer to them as "Medea's." At first they had been given the name by Medea's young relatives. From them the new name was adopted by the postwar settlers, and subsequently also by other people they didn't know, who, if they had heard of a Medea, knew only the other, mythical one.

Getting down to the water was awkward, over uneven boulders sprinkled with coarse shingle. The rocks were scattered around at random as if this had once been a playground for troll children. Here there were none of the pretty gemstones, chalcedonies, carnelians, the different-colored Crimean jaspers which you found in the Bay of Koktebel; but to make up for it there were any number of light-colored figure-of-eight pebbles with a dark, drawn-in waistband, and quantities of exotic flotsam and jetsam thrown up by storms. And then, right down by the water's edge, there was the shining white sand with never a tinge of yellow.

They all went down to the sea, abandoning their belongings, and all as one fell silent. There was always this moment of respectful silence in the presence of the relative eternity lapping softly at their feet.

Katya was the first to take off her slippers and proceed with her affected ballerina's walk down to the water. Now that she was walking with her back turned to Artyom, he could at last look at her without fear of catching her hostile, mocking glance. But even looking at her back, it was obvious she had no need of anyone or anyone's friendship.

Artyom was suffering, looking at her erect back and her little head with its sleek bun on the very top, à la Mary Poppins. She bent her body as she picked her way over the stones, turning her feet so that the toes pointed outward, and her firm calves, convex on the inside, gave a little wobble at every step. She walked along the water, and she too was suffering even as she indulged herself. She knew that she was walking well, but the only person looking was that utter drip Artyom, while Uncle Georgii, if he was looking at all, would be looking disapprovingly, and that new neighbor didn't even know she was there. She walked on, the spirit of ballet incarnate, but the most dreadful thing that could happen had already happened: she had been expelled from ballet school because her *jeté* was hopeless. She could turn out her feet splendidly, her *allongé* was fine, but her *jeté* was a flop. More specifically, she could walk weightlessly, as if she were flying, but on stage her *ballon* was leaden and her teachers knew it would never improve. She stepped into the water by the shore, which was gently stirring pink seaweed brought from far away; she ran her ballerina's foot over it, and it was cold to touch but with a pleasant velvety feel.

"Is it very cold?" Nike called to her daughter.

"Eleven degrees," Katya replied unsmilingly.

"Terrible!" Nike exclaimed.

"When it's thirteen it's all right for swimming," Masha remarked, heading for the water.

The littlest ones, all three of them, followed after her. Alik was leading Liza with one hand and trying to take Tanya's hand with the other.

"We've got a lady's man in the making," Nike murmured.

"What do you mean! He's just very kindhearted," Georgii protested.

Nike was about to make a further reply, but suddenly Medea's voice was heard. "I like this latest generation of children. These two, and Tom's little Revaz, and Brigita, and Vaska."

"But aren't they all the same?" Nike asked in surprise. "Are these really any different from Katya and Artyom, or from us when we were little?"

"There was a time when generations were counted thirty years apart, but now I think they change every decade. Katya, Artyom, Shusha's twins, and Sofiko—they are very purposeful. They will be businesspeople. But these little ones are so tender, so full of love, for them relationships are everything, emotions . . ."

Medea had no time to finish speaking before a shriek came from Liza down at the water's edge: "Let go, let go of his hand! Make her let go of him!"

Liza was trying to pull Alik's hand out of Tanya's, and Tanya, with her head lowered, was pulling it toward herself.

Everybody laughed. "Women!"

Nora rushed to Tanya, caught her up in her arms, and started whispering something to her. Only a few days had passed since she had met these people, and she liked them all; she felt drawn to them, but she couldn't understand them, and somehow they treated their children differently from the way she treated her daughter.

"They are too strict with the children," she thought in the morning.

"They give them too much freedom," she concluded in the afternoon.

"They spoil them terribly," it struck her in the evening.

Admiring them, envying them, and disapproving of them all at the same time, she had not yet worked out that they apportioned part of their lives to their children but not all of it.

"Collect some firewood, Artyom," Georgii quietly ordered his son.

The boy blushed. His father had noticed him staring at Katya. He bent down and picked up a splintered plank which a storm had brought in.

"Collect it higher up, there's a lot of dry stuff there," Georgii advised, and Artyom went back up the shore, relieved.

Georgii himself picked up two water churns.

"I'll come and get the water with you," Butonov offered.

Georgii would have preferred to go on his own to this ancient place which Medea had pointed out to him when he was a boy but, out of politeness, did not object.

It had the makings of a warm, even hot day. In this hidden spot, as Medea had long known, the natural world lived more intensely: in the winter it was colder here, and in warm weather hotter; in this seemingly sheltered spot the winds whirled with furious force. And the sea cast up onto the shore unheard of rarities: fish which no one had seen on this coast for a hundred years; shellfish, cockles, and mussels which inhabited the depths of the sea, and little starfish the size of a child's hand.

Medea put on her bathing costume. It had been a daring novelty of Parisian fashion in 1924, and had been brought to Medea by a certain literary celebrity of those years. The whole outfit had completely lost its color and had short little sleeves and something resembling a skirt. It had all been skilfully restored by Nike with the aid of scraps of navy blue and maroon knitted material, and on Medea it did not look ridiculous. Although during the August party, which was always held at the house to celebrate Medea's birthday and the end of the season for the children, when Medea had an endless queue of people wanting to wear it, the costume looked totally clownish on anybody other than herself.

"Are you going to swim?" Nike asked in surprise.

"We'll see," Medea replied noncommittally.

Nora felt a pang when she thought of her own mother, prematurely aged, her swollen white legs lined with blue veins, hysterically and frantically embattled with the evils of old age, her constant tearful demands and ultimatums, her insistent advice and recommendations.

"Lord, what incredibly normal human relationships. There's nobody demanding anything from anyone else, not even the children," she sighed.

At just this moment the wailing Liza rushed to her mother demanding that Tanya should without delay surrender a pipefish which they had just found, because she saw it first but Tanya had grabbed it. Nike was sitting cross-legged. She didn't turn a hair, only rummaged behind her and, without looking around, pulled a flat stone from behind her back, adroitly picked out of a pile of pebbles a little reddish one, and started rubbing the red one over the grey one. She did not try to calm her daughter, made no attempt to resolve the dispute fairly, and accordingly Nora, who was all ready to try to persuade her daughter to show magnanimity and hand over the shell, also stayed seated.

"I'm just going to draw something, but you'll never in your life guess what," Nike said into space, and Liza, still shedding tears, was already following the deft movements of Nike's hand.

Her mother shielded the drawing with her hand, and Liza moved around to the side of her to get a peep. Nike turned away.

"Mum, show me," Liza begged.

Nora was overcome by admiration of Nike's pedagogical abilities.

A little later the same day she was again filled with admiration for her abilities, this time culinary. On a campfire, in an ancient battered pot, Nike made a soup out of dried packet soups into which she threw heaven knows what: crumbs and bits of bread swept off the table after breakfast and wrapped in a linen cloth, chopped leftover pieces of yesterday's sorrel, and even hard little leaves of thyme picked on the way down to the cove.

This was the Medea or, more accurately, the Matilda school of culinary art, ideally suited to the larger family of slender means. To this day Medea never threw anything out, even making a crunchy bisque out of potato peelings with herbs and salt: the ideal accompaniment for beer, according to Georgii.

Nora knew nothing of this. She helped herself to soup out of the communal pot with a wooden spoon, placing a piece of bread under it as Medea did; she drank the thick, fragrant broth with a long-forgotten childish hunger and looked over constantly to where the little ones were sitting at a separate rock table. This was another family tradition: feeding the children at a separate table.

"Some more for Medea, please, Nora," Georgii said, proffering Medea's empty bowl.

Nora leaned over the pot in confusion.

"Use the mug, the mug, we haven't got a ladle," he said.

"They're a couple," Nike thought. "A perfect couple. He ought to have an affair with her. He's been so low these last few years."

Nike had a hunter's flair for knowing where the lovebirds were waiting to be flushed out, even other people's. Yesterday evening she had allocated Butonov to herself. Actually, of course, there was no one else to choose, and he was good-looking, had a fantastic body and an easygoing manner. Admittedly he didn't have that spark which Nike looked for; and the fact of the matter was that he hadn't been transmitting any call signals.

"We'll just have to wait and see," Nike decided.

Butonov was sipping his soup, speaking to no one, looking at no one. Masha was sitting next to him, looking sad and somehow hunched up. Her arm was still burning, as if it had been slapped, and she wanted to try out his touch again. She had sat next to him quite deliberately, and in passing a spoon and the bread she had touched him twice, but there had been no recurrence of the burn, only a kind of dullness inside her. He was sitting next to her with his body as still as a Buddha's and radiating a rocklike strength. Masha was fidgeting. She just couldn't get comfortable, and eventually realized to her disgust that all this fussing was a subconscious attempt to interest him. She put her spoon down, stood up, and went to the sea, and as she went, she threw off the man's white shirt she had been wearing to shield herself from the sun. She plunged headlong into the water and immediately started swimming, without breathing and thrashing up a cloud of spray with her arms and legs.

"The girl's quite frantic," Medea thought.

Butonov looked in her direction. "That water is quite cold."

"Katya says it's eleven degrees, and she's our thermometer," Nike said, turning to him.

"Ah, you're up for it," Butonov noted to himself, directing a sober, steady gaze at her and, without hurrying, went down to the water. Masha was already coming out, shaking her head and getting her breath back.

"It's like swimming in a hole in the ice," she said with her teeth chattering.

"Yes, it's a strong sensation," Butonov agreed.

Masha lay down on the hot rocks, covering herself with the white shirt. Cold and heat flooded her body simultaneously.

Butonov sat down beside Medea.

"I hear, Medea Georgievna, that you swim all through the winter."

"No, my dear young man, it must be twenty years since I last did that."

They finished the soup, and Nike told Katya to wash out the pot.

"Why is it always me?" Katya asked indignantly.

"Just because," Nike smiled, and Nora was overcome for the umpteenth time: no remonstration, no explanation, no arguing.

Katya took the pot grumpily and went toward the water.

"Hey, Katya! You've forgotten something!" Nike called after her.

"What now?" Katya asked, turning round.

"Your smile!" Nike replied, demonstrating an ear-to-ear smile.

Katya made a deep theatrical curtsy, clasping the pot to her bosom.

"Ten out of ten," Nike appraised it.

She doesn't think twice about screwing up her beautiful face, pulling it out of shape with her fingers, and contorting her body to show the children a monkey which has been given a laxative, or a hedgehog which wants to kiss its mother but can't because of its prickles. She's not in the least afraid of making herself look ugly! Nora found this both amazing and beyond comprehension.

Medea didn't see this. She had turned her back to the sea and raised her eyes to the hills, the near at hand and the far away. Two thoughts were simultaneously in her mind: that when she was young she had loved the sea more than anything else in the world, but now looking at the mountains was much more important to her; and also, that behind her back, among these young relatives of hers, the languor of love was developing and the air was full of their mutual attractions and the subtle stirring of hearts and bodies.

CHAPTER 6

The ring which Medea had found in the coves truly had once belonged to Alexandra. In Medea's memory the summer of 1946 was the time they had been closest as sisters, meeting then for the first time after the war. Throughout the war Medea had gone nowhere, not only not leaving the Crimea, but not even going out of the Village. Alexandra too had stayed the whole time in Moscow, flatly refusing to be evacuated to Kuibyshev, to which families of the military were moved at the beginning of the war. That year, in 1946, it was as if the age difference between them had been evened out and Medea could finally stop worrying all the time about what her younger sister might get up to next.

Alexandra was a war widow with three children, worn down by the years of hardship and already past her prime. There was nothing to suggest that this would be the moment she would pull off another of her stunts.

The loss of the ring had been unimportant in every respect. Alexandra was always losing things. Possessions did not stay with her for long, and she did not become attached to them. Nevertheless, Medea could not get the finding of this ring which had been lost thirty years before out of her head, perhaps because she knew that, apart from the usual links of cause and effect, there are other links between events, sometimes evident, sometimes hidden, and sometimes completely unfathomable.

"Never mind, if it's something I need to know it will be explained," she decided, with total confidence in the One to whom all things are known, and stopped worrying.

Alexandra had a whole collection of rings. Almost since child-hood she had been tricking herself out in all sorts of frippery, and this despite the fact that she was young at just the time when this harmless feminine weakness was most heavily frowned on by public opinion. In the 1920s, when Medea was shielded from trouble by being an orphan with many children to look after, by her unsmiling seriousness and her unremitting concern for the younger ones, Alexandra, frivolous by nature but nobody's fool, inflated her forgivable weakness like a balloon until it seemed she might at any moment fly off wherever she fancied in pursuit of who knows what.

Over time, her innocent failing developed to such an extent that all manner of ideological missionaries from the Russian League of Communist Youth and elsewhere called off all at-tempts to lay claim to her soul. Her civic deficiencies were man-ifest, and her incurable frivolity became a diagnosis freeing her from participation in the great cause of building—well, exactly what, Alexandra didn't bother to find out.

Medea, the only member of the family to have received a full grammar-school education, had not really been properly taught during the times of war and revolution, and she longed to give her younger siblings a good start in life. With Alexandra she clearly failed. Alexandra was a poor student, although not with-out ability. In the municipal school she attended, there were still teachers left from the old grammar school, and it was not a bad school. Medea would sometimes come to collect her sister, and the old geography teacher, Nikolai Leopoldovich Velde, a great expert on the Crimea, would sit Medea down in the teachers' common room, volubly curse today's pupils for their lack of in-terest in studying, and lapse with heartfelt nostalgia into remi-niscing about the days when he used to take well-bred young ladies on excursions to the wildest and most remote corners and crevices of Karadag. In this there could be detected a secret hope that everything might yet return to normal—that is, to life as it was before the war and before the Revolution.

But although life did not return to normal, things gradually settled down and became more tolerable. The boys grew out of infancy. Like all the Sinoply men, they were drawn to the sea. Fishing, since time immemorial a favorite pastime of boys, was a means of putting food on the table for them from an early age, and old Uncle Grisha Porchelli, a descendant of Genoese settlers who had worked for Harlampy since he was a lad, took them with him when he went out night fishing for mullet, which was not the easiest of pastimes.

In 1924, Alexandra finished her secondary schooling in the seventh grade. Medea racked her brains wondering where she could find her a job. Although the famine had passed, unemployment was still terrible.

Medea spent two days mulling, even in her dreams, over how best to fix her up, and on the third day as she was going to work early in the morning—she was working at the time in the obstetrics unit of the Theodosia city hospital—she ran into Nikolai Leopoldovich Velde, who was out taking his morning constitutional in the direction of the Quarantine district. She had barely opened her mouth to tell him about her problem before he told her, as if he had already thought everything through and decided the matter for her, to come and see him after work.

When Medea went to see him, he had the whole business practically sewn up. He had prepared her a letter addressed to the director of the Karadag research station, who was an old friend of his.

"I don't know what sort of staff numbers he has there, but the station is under the auspices of the State Science Committee now, so perhaps they have got a bit of extra funding; the more so in the summer because they receive visiting scientists and have more work." He held out the envelope for her.

As Medea accepted the envelope, which was made of grey poor-quality paper, she immediately had a sense that things were going to work out. Every time she encountered these old ties or had dealings with old, prerevolutionary people, everything fell into place.

She knew the station very well. She knew its present director, and she even remembered Terentii Ivanovich Vyazemsky, who had founded it. That first summer she had stayed at the Stepanyans' dacha in Sudak. He used to come and visit them on matters concerning the station, a neglected old man in a frock coat which had acquired a reddish tinge with age, with a woman's scarf tied in the manner of an old fashioned cravat; and he was accompanied by a second, no less remarkable personage, but of a completely different kind, with a round face, a paunch, thick salt-and-pepper eyebrows, and with an equally strong Jewish accent in Russian and French: Solomon Solomonovich Krym, a member of the prerevolutionary Russian Duma and a local celebrity.

Stepanyan, a great philanthropist and patron of the arts, declined for some reason to support his petitioners on that occasion, and in the evening, after supper, related what an original and unusual person this Dr. Vyazemsky was—a physiologist, a crusader for temperance, and a proponent of the strangest ideas. He was particularly keen for many years on the most unusual of these: he was concerned that, by locking its intellectuals up in prison, the state was losing their wonderful mental energy, which it could be putting to good use for the benefit of the state itself, and that by establishing penal scientific laboratories that energy could be conserved in the interests of society. Terentii Ivanovich enthusiastically propounded this idea to the then minister of education, Count Delyanov, who thought the whole notion bizarre and even dangerous, although it was successfully taken up by the state a few decades later.

"*C'est un grand original,*" Armik Tigranovna murmured, and sent the children upstairs to bed.

At that time everybody fortunately forgot the harebrained idea of the magnanimous madman. A few years later he sank all his fortune in a better-conceived project: creating a research station on his estate at Karadag which would be at the disposal of any serious scientist, even if he lacked formal academic qualifications and even, and indeed so much the better, if he were not in good health, because he could then restore his health right here in the course of productive scientific work, even if he were in straitened circumstances, because Dr. Vyazemsky would also open a sanatorium here and use the income from it to underwrite the expenses of research work.

The very next day Medea and her sister went to the station. The director kissed Medea on both cheeks. His older daughter, Xenia Ludskaya, had been in Medea's class at the grammar school, had worked with her at the hospital, and had died in 1919 of typhoid.

Old Ludsky went off to arrange for the station's external hygiene worker, or, in prerevolutionary parlance, the yard-sweeper, to vacate a small corner room in the station's residences for Alexandra. Then they drank tea at length, recalling mutual acquaintances, of whom there were more than a few, and parted on the warmest of terms.

Three days later Alexandra moved to the station and started learning everything she would need to know to facilitate the fieldwork of the students coming that year from Moscow, Leningrad, Kazan, and Nizhny Novgorod. She was a great success that first season and had lots of fun. First she had an affair with a category-two research worker from Kharkov, and when he left after collecting the requisite number of earthworms, the nicest geologist turned up who was compiling a large-scale geological map of Karadag, and she was allocated to him since his surveying could only be done with a partner. They proved excellent partners, both tall with a hint of rust in their hair, and hazel eyes, both cheerful and fun loving, and the geologist, whose name was Alexander, which both of them also found amusing, marked a faint cross on his new map in all the good, private locations they found, and from July until the last days of October, Alexandra never spared herself in underpinning the upward progress of science, beginning with the Beregovoy Ridge, and charting all its five massifs, from Lobovoy to Kok-Kai. After that the weather broke and the geologist departed, postponing the culmination of his efforts to the following year.

The winter didn't drag. Alexandra worked hard in the library and the station museum and proved to have the requisite degree of common sense, literacy, and numeracy to cope with the demands made of her. In late March all manner of scientists began arriving and things livened up again. In addition the gliding center, which had been in decline for a few years, revived and broad-shouldered sportsmen and romantic inventors were soon to be found not far away on St. Clement's Hill in quiet Koktebel. As a result, by the time last year's geologist returned, Alexandra was already in love with a glider pilot whom she swapped a month later for his twin brother, who resembled him so closely that Alexandra barely noticed the moment of transition.

Medea made no attempt to pry into her sister's personal life, and was only glad that she had a good job where she was not ill treated and, indeed, on the contrary, spoiled. She was much more worried about the younger ones. Dimitry showed great promise in mathematics and dreamed of going to the artillery college. Medea did her best to tactfully steer him away from the military profession, but he was profoundly sensitive to her maneuvering, clammed up, distanced himself from her, and, although he never said a word, left her in no doubt that he considered Medea a bourgeois relic and ballast left behind by the *ancien régime.* Constantine, although only two years older, had no leanings in that direction and continued to go out fishing with Uncle Grisha Porchelli, and seemed to dream of nothing more complex than standing nets and dragnets.

A certain coolness which developed between Medea and her younger brothers upset her deeply, the more so since she now saw Alexandra quite infrequently as well. Alexandra would come to Theodosia a couple of times a month, run around to see her friends, and in passing, over supper, tell Medea about life at the station, mainly about her trips out and things she had found, leaving her tempestuous private life strictly private. Medea had little trouble, however, in guessing that her kid sister was not missing out on anything, diving for pearls in any sea, and sipping honey from any flower. This led her to reflect sadly that her own life was not fulfilled, and probably never would be.

She was not in demand. Her iconic face, her small head, even then bound with a scarf, her flat-chestedness—in the estimation of the men of Theodosia, her general thinness did not attract admirers.

"Evidently my intended was killed in the war," Medea decided, and quickly reconciled herself to the idea. She thought, however, that she needed to get Alexandra married off as soon as possible.

Alexandra had been working at the station for three years. It would have been closer to the facts to say three seasons. Meanwhile her future husband was already packing his bags in Moscow, on Polyanka Street, in preparation for a research visit to Karadag.

Alexei Kirillovich Miller belonged to a rather prominent St. Petersburg family which had what at one time was a slightly dangerous aura of "progressiveness" and long-established humanitarian traditions. His most prominent ancestor was one of Peter the Great's Germans; both grandfathers, paternal and maternal, were professors. His father had shown promise of going far in the natural sciences and had been educated in England but died young, before reaching thirty, on an expedition to the North. Alexei Kirillovich, brought up by a rich aunt, an educated woman very active in the publishing business of her husband, also studied in England for a time but, because of the outbreak of war with Germany, returned to Russia before receiving his doctorate.

Congenital shortsightedness, which was actually quite minor, exempted him from military service, and after defending his doctoral dissertation at Moscow University, he remained there, first as an assistant professor and subsequently as a full professor. He was an entomologist and studied insects with complex social behavior. In effect, he was one of the first specialists in sociozoology. His favorite research subjects were earth wasps and ants. These wordless creatures were able to tell the observant researcher about the interesting and highly enigmatic events occurring in their city-states of many thousands of inhabitants, with all their complex administrative, economic, and military structures.

Many years later, finding himself in southern Germany with the indefinite status of displaced person and the position of research worker in a secret scientific institution which brought together the intellectual potential of occupied Europe, organized in accordance with the principle once proclaimed by the late Terentii Ivanovich Vyazemsky, he even wrote a short work full of deeply pessimistic elegance, in which he tried to separate out common behavioral patterns in colonies of social insects and in the prisoner-of-war camps where he had spent almost a year as a translator before being transferred to the laboratory.

This work, in which he provided a sad theoretical basis for

racism as a biological phenomenon, perished in early 1945 during the bombing. Unfortunately together with its author.

But in that summer of 1925 in the Crimea he first succeeded in observing from start to finish the drama of the conquest of one race of ants by another, beginning with the first invasion of the newcomers, relatively smaller, but with more massive jaws. Sitting over an anthill by the hour and peering into the deceptively purposeful life of beings incapable of existing as individuals, he felt himself almost like the Lord God and well able to understand but unable to express in his customary scientific language the notion that in the innocent to-and-fro of the ants there was both a mystery and a destiny and a lesson for humanity. Not only biology was at work here, there was much else besides: he had the presentiment of an imminent discovery, he was in an excellent mood, and he felt a surge of energy.

Alexei Kirillovich was not yet forty. He belonged to that breed of people who are respectable from birth, fixed at a predetermined age once and for all. Possibly he had been feeling so good these last few years precisely because this personal age of his, which was independent of the passing of years, currently coincided with his age by the calendar.

He had gone bald early, but even before the hair fell naturally from his round head with its gleaming, symmetrical bumps, he had begun to shave it and to grow a small beard and mustache. To complete his image, spectacles in a gold frame were required, and a prerevolutionary-style linen or silk suit of a size even more expansive than was demanded by his early but entirely muscular stoutness. He was light on his feet, an excellent swimmer, and, something you would hardly have suspected of him, an excellent player of all ball games, from tennis to soccer. His English schooling, no doubt.

That year volleyball was all the rage at the Karadag station. In the hour before sundown a very varied, socially mixed group of local and visiting researchers and students on field trips would pick their way back to shore over slippery rocks after their evening dip and play a relaxed game of ring volleyball. The prim and proper Alexei Kirillovich took the ball lightly on his sensitive phalanxes, passed it with precision, and, rising to the most difficult passes, rolled under the ball like an ocean wave. Alexandra leapt in a flurry of elbows and long shins with their sural muscles attached high up to the tendons, lost the ball, shrieked and chortled, opening her mouth so wide in the process that her pink gullet showed.

"What a charming young woman," Alexei Kirillovich thought to himself in an abstract, contemplative sort of way. He had married long ago; his wife was a professor, a hydrobiologist with a reputation no less solid than his own. Many years before, she had left her first husband for Alexei Kirillovich, then still a student, and they had married in the Registry Office.

There had been a time when she, born and brought up a Lutheran, had even thought of converting to Orthodoxy in order to legitimize her marriage officially, but in the postrevolutionary years the idea was dropped and even seemed risible. The profound disagreements between the denominations dissipated without a trace in the air of a new world which had no interest whatsoever in any Articles of Schmalkalden.

The couple lived in civil marriage in peace and harmony, exchanging professional information over the dinner table and not inclining in the least toward adultery. That merest flicker of a flame catching light in his bosom under its thick coat of furlike hair might well have remained unnoticed even by Alexei Kirillovich had not Alexandra herself felt attracted to this droll, old-fashioned professor, and had she not assiduously fanned the flame of unfocused, barely smoldering interest.

At first she gave him three days, but he made no approach beyond positioning himself opposite her in the volleyball circle and only passing the ball to her. Then she gave him another two days. Every evening they went swimming together with a noisy group of friends, then played ball, and still he made no approach, only casting quick, frightened glances in her direction and intriguing her more and more. They did not see each other during the working day: he went off to his plots to watch the ants, and she helped the botanists with their work in the herbarium.

For people of strong moral principles and decent physical habits, such as Alexei Kirillovich undoubtedly was, life lays the simplest traps, but also the most effective. The final twist came when he had all but emerged as victor in a contest which had never begun. Actually, the twist came in Alexandra's ankle in a moment of abandon on the volleyball court. It was impossible for her to stand on it.

The male research workers took turns carrying Alexandra from the shore to the house. First, two postgraduates bore her on hands linked to make a seat; then Botazhinsky, an ichthyologist, carried her piggyback; finally, for the last third of the way, it was Alexei Kirillovich's turn. That evening she was his, elbows, knees, sprained ankle and all.

He could remember perfectly well carrying her to the corner room and then going over to Junge's dacha to get a bandage from the dispensary, a prerevolutionary German bandage from the supplies of the late Vyazemsky, no less, and returning to Alexandra to wrap her swollen and inflamed foot. The half-hour which passed between the act of bandaging and the moment when, without even closing the door, he plunged into the muscular grip of the novice volleyball player, disappeared without trace from his memory.

Possibly, Alexandra conceived that very evening, and two months later, departing before the end of his period of research leave, Alexei Kirillovich went back to Moscow leaving her unambiguously pregnant and quite certain that he would be returning for her in the very near future. However, the rearrangement of his former life which this romantic history entailed needed more time than he had supposed.

His wife took Alexei Kirillovich's announcement of the new circumstances with Lutheran calm and even perhaps rather coldly. The only condition she stipulated was, however, unexpected and not easily met: she asked him to resign from the university where they both worked. Before September he had no means of looking for teaching work since the higher education institutions were all on vacation. In September a vacancy came up at the Timiryazev Academy, but now there were problems with accommodation. The apartment on Polyanka Street went to his wife. The Timiryazev had staff accommodation, but time was needed to complete the necessary applications and obtain the essential signatures and resolutions.

Time passed. Alexandra was not conspicuously pregnant and did not have to let out her clothes until the seventh month. She received weekly letters from Alexei Kirillovich and, thanks to her carefree nature, gave not a thought to what would happen if he were to disappear as unexpectedly as he had appeared. Or perhaps her equanimity was based on confidence that if need be Medea would take on this child too, as she had once taken on Alexandra and her brothers.

In the meantime neither sister said anything, although Medea did go through the old linen and set aside a few bits and pieces for diapers. Only when she saw an old-fashioned baby's bonnet in Medea's hands, on the border of which she was finely embroidering a crisscross pattern, did Alexandra tell her about Alexei

Kirillovich, tossing her hair and perhaps protesting a little too much: "I do like him *very* much . . . he really is a *very* interesting man . . . he is someone you *already* know *very* well . . ."

Medea did indeed remember him from the days of her childhood, when Alexei Kirillovich, who was a student at the time, had rented a room in their house before he went to England. The Crimea attracted a lot of naturalists then. Now both the Sinoply sisters were waiting for Alexei Kirillovich's return.

He, meanwhile, had been allocated his accommodations, a winter dacha beside the Timiryazev park. The dacha was so run-down it had to be hastily redecorated, and additionally Alexei Kirillovich had a major new lecture course to prepare on general entomology, as well as a special course on "orchard pests."

Alexandra's son didn't, however, wait for them to move to Moscow and was born under the supervision of his Aunt Medea at the same Theodosia city hospital in which Matilda had given birth to all of her children. Only Dr. Lesnichevskii was no longer in the land of the living.

Two weeks later, without advance warning, Alexei Kirillovich arrived at Medea's door. He knew from Alexandra's letters that shortly before the birth she had moved in with her sister. He found a young woman sitting by the window on a bentwood Vienna chair with cropped ginger hair half-concealing her face, and a round-headed baby sucking at her bluish-white breast. This was his family. It took his breath away.

Two days later, Alexei Kirillovich and his new family departed for Moscow. There was no need for Medea to travel with them, but by now she had become so attached to her nephew, whom she had already christened, becoming his godmother in the process, that she took time off work and went with them to help Alexandra settle into her new home. That month, the first month of little Sergei's life, she vicariously experienced to the full the motherhood that would never be hers.

Sometimes it seemed to her that her own breasts were filling with milk. She returned to Theodosia with a sense of profound inner emptiness and loss. "My youth is over," Medea guessed.

CHAPTER 7

Valerii Butonov came from the Rastorguevo district of Moscow. He lived with his mother, Valentina Fyodorovna, in a low private house which had long been threatening to fall apart. He had no recollection of his father and as a boy was convinced that his father had died in the war. His mother did not particularly insist on that, but neither did she undermine the legend. Valentina Fyodorovna's short-stay husband had signed up for contract work somewhere in the Russian North even before the war. He had sent back one letter of little interest and then dissolved forever in the polar wastes.

Like most boys his age, Valerii spent his protracted childhood hanging on rickety fences or driving a captured German penknife, his most precious possession, into the run-down suburban soil. In this activity he had no equals, winning with his knife easily and lightheartedly, like a latter-day Alexander the Great, all the cities and states gambled on the barren patch of land behind the Rastorguevo bus station.

The neighborhood kids, having ascertained his total superiority, stopped playing with him, and he spent many hours in the courtyard of his house, implanting the penknife in the pale walleye where the lower branch of an enormous pear tree had been sawn off, gradually moving farther and farther away from his target. Over these long hours he gained an insight into the mechanics of throwing, knew it inside out with both hand and eye, but derived the greatest pleasure from the lightning moment when the knife in his hand and his chosen target came into alignment, culminating in the quivering of the haft in the heart of his target.

Sometimes he would take a different one, a kitchen knife, and choose a different target, and with a crunch or a moan or a thin whistle the knife would penetrate it. His mother's old house, already falling apart, was covered in scars from his boyhood practicing. Perfection proved boring, however, and in the end he packed it in.

New vistas opened up when he moved from primary school to the newly introduced ten-year secondary school where much was new and unfamiliar: urinals, porcelain washbasins, a stuffed owl, a picture of a naked man with no skin, wonderfully shaped glass vessels, metal contrivances with valves. The place that really fascinated and delighted him, however, was the sports hall, which, for those times, was very well equipped. From the fifth grade on, he honed in on the horizontal bars, the parallel bars, and the leather vaulting horse.

A physical giftedness, so much admired in the classical world, and just as rare as musical or poetic talent, or a talent for chess, became apparent in Butonov. He didn't know that the modern world rated his talent lower than intellectual gifts, and reveled in progress which became more striking with every passing month.

The physical education mistress sent him to the Central Sports Club gymnastics section, and by the new year he was taking part in the first competitions in his life. The trainers were astonished by his phenomenal grasp, his natural economy of movement, and his self-discipline. He achieved results immediately which usually had to be diligently pursued for years.

He wasn't yet twelve years old when he was first sent for trials. On that occasion the junior athletes were not taken outside of Moscow; they were simply put up in a military hotel on Commune Square, in four-bedded rooms with a red carpet, a decanter and telephone on a hardwood table, in the ponderous opulence of the Stalin style with a military nuance.

It was during the school year, so in the mornings the gymnasts dispersed to their schools and, when they returned, had lunch in the local military cafeteria with thirty-ruble vouchers. The sports complex was located in the right-hand wing of a low, squat building, at the heart of which was the Great Hall. It was there that the future flowers of Soviet sport passed the best hours of their happy childhood. Entry was possible only with a pass, and everything together, the vouchers for lunch, the top-quality calorific food with chocolate, condensed milk, and cakes, the pass itself with his photograph in its little booklet, and especially the dark blue woollen tracksuit with a white stripe by the collar which was issued free, inspired a due respect in the youthful Butonov for his own body, which was deemed worthy of these heaven-sent goodies.

He wasn't too good at school, always carrying some unredeemed failing mark, which he usually put right by the end of the term for fear he would be banned from training. Since he was the sports star of the school, his teachers usually bit the bullet and awarded him highly questionable passing marks without too much trouble.

By the age of fourteen he was a strikingly built youth with regular facial features, his hair cut short in the sporting fashion, disciplined and ambitious. He was a member of the youth gymnastics team, training under the master of sport schedule and aiming for first place in the forthcoming All-Union Competition.

His trainer, Nikolai Vasilievich, was an intelligent sports insider who had seen it all, had high hopes of him, and anticipated a major athletic career. He took a lot of trouble with Valerii, and his straightforward way of calling him "my son" was very meaningful and important to the boy. Valerii looked for shared features with his idol: he was glad their hair was the same color and their greyish-blue eyes similar; he narrowed his eyes the way Nikolai Vasilievich did, imitated the rolling, springy way he walked, and even bought himself white handkerchiefs like the ones Nikolai Vasilievich had.

He did not, however, win the All-Union Competition, even though he was sure he had. He performed excellently, felt like a knife in flight, and knew he had hit the target; but there were other important things he did not know, which his trainer knew only too well, about the secret mechanisms of success, about friends in high places, about rigged judging and the barefaced corruption of sport. The two decimal points which relegated Butonov to second place seemed to him such a cruel injustice that in the changing room he threw off his free Central Sports Club outfit and went back to Rastorguevo wearing his school trousers over his bare body.

Nikolai Vasilievich might just have succeeded in getting him back, papering over the defeat with meaningless words, slippery, half-true explanations of what had happened, but unfortunately one of Valerii's older teammates—Butonov was the youngest on the team—revealed the secret side of his unjust defeat to him. It was a fix, and his own trainer was implicated. The boy who won had been trained by the son-in-law of the head of the federation, and the panel of judges was not independent—not bribed exactly, but tied hand and foot.

A number of things fell into place now: why the day before his performance Nikolai Vasilievich, who had taught him to reach for the sky, had told him for no apparent reason, "Okay, Valerii, don't get too wound up. For you at your age second place won't be bad, not bad at all."

The trainer came out several times to Rastorguevo. The first time Valerii went up and hid in the attic like a little kid. The second time he came out but talked through his teeth, refusing eye contact. The third time Nikolai Vasilievich talked to Valentina

Fyodorovna, but she only held her arms out wide and bleated, "I'm sure it's all fine by me, what is there to get upset about, but it's up to Valerii . . ." She too liked the free Olympic suits and saw nothing wrong with second place.

Valerii, however, was implacable. Nikolai Vasilievich was afraid the boy would defect to the Worker Reserves or Spartak and someone else would get the credit for his three years' work, but that did not happen. The monstrous secret self-esteem of Butonov which had flourished in the shade of the Rastorguevo pear tree drove him on now to seek a different path, more certain, where there were no humiliating possibilities of defeat, no corrupt, rotten fixes, and treachery.

The summer holidays had begun, but he didn't go to any trials, just lay for days at a stretch under the pear tree, all the time wondering how what had happened could have happened, and after a week was vouchsafed a revelation: you shouldn't allow yourself to become dependent on circumstances or other people. Had he been musing under a fig tree, the revelation might have been of a more sublime nature, but that was the best that could be expected from a Russian pear tree.

Two weeks later he enrolled in the circus college. How wonderful it was! Every day Butonov came to train and experienced the delight of a five-year-old boy on his first visit to the circus. The training ring was entirely real: it smelled just as it should, of sawdust, animals, and talcum powder. Balls, colored clubs, and physically perfect girls flew freely through the air. This was a special, wholly unique world: that was what every cell in his body told him.

There was no question of competition here; each person was worth exactly what his profession was worth. The aerial gymnast could not be incompetent: his life was on the line. No telephone call could halt the bear when it reared up with its immobile muzzle completely incapable of expression and went to savage its trainer. Being related to the director, enjoying the support of someone higher up, was not going to help you turn a backward somersault.

"This is not like sport," a sadder but wiser Butonov reflected. "Sport is corrupt. This isn't."

Although he would have been hard-pressed to articulate the thought fully himself, he was profoundly aware that at the very peak of artistry in the Soviet Union, in the zone where you are totally master of your profession, there is a tiny platform of independence. Up there, on the summit of Mount Olympus, were the stars of the circus, who freely crossed frontiers into other countries, and wore unimaginably beautiful clothes, and were rich and independent.

The boy had intuited something crucial, although in many respects the circus was exactly the same as other Soviet institutions—the warehouse, the bathhouse, or academe. It had its Party committee, its local committee, its official subordination to superior institutions—and its unofficial subordination to any telephone call from the mystical heights. Envy, intrigue, and fear were the powerful levers of circus life, but this was something he had yet to learn. And in the meantime he lived that half-monastic life which sport had taught him. Although no formal vows had been taken, ascesis was observed, the rules of prayer were replaced by morning exercises and evening training, fasting was replaced by dieting, and the code of obedience by total subordination to the discipline of the trainer. The Master, as he was called here. As for chastity, which was not by any means esteemed in itself, a true sportsman's life was organized in such a way that the ferocious physical demands and the harsh regime made terrible inroads into the free and easy party mood which draws two young people to pool their energies for the giving and taking of mutual pleasure.

The school remembers Butonov to this day. He acquired all

the arts of the circus effortlessly: acrobatics, juggling, tightrope-walking, and each of these arts laid claim to him. Butonov had no equal in gymnastics.

From the first months of his studies he was invited to take part in existing routines. He refused, because he knew exactly what he wanted to be: a trapeze artist. To work the air . . . Butonov's teacher, replacing the discredited Nikolai Vasilievich, was an aging circus artist of indefinite nationality but from a circus dynasty, who looked like a Russian peddler but had the Italian name of Antonio Muzzetoni, and was popularly known as Anton Ivanovich.

Muzzetoni the Elder was born in a three-axled caravan on a faded red and blue circus horse blanket, on the road from Galicia to Odessa, to a lady horse rider and an acrobat. His face was etched with many deep vertical and horizontal wrinkles which were as intricate as the innumerable stories he told about himself.

In these, truth had blended with fiction so long ago that he himself no longer remembered what was embellishment. Seeing the exceptional gifts of his new pupil, he was already considering the possibility of eventually incorporating him into the troupe of aerial gymnasts in which his own son, nephew, and twelve-year-old granddaughter Nina flew from trapeze to trapeze.

By the end of his second year of training Butonov had matured greatly in knowledge, skill, and good looks. He was approximating ever more closely to the archetypal image of the builder of Communism familiar from red and white posters drawn with straight, uncomplicated horizontal and vertical lines, and with a deep transverse mark on the chin. His image needed a certain amount of further work, as was evident from the unimpressive ducklike end of his nose, but this was compensated for by the line of his shoulder, the quite un-Slavic long legs, and the refinement of his hands (heaven knows where that came from). And to cap it all, his quite incredible immunity to the female sex.

The circus girls, as in earlier days the girls at school, hung on him. Here everything was so exposed, so near at hand—the shaven armpits, and the contours of the groin, the muscular buttocks, the small, firm breasts. The other young circus artists of his age enjoyed the fruits of the sexual revolution and the artistic license flourishing in the backyards of Socialism, in an oasis on Fifth Street in Yamskoye Polye, but he viewed the girls with distaste and irony, as if Brigitte Bardot herself were waiting for him on a crumpled sofa back there in Rastorguevo.

Valentina Fyodorovna couldn't believe her luck: her son didn't drink, didn't smoke, didn't chase after women, had a good maintenance grant, and treated her well. She boasted to her neighbors: "Your Slavka is a right thug, but in all my born days I've never had a cross word from my Valerii."

At the end of his second year Butonov was awarded an apprenticeship: he was one of a number of privileged students excused the standard curriculum, attached to a master and allowed to work in an act. Anton Ivanovich put him into his son's program. Giovanni, or Ivan, although not endowed with his father's talents, had nevertheless been schooled by him. From his earliest days he had been flying beneath the big top, turning his somersaults; but his real passion was for cars. He was one of the first circus people to import a foreign car into Russia: a red Volkswagen. It might have been old hat for Germany, but it was thirty years ahead of the sluggish progress of the Soviet car industry.

Having carefully placed an old blanket under his extremely valuable back, he spent hours lying under the car. His ill-tempered, sluttish wife Lyalya remarked caustically, "If I got to lie under him as much as he lies under that car, he would be worth his weight in gold."

The younger Muzzetoni's relations with his father were less than straightforward. Although the son was already past thirty and, in Butonov's eyes, getting on a bit (indeed by circus standards this was almost pensionable age for an "aerial"), he was as scared of his father as a little kid. They had been working together for many years now: Anton Ivanovich had broken all records for longevity under the big top. He had always, since he was a boy, been the first to master the riskiest stunts. In the 1920s he was the only person who could perform a triple screw somersault, and it was eight years before another gymnast appeared who could duplicate the feat. Of his son Anton Ivanovich would say with carefully contained exasperation, "The one thing Ivan is perfect at is falling."

This aspect of the profession really was very important. They were working right up under the big top, and although they had the double reassurance of the lunges fastened to their belts and the safety net, serious injury was still possible. The younger Muzzetoni was considered a virtuoso at falling; the elder was a trailblazer by nature and had grown mightily tired of waiting for his son to deliver something he simply did not have in him.

That year, however, all the performers were preparing for a major circus festival in Prague, and Anton Ivanovich set to work on his son, brooking no contradiction. He was to revive the trick which had spread old Muzzetoni's fame the length and breadth of the country before the war.

Giovanni submitted reluctantly to his father. The old man always forced him to work with total dedication. Valerii, who was invariably present at rehearsals, felt his muscles quivering. He wanted desperately to try himself in the long and complex flight, but Anton Ivanovich was having none of it: he kept him paired with his nephew Anatolii. They performed their meeting flights with synchronized precision, but this was not going to set anyone back on their heels: all trapeze artists began that way.

The rehearsals lasted for a good six months, but the day finally came for them to go to the Central Directorate at Izmailovo to present their program to the Artistic Council. At stake was the trip to Prague: for Butonov, his first trip abroad.

There was turmoil at the directorate, a coming together of the star performers and the administrative bosses of the circus. Everybody was on edge. The time for the displays was approaching. Anton Ivanovich climbed up to check the mountings, which were partly outside the top of the marquee, and scrupulously went over every nut and every bolt, running his hands along the cables. The safety inspector of the arena was his old rival Dutov, and although the conditions of Dutov's job were such that any failure of the safety equipment would land him in jail, Anton Ivanovich was taking no chances.

Ivan was allocated a dressing room to himself, and Anatolii and Valerii shared another. The girls were put in a third. There were three of them, two young gymnasts and twelve-year-old Nina, Ivan's daughter and an undoubted future star.

The artists were already putting on their maroon costumes with the gold stars when Valerii heard swearing in the corridor: some access was being obstructed by Ivan's car and a circus wagon could not get through. Ivan gave a reply, the voice made some demand. Anatolii went over to the door and listened.

"Why are they going on at him? He's parked it fine."

Valerii didn't believe in interfering in other people's business and didn't even bother to look out. Everything quieted down.

A few minutes later there came a knock at the door of their dressing room, and Nina stuck her head in. "Valerii, Toma wants you to come."

Toma, one of the young gymnasts, had been coming on to him for a long time, and Butonov was both flattered and irritated.

He went to look in on her.

"Well, what do you think of my makeup, Valerii?" she asked, turning her little round face to Butonov as if to the sun.

Her makeup was the usual: a pinkish-yellow base with two delicate maroon wings of blusher, and the eyes heavily outlined in blue and drawn up to her temples.

"It's fine, Toma. The Cobra Look."

"Oh, you are beastly, Valerii." Toma skittishly tossed her head, which was drenched with lacquer like a doll's. "You only ever say horrid things."

Valerii turned and went out into the corridor. A grey-haired man in overalls and wearing a tartan shirt was emerging from the door of Ivan's dressing room. It was the shirt that caught Butonov's attention, and that was why he remembered the encounter later. They were on in ten minutes.

Everything went like clockwork, worked out second by second: blackout, a leap, lights, a push, a trapeze, a drumroll, a pause, music, blackout again. The score even indicated when to breathe in and out. Everything was going splendidly.

Giovanni saved his strength during this number, standing with his chest thrust out there in the heights immediately under the big top, godlike, holding the light on himself while the juniors went through their paces. Their work was clear-cut and competent but nothing out of the ordinary. The jewel in the crown, the triple screw somersault, was all Giovanni's. Not all the members of the Artistic Council had seen the trick, which was very rarely performed.

Old Muzzetoni was a shrewd director and had everything in place for maximum effect: the light flexible, floating; the music building up. Then suddenly a complete break: all the light on Giovanni up there under the roof, the arena in darkness, the music fortissimo and then cut.

Giovanni was sparkling, his head in gold, and wearing greaves devised by a clever designer to disguise his bowlegs. A hushed drumroll. Giovanni throws up his golden head. He is a demon incarnate. A momentary touch to his belt to check the carabiner.

Butonov had noticed nothing, but Anton Ivanovich's heart had almost stopped. Giovanni was taking too long checking it, something was wrong. Everything was still on course; he wasn't behind yet. The drumroll stopped. One, two, three, one second too many, the trapeze was going back, the push, the leap, Giovanni was still in flight and nobody knew, but already Anton Ivanovich could see that the formation was flawed and he could never complete that final pirouette. He was right.

Anatolii sent him the trapeze at the right moment, but Ivan missed it by twenty centimeters. He wasn't in the right place at the right moment; he stretched out in mid-flight for the trapeze, attempting the impossible feat of following it back, and hurtled out of the geometry he had perfected, plunging down to the outer edge of the net where it was most dangerous to land, where the tension was greatest, where he was most likely to be jarred and thrown out . . . He hit the edge, as his father knew he must.

The net stretched and threw Ivan up. But not out. Farther inside the net. He really was good at falling. It was a disaster, of course it was, but at least the boy hadn't been hurt.

But he had been. They lowered the net. The first to get to him was Anton Ivanovich; he grabbed the carabiner: the link was loose. He cursed under his breath. Ivan was alive but unconscious. He had taken a hard knock. Was it his skull? His spine? He was laid on a board. The ambulance arrived seven minutes later. He was taken to the best place of its kind, the Burdenko Institute. Anton Ivanovich accompanied his son.

Butonov saw his master only two weeks later. He had heard that Ivan was alive but unable to move. The doctors were working their magic on him but could give no assurance they would get him back on his feet.

Anton Ivanovich had lost so much weight he looked like an Italian borzoi. A dark suspicion was haunting him: he could not imagine how Ivan could have noticed the loose carabiner only immediately before the leap. Privately he knew that an upset of that kind would not have put him off; he would just have kept his cool. Indeed, something very much the same had happened to him once, and he had taken the belt off, unfastened himself completely, and just gone ahead. But Ivan had panicked, lost his cool, gone to pieces. Something else that didn't fit was why, immediately before he was due on, he had been ordered to move his car although it was perfectly well parked. Anton Ivanovich checked afterward himself: the wagon had had room to get through.

When Anton Ivanovich mentioned his misgivings to Butonov, he blurted out, "That workman from the estates office wasn't the only person who paid Ivan a visit."

Anton Ivanovich caught him by the sleeve. "Tell me about it."

"While he was away moving his car, Dutov went into his dressing room. I saw from the corridor, he came out in a tartan shirt."

By this time Valerii knew that Dutov himself was the safety inspector for the arena.

"Damnation! I'm a bright one. What a silly old fool I am," Anton Ivanovich said, clutching at his sagging face. "So that's what it was all about. That fits."

Butonov visited Ivan in the hospital. He was encased in plaster from his chin to his sacrum and looked like a mummy. His hair had thinned, with two deep bald patches encroaching from his brow. He blinked to say hello and could hardly speak. Valerii, swearing to himself for having gone in, sat there for ten minutes or so on a white visitors' stool trying to think of things to say. "Um, er," was followed by silence. He had had no idea until then just how fragile a human being is, and he was profoundly shocked.

The autumn was dull and wet. The pear tree in Rastorguevo had lost its leaves and stood there black, looking as if it had been burnt, so Butonov wasn't able to lie beneath it to see whether some new revelation might come to him.

There was half a year left before he would graduate from the circus college. The visit to Prague, of which he had had such high hopes, had gone down the tubes. The circus college too was in the process of going down the tubes. Butonov couldn't stop picturing Ivan's lackluster eyes. One minute there had been Ivan, Giovanni Muzzetoni, the famous circus performer, everything Butonov wanted to be: independent, rich, able to travel abroad, and driving around in the best car Butonov had ever seen. (He had got rid of the humpbacked red Volkswagen long ago, and now had a spanking new white Fiat.) And in a single instant it was all gone. Butonov had been wrong, there was no independence, it was all a sham. And now Ivan was going to be paralyzed until the day he died.

Butonov did not turn up to take his final winter exams. In the circus college, in addition to the special subjects, you were taught the usual school subjects and couldn't get a leaving certificate without passing in those despised disciplines too. Butonov never went back to the college again. He lay about on the divan for six months waiting for his military draft papers. He turned eighteen in February, and had his hair cropped by the army in early spring. He was first invited to enroll in the Central Army Sports Club, his top-grade certificate in gymnastics having made a suitable impression, but to the amazement of the enlistment office he turned the offer down. Butonov didn't care about anything anymore, but he didn't want to go back into sport. He had joined the army, and that was that.

But it didn't work out that way, as it never does. There was no escaping a talent which marked him out, and some extraordinary opportunity invariably came his way. Butonov could shoot better than anyone else, with a semiautomatic, a carbine, or a pistol as soon as he got it in his hands. Even the lads from Siberia who had been hunting since they were children couldn't match his keen eye and steady hand.

At the training review Butonov was spotted by the colonel, who was a great shooting enthusiast. Within a year he was in the Central Army Sports Club team, but now in marksmanship. It was back to training, trials, back to working out. His military service passed in a thoroughly agreeable manner, at least in the second half of his term.

He returned to Rastorguevo, having put on seven kilograms in weight and three centimeters in height, and his demobilization papers were issued on time, without the usual delays, almost to the day. Most importantly, however, he again knew precisely what he wanted to do. He rapidly obtained a high school diploma without difficulty as an extension student and that same summer enrolled at a physical education institute, but again surprised the world by registering for the faculty of sports medicine.

The diagram which Butonov remembered from his school days of the man with his skin removed and his muscles exposed was now the focus of his interest. He studied anatomy, the bane of freshmen, with immense enthusiasm and great respect. Butonov, whose memory wasn't good enough, who forgot books without a trace as soon as he had read them, now grasped everything, remembered everything in what everyone else found the dreariest activity imaginable.

Butonov had one other peculiarity which, along with his physical giftedness, made him the man he was: an ability to accept instruction. His trainer Nikolai Vasilievich, who betrayed him, and poor Muzzetoni both appreciated his capacity for gladly subordinating himself, for getting to the heart of a new technique and somehow assimilating it from the inside.

Butonov met his third and final teacher in his third year at the institute. He was a small, nondescript-looking fellow, a China-Eastern Railroad man with the cover name of Ivanov, and he had a dark and tortuous past. He was born, or so he said, in Shanghai, knew Chinese to perfection, had lived many years in India, had been to Tibet, and in semi-European Russia was an ambassador of the mysterious Orient. He knew his way around in the martial arts, which were just coming into fashion, and he taught Chinese massage.

The Deutero-Ivanov was delighted by Butonov's unusual flair for the physical: there was independence and cleverness in his fingers. Butonov could instantly locate a slipped disk, or a ridge of deposited salts, or where there was simply a muscular spasm, and his hands assimilated the arcane science of pressure points by themselves, without the need of involving his head. If Butonov had had the words and a certain versing in the humanities, he could have talked about a back in good heart, of joyful legs, clever fingers, and also about lassitude in the shoulders, lethargic hips, or drowsy arms, all of which peculiarities of the life of the body he could diagnose at any given moment in the person lying before him on the massage table.

The Deutero-Ivanov invited him around to his half-empty one-room flat hung with Tibetan icons. A fine connoisseur of the Orient, he tried to interest his exceptional pupil in the nobility of yoga, the wisdom of the Bhagavad Gita, the elegant Chinese divination method of Ba-Goa; but Butonov proved totally immune to the domain of the spirit.

"That's all a bit too up in the air," he would say, making a slight movement with the abducent muscles of his right hand.

His teacher was disappointed, but at least Butonov mastered

the practicalities of yoga and pressure-point massage very rapidly and with all their subtleties.

Ivanov himself was enjoying major success in those years not only as a brilliant masseur whose services were enjoyed by a variety of stratospheric celebrities: a world champion weightlifter, a ballerina of genius, a notorious author. He took part in various seminars in people's homes, sophisticated entertainments of those years; he conducted specialized courses on yoga. He involved Butonov too in his activities, at least in the part visible on the surface. Butonov had no intimation of the other side of Ivanov's activity—informing for the secret police—and it was not until many years later that he understood that his teacher had been wearing invisible epaulettes.

His teacher promoted Butonov to be his assistant. He led his audience of yoga enthusiasts straight along the exalted path of liberation to moksha, while Butonov contorted himself on the mat, teaching them the lotus position, the lion, the snake, and other inhuman configurations.

One of the groups met in the appropriately large apartment of a top academician, invited there by his daughter. The participants of these meetings were all as one constituted of doughy flesh, and it was for Butonov to teach them that sensitivity to the physical body with which he himself was so endowed. They were scholars, physicists, chemists, mathematicians, and for all of them Butonov felt a quite inexplicable slight contempt. Among them was a tall, somewhat plump girl called Olga, a mathematician with heavy legs and a rather coarse face, which changed in the course of the exercises from its natural delicate pink to an alarming red.

Two months after they met, to the disapproving amazement of friends on both sides, Valerii and Olga got married. The mistress of the apartment, upon learning of the proposed alliance, clicked her tongue and wondered, "What on earth is poor Olga going to do with that magnificent beast?"

But Olga didn't do anything with him in particular. She was a cold, cerebral person, which may perhaps have been related to her profession: by now she had already defended her doctoral dissertation on topology, an abstruse area of mathematics, and the meticulous mental jewelry making that went on in her large head beneath its covering of long, badly washed hair was the main thing that gave meaning to her life.

Butonov was not particularly awed by the twisted symbols which ran, like birds' footprints in the snow, over the papers on his wife's table. He just muttered skeptically to himself when he looked at the little signs, infrequently accompanied by human words on the left hand side of the sheet: "from this it follows, as is evident from the above . . ."; "let us consider the definition . . ."

Olga had an accommodating, slightly sluggish personality. Valerii was amazed by how little she moved about and how generally lethargic she was: too lazy even to do the few yoga exercises which would relieve her constipation.

Valentina Fyodorovna took an immediate dislike to her son's fiancée, in the first place because she was four years older than Valerii, and in the second place for her lack of thrift. But Olga just smiled unconcernedly and, to Valentina Fyodorovna's considerable annoyance, failed even to notice her dislike.

Their connubial bliss was exceedingly moderate. Butonov, who from childhood had sought out muscular pleasures, had somehow neglected a small group of muscles controlling quite special delights. Achievements in this area of endeavor didn't win awards or get you onto teams, and his instincts were faced down by youthful vanity.

There was one more factor contributing to his surprising reserve toward women, and that was that they had been falling in love with him from the moment he wore his first trousers. Their wearisome infatuation pursued him like a rain cloud, and as he got older, he began to feel this relentless interest in him as an intrusion on his body and tried desperately to safeguard his most prized asset, whose value was only emphasized the more by the amazing availability of women's hungry bodies and the endless propositions he was bombarded with.

His first sexual experiments were neither particularly successful nor particularly significant: a thirty-year-old neighbor; the dinner lady in the Central Sports Club canteen; a swimmer in his class whose face appeared to have been washed off by her sport; and all of them really keen, gasping for it, eager to continue the relationship. For Butonov himself these encounters ranked little higher than an agreeable wet dream climaxing on the boundary of sleep before the image of his temptress was finally dissipated by the banging of doors in the corridor and the sound of the toilet flushing on the other side of the wall.

All was tranquil and well ordered in the Butonovs' life. They got married three months after Olga defended her doctoral dissertation, and three months after that she became pregnant; and three months before her thirtieth birthday she gave birth to a daughter. While she was carrying, giving birth to, and feeding with her large but nutritionally disappointing breasts the very small baby girl produced by two such large parents, Butonov completed his sports medicine course and sold himself to the tennis players.

His job was to keep an eye on the health of the healthiest people on the planet, treating their injuries and massaging their muscles. In his free time he did exactly the same thing, but on a private basis. He earned good money; he was independent. His patients were referred to him by his teacher, and all doors opened for him, from the restaurant of the All-Russian Theater

Society to the Communist Party Central Committee's ticket office.

A year later, international tennis did finally take him abroad, first to Prague—he finally made it to Prague—and later also to London. What more could anyone aspire to?

To Butonov's credit it needs to be said that he received his high fees for work well done. He maintained the bodies of the tennis players, ballerinas, and actors entrusted to him in a state of irreproachable fitness, but additionally busied himself with heavy posttraumatic rehabilitation. His vanity had finally found a worthy foundation. It was said that he could work miracles. The legend of his hands grew, but he had no illusions as to what legends were worth and worked now as he had as a gymnast to the fullest extent of his abilities, and these gradually extended further and further.

The achievement he was proudest of was Ivan Muzzetoni, on whom he had been working from the moment Ivanov showed him the first techniques and approaches to the spine. Butonov brought Ivanov to see Muzzetoni more than once. On one occasion Ivanov sent an illustrious Chinaman to singe Ivan's back with aromatic herbal candles.

The main labor, however, was Butonov's. For six years in a row, twice a week, almost without fail, he wove his spells over the paralyzed back, and Ivan rose up and could walk around the apartment supporting himself on a special walking frame, and slowly, very slowly, was restored to life.

Anton Ivanovich, his face now even more wrinkled, worshiped Butonov. His granddaughter Nina, who had fallen in love with Butonov at the age of twelve, evaluated men on the basis of only one criterion: the extent to which this or that admirer resembled Butonov. Bad-tempered Lyalya Muzzetoni, who had been planning for ten years to divorce Ivan, was transformed after his accident into a quite different person: admirably controlled and optimistic. She knitted sweaters to order, taking over as the breadwinner and never complaining. She usually presented Butonov with a woolly masterpiece on his birthday.

In the middle of October, Butonov came to see Ivan, looking fed up and generally out of sorts. He worked on Ivan for an hour and a half and was about to leave without his usual cup of tea or coffee. Lyalya waylaid him, brought in the tea, and got him talking.

Butonov grumbled that he was off the next day on an idiotic trip to Kishinev, a town which was of no use to anyone, accompanying a group of athletes making guest appearances.

Lyalya suddenly livened up and said enthusiastically: "Oh, but you must go! It's absolutely marvelous there at this time of the year, and so that you don't get bored, I'll give you an errand. You can take a present to my friend." She dug about in a cupboard and pulled out a white mohair sweater.

"They live on the outskirts, Chovdar Sysoev's famous equestrian troupe. Haven't you heard of them? He's a scary old Gypsy, and Rosa is his rider." Lyalya pushed the sweater into a plastic bag and wrote the address.

Butonov took the parcel without a great deal of enthusiasm.

His first half-day in Kishinev was free and, having slept the night in a hotel, he went out into the street early in the morning and headed off into the unfamiliar city as instructed, in the direction of the bazaar. The city had little to recommend it, lacking any hint of architectural interest, at least in the part which revealed itself to Valerii through the morning mist as it dissolved before his eyes. The air was balmy, though, southern, with the smell of sweet fruits rotting on the ground. The smell must have been coming from far away, because there were no trees at all in the streets of the new town. Only crimson asters, which had completely faded and had no scent whatsoever, were growing out of rectangular lawns bordered by concrete slabs. It was warm and the place had a touristy feel to it.

Valerii came to the bazaar. Horse carts and oxcarts and their attendant horses and oxen completely clogged the small square; dumpy men with warm fur hats and drooping mustaches were dragging baskets and crates, while women arranged mountains of tomatoes, grapes, and pears on their counters.

"I should take some home," Valerii thought fleetingly before spotting right in front of him the battered back of a bus with the number he needed. The bus was empty. Valerii got in, and a few minutes later the driver climbed into the cabin and, without saying a word, drove off.

The road ran for a long time through the suburbs, which became increasingly more attractive, past modest little houses and small vineyards. There were frequent stops. In one stretch of the journey children piled in, then they all got off simultaneously when they reached the school. Finally, almost an hour later, they reached the end of the bus route, a strange, transitional place, neither town nor country.

Valerii did not yet know what an important day in his life had begun that morning, but for some reason he remembered every detail very clearly. Two small factories stood on either side of the road blowing smoke in each other's faces, in total defiance of the laws of physics which dictated that the wind should carry their grey smoke in the same direction.

The observant Butonov shrugged. Greenhouses were ranged along the road, and that seemed odd too: what on earth did they need greenhouses for, when it was seventy degrees in late October and everything was ripening splendidly without them?

Farther along the road were some industrial buildings and stables. Butonov headed toward them. Still at a distance, he saw the gates of the stables open, the gap filled with a velvety blackness and out of it, its white teeth gleaming, came a tall black stallion which, because of its unexpectedness, seemed to Butonov to be enormous, like the steed of the Bronze Horseman statue in St. Petersburg. But far from there being a bronze horseman, the stallion was being led by the reins by a small curly-haired boy who, on closer inspection, turned out to be a young woman in a red shirt and dirty white jeans.

Butonov looked first at her boots, which were light, with a thick toe cap and a rough heel, very suitable boots for horse-riding; and then his eyes met hers. Her eyes were mirror-black and crudely extended with black makeup; her gaze was alert and unfriendly. They all stopped. The stallion neighed and she patted its withers with a surprisingly white hand with short red nails.

"Looking for Chovdar?" she asked rather rudely. "Over there." She pointed in the direction of the nearest shed before putting her foot in a very high stirrup and vaulting up into the saddle, giving Valerii a dose of a sweet, alluring, and wholly un-perfumelike smell.

"No, I'm looking for Rosa." Butonov had already worked out that this was Rosa.

"I have a parcel from Lyalya Muzzetoni." He pulled the plastic bag out of his carryall and held it up.

Without getting down from her horse, she took the bag and threw it with a sweeping gesture through the open stable door, gave a flash of her teeth suggestive of a snarl rather than a smile, and asked hurriedly, "Where are you staying?"

"The October Hotel."

"Right, okay. I'm busy at the moment." She waved her hand and with a cry galloped off.

He looked after her with a feeling of irritation, admiration, and something else he would have to analyze for a long time yet. One way or another this was the last day in his life when he still had absolutely no interest in women.

That night Valerii lay for a long time in the hotel bed with its smell of detergent, remembering the insolent Gypsy girl, her magnificent stallion, and the small yellow horses of some rare breed which he had observed in the paddock behind the stable while waiting for the bus back to town. "Obnoxious little person," Valerii decided, drifting off into a dream of horses, the smells of the stable, and the lazy pleasure of a warm day doing nothing. A long, quiet tapping at the door brought him back up out of that state. He raised himself slightly from the pillow.

He had evidently forgotten to lock the door. It opened slowly and a woman entered the room. Valerii said nothing, peering. He thought at first it was the maid.

"Ah, so you were expecting me," the woman said in a slightly hoarse voice, and then he recognized her: it was this morning's horse-rider.

"I decided that if you asked who was there I'd turn and go away," she said without a smile, and sat down on the bed.

She took off the same boots he had approved of that morning. First she stepped on the back of the left one and took it off, then pulled the right one off with her hands and with a certain amount of effort threw it over into the corner.

"Well, what are you gawking at?"

She stood up beside the bed and he saw how small she was. He also just had time to reflect that he didn't like such sharp little women in the slightest.

She pulled off the white sweater she had so recently been presented with, undid the button on her dirty white jeans, and, without taking them off, dived under the blanket, put her arms around him, and said in a tired, serious voice, "I've had the hots all day. I wanted you so much."

Butonov breathed out all the breath in his lungs and forgot for the rest of time what kind of women it was he usually liked.

Everything he discovered about her, he learned later. She was not a Gypsy at all, but a Jewess from the family of a professor in St. Petersburg. She had run off with Sysoev seven years ago. Her parents were bringing up the daughter from her first marriage and didn't trust her. But the most important and surprising thing was that by morning he had discovered that in his not quite twenty-nine years there was a whole continent he hadn't discovered, and it was wholly incomprehensible how this slight girl, so hot outside and inside, had managed to immerse him in herself so completely that he seemed to himself to be a pink sweet dissolving in a thick sweet liquid while all his skin groaned and melted with tenderness and joy, and every touch, every slipping and sliding of skin pierced him through to the heart, and all that was surface seemed to end up inside, in the very deepest part of him. He felt himself turned inside out and accepted that if she had not plugged his ears with her slender little fingers, his soul would undoubtedly have flown out and away.

At six o'clock in the morning the weird little watch she had not taken off all night tweeted feebly. She was sitting on the windowsill with her legs wrapped around his loins. He was standing in front of her and could see a mound bulging beneath her belly button, indicating his presence.

"That's it," she said, and stroked the bulge through the thin membrane of her stomach.

"Don't go," he begged.

"I've gone already," she laughed, and he noticed the vampire-like way her little upper fangs protruded.

He ran his fingers over her teeth.

"No," she laughed, "I'm not a vampire. I'm a common little whore. Do you like it?"

"Very much," he replied honestly, and she jumped off, leaving his arrow unloosed.

She went into the shower. Her legs were slightly bowed and

not joined very attractively to her body, but this only fanned the flames of his desire for her. He picked out of the devastated bed the broken golden chains which had slipped from her neck during the night.

The water was beating down in the shower. He fingered the chains and looked out of the window. There was the same shining mist as yesterday, and you could tell the sun was hiding beyond its disappearing radiance.

She came into the room covered in large drops of water. He held out the chains to her. She took them, let them fall to their full length, and tossed them onto the table. "You can give them back when you've had them mended. Is today Wednesday?"

She shook the last of the water from her little breasts and pulled the jeans onto her slender wet body with difficulty. There were still large drops of water in her springy black hairstyle which nobody was yet calling "Afro" and which belonged solely to her. A few small scars, already arousing and loved, which you didn't need to touch to feel their hardness, marked her body beneath her breasts, to the left of her belly, and on her right forearm. She did not seem feminine in the least, but by comparison, all the women he had known before now seemed like semolina pudding or boiled cabbage.

"Do you know what, Valerii? We'll meet in exactly one week's time at the Central Post Office in St. Petersburg. Between eleven and twelve."

"How about today?" Butonov asked.

"No, impossible. Sysoev will kill you. Or maybe me." She laughed. "I'm not sure exactly who, but definitely someone."

They met up three times more in the course of a year, and then she disappeared. Not just from Valerii, but altogether. Neither her parents nor Sysoev knew who she had gone off with or where to.

From then on, Butonov never refused a woman. He knew that miracles don't happen, but if you kept on the edge of the possible, at the limit of your concentration, then here too, in the physical depths themselves, lightning strikes and everything is lit up, and that same feeling flares within you of a knife hurled at a target, which shudders and dies right there in its heart.

CHAPTER 8

Getting back home from the coves after nine at night, the grown-ups put the sleeping small children to bed before settling down in Medea's kitchen for a cup of tea. Although they were all tired, they did not want to part: something was in the air, a vague sense of "to be continued." Even Nora, the conscientious mother, agreed to put her daughter to bed in a strange place in order to sit here and enjoy the tea.

The only person not in the kitchen was Masha. When they were halfway back, she had a disgusting sensation like an itching in her blood, and knew one of her rare and inexplicable attacks was coming on. Her husband Alik, a doctor who thought through every illness as if it were a puzzle in its own right, believed Masha must have a rare form of arterial allergy. She had suffered one of these attacks right in front of him one time when they had gone to celebrate the New Year holiday in the country. Masha had touched the cold nozzle of the water dispenser, and it left a mark on her arm like a burn. Within two hours her temperature went up, and by evening she was completely covered in an allergic rash.

This time something similar had happened, not from touching inanimate metal but from being fleetingly touched by Butonov. Or perhaps she had just got too hot in the spring sunshine. At all events, her right arm was scarlet and slightly swollen.

No sooner had she got home than Masha went to bed, covering herself with every blanket she could find. While she was shivering with the fever and tormented by thirst, she kept dreaming the same obsessive dream in which she seemed to be getting out of bed, going to the kitchen, and trying to scoop water from a bucket, only there was very little and the mug just scraped over the metal without getting any water. Parallel with this, rough lines of verse were shaping themselves, lines in which the seashore figured, and hot sun, and a vague sense of anticipation, along with an entirely real thirst.

Georgii went out to smoke, sat on the bench by the house, and looked back out of the darkness, like someone looking from the darkened auditorium onto a theater stage, at the lit rectangle of the open kitchen door. The light came from two inconstant sources: a yellow light from the oil lamp and a low red glow from the hearth. Faces which in the course of the day had caught the dangerous spring sunshine now seemed heavily made up. Next to dark Medea sat light-colored Nora with her hair pinned back and her fringe tucked up. Nike had told her to rub some of their yogurtlike kefir on her face and now her skin had a dull gleam. When she gathered up her hair like this, her forehead looked too high and steep, the way it is in babies and medieval German Madonnas, and this fault made her face seem even sweeter.

Georgii could also see Butonov's powerful back in his pink T-shirt, and Nike's winged shadow with the neck of the guitar and her hands flickering on the wall. In the middle of the table, like a precious globe, stood the samovar, but it wasn't boiling for the tea. Although Georgii had finally run an overhead cable through to the kitchen, for some reason the electricity was cut off in the Village today.

Along with the light, song poured out into the night, sung in Nike's strong, simple voice supported by the uncomplicated chords of hands unschooled in music. At the time, everyone was singing Okudzhava, but Georgii, unlike the rest of them, did not like his songs. They irritated him with their cuffs and their velvet camisoles, their blues and their gilding, their smells of milk and honey, with all their romantic charm; but mainly, perhaps because they were captivating, and crept into your heart uninvited, and because you could still hear them long afterward and they left a residue in your memory.

For many years he had been working in the field of paleozoology, the deadest of sciences, and this had given him a strange view of the world: he divided everything into hard and soft. Soft caressed the feelings, smelled, was sweet or repellent. It was associated with emotional reactions. Hard, on the other hand, determined the essence of a phenomenon, hard was its skeleton.

Georgii could pick up one-half of an oyster shell buried in the hillside somewhere in Fergana or here, near Alchak, and tell straightaway in which of ten phases of the Paleogene Period this fleshy, long-vanished animal had lived, together with its adductor muscle and primitive nerve ganglions, all the stuff that made up its unimportant soft matter. These songs seemed to be nothing but soft matter. As distinct from, say, Schubert's *Lieder*, in which he could feel the firm musical framework. Luckily he did not know German, so the words were no problem.

Georgii crushed his cigarette end with a flat stone and went back to the kitchen, sitting in the darkest corner, from where he had a good view of Nora and her sweet, sleepy face. "She's a real northern girl, and not very happy by all appearances," he mused. "A Petersburg girl. There is an anemic blonde type with transparent fingers, fine blue veins, slender ankles and wrists. Her nipples are probably pale pink too . . ." He suddenly felt hot.

As if sensing his thoughts, she half-hid her face with her slender hands.

The days of Georgii's youth, with their geological parties, their local cooks, obliging laboratory assistants always ready to offer up their muscular hips to the biting mosquitoes, their geologist girlfriends, were long past. From an Armenian mixture of stubbornness and lethargy, but also because he adhered to the mythology of family life instilled in him by his mother, despite the universal acceptance of promiscuity and all the habits of his circle and the derision of his friends, he preserved a grim fidelity to fat Zoyka but could never remember, no matter how hard he tried, what it was about her that had attracted him fifteen years ago. Nothing, except the touching way she folded her white socks carefully together, placing one on top of the other.

He went out of the kitchen again to escape from the disturbing atmosphere which was bubbling away furiously in there, irritating and arousing him.

"He's gone," Nora thought, disappointed.

Nike meanwhile was busy with her favorite art of seduction, fine as lace, invisible but palpable, like the smell of a pie fresh from the oven, instantly filling any space. It was a necessity for her soul, a food almost spiritual, and Nike knew no better moment than when she was turning a man in her direction, breaking through the typical male's self-absorption in the life taking place deep within himself; arousing interest in herself, deploying her lures, spreading her bait, drawing the bright threads toward herself, and already, while he is still talking to someone at the other end of the room, he is beginning to listen to her voice, picking up the intonations of her joyful friendliness and that other indefinable something which makes the male butterfly struggle dozens of kilometers to mate with the indolent female—and already, against his will, the man Nike has targeted is being drawn to the corner where she is sitting with her guitar, or without her guitar, large, jolly, russet Nike with the appeal in her eyes. Perhaps, indeed, this was the moment of her greatest triumph, with which no physiological delights could compare, when the game bird began to wander its way absentmindedly through the rooms with an empty glass in its hand, responding to the lure, while Nike, radiant, anticipated her victory.

Butonov, sitting motionless in the middle of the bench opposite her, was already in Nike's hands. For all his bright feathers he was a fairly simple game bird who rarely refused women but also did not allow them to tame him, preferring one-night stands to long-term relationships.

Right now he wanted to go to bed, and he was wondering whether to save this gingersnap for tomorrow. Nike for her part had not the least intention of putting off till tomorrow something that could be done today. She got up casually and put the guitar in the armchair of Medea, who had already turned in.

"The rest is silence," she said, giving Butonov a smile which promised a continuation of the evening.

Butonov did not recognize the quotation.

"We'll just check how the children are," she said, seemingly addressing Nora.

Butonov gathered that he was to wait.

The women went into the dark house and looked into the children's room. Nothing needed to be done: they were all worn out and sound asleep after their excursion; only Liza was sighing sweetly in her sleep as usual. Tanya was spread out across a very wide ottoman, to one side of which Katya was lying straight and elegant, not forgetting her deportment even in sleep. In the middle of the room stood a large communal chamber pot.

"If you like, you can sleep here," Nike said, indicating the ottoman, "or if you prefer, you can sleep in the little room—it's made up."

Nora lay down beside her daughter. It was already past three in the morning and there was little time left for sleep.

Nike returned to the kitchen and put her hand lightly on Butonov's neck in passing. "You've got sunburnt."

"I have a bit," Butonov responded, and it suddenly seemed to Nike that there had been no conquest. "Okay, let's go, shall we?" Butonov suggested without turning around, his voice expressionless.

Something was wrong here. The game wasn't being played to Nike's rules, but she didn't stoop to flirting to try to obtain the requisite intonation; she squeezed her breast lightly against the firm back covered in stretched pink material.

What followed, on Ada's territory, does not merit detailed description, but both participants were left wholly satisfied. After Nike had gone, Butonov relieved himself in the planked toilet at the end of the plot, which he had been unable to do earlier in a long day in the company of many people, and fell soundly asleep.

When Nike returned home, it was already getting light and she didn't feel in the least like sleeping: on the contrary, she was full of energy, and her body, as if appreciative of the pleasure it had just enjoyed, was ready for hard work and more fun. Humming something from a few years back, she scrupulously washed the dishes and cooked the porridge for breakfast. She was stirring it in a large saucepan using a long spoon when Medea came in for her cup of coffee.

"I hope we didn't disturb you too much last night," Nike said, kissing Medea's shriveled cheek.

"No, child, no more than usual." And Medea touched Nike's head. She liked Nike's head: her hair was just as springy and slightly crackly as Samuel's.

"I thought you were looking very tired yesterday," Nike half-said, half-inquired.

"You know, Nike, I never used to notice it, but the whole of this last year I seem to have been tired all the time. Old age, do you think?" Medea replied artlessly.

Nike turned down the flame in the Primus. "Haven't you had enough of that hospital of yours? Perhaps you should give it up?"

"I don't know, I don't know. I'm used to working. An affliction of slaves, Armik Tigranovna used to call it." Medea stood up, the conversation over.

Masha came in wearing a jacket over her nightdress, her face pink and inflamed and covered in little spots.

"Masha! What's wrong with you?" Nike gasped.

Masha drank thirstily from a mug and, when she had finished, said in an odd voice, "The bucket's full, though. I've got an allergy."

"It isn't German measles, is it?" Medea asked anxiously.

"Where would I have got that from? It'll be gone by this evening," Masha said with a smile. "I had a terrible night. Fever, shivering. But now it's all over."

In her pocket was the crumpled piece of paper on which she had written her poem that night. For the moment Masha liked it very much, and she repeated it to herself: "A floating basket brings a child who nameless lies beside the river. Pharaoh's daughter, heart aquiver, clothes the babe and with her song moves his destiny along. A fish is caught, it takes the bait and thrashes on the bank in netting. On that riverbank, forgetting everything, my name, my state, I sit in silence and I wait. I run the sand through fingers swelling. In that hot sun something's jelling. I sleep, I bake, and still I wait. But wait for what? There is no telling."

In fact, however, she had no trouble at all in telling. After yesterday's confusion and her terrible night, everything was crystal-clear: she had fallen in love.

And she was feeling weak, as you do after a fever.

CHAPTER 9

Throughout her life Alexandra changed not only her men, of whom she grew bored easily, but also her profession. She met her third husband at the Maly Theater, where she worked from the mid-1950s as dresser to an ancient celebrity. Her husband, while collecting a decent state salary there, restored priceless antiques which the theater élite, the Actors of Merit of the USSR and the Actresses of the Soviet People, who had an eye for fine furniture, bought for a song.

Alexandra, always ready for love, had little interest in wealth but worshiped brilliance. Her marriage to Alexei Kirillovich had not been brilliant. They were the three most boring years of her life, and they ended in scandal: Alexei Kirillovich caught her in flagrante delicto with the handsome deaf-and-dumb boiler-maker who serviced the Timiryazev dachas.

Alexei Kirillovich was deeply shocked and walked out forever, leaving his wife in the embraces of her huge Gerasim. Alexandra cried right up until the evening.

She saw Alexei Kirillovich only once after that, in court for the divorce, but right through to 1941 she received alimony from him through the post. Alexei Kirillovich did not require access to his son.

The boilermaker, needless to say, was an episode of no significance. She had various brilliant liaisons: with a dashing test pilot, with a famous Jewish academician who was a witty but indiscriminate philanderer, and with a young actor, a casualty of early fame and even earlier alcoholism.

Her second husband, Yevgeny Kitaev, was a military man, well built, a lover of Ukrainian folk songs with a powerful voice. She had a daughter, Lidia, by him before this marriage too hit the buffers. They didn't get divorced but they lived apart, and her second daughter, Vera, born just before the war, had a different father, a man with such an illustrious name that Kitaev modestly kept silent about the vagaries of his family life until the day he was killed. Alexandra's last daughter, born in 1947, three years after his death, also bore his jolly surname.

When Alexandra passed fifty, however, and admirers ceased to swarm to the no longer gleaming beacon of her red hair, she heaved a sigh and said to herself, "Oh, well, time's up . . ." She cast her keen feminine eye around, and rather unexpectedly it came to rest on the theater's cabinetmaker, Ivan Isaevich Pryanichkov.

He was not old, about fifty, a year or two younger than she; not tall, but broad shouldered. He wore his hair longer than was customary among the working class, more in the fashion of an actor. He was invariably clean shaven, and his shirts peeped out freshly from beneath his blue work coat. Walking down the corridor behind him one time, Alexandra analyzed the complex and astringent aroma emanating from him and associated with his profession: turpentine, varnish, rosin, and something she couldn't recognize. The smell struck her as really quite attractive.

The cabinetmaker had a certain special dignity of his own. He did not fit into the usual theater hierarchy. He might have been expected to occupy a modest position somewhere between a stage mechanic and a makeup artist, but he stalked the theater corridors acknowledging greetings with a nod like an Actor of Merit of the USSR and closed the door to his workshop as firmly as an Actor of the Soviet People. One time, toward the end of the working day when the workers in the workshops had not yet left and the actors and all those needed for the production of the night's performance had already assembled, Alexandra Georgievna knocked on his door. They exchanged greetings. It transpired that he did not know her by name, although by this time she had been working in the theater for three years. She told him about the walnut cabinet she had inherited from her late mother-in-law, cast a quick glance around the walls of his workshop, at the shelves with great bottles of dark and reddish fluids and at the various tools symmetrically hung up or lying around.

Ivan Isaevich was holding a brown hand with a dark outline around the nails on the light-colored top of a dismantled side table, stroking down a jagged flower with a rough finger, and when Alexandra Georgievna finished her tale about the cabinet, he said, without looking her in the eyes, "When I finish this marquetry for Ivan Ivanovich I can come and take a look at it."

A week later he came to see her in Uspensky Lane, where she lived in two and a half rooms with her daughters Vera and Nike. The bowl of broth he was offered with a piece of yesterday's meat kulebyaka, and buckwheat porridge which seemed to have been baked in a Russian stove, made a deep impression on Ivan Isaevich, who led a clean, worthy, but nevertheless bachelor existence, without good home cooking.

He liked the solicitous movement with which Alexandra Georgievna took the bread out of the wooden bread bin and opened the napkin in which it was wrapped. An even deeper impression was made by the brief glance she threw at the end of the buffet, where a small icon of the Mother of God of Korsun was hanging and which he had not noticed immediately precisely because it was not hanging in the corner in the officially approved manner, but hidden—and the quiet sigh, "Oh, Lord," which she had learned from Medea already in childhood.

He was an Old Believer but had left home as a youth, renouncing his faith. Having swum away from his home shore, however, he never did reach another and had lived all his life at war with himself, sometimes appalled at having turned his back on his parents' world, sometimes anguished by the impossibility of uniting with the thousands of his frenzied and energetic Soviet fellow citizens.

He was touched by her prayerful sigh, but only much later, when he was already her husband, did he realize that the crucial point was the amazingly simple way she had solved the problem which had tormented him all his life. For him the worship of a righteous God simply could not be reconciled with the living of an unrighteous life, but Alexandra brought everything together in a splendidly straightforward way: she painted her lips and dressed to kill, and could throw herself into having fun with total abandon, but when the time came, she would sigh and weep and pray, and suddenly give generous help to someone in need.

The cabinet turned out to be an object of no importance, walnut veneer, with a lost key and damaged key plate. Ivan Isaevich laid out his tools and unscrewed the front leaf while Alexandra Georgievna got herself ready and ran to the evening performance to cloak her decaying prima donna in a merchant's talma of heavy silk. The old woman played mothers-in-law in Ostrovsky almost all the time.

Ivan Isaevich, left with her daughters, quietly got everything ready, cleaned the surface, removed the veneer where it was damaged in one place, and thought about the widow: a good woman living a pure life; her children well brought up; she herself, he could see, was well educated; although why on earth she was working as dresser to an old dame renowned for her difficult personality he couldn't imagine.

He had to leave before the owner returned, as she was held up longer than usual. The old prima donna had summoned the principal producer after the performance and ordered him to replace a young actress "who's an uppity young madam, even

though she's incapable of articulating her lines properly herself."
By the time feathers had been unruffled and Alexandra had
calmed her grand old lady down and changed her clothes, it was
already half-past midnight, and Alexandra had to walk home because that evening the actress either forgot to give her a lift
home in her personal taxi, as she usually did, or chose not to.

Ivan Isaevich arranged his dates with the walnut cabinet after
first glancing at the theater schedule and choosing days when
Ostrovsky was not being performed and Alexandra Georgievna
would be at home. The first evening she sat at a side table writing letters; the second, she sewed a skirt for her daughter, then
sorted the cereals while quietly humming a catchy melody from
an operetta. She offered Ivan Isaevich first tea, then supper. She
was taking to "the furniture man," as she had christened him to
herself, more and more for his earnest restraint, his laconic way
with words and movements, and for his behavior in general
which, although "a trifle wooden," as she described him to her
bosom friend Kira, nevertheless was "all man."

At the very least he was clearly ahead of her principal suitor,
an Actor of Merit recently widowed, with a sonorous voice, garrulous, vain, and as quick to take offense as a schoolgirl. He had
recently invited her to his large and splendid Stalinist apartment
adjacent to the Moscow City Soviet, and the following day she
lengthily derided him on all points to Kira: how he had laid the
entire table with old banqueting china, but placed in the enormous crystal cheese dish a solitary dried-out segment of cheese,
and in a half-meter-sized hors d'oeuvre dish an equally dried-
out piece of sausage; how, with a voice like thunder which filled
the whole enormous room right to its four-meter-high ceiling,
he spoke first of his love for his late wife and then equally reso-
nantly tried to entice her into the bedroom where he promised
to show her what he was capable of; and finally, when Alexandra
was ready to go home, he had produced his wife's jewelry box

and, without actually opening it, announced that its contents would all fall to the woman whom he now chose to be his new wife.

"So what did you do, Alexandra, make your excuses or go into the bedroom with him anyway?" enquired her friend, to whom it was vital to know every last detail of Alexandra's life.

"Shame on you, Kira," Alexandra Georgievna chuckled. "It was obvious the only place he has unbuttoned his trousers for a long time is the toilet! I pouted my lips and said, 'Oh, what a shame I can't go into your bedroom, because today I am men-stru-a-ting!' He almost sat down on the floor. No, no, he's look-ing for a cook and I'm looking for a man in the house. He's out."

Ivan Isaevich worked unhurriedly; he never did hurry any-way, but on the fifth evening of unhurried work the cabinet was nevertheless finished, and he specially left a little bit early in order to put the last layer of shellac on tomorrow. He would be sorry to leave this house never to return, and he looked hope-fully at a dubious moderne three-leaved mirror which was man-ifestly defective.

He liked Alexandra Georgievna and everything about her house, and he felt as if he were observing her life from a hide created by using the walnut cabinet: unsmiling Vera, the student, always scuffling among her papers like a mouse; deep-pink Nike; and her older son, who dropped in for a cup of tea with his mother nearly every day. He saw here not the fear and respect for one's parents which he was used to from his own childhood, but the lighthearted love of children for their mother, and a warm friendship between all of them. He was surprised and de-lighted.

Alexandra Georgievna agreed to the mirror, so now Ivan Isaevich came to see her twice a week, on her days off. She even found his presence slightly wearing: she couldn't invite guests around and couldn't go out herself.

The way she saw things, she had the furniture man eating out of her hand, but she herself was unsure: of course he looked like a regular he-man, and he knew his own mind, but he was still a drudge. In the meantime he turned up with a child's cot shaped like a little boat: "It worked for the children of the gentry, and it'll be just right for Nike," he said, and presented it.

Alexandra sighed: she really was tired of being husbandless, on top of which a year ago her patroness had charitably presented her with a plot of land in the Maly Theater's village to build her own dacha and she could hardly put a house up on her own. Everything was pointing the same way, in favor of slow-moving Ivan Isaevich; and in him too the currents which lead a lonely man to family life were swirling beneath the surface of consciousness.

As the furniture-mending prelude to their marriage continued, he became even more persuaded of Alexandra Georgievna's exceptional qualities. "She's a thoroughly decent person, not some kind of flirt," he thought, having disapprovingly in mind that Valentina with whom he had lived a few good years before she was unfaithful to him with a captain who had turned up from her home province. It was certainly true that his lumbering Valentina lagged far behind Alexandra.

By now winter was coming to an end, and Alexandra's long-running affair with the ministry official who had once secured for her the job at the Maly Theater was also coming to an end. A bribe taker and thieving bureaucrat, he was generous toward women and had always helped Alexandra; but now he had another strong liaison, saw Alexandra infrequently, and the end result was that she was a bit short of money.

In late March she asked Ivan Isaevich to go with her to the dacha plot, where the building of her house had been begun last year but not finished. From then on he began to accompany her regularly on these Sunday trips.

They met by the booking office at the station before eight o'clock in the morning. He would take from her the bag with the food she had prepared; they would get into the empty train and with barely a word travel to their station, and then walk two kilometers in silence along the main road. Alexandra had her own thoughts and paid little attention to her companion, while he was pleased by her intense silence because he didn't like to talk much himself and there was in any case very little for them to talk about, since neither of them cared for theater gossip and they had yet to gain a life in common.

Gradually a genuine topic for discussion did arise between them: the practicalities of building a house. Ivan Isaevich's advice was always intelligent and practical; the workmen who reappeared at the end of April to complete the building they had begun treated him as the owner and, under his watchful eye, worked quite differently from last year.

The question of matrimony was still not moving forward. Alexandra had become accustomed to not lifting a finger without consulting him, and having him there gave her a quite unprecedented feeling of security. The anxieties, extending over many years, of a lone woman wholly responsible for her family had exhausted her, and then the material support of men, of which she had been readily able to avail herself without raising unnecessary moral issues, had somehow dried up of its own accord.

She was constantly discovering new virtues in Ivan Isaevich but squirmed every time he clumsily misused the Russian language. Although Alexandra Georgievna's own education had been nothing special—incomplete secondary schooling and her training as a laboratory assistant—her upbringing under Medea's tutelage had given her irreproachable, grammatically correct speech, and from the Pontic seafarers she had probably inherited a drop of royal blood and honorary kinship with those queens who always had their profile toward the spectator as they spun wool, wove tunics, and made cheese for their husbands, the kings of Ithaca and Mycenae.

Alexandra was conscious that their mutual inspection was dragging on, but she had not yet freed herself of the quite mistaken belief that she was so much better than he in every respect that he should consider her choosing him to be great good fortune: she took her time, still not giving that wordless indication of consent which Ivan Isaevich was so much waiting for. A great and irreparable misfortune which occurred that summer brought them together and united them.

Tanya, Sergei's wife, was a general's daughter, and this was not a stereotypical characterization of her, but a simple biographical fact. From her father she inherited ambition, and from her mother a pretty nose. Through the general's exertions she received a dowry of a new one-room apartment in Cheryomushki and a large secondhand Victory car. Sergei, who was both fastidious and independent, would not touch the car, and did not even obtain a driving license: Tanya was the driver.

That last preschool summer, their daughter Masha was living at the general's dacha with her grandmother, Vera Ivanovna, the general's wife, who had an impossible, hysterical personality, as everybody knew. From time to time, the granddaughter would have a row with her grandmother and call her parents in Moscow, asking them to come and take her home. This time Masha rang late at night from her grandfather's study. She did not cry but complained bitterly: "I'm bored. She doesn't let me go anywhere and doesn't let girls come to play. She says they'll steal things, but they won't steal anything, honestly . . ."

Tanya herself had not entirely forgotten her upbringing under Vera Ivanovna and promised to collect Masha in a few days' time. This entailed major disruption of the family's plans. They had been intending to drive all together to the Crimea in two weeks' time, to Medea; the holiday had been written into her timetable, they had arranged it all with her, and it was quite impossible to move the trip forward.

"Perhaps Alexandra could look after Masha just for a week?" Tanya enquired, angling cautiously.

Sergei was not keen to take his daughter from "the Junta," as he called his wife's family. He felt it was unfair to his mother, whose dacha had only just been finished, to say nothing of the fact that the Junta's dacha was enormous and provided with servants, while Alexandra had two rooms and a verandah.

"I do feel sorry for Masha," Tanya sighed, and Sergei gave in.

They decided to play truant in midweek and set off early in the morning. They never made it to the general's dacha: a drunk truck-driver swerved over onto the wrong side of the road, crashed into their car, and both died instantly in the head-on collision.

Toward the evening of that day, when Nike was worn out waiting for her much loved friend and cousin, and had arranged her dolls in a row for her, and herself beaten the raspberry mousse, the general's Volga arrived and the dumpy general climbed out and walked unsteadily toward the house. Seeing him through the net curtain, Alexandra came out onto the verandah and stopped on the top step, anticipating news which had already reached her as a terrible inarticulate heaviness in the thickening evening air.

"Lord, Lord, wait, I can't, I'm not ready for this . . ."

The general slowed his progress up the path, time slowed and stopped. Only the swing which Nike was sitting on did not stop completely, but very slowly glided down from its high point.

In this moment of frozen time Alexandra saw a large part of her and Sergei's life, and even that of her first husband, Alexei Kirillovich, in that summer at the Karadag station: the newborn Sergei in Medea's arms; their joint departure for Moscow in the expensive old-fashioned railway carriage; Sergei's first steps at the Timiryazev dacha . . . and he in his little jacket, his head shaven, when he went to school. And Alexandra saw much more, like so many forgotten photographs, while the general stood on the path with his leg poised to take a step.

She watched it through right to the end, to Sergei's coming around to Uspensky Lane the day before yesterday to ask her to keep Masha at the dacha for a few days until they could all go to the Crimea, and his awkward smile, and the way he had kissed her hair, which she wore pinned forward in a roll: "Thanks, Mum, you do so much for us."

And she had dismissed his thanks: "Nonsense, Sergei. What sort of favor are we doing when we all worship your little Masha."

General Pyotr Stepanovich Gladyshev reached her at last, stopped, and said in a slow, thick voice: "Our children . . . a crash . . . both of them killed."

"With Masha?" was all Alexandra could find to say.

"No, Masha is at the dacha. They were on their way . . . they were going to collect her," the general wheezed.

"Come into the house," Alexandra ordered him, and he obeyed and climbed the steps.

They had a bad time with the general's wife, Vera Ivanovna. For three days she shrieked and screamed, hoarsely, dementedly, and fell asleep only when given injections; for all that, she wouldn't let poor Masha out of her sight. Swollen and bloated, Vera Ivanovna brought Masha to the funeral. The girl immediately rushed to Alexandra and stood, squeezing against her, through the whole immensely long secular funeral service.

Vera Ivanovna beat against the sealed coffin and finally started shouting out snatches of a Vologda folk lament, torn from the depths of a simple, peasant soul which had been spoiled by her exalted status. Alexandra stood like stone with a firm hand resting on Masha's black hair. Her two elder daughters stood to the right and left of her, and behind them, holding Nike by the hand, Ivan Isaevich protectively stood sentinel over the family's grief.

The funeral party was held at the general's apartment on Tinkers Embankment. Everything, including the china, was brought in from some special place which fed high-ranking persons. Pyotr Stepanovich got utterly, terribly drunk. Vera Ivanovna kept demanding that Masha should come to her, but the little girl held on to Alexandra for dear life. So the three of them sat through the whole evening, two mothers-in-law united by a shared granddaughter.

"Alexandra, let me come and stay with you, Alexandra," the little girl whispered in her ear, and Alexandra, who had promised the general not to take away their only child, comforted her by promising to let her stay just as soon as Grandma Vera was feeling a bit better.

"We can't just leave her all alone, can we now?" she reasoned with Masha, herself thinking how desperately she wanted to take Masha back to her two and a half rooms in Uspensky Lane.

This was the evening when Alexandra first noticed a scattering of ginger freckles on Masha's pale face, the hereditary freckles of the Sinoply family, little indicators of the continuing presence of long-dead Matilda.

"Masha ought to be taken away from that place. I could help," Ivan Isaevich murmured late that evening as he saw Alexandra home from Tinkers Embankment, not addressing her directly in order to avoid having to call her Alexandra Georgievna, which by now was just too formal.

"Ought to be, certainly, but how's it to be done?" she replied equally unspecifically.

Medea did not come to her godson's funeral. Her late sister Anelya's adopted daughter Nina was ill in the hospital after a serious operation; Medea had taken her two little children from Tbilisi to stay with her and now had no one to leave them with.

In late August, Ivan Isaevich finished installing fencing around the dacha, put grilles on the windows, and installed an ingenious lock: "No self-respecting thief is going to be breaking in here, and it's a deterrent to vandals."

All this dark time, from the day of the funerals, he had not left Alexandra's side, and here, in this sad place, they began their life as man and wife. The tragedy seemed to cast a shadow on their relations for all time, and Alexandra herself no longer seemed able to throw herself into celebrating life as she had from her earliest youth come war, peace, or universal flood. Ivan Isaevich had no inkling of this. He was a different kind of person, who didn't have the words in his vocabulary or the sights in his memory that Alexandra had. He saw his wife as a superior, perfect being. Even when he did work out that her youngest daughter Nike could not possibly have been fathered by the Colonel Kitaev whose surname she bore but who had died four years earlier, he would sooner have believed in an immaculate conception than in any other explanation.

Alexandra, purely from a desire to preserve his exalted faith in her, had to concoct a story about how she had been planning to marry a test pilot who crashed the day before the wedding. The story was not a complete fabrication: there really had been a pilot. There was even a photograph of him with a breezy inscription, and alas he really had died in a crash during a test, but there had never been any suggestion of marriage between them, and it was not he who was Nike's father. He had crashed five years after she was born, and Nike remembered him because he always brought long boxes of chocolates called "Nuts of the South" which you couldn't get later on.

So positive, however, was Ivan Isaevich's attitude toward his wife that even in this questionable part of her biography he discerned merit: a lesser woman would have had an abortion or some such disgusting thing, but Alexandra had had the baby and brought it up, denying herself in all things. He was eager to ornament her bitter life by any means within the scope of his imagination: he brought her the best things he could find in Eliseev's delicatessen; he gave her presents, sometimes completely absurd; he guarded her sleep in the morning. What he most appreciated in intimate relations with his wife was the very fact that they occurred at all, and in the depths of his simple soul at first supposed that his demands could only be a source of vexation to his noble wife. It was some time before Alexandra succeeded in getting him more or less attuned to the extracting of modest and muted matrimonial joys. Ivan Isaevich's fidelity much surpassed what the concept usually entails. He served his wife with his every thought and every emotion, and Alexandra, taken aback by such an unexpected gift so near to the falling of the curtain on her womanly biography, accepted his love gratefully.

General Gladyshev had built so many military and semi-military installations in the course of his career and had received so many decorations for his broad but short chest that he was almost not afraid of the authorities. Not, of course, in the sense in which a philosopher or an artist in some namby-pamby bourgeois state is not afraid of the authorities, but in the sense that he had held his ground under Stalin and outlived him, had got on fine with Khrushchev, whom he had known from the war, and was confident that he could find a common language with any other authorities.

He was afraid only of his wife, Vera Ivanovna. Only Vera Ivanovna, his faithful spouse and partner through thick and thin, disturbed his calm and jangled his nerves. She regarded her husband's high rank and senior position as effectively her own private property and was fully capable of demanding all that, in her perception, was her due. When the need arose, she had no hesitation in raising the roof. It was these outbursts that Pyotr Stepanovich feared most of all. His wife had a powerful voice, the acoustical properties of their tall rooms were first-rate and the sound insulation inadequate. When she started shrieking, he surrendered with alacrity: "What must the neighbors think? You've completely taken leave of your senses."

After her hungry Vologda childhood and penniless youth, Vera Ivanovna was knocked sideways by the loot of which Pyotr Stepanovich—who was not a covetous man, but neither was he a fool—shipped back one full goods wagon from defeated Germany at the end of 1945, since which time Vera Ivanovna had been unable to stop herself from buying more and more possessions. Cursing her for a lunatic and a madwoman, he did not consider her to be either of those things in a literal sense. For this reason when one night a few months after the death of their daughter he was awakened by the muttering of his wife, who was standing in a piglet-colored nightgown in front of the open drawer of a lady's escritoire, from Potsdam as he recalled, it never occurred to him that the time might have come to commit her to a lunatic asylum.

"She thinks she will get all my things now, they'll all be left to her, the little murderess," Vera Ivanovna said, wrapping a Chinese fan and some little flasks in a light towel.

"What are you doing at this time in the night, Mother?" Pyotr Stepanovich asked, raising himself on his elbow.

"We need to hide them, Pyotr, hide them. That's what she thinks will happen." Her pupils were so dilated they almost merged with the black rims of the irises, and her eyes seemed not grey but black.

The general was so irate that the foreboding which had stirred briefly in his heart promptly dissolved. He hurled a long and elaborate curse in her direction, took the pillow and a blanket, and went to sleep the rest of the night in the study, trailing the long ribbons of his army-issue underpants behind him.

Madness, as anyone knows who has observed it at close quarters, is the more infectious the more sensitive the psyche of the person finding themselves in the proximity of the mad person. The general simply did not notice it. Motya, a distant relative of Vera Ivanovna's who had been subsisting in their apartment since she was young, did notice certain strangenesses in the mistress's behavior but paid them no special attention since she, having twice experienced famine in Russia, had long been slightly deranged herself. She lived in order to eat. Nobody in the family saw how or when she did it, although they did know that she ate at night.

She feasted in her narrow, windowless room, intended as a larder, with the latch down. First she gorged on what she had gathered during the day from food left by the family; then what she considered the food due to her herself; and finally, and sweetest of all, what she had slyly stolen with her own hands out of the Kremlin-supplied food orders: a makeweight piece of sturgeon, a lump of dry sausage, and chocolates if they arrived in paper bags rather than sealed boxes.

Her quarters were off limits to all members of the household: not even the cat was allowed in; and even the general, insensitive as he was to anything mysterious, was aware of some kind of unpleasant secret in there. She carried in cereals and flour which she had poured into paper bags, and tinned food. A day before her annual trip to her sister's in the country, she would slip out the door, unnoticed by her mistress, with two large bags that she would take to Yaroslavl Station and put in the left-luggage section. All these foodstuffs were intended as a present for her sister, but year after year the same story repeated itself: the first evening she was there she would put on the table a tin of stew covered with delicious, cheap oil, intending to present the rest later; but her sick soul prevented her from carrying through this act of heroism, and she would revert to guzzling her supplies at night, in the dark and alone; and her sister, observing the midnight feasts from her place above the stove, only felt great pity for her greed and forgave her. Even though she was older than Motya, she lived off her vegetable garden, kept a cow, and didn't suffer from gluttony.

It was no wonder, then, that Motya, constantly occupied with her search for food, failed to notice either the stupors into which Vera Ivanovna would fall or the abnormal agitation which would have her pacing around the apartment from room to room like a wild beast in a cage; and if she had noticed anything, she would have given it her customary explanation: "Vera is Satan incarnate."

Pyotr Stepanovich didn't notice anything either, since for many years he had been avoiding contact with his wife, getting up early and not breakfasting at home. The moment he arrived at his enormous office, his secretary would bring him tea. He would return home late, in the old days after midnight, having sat out some sixteen hours at a time in his department; what he enjoyed most of all were tours of inspection to installations, and he was often out of Moscow. He did not exchange two words with his wife if he could help it. He came home, had supper, burrowed into her silk-covered, down-filled duvets as fast as he could, and rapidly fell asleep like the healthy man he was.

So it happened that all the monstrous power of Vera Ivanovna's insanity fell upon Masha. She started school here, on Tinkers Embankment. She was wakened, taken to school, and brought home again by Motya, but from dinnertime on, Masha spent all her time with her grandmother.

Masha sat down at the table. Grandma Vera sat down opposite and didn't take her eye off her for a moment. She didn't keep scolding Masha; she just stared at her with grey, unblinking eyes and from time to time whispered something incomprehensible. Masha pushed her silver spoon around in the bowl and couldn't raise it to her mouth. Under Vera Ivanovna's chilling gaze the soup quickly got cold and Motya, who had a vested interest, quickly took it off to who knows where and put a large plate with the main course in front of Masha, which very soon was carried off almost untouched to wherever it was the soup had gone. Then Masha ate a piece of white bread with stewed fruit, which was to remain her favorite food for the rest of her life, and her grandmother would say to her, "Let's be off."

She would sit down obediently at the piano on three thick encyclopedia volumes and lower her fingers to the keys. In her life she never came across any cold more piercing than the chill that flowed through her bones from the black and white teeth of the hated keyboard. Vera Ivanovna knew that the girl hated these exercises. She would sit to one side of her, watching and ceaselessly whispering something, and tears welled up in Masha's eyes, ran down her cheeks and left cold, damp tracks.

Then she was sent to the corner room. A framed photograph of Tanya stood in there on a table, and there were many more in a cardboard box. Masha would open her exercise book and push one of her mother's photographs between the pages, most often the one where she was standing in the doorway of a house in the countryside; to one side you could see part of a hedge and a flowering shrub, and she had such a broad smile that it barely fitted on her narrow face. It was a snapshot Sergei had taken, and the happiness of the summer morning was plain to see, and reflections of the first night they had just spent together after Tanya herself had proposed to Sergei. He had long been silently in love, but hesitating and putting the moment off, embarrassed by the shadow her father's rank cast over her.

Masha practiced her writing, sometimes staring motionlessly

at the photograph for a long time. She sat for hours at her lessons. She was not allowed out for walks for some special reason of Vera Ivanovna's. Occasionally, Motya would take Masha with her to the shop, or the baker's or the shoemaker's. Nearly all the shops were downstairs on the ground floor of their apartment block, so it wasn't a long walk. Occasionally they walked to Solyanka, where there was Masha's favorite house, with the caryatids—the giants, as she called them. An even greater delight was that the River Yauza, the little churches, the fences around the building sites which she could see from their window on the eleventh floor suddenly became much larger, didn't look so toy-like, but in compensation sprouted little details and attractive touches.

At night, after Motya had put her to bed, the most dreadful part began: she could not sleep; she turned over and over in the large bed and kept waiting for the moment when the door would creak and Grandma Vera would come into her room. She came in very late, at an hour which Masha had no way of knowing, wearing a cherry-red dressing gown, and with a long smooth plait down her back. She would sit beside the bed, and Masha would curl into a ball and screw up her eyes. She remembered one such evening particularly clearly because of the illuminations with which the block had been decorated for the October Revolution festivities. The light fell in yellow and red stripes, and Vera Ivanovna, sitting in a shaft of red light, moaned in a clearly audible whisper: "Murderess, little murderess. You phoned them and that's why they set out . . . you made it all happen . . . live with it now, live with it and gloat over what you've done."

When Vera Ivanovna went away, Masha could finally cry. She buried her face in the pillow and fell asleep in her tears.

On Sundays dear Alexandra, for whom Masha had been waiting all week, would finally come. Masha was handed over to her until dinnertime, a few hours. Downstairs by the entrance Ivan

Isaevich would be waiting for them, Uncle Vanya, sometimes alone but more often with Nike, and they would go for an outing: to the zoo, or the planetarium, or to somewhere in Durov. The partings always proved more powerful for her than the meetings, and just the brief outing itself reminded her of other people, who had the good fortune to live in Uspensky Lane.

Alexandra took Masha there several times. She could see the little girl was unhappy, but could never have imagined that what was upsetting her most was the appalling accusation of the crazy old woman. Masha said nothing about it because what she feared most of all was that her beloved Alexandra and Nike would find out what she had done and stop coming to see her.

Late in the autumn Masha had a terrible nightmare for the first time. In it nothing happened at all. It was just the door to her room opening, and someone terrifying was going to come in. She could feel the monster coming nearer down the corridor, and the horror grew and grew until Masha woke up with a scream. Who was pushing the door open and why? And it was never quite where the real door was . . . Motya usually came running in when she screamed. She would tuck her in again, stroke her, and make the sign of the cross, and then when it was already almost morning Masha would fall soundly asleep.

If before she had been unable to sleep, waiting for her grandmother to come, now even after she left, Masha could not sleep for a long time, terrified of the nightmare which visited her more often the more she feared it. In the mornings Motya had trouble getting her out of bed. She sat half-asleep through her lessons, came back home half-asleep and performed her musical servitude in front of Vera Ivanovna, and then she fell into a fitful catnap which saved her from nervous exhaustion.

The location above the River Yauza where their apartment block stood had long been considered an unholy spot. Above it was Louse Hill, and along the shore itself there once sprouted the hovels of tinkers and potters. On the opposite bank had sprawled Khitrov Market, whose environs were populated by rag-and-bone men, prostitutes, and tramps. It was their descendants who inhabited the tenements built here at the turn of the century, and these were the people, crammed now into moldering communal flats, who pointed to the vast building which rose up higher than any of the neighborhood churches, a flight of architectural insanity not without irony, with a spire, arches, colonnades above tiers of diverse heights, and said, "That's an unholy place."

Many residents of the block died unnatural deaths, and the narrow windows and stunted little balconies attracted suicides. Several times a year the emergency services would drive up to the block with sirens wailing and scrape up the flattened human remains which some compassionate soul had covered with a sheet. Statistics, a science so much cherished in Russia, had long ago established that the number of suicides rose on sunless winter days.

That December was unusually dismal. The sun did not once break through a blanket of cloud. It was the ideal time for a last flight.

The Gladyshevs usually dined in the dining room but ate their supper in the kitchen. One evening as Masha was finishing the potato fritters which Motya had cooked country style, Vera Ivanovna came into the kitchen. Motya informed her that someone else had "made the leap" today. The daughter of a famous aircraft designer had thrown herself from the seventh floor.

"Unlucky in love, I expect," Motya commented.

"They spoil them. That's what it leads to. You shouldn't let girls out," Vera Ivanovna responded sternly. She poured some boiled water into a glass and went out.

"Motya, what happened to her?" Masha asked, tearing herself away from the potatoes.

"What do you mean? She killed herself. It's stone paving down there you know, not straw. Oh, this sinful world." She sighed.

Masha put her clean plate in the sink and went to her room. They lived on the eleventh floor. There was no balcony in her room. She moved a chair over and climbed up onto the broad windowsill. A rudimentary little balustrade was squeezed in between the tenth and eleventh floors. Masha tried to open the window, but the bolts were paint-stuck.

Masha got undressed and put her things on the chair. Motya came in to say good night. Masha smiled, yawned, and fell asleep instantly. For the first time in her life at Tinkers Embankment, she fell into a light, happy sleep; for the first time she did not hear the quiet curses with which Vera Ivanovna came into her room at midnight; and the door of the terrifying nightmare did not open that night.

Something had changed in Masha from the day she heard about the girl who had "made the leap." Evidently there was a possibility she hadn't known about, and knowing about it made her feel better.

The next day Alexandra rang to see if she would like to go with Nike to a winter camp run by the Theater Society. Masha would have liked to go anywhere in the world with Nike. Nike was the only girl left from her old life: all her other friends in the southwest region of Moscow, where she had lived before, had vanished without trace, as if they too had been killed along with her parents.

For the few days remaining before New Year, Masha lived in a state of happy anticipation. Motya packed her case, covered it in protective canvas, and sewed a white square to it on which she wrote Masha's name. The general's chauffeur brought over her skis from the southwest. He couldn't find the poles but bought some new red ones in Children's World, and Masha stroked them and smelled them. They smelled more delicious than any food.

She was to be taken to Pushkin Square on the morning of December 31. She would meet Nike at the place from which the buses would be leaving. She imagined that all her friends from her old home would be there too: Olya, Nadya, and Alyona.

On the evening of the thirtieth her temperature rose to almost 104 degrees. Vera Ivanovna called the doctor and rang Alexandra Georgievna to inform her. That was the end of the trip.

Masha lay for two days in a high fever, opening her eyes from time to time and asking: "What's the time? It must be time to go. Aren't we going to be late?"

"Tomorrow, tomorrow," Motya kept saying, hardly leaving her bedside.

In occasional lucid moments Masha saw Motya and Alexandra, Vera Ivanovna and even her grandfather, Pyotr Stepanovich. "When am I going to the camp?" Masha asked in a clear voice when the illness released its grip on her.

"But the holidays are over, my dear. What camp could you be going to?" Motya responded.

It was the end of the world.

In the evening Alexandra came and comforted her for a long time, promising to take her to stay in the summer at her dacha in Zagoryanka.

That night the nightmare came back. The door from the corridor opened and somebody terrifying was slowly approaching her. She wanted to scream but couldn't. She sat bolt upright, jumped out of bed in a strange state between sleeping and waking, moved the chair over to the windowsill, climbed up on it, and heaved the bolt with a strength which came from who knows where. The inner window frame opened. The second opened easily, and she slipped down off the sill before she even had time to feel the icy touch of the tin cowling. The hem of her nightdress snagged on its jagged edge, pulling her in just enough for her to fall lightly onto the snow-covered balustrade of the tenth floor.

An hour later Motya finished gorging herself and came out of her storeroom. A cold draft blew over her. Ice-cold air was coming from the open door of Masha's room. She went in, saw the open window, gasped, and rushed to shut it. On the windowsill a small, uneven pile of snow had drifted. Only after she had closed the window did she notice that Masha was not in bed. Her legs buckled under her and she fell to the floor. She looked under the bed. She went over to the window. It was snowing heavily. She could see nothing other than the slow snowflakes.

Motya shoved her bare feet into felt boots, threw on a shawl and an old overcoat of her mistress's, and ran to the lift. At the bottom she ran through the large vestibule with its red carpeting, squeezed through the massive door out to the street, and ran around the corner of the house. The snow was loose and level and sparkling prettily.

"Perhaps she's been covered over already," she thought, and walked along, kicking through the thick snow under the windows of their apartment with her boots. The little girl wasn't there. Then she went back up and woke the master and mistress.

Masha was out on the balustrade for a further hour and a half before she was found. She was unconscious but hadn't a scratch on her. Pyotr Stepanovich went out to the ambulance with the girl tucked up in blankets and then came back to his apartment. Vera Ivanovna sat throughout that hour and a half on the edge of her bed, not moving an inch or saying a word. After Masha had been taken away, the general led Vera Ivanovna into his office, sat her in the cold leather armchair and, taking her firmly by the shoulders, gave her a good shake: "Tell me what happened!"

Vera Ivanovna smiled an out-of-place smile. "She was behind it all. She killed my Tanya."

"What?" Pyotr Stepanovich demanded, guessing at last that his wife was mad.

"She's a little murderess, she was behind it all, she . . ."

The next ambulance took Vera Ivanovna away. The general didn't wait for morning but called it immediately. That night he went down in the lift for a second time to liaise with the emergency services. Coming back up, he vowed not to spend another day under the same roof as his wife.

In the morning he rang Alexandra Georgievna, told her very tersely what had happened, and asked her to take Masha to live with her as soon as she was discharged from the hospital. The next day the general went off on a tour of inspection to Vladivostok.

Masha saw her grandmother only once more after that, at her funeral. Pyotr Stepanovich was as good as his word: Vera Ivanovna lived out the eight years of life remaining to her in a privileged clinic far from all her antique furniture, porcelain, and crystal. Masha did not recognize the dead, wizened old woman with sparse grey hair as the fine-looking Grandma Vera with the splendid mane who used to come in a cherry-red dressing gown into her room when she was seven years old to utter whispered curses at her in the night.

A week after this disaster with a relatively happy ending, the nondescript, provincial-looking Jewish Dr. Feldman pushed Alexandra Georgievna into a lumber room under the stairs which was piled up with old hospital beds, bundles of torn laundry, and boxes, and sat her down on one rickety stool and himself on another with three legs. An old knitted shirt with a stretched collar and a badly knotted tie looked out of the opening of his hospital coat. Even his bald head seemed untidy, with irregularly sized little clumps of hair resembling fur about to molt.

He folded his Hippocratic hands professionally in front of him and began: "Alexandra Georgievna, if I'm not mistaken. It's completely impossible to speak privately here. This is the only place we won't be interrupted. I have something serious to say to you. I want you to understand that the mental health of this child is entirely in your hands. The girl has been so profoundly traumatized that it is difficult to foresee the remoter consequences. I am quite sure many of my colleagues would insist that she become an inpatient and be given serious drug-based treatment. That may not yet be necessary: there's no way of establishing a clear prognosis, but I think that there is a chance of burying the whole sorry business." He looked awkwardly aware of having used an inappropriate expression. "I mean that the mind has formidable defense mechanisms, and perhaps these will become operative here. Fortunately, Masha is not fully aware of what happened. She hadn't consciously formulated the intention of committing suicide, and is not aware of having attempted it. What happened to her may be regarded rather as a reflex, like when someone quickly pulls back their hand when they've taken hold of something hot. I have spoken to Masha a lot. She is reluctant to open up, but when she does, she talks sincerely, honestly, and you know"—he abandoned his quasi-scientific discourse—"she is an enchanting little girl, so clever and bright eyed, and somehow with very good moral instincts. A delightful child." His face lightened and he even became likable.

"Just like someone else I know," darted through Alexandra's mind.

"Some people are crippled by suffering, but others, you know, are somehow raised up by it. What she needs right now is a hothouse, an incubator. I would take her out of school this year in order, you know, to rule out mischance: a bad teacher, unkind children. It would be better to keep her at home until next year; and make sure she has a very, very protective environment." He became animated. "And absolutely no further contact with that grandmother! None at all. She has instilled a guilt complex in her for the death of her parents, which is something not every adult could cope with. All of this can be squeezed out. Try to avoid reminding her about this period, and it would also be best not to remind her about her parents. Here is my telephone number. Call me." He took out a slip of paper he had already prepared. "I am not going to abandon Masha. I shall be keeping an eye on her. Thank you, that's all I needed to say."

Alexandra had not expected Masha to be allowed out so soon. Her belongings, moved for the second time in half a year to a new home by the general's chauffeur, hadn't yet been sorted and stood there together with the no longer needed suitcase and skis. Alexandra went home immediately after her talk with the doctor to get Masha's things, and the same day took her back to Uspensky Lane.

It was the middle of January. The New Year's tree had not yet been taken down, the table was still moved to one side for the holiday, and they even had a visitor: Alexandra's oldest daughter Lidia, who was pregnant. The food was nothing special, not fare for a celebration: a pickled salad, rissoles with macaroni, and some slightly burned biscuits which Nike had cooked in a rush just before Masha arrived.

But then again, as far as the love prescribed by the doctor was concerned, things could not have been better: Alexandra's heart was simply overflowing with prayerful gratitude that Masha's life had been spared by a miracle and that she was well and living in her home. None of her own children seemed to her at that moment as dearly loved as this fragile, grey-eyed little girl who didn't seem at all like the rest of them.

Nike cuddled her and hugged her and did everything she could think of to keep her amused. Masha sat at the table for a time and then moved to a little child's wicker armchair which Ivan Isaevich had brought from somewhere a few days before her arrival: he had spent two days mending a broken arm and fixing a piece of red material and a fringe to the seat.

Made drowsy by her pregnancy, Lidia soon left. She and her husband were living in Ivan Isaevich's old room now.

Although the whole family had been looking forward to Masha's arrival, her timing was unexpected, and the result was that they had nowhere for her to sleep. Nike went off to sleep in her mother's bed, and Masha was put in Nike's little boat, which she had almost grown out of over the summer. Masha's eyes were drooping, but when they put her to bed, sleep departed. She lay there with her eyes open and thought about going to the winter camp with Nike next year.

Having washed the dishes and put them away, Alexandra came over and sat down beside the little girl.

"Can I hold your hand?" Masha asked her.

Alexandra took Masha's hand, and she was soon asleep. But when Alexandra tried to carefully free her hand, Masha opened her eyes and said, "Can I hold your hand?"

Alexandra sat this way till morning beside her sleeping granddaughter. Ivan Isaevich wanted to relieve her at her silent vigil, but she just shook her head and motioned to him to go off to bed. It was the first night of many. Without someone to lead her through the night, her grandmother or Nike, Masha could not sleep, and even after falling asleep she sometimes woke with a scream, and then Alexandra or Nike would take her to their own bed and comfort her. It was as if there were two little girls: the daytime Masha, calm, loving, and outgoing, and the nighttime Masha, haunted and afraid.

They put a folding bed beside Masha's, and it was usually Nike who slept there. She was better than her mother at watching over Masha's fragile sleep and, if she was disturbed, could get back to sleep again right away. Nike was altogether more help to her mother than her older sister Vera, who was a college student, passionately interested in scholarship of every description, and, in addition to her studies at the institute, attending courses in German, Alexandra thought, or in some obscure branch of aesthetics.

Nike was twelve and had already attained a good height and acquired all sorts of feminine skills; a cluster of little spots in the middle of her forehead testified that the time was approaching when her gifts would be called upon.

Masha moved to Uspensky Lane just as Nike was losing interest in the traditional amusement of little girls, playing with dolls, and the live Masha promptly replaced all the Katyas and Lyalyas she had been practicing her inchoate maternal instincts on at such length. The whole contingent of dolls along with a pile of little coats and dresses which nimble-fingered Alexandra never tired of sewing for them passed to Masha, and Nike now felt herself the matriarch of a large family consisting of her daughter Masha and lots of doll granddaughters.

Many years later, after Katya had been born, Nike confessed to Alexandra that she must have used up the first flush of her maternal feelings on her cousin, because she never felt for her own children a comparable all-consuming love, the taking of another person so completely into her heart as she did in the first years Masha lived in their house. It was particularly true of that first year, when her whole life was colored by compassion for Masha, holding her hand at night, braiding her hair in the morning, and taking her out after school for walks down Strastnoy Boulevard. Nike occupied an enormous place in Masha's life, which it was difficult to define: she was her best friend, her elder sister, the best at everything, ideal in every way.

The following year, when Masha went back to school again, Nike would take her there in the morning and Ivan Isaevich would collect her in the afternoon. After her classes he would either take her home or cart her off with himself to the theater.

Soon after Masha's arrival Alexandra's illustrious patroness died, and she stopped working at the theater. Now she was managing a small private atelier which dressed the government's wives. It was an illegal business activity, but Alexandra still had certain backers from her earlier years.

The crepe de Chine offcuts from vast dresses for government officials' wives went to provide outfits for the dolls, but both Nike and Masha developed a lifelong aversion to anything pink, light blue, flounced, or pleated. When they were a little older, both of them took to wearing men's shirts, and jeans when those became available in Russia.

Despite dressing in what seemed to Alexandra a thoroughly unfeminine manner, by the age of sixteen Nike was a runaway success. The telephone rang night and day, and Ivan Isaevich looked at Alexandra, expecting that any moment now she would put a stop to her daughter's turbulent lifestyle.

Alexandra, however, seemed if anything to be delighting in Nike's conquests. At the end of the ninth grade Nike embarked on a headlong romance with a youth poet who had become wildly fashionable, and without finishing her last term flounced off with him to Koktebel, announcing this ex post facto by telegram when she was already in Simferopol.

Masha had become Nike's confidante from the age of eleven, and received her confessions with secret horror and admiration. Nike raked in pleasures large and small with both arms, and any sour little berries or pips she just spat out without giving them a second thought. She also spat out, as it happened, her schooling.

Alexandra did not tell her off, did not go in for senseless dressings down, and, mindful of the days of her own youth, quickly found Nike a place in a college of theater design where she had good contacts from when she worked in the theater. Nike did a bit of drawing, passed the exams with the requisite Grade Fours, and joyfully threw out her school uniform. A year later she was already more or less married.

Masha was now the last child of elderly parents, and the entire life of the family revolved around her. Her night fears had stopped, but her early contact with the dark abyss of madness left her with a subtle awareness of the mystical, a sensitivity toward the world, and an artistic imagination: all the things which go into creating an aptitude for poetry. By the age of fourteen she was wildly enthusiastic about Pasternak's poetry, adored Akhmatova, and was writing secret poems in a secret notebook.

CHAPTER 10

Toward evening, clouds built up over the mountains in the place known as Rotting Dell, and in the house an atmosphere built up of silent expectation. Nike was expecting Butonov to look in. As she saw it, after their nocturnal romp it was for him to make the next move. The more so since she could not remember whether she had told him she was preparing to leave.

Masha was waiting too, her expectation all the more tense since she could not decide who she wanted to see more: her husband Alik who was taking some of his holiday entitlement to come down for a few days, or Butonov. She could still see him running down the hill, leaping over the thorn bushes and jumping up and down on the scree. Perhaps her infatuation might indeed have been dispelled if she had sat in the kitchen and talked to him.

"He's completely thick," she recalled Nike's words, resorting to a saving but meaningless logic which proposed that someone who was completely thick couldn't be the object of an infatuation.

The person most acutely tormented by expectation was little Liza. That morning, after all her petty squabbling and displeasure with Tanya the day before, she had discovered that really she couldn't live without her. She had been waiting all day for her to come, pestering everyone, and now in the evening, tired of waiting, was wringing her hands and throwing a tantrum. Nike never took Liza's excessive demands on life too seriously, but this time she smiled: she too was having an affair of the heart. "She's just like me. If I want something, I want it now."

And right now the wishes of mother and daughter partly co-incided. Both were eager to continue their romance.

"Oh, do stop it. Get dressed and let's go to see your Tanya," Nike mollified her daughter, who ran to put on her best dress.

With the buttons on the back of her dress undone and with a whole armful of toys, Liza returned to Nike in the kitchen to ask which toy she could give to Tanya.

"Whichever one you don't mind parting with," Nike smiled.

Medea looked at her tear-stained granddaughter and thought to herself, "So hot-blooded. How enchanting she is."

"Liza, come here. I'll do up your buttons," Medea commanded, and the little girl obediently came over and turned her back.

It was difficult to get the small buttons into the even smaller buttonholes. Her fair hair still had that familiar sweet baby smell.

Fifteen minutes later they were at Nora's, sitting in her little house decked with arrangements of wisteria and tamarisk. The tiny summer house had a Ukrainian coziness about it, was cleanly whitewashed, and the earthen floor was covered with mats.

Liza had hidden the hare she had brought under her skirt and was trying to intrigue Tanya, but Tanya had her eyes down and was eating her porridge. Nora, as ever, was complaining mildly that they had got very tired yesterday, that the sun had been too hot, that the walk had really turned out to be very long. She went on and on. Nike sat by the window constantly glancing over toward the owners' residence.

"Valerii hasn't come out all day, either," Nora said, nodding in the direction of the Kravchuks' house. "He's watching television."

Nike got lightly to her feet, turned at the door, and said, "I'm just going to see Aunt Ada for a minute."

The television was turned up full volume, and there was a big meal on the table. Landlord Mikhail didn't like small portions, and Ada's saucepans, for all the modest size of her family, were practically the size of buckets. She worked in the kitchens of one of the sanatoriums and had all the resources of the state catering organization at her command, which also reflected gratifyingly on the rations of the two pigs she kept.

Valerii and Mikhail were sitting looking slightly dazed after their heavy meal, while Ada herself had just gone down to the cellar for the stewed fruit. She came into the room behind Nike with two three-liter jars. Ada and Nike kissed.

"Plums," Nike guessed.

"Nike, do sit down. Mikhail, pour something," Ada ordered her husband.

Butonov stared fixedly at the television.

"I won't, I just came in to say hello. My Liza is visiting your lodgers," Nike excused herself.

"You don't come to see us yourself. You only visit our tenants," Ada reproached her.

"No, really, I've come 'round several times, but you were either out at work or driving around looking up your friends," Nike said.

Ada furrowed her little brow and rubbed her nose, which was barely visible on her fat face.

"That's right enough, we went to Kamenka to see my godmother."

Mikhail had meanwhile already poured her a glass of chacha. He was good at all sorts of practical things, as Valerii had already heard from his neighbor Vitka: distilling chacha, smoking meat, salting fish. No matter where Mikhail lived, in Murmansk, in the Caucasus, in Kazakhstan, what interested him most was what people ate, and he made a mental note of all the best practices.

"Here's to our meeting," Nike exclaimed. "Your health!"

She held out the glass to Butonov too, and he finally tore himself away from the television. She gave him a look which Butonov did not like. Right now he didn't like Nike. Her head was tightly bound with an ancient green scarf which concealed her lively hair and made her face seem too long, and her dress was the color of dilute iodine. Little did Butonov know that Nike had put on precisely the things which most suited her, and in which she had posed for a famous artist. It was he who had told her to wear the scarf tight, and had gazed at her for a long time almost in tears, repeating over and over again, "What a face . . . my God, what a face . . . it's a Fayum portrait."

But Butonov knew nothing about Fayum portraiture, and was just feeling ratty that she had come trolloping over here to him without an invitation, a right he hadn't conferred on her yet.

"This is a friend of our Vitka. He's a famous doctor," Ada boasted.

"Yes, we went to the coves with Valerii yesterday. We're already acquainted."

"You always were quick off the mark," Ada said waspishly, alluding to something Butonov didn't know about.

"Yes, that's the truth," Nike replied brazenly.

At that point Liza started squealing and Nike, vaguely aware that something wasn't right with her new romance, slipped out through the door, swishing her long iodine-colored dress as she went.

Nike spent the evening with Masha. Nobody came to see them. They had plenty of time to smoke a cigarette together, to sit in silence together, to talk together. Masha confessed to Nike that she had fallen in love, read the poem she had written during the night and another two besides, and Nike for the first time in her life reacted wryly to her favorite cousin's poetry.

All day she had been unable to find a moment to tell Masha

about yesterday's conquest and now it had soured completely, and in any case she did not want to upset Masha with this fortuitous rivalry. Masha, however, was engrossed in her own thoughts and didn't notice anything.

"What should I do, Nike? What should I do?"

She was so concerned about her newly acquired condition of being in love, and was looking up at Nike with such expectation, the way she did as a child. Nike, suppressing her irritation with Butonov, who had evidently decided to punish her for some reason, and with her daft niece who had found a fine one to fall in love with, the idiot, shrugged and replied, "Give him one and calm down."

"What do you mean, 'Give him one'?" Masha asked.

Nike got even more exasperated: " 'What do you mean? What do you mean?' Are you a child? Just grab him by the balls."

"It's as simple as that?" Masha asked in astonishment.

"It's simpler than a steamed turnip," Nike snorted, and thought, "What a hopelessly innocent idiot. Love poems and all! If she wants to land in the shit, so be it."

"You know, Nike," Masha suddenly decided, "I'll go to the post office right now and ring Alik. Perhaps he'll come and everything will settle down again."

"Perhaps he'll come! That's just the problem!" Nike laughed unkindly.

" 'Bye!" Masha said, suddenly jumping up from the bench and, grabbing a jacket on the way out, ran to the road. The last bus to town, the ten o'clock, was leaving in five minutes' time.

At the city post office the first person Masha saw was Butonov. He was standing in a telephone booth with his back to her. The telephone receiver seemed tiny in his big hand, and he had to dial with his little finger. Without having talked, he hung up and came out. They said hello. Masha was standing at the end of the queue, with two other people in front of her. Butonov took a step to one side, letting the next person in, looked at his watch, and said, "It's been engaged for forty minutes now."

The streetlamps, flickering bluish wands, were very close together and gave off something like daylight; the light was stark, like in a horror movie when something's about to happen, and Masha felt frightened that this big, movie-star-like man in his blue denim shirt might make her reasonable and well-ordered life collapse. But he moved toward her, his mind still on the same tack.

"Women gossiping, or the telephone's out of order."

Now it was Masha's turn. She dialed the number, desperately hoping to hear Alik's voice, which would settle everything down again, but nobody answered.

"Engaged too?" Butonov asked.

"Nobody home," Masha answered, swallowing hard.

"Let's take a walk along the embankment and then try calling again," Butonov suggested.

He suddenly noticed she had a nice face and a round ear which stuck out touchingly on her closely cropped head. In a friendly gesture he put an arm on the thin velveteen of her jacket.

Masha's head came up to his chest, and she was thin and angular like a boy. "She'd make a good partner as a trapeze artist," he thought.

"I heard there's some kind of barrel on the embankment and a special wine."

"Novy Svet champagne," Masha responded, already walking.

They walked down to the embankment, and Masha suddenly saw them from one side, as if they were on a screen, walking quickly, looking both relaxed and purposeful at the same time, whirling past the backdrop of a resort with oleanders planted in urns and carried out and placed at the sanatorium entrances, past the fake plaster pillars, the glittering eternally green boxtree, past the shoddy palms worn out by pavilion living, and the local prostitute Serafima with her fat face, and several sturdy miners with goggling eyes were there to be glimpsed in the depths of the frame, and the soundtrack was "Oh, the Sea at Gagry," of course. And while all this was going on, her feet were joyfully dancing along in time to his walking, and her body was full of a holiday lightness and even a kind of wordless merriment, as if the champagne were already working.

Butonov liked the little cellar Masha took him to. The champagne they were brought was cold and delicious. The movie which had started on the way there was still running. Masha saw herself sitting on a round stool, as if she was positioned slightly to the right of herself and back a bit; she saw Butonov, who had been moved a half-turn toward her; and most amusing of all was that at the same time she could see the gold-toothed barmaid in her gold jacket, who was behind her back, and the boys who were half loaders, half waiters, who were dragging crates from the cellar through the back entrance. Everything took on the expansiveness of cinema and at the same time the flatness of a movie.

Masha also noticed that she herself looked pretty as a shadow on the screen, sitting calm and upright, with a good figure and her hair coming attractively together at the back, like a narrow promontory, onto her long neck.

Oh yes, a movie allowed you to act, allowed easy ways, passion, the bursting of champagne bubbles, he and she, a man and a woman, the sea at night, Nike, you are a genius, you are so gifted, no heaviness of being, no forced striving toward self-cognition, toward self-improvement, toward self—

"Isn't it a breeze here," she said, affecting Nike's intonation.

"Nice little wine. Some more?"

Masha nodded. Clever Masha, educated Masha, Masha the first in their entire company to begin reading Berdyaev and Florensky, who loved the commentaries to the Bible, Dante, and Shakespeare more than the originals; who had taught herself English and Italian, if you didn't count the second-rate extramural course at the teacher training institute, who had written two slim volumes of poetry, admittedly yet to be published; Masha, who could talk to a visiting American professor about Ezra Pound and about the Nicene Council with an Italian Catholic journalist, said nothing. There was nothing she wanted to say.

"Some more?" Butonov looked at his watch. "Well then, shall we try calling once more?"

"Where to?" Masha asked in surprise.

"Home, that's where to," Butonov laughed. "You're priceless."

The movie ambience seemed to recede slightly, giving way to her earlier disquiet, but the holiday-resort scenery was rerun as they retraced their steps to the post office. Butonov got through immediately, asked a few short, businesslike questions, learned from his wife that his trip to Sweden had been postponed, and hung up.

Masha phoned immediately after him, and now the thing she most wanted was for Alik not to be home. He wasn't. She didn't bother ringing Alexandra. She and Ivan Isaevich went to bed early, and anyway Nike would be in Moscow tomorrow and she had already written Alexandra a letter.

"Didn't you get through?" Butonov asked absently.

"There's nobody at home. My husband's taken off somewhere."

The words were a complete lie. She didn't believe anything of the sort. Most likely Alik was on duty. Moreover, the casual way she said it made it even more of a lie.

But in the context of the movie, which still running, everything was just fine.

"Well, then, shall we go?" Butonov asked, and looked at Masha doubtfully. "Perhaps we should take a taxi?"

"No, there aren't any taxis here. All our lives we've walked home at night. It's a two-hour walk."

They turned off the lit road onto a side street and walked some fifty meters. No streetlamps or oleanders were in evidence here; the street was abruptly, rustically, black. In addition the road would sometimes veer off uphill, stumble, and come back down again. The darkness on the ground was impenetrable, but the sky was less uniformly black. Over the sea the sky seemed lighter, and the western horizon retained a faint memory of the sunset. Even the stars seemed insignificant, as if only turned on at half-power.

"We'll cut a bit off here," Masha said, plunging down a much-trampled clay path to what was either a flight of steps or a small footbridge.

"Can you really see anything?" Butonov asked, touching her shoulder.

"I'm like a cat, I have night vision."

In the darkness, unable to see her smile, he decided she was joking.

"It occurs in our family. Actually it's very useful: you see things that nobody else can."

It was a highly meaningful feminine way of giving a signal, throwing a line in order to reduce the distance between two people which was as vast as the depths of the sea, but which could shrink to nothing in an instant.

It would be too much to say that Masha had thought up a plan. It was more as if a plan had thought up Masha. Like the ball in a children's game, she had slipped through some opening and was now rolling along a channel from which the only way out was into the empty hole of a pocket enmeshed in a fine lattice of strings. All this, however, would be for Masha to reflect on later, in the hours of her long winter insomnias.

Meanwhile she was leading Butonov by the hand across the bridge and up the steps, and then up along a track and, having indeed cut off about a kilometer and a half, she brought him out onto a firm earthen road lined with pyramidal poplars. This was a shortcut which had developed from a footpath; it led to the main road. At the main road their hands separated. Butonov marched ahead with a quick, confident step, and Masha had trouble keeping up. His mind was on Moscow matters, the postponement of his trip, and he was wondering what might be behind it. Butonov's back, which Masha could see two paces ahead of her, was the embodiment of total self-absorption, and there were moments when she wanted to hurl herself at it with sharp little fists, to rip that blue shirt and scream.

They entered the Village, and Masha registered that in a few minutes they would part and that this could not be allowed to happen. "Stop!" she said to his back as they were walking past the Hub. "This way."

He obediently turned aside. Now Masha was in front. "Here," she said, and sat down on the ground.

He stopped beside her. It suddenly seemed to him that he could hear her heart beating, and she herself felt her heart was a tocsin for the whole neighborhood to hear.

"Sit down," she requested, and he squatted down beside her.

She took his head in her hands. "Kiss me."

Butonov smiled, the way one smiles at a pet. "You really want me to?"

She nodded.

He did not feel the least bit aroused, but the practiced habits of a conscientious professional obliged him. He pressed her to himself and kissed her and was amazed how hot her mouth was.

Always one for respecting the rules, he duly observed them

now: first undress your partner, then undress yourself. He ran his hand along the zipper of her trousers and met her own hands feverishly undoing the stiff zipper. She slipped awkwardly out of her clothes and started tugging at the buttons of his shirt. He laughed.

"Don't they ever feed you at home?"

Her comical enthusiasm excited Butonov somewhat, but he was not altogether ready yet and played for time. The feverish groping of her hands—"Nike, Nike, I've got his balls!"—her desperate groan, "Butonov! Butonov!" and he could feel that he was ready to perform.

He found her more attractive inside than out, and unexpectedly hot.

"What have you got in there, a stove?" he laughed.

But she was far from laughing, her face wet with tears, and she only murmured, "Butonov, you're wonderful. Butonov, you . . ."

Butonov detected that this girl was well ahead of him in her sexual achievements, and guessed that she belonged to the same breed as Rosa—quick firing, frantic, and even outwardly a bit similar, only without the African hairstyle. He grasped her little head, squeezing her ears painfully, and thrust so deep he could feel the pounding of her heart as if he were inside her rib cage. He was afraid he might have hurt her, but it was already too late.

"Forgive me, forgive me, little one."

When he got to his knees and looked up, it seemed to him that they had been caught in the beam of a searchlight: the air was lit up with a bluish light and every blade of grass was clearly visible. There was no searchlight: high in the sky a round moon was riding, enormous, completely flat and silver-blue.

"Sorry, the show's over." He slapped her on the hip.

She got up from the ground, and he saw that she was well proportioned, except that she was slightly bowlegged and, as with Rosa, her legs were set in such a way that they didn't quite come together at the top. He liked this narrow chink of light: it was certainly better than fat thighs rubbing against each other till they got red marks, like Olga's.

He was already dressed, but she was still standing naked in the moonlight and he misunderstood her languor. Now all he wanted was to sleep, and before doing so he wanted to finish thinking through why his trip might have been set back.

The Village was now as clearly visible as the palm of his hand, and Butonov saw a path which led directly to Vitka's house, to the back of Ada's yard. He gave Masha a squeeze and ran his finger along the thin ridge of her spine.

"Do you want me to see you back or will you run up there on your own?"

"On my own." But she didn't go, she held him back. "You didn't say you loved me."

Butonov laughed. He was in a good mood. "Well, what have we just been doing right here?"

Masha ran home. Everything was new: her hands, her legs, her lips. Some physical miracle had occurred. What delirious happiness! Could this be the thing Nike had been hunting for all her life? Poor Alik.

Masha looked in on the children: in the middle of the room stood an already packed rucksack. Liza and Alik Junior were sleeping on folding beds. Katya was stretched out on the ottoman. Nike wasn't there. "She's probably gone to sleep in Samuel's room," Masha surmised. She was greatly tempted to waken her without more ado and lay everything out before her but decided she shouldn't disturb her in the middle of the night. She didn't open the door to Samuel's room, and tiptoed through to the Blue Room.

Butonov's adventures that night were not yet over. He found the door to Vitka's house half-open and was surprised: he remembered latching it from outside, although he hadn't padlocked it. He went in, making the door creak, threw his sneakers down on the mat, and went through to the second room, where he usually slept.

On the high bed, made up in the complicated Ukrainian fashion with a valance, a bedspread, a mound of pillows which Ada rearranged in strict order every morning, on the white woven blanket with her long hair spread out over the chaotically disordered pillows, slept Nike. The truth was that she had been wakened by the sound of the door creaking. She now opened her eyes and beamed a slightly theatrical happy smile: "A surprise just for you! With home delivery!"

Butonov always performed better on the apparatus the second time. Nike was straightforward and fun, and didn't darken their last night with foolish reproaches or say any of the things that might have been said by a woman scorned.

Butonov, still conducting himself by the same rules for treating a lady, the first of which he had been unable to implement this evening because of Masha's alacrity, now availed himself of the second and most important one: never explain yourself to a woman.

At dawn, to their complete mutual satisfaction, Nike left Butonov, not forgetting to write her telephone number in his little black book. When she got back, Medea was already sitting with a cup from which there rose the aroma of morning coffee, and there was no telling from her expression whether she had seen Nike's return through the kitchen window. Actually there was really no need to try to hide anything from Medea: the young people were always sure she knew everything about everyone. Nike kissed her on the cheek and immediately went out.

Medea's perspicacity was in general greatly exaggerated, but this night she really had found herself right at the epicenter: some time after two in the morning, having patiently but fruitlessly waited for sleep to come, she had gone out to the kitchen to take some of her "sleeplessness potion," as she called the spoonful of poppy seeds she boiled in honey. The moon came out at the same time as she did, lighting up the mound on which a young couple were disporting themselves, their white, unidentified bodies gleaming dazzlingly. A little later, when she had finished drinking her decoction with little mindful sips and was lying in her room, she heard the adjoining door open and springs creak softly. "Masha's back," Medea thought, and dozed off.

Now, seeing Nike return, Medea was puzzled for a moment: there was, after all, only one young man to go around the entire neighborhood, the athlete Valerii with his iron body and the long, priestly hair constrained by a rubber band. Medea noted this occurrence with a certain bafflement and filed it away where she kept her other observations of the life of her young relatives with their ardent romances and unstable marriages.

Nike came in again with a pile of laundry she had just taken off the line. "I washed it ready for the Lithuanians. I'll iron it before I leave."

At midday a neighbor took Nike, Katya, and Artyom off to Simferopol. Half an hour previously Nike had taken a stack of fresh laundry into the Blue Room, which Masha was relinquishing in favor of the Lithuanians, and here it was that, having a moment alone with Masha for the first time that morning, Nike received her confession and was immeasurably surprised.

"Nike, it's so awful!" Masha's gaunt face beamed at her. "I'm so happy! It was all so simple . . . and amazing! If you hadn't said, I'd never have dared."

Nike sat down on the stack of laundry. "Never have dared what?"

"I grabbed him like you said." Masha gave a rather silly giggle. "But you were absolutely right. You always are. I just had to stretch out my hand."

"When?" was all Nike could ask in a strangled voice.

Masha embarked on a detailed account of how at the post office . . . But Nike stopped her. She no longer had time for long explanations and asked just one, seemingly quite odd, question: "Where?"

"At the Hub! It all happened right at the Hub. Like in an Italian movie. Now we can put a cross there in memory of my unshakable fidelity to my husband." And Masha smiled her clever smile, just the same as it always had been.

Nike had never imagined that her crosspatch advice would be acted on with such precipitate literalness. But Butonov was obviously no dud.

"Well then, Masha, now you'll have something to write poetry about, love lyrics," Nike predicted, and was entirely correct.

"What a mess . . . Should I perhaps make her a present of this sports doctor?" Nike wondered. "Never mind, I'm leaving anyway. What will be, will be."

CHAPTER 11

The small leather trunk bound with strips of molded wood, lined inside with glued white-and-pink-striped calico, full of partitioned boxes which interacted ingeniously to form a series of little shelves and compartments, had once belonged to Elena Stepanyan. This was the trunk with which she had returned from Geneva in 1909; and she had traveled with it from St. Petersburg to Tiflis; she had come with it to the Crimea in 1911. With this small trunk she returned to Theodosia in 1919 and there, immediately before her departure for Tashkent, she had presented it to Medea.

Three generations of little girls had swooned over it longingly, persuaded that Medea's little trunk was full of treasure. There were indeed a few poor treasures in there: a big mother-of-pearl cameo, without its frame, which had helped feed them in the lean year of 1924; three silver rings and an inlaid Caucasian belt for a man, and for one with a very slender waist at that. But apart from these insignificant treasures the little trunk housed everything Robinson Crusoe could ever have dreamt of. There stayed there, securely packed and faultlessly tidy, candles, matches, threads of every color, needles and buttons of every size, spools for no longer extant sewing machines, fastenings for trousers and fur coats, hooks for fishing and needles for knitting; postage stamps—tsarist, Crimean, German occupation; shoelaces, braid, lace edgings, and insertions; thirteen locks of hair of various colors from the first haircut of yearling babes of the Sinoply family, wrapped in cigarette paper; a hoard of photographs; old Harlampy's pipe; and much more besides. In the two lower drawers were letters, arranged by year and all of them in their original envelopes, neatly slit open down the side with a paper knife.

Here too various documents were kept safe, including some which were quite curious, for example a form concerning the requisitioning of a bicycle from Citizen Sinoply for the transport needs of the Volunteer Army. It was a true family archive, and like any worthwhile archive, it concealed secrets not to be made public before the time was ripe. These secrets were in trustworthy hands, and as far as it lay within Medea's power, they were kept fairly scrupulously. At least the greatest and earliest of them was.

This secret was contained in a letter addressed to Matilda Tsyruli and dated February 1892. The letter had come from Batumi, was written in extremely bad Russian, and was signed with the Georgian name Medea. The present Medea knew, of course, of the existence of her Batumi namesake, Matilda's sister-in-law, the wife of her elder brother, Sidor. According to family legend, the Georgian Medea had died of grief at the funeral of her husband, who had been killed in an accident. It was in her honor that Medea had received her own name, which was unusual among Greeks. The letter, with its spelling and grammar corrected, ran as follows:

Matilda, my dear friend, we heard it said a week ago that they had drowned, your Teresii and the Karmak brothers. The day before yesterday his body was washed ashore at Kobulety. The witnesses who identified him were Vartanyan and Kursua the Cap. He was buried and may the Kingdom of Heaven be his, I can say no more. When you ran away, his temper became even more foul, he beat up Uncle Plato, and was always fighting with Nikos. God granted you a lucky escape. My legs are very bad. Last win-

ter I could hardly walk on them. Sidor helps me, great will
be his reward. Get married straightaway now. I send you
my love, and God be with you. Medea.

Medea found this letter a few years after the death of her parents and had kept it from her brothers and sisters. When the
young Alexandra started on her first escapades, Medea had told
her the story with some vague didactic intention, as if trying to
conjure Alexandra's destiny, to forestall the misfortunes and the
difficult search for the meaning of her life which, this letter
seemed to testify, had been the lot of their mother Matilda. Medea
was deeply convinced that frivolity led to unhappiness, and had
no inkling that levity can equally well lead to happiness or, for that
matter, lead nowhere at all. From childhood, however, Alexandra
behaved exactly as her wayward heart dictated, and Medea could
never understand waywardness, whims, urgent desire, caprice, or
passion. The second family secret was linked precisely to this peculiarity of Alexandra's and, until its time came, had been hidden
from Medea herself on the lower shelf of a single wardrobe, in the
officer's map case of Samuel Yakovlevich.

Medea had made herself a little corner of her own in the small
room where Samuel had spent the last, agonizing year of his life.
She placed her husband's chair with its back to the window, put
the small trunk at its side, and laid out on it the few books which
she read constantly. She continually changed the white curtains
in the room for even whiter ones, and dusted the whitish
Crimean dust off the bookshelf and the cupboard where
Samuel's things were kept. She did not touch his belongings.

For the whole of that year she read the Psalter, one kathisma
each evening, and when she got to the end, she started again at the
beginning. Her Psalter was an old one, in Church Slavonic, left
from her school days. Another, Greek, which had belonged to
Harlampy, was difficult for her because it was written not in the

language of the Pontic Greeks but in modern Greek. She also had in the house a Russian-Hebrew parallel-text Psalter published in Vilnius at the end of the nineteenth century, and this, together with two other books in Hebrew, now lay on the lid of the small trunk. Medea tried sometimes to read the Psalter in Russian, but although this made the meaning clearer in some places, the mysterious veiled beauty of the Church Slavonic was lost.

Medea well remembered the brown face of the young man with the thick, crudely split upper lip, his pointed nose, and the big flat lapels of his brown jacket, who came firmly up to Samuel sitting on a bench near the Theodosia bus station waiting for the bus to Simferopol. The young man was pressing three books to his side with his elbow. He stopped next to Samuel and asked him very directly, "Excuse me, are you a Jew?"

Samuel, tormented with pain, nodded silently, choosing not to come out with one of his customary dazzling jokes.

"Please take these. Our grandfather has died and nobody knows the language." The young man began pushing the dog-eared volumes into Samuel's hands, and it became clear that he was terribly confused. "Perhaps you will read them some time. My grandfather's name was Chaim."

Samuel silently opened the top one.

"The Siddur. I studied so badly in the *heder*, young man," Samuel said thoughtfully, and the youth, seeing his indecision, hurried to say,

"Do please take them. I can't just throw them out, can I? What use are they to us? We aren't religious."

And the brown youth ran off, leaving the three volumes on the bench beside Samuel. Samuel looked at Medea with large eyes: "There, do you see that, Medea," he halted, because he guessed that she could see everything he could see and a few more things besides, and deftly wriggled out of his predicament. "Now we'll have to drag all this weight to Simferopol and back."

The last leaf of hope had fallen from the tree. Believing not in chance but in God's providence, she understood this clear sign without any room for doubt: prepare yourself! From that moment she had no need of any biopsy, which was why they were going to the provincial hospital. They looked at each other, and even Samuel, who habitually blurted out everything that came into his head, said nothing.

They didn't bother with a biopsy in Simferopol but operated on him two days later, removing a major part of his large intestine, made an outlet in his side, a colostomy, and three weeks later Medea brought him home to die.

After the operation, however, he gradually felt better and better. Strangely enough he grew stronger, although he was extremely emaciated. Medea fed him only porridges and gave him herbal drinks, picking the herbs herself. A few days after his return from the hospital, he began reading those ancient books, and in the last year of his life the most useless pupil of the Olshansk *heder*, blessing unknown Chaim, returned to his people; and Orthodox Medea rejoiced. She had never studied theology and perhaps just because of that felt that the bosom of Abraham was situated not all that far distant from the regions inhabited by the souls of Christians.

This last year of his life was wonderful. The autumn outside was so still and mild, and unusually generous. The old Tatar vineyards, not pruned or tended for many years, bestowed their last harvest on the earth. In the following years the vines degenerated finally, and centuries of hard work went to waste.

Pears and peaches broke their boughs and tomatoes their stems. There were queues for bread, and not the remotest prospect of sugar. Housewives boiled and marinated tomatoes, dried fruit on their roofs, and the knowledgeable ones like Medea made Tatar pastilla without sugar. The Ukrainian pigs fattened on all the sweet windfalls, and the honeyed aroma of moldering fruit hung over the Village.

Medea was managing the hospital then. Only in 1955 was a doctor sent, and until then she was the only nurse in the Village. In early morning she would come into her husband's room with a bowl of warm water, take off the clumsy, crudely made apparatus from his sick side, and cleanse and wash the wound with a decoction of chamomile and sage.

He grimaced not with pain but with embarrassment and muttered, "What justice is there in the world? I get a bag of gold and you get a bag of shit."

She fed him watery porridge, gave him a herbal infusion to drink from a half-liter mug, and waited, placing a trough beneath his side until the porridge, having completed its short passage, poured out of the open wound. She knew what she was doing: the herbs sluiced the poison of his illness out of him, but the food was hardly assimilated. His death, for which both of them were readying themselves, was to come from starvation, not from poisoning.

Samuel at first turned away squeamishly, embarrassed at the exposing of this unpleasant physiology, but then he detected that Medea was not having to make the slightest effort to conceal revulsion, and that she was much more concerned about the inflamed edge of the wound or a delay in the outpouring of porridge which had only slightly changed its appearance than about the unpleasant smell emanating from the wound.

The pain was very great, but inconsistent. Sometimes several days would pass peacefully before some internal obstruction would form; then Medea would rinse the stoma with boiled sunflower oil, and everything would settle down again. After all, this too was life, and Medea was prepared to bear the burden indefinitely.

In the mornings she would spend three hours or so by her husband's side, going off to work at half-past eight and running home at lunchtime. Sometimes, when Tamara Stepanovna, an old registered nurse, was on duty with her, she could leave at lunchtime and she didn't have to go back to work in the afternoon.

Then Samuel could go out to the yard. She would arrange him in the chair and sit herself beside him on a low bench, cutting the skin off pears with a little knife whose blade had been almost completely worn away, or peeling blanched tomatoes.

Toward the end of his life Samuel became taciturn, and they sat quietly, enjoying each other's presence, the stillness, and their love in which there was now no fault. Medea, ever mindful of his rare natural lack of malice and the event which he considered his ineradicable disgrace, but which she saw as a true manifestation of his meek soul, rejoiced now in the quiet courage with which he bore his pain, fearlessly approaching death and literally pouring gratitude out of his heart to all God's world, and in particular to her, Medea.

He usually had his chair so that he could see the table mountains and the rounded hills in their pink and grey haze. "The hills here are like the hills of Galilee," he repeated after Alexander Stepanyan, whom he had never seen, any more than he had seen the hills of Galilee. He knew of him only from what Medea had told him.

The book from which he had read excerpts worse than anyone else at the celebration of his Jewish coming of age half a century before, he now read slowly. Forgotten words rose like air bubbles from the bottom of his memory, and if they didn't and the square letters chose not to reveal their hallowed meaning to him, he looked for an approximate paraphrase in the parallel Russian text.

He quickly realized that the book did not lend itself to exact translation. On the bourne of life things began to reveal themselves of which he had had no idea: that thoughts are not fully conveyed by words, but only with a large amount of approximation; that there is a certain gap, a breach, between the thought and the word, and it is filled in by hard work on the part of consciousness, which makes up for the deficiencies of language. In order to break through to the thought itself, which Samuel now imagined as resembling a crystal, you had to leave the text behind. In itself language clogged the precious crystal with inaccurate words whose boundaries fluctuated over time, with the physical appearance of words and letters, and with the different sound of the spoken word. He noticed that a certain shift of meaning occurred: the two languages he knew, Russian and Hebrew, had slightly different ways of expressing thought.

"National in form," Samuel smiled, paraphrasing Stalin, "and divine in content." Even now he couldn't stop joking.

He had little strength left. Everything he did he did very slowly, and Medea noticed how his movements had changed, how meaningfully and even solemnly he raised the cup to his mouth, and wiped with his withered fingers the mustache he had grown over the last few months and the short beard streaked with grey. But, as if in compensation for this physical decline, or perhaps it was the effect Medea's herbs had, his mind was clear and his thoughts, although slow, were very precise. He understood that he had little of his lifetime left, but surprisingly enough the sense of always being in a rush and the fussiness which had always been a part of him completely left him. He slept little now, his days and nights were very long, but this did not burden him: his consciousness had become attuned to a different timescale. Looking into the past, he was amazed at the instantaneousness of the life he had lived, and at the length of each minute he was spending in the wicker chair, sitting with his back to the sunset, his face to the east, to the darkening, lilac-blue sky, to the hills which in the course of half an hour could turn from pink to a brooding blue.

Looking in that direction, he made another discovery: it transpired that all his life he had lived not only in a rush, but also in a state of profound fear, which he had hidden even from himself. More exactly, many fears, of which the most acute was the fear of killing. Remembering now that appalling event in Vasilishchevo, the shootings which he was to have conducted and which he had not in the end seen, having ignominiously collapsed in a nervous fit, he now thanked God for that weakness so unbecoming in a man, for his behaving like a high-strung lady, which had saved his soul from damnation.

"I'm a coward, a coward," he admitted to himself, but even here could not miss an opportunity for ironic creativity: "She loved him so because he was a coward, he loved her for forgiving that in him." "And I always hid my cowardice," as Samuel now judged himself, "by running after women."

A psychoanalyst might have extrapolated from Samuel's case some complex with a mythological name, and would at the very least have explained the dentist's heightened sexual aggression as a subconscious driving out of fear of the bloodiness of life by means of simple thrusting movements in the yielding soft tissue of generously endowed ladies. Marrying Medea, he hid from his eternal fear behind her courage. His pranks and jokes and the constant desire to get those around him to smile were associated with an intuitive realization that laughter kills fear. He found out now that a mortal illness too could free you of the fear of living.

The last fierce dog waiting to bite every Jew's heel was cosmopolitanism. Even before the term became generally accepted, sprouting its rigid expanded definition of "a reactionary bourgeois ideology," from Zhdanov's first publication Samuel anxiously followed the newspapers in which this bubble sometimes expanded and sometimes shrank. From his socially insignificant but materially more than tolerable position as district dental prosthetist, ever since his disgraceful flight from the ranks of the directly involved perpetrators of history into the herd of passive observers under experiment, Samuel foresaw the next of Stalin's migrations of the peoples. The Crimean Tatars, the Germans, in part the Pontic Greeks, and the Karaims had already been deported from the Crimea by this time, and he had the inventive idea of preempting the blow and taking contract work in the north of Russia for five years or so, by which time, with any luck, it would all have blown over.

Even before his illness he often walked with his friend Pavel Nikolaevich Shimes, a consulting physiotherapist at the Sudak sanatorium, through the manicured park which had formerly adjoined the Stepanyans' dacha, and they had whispered discussions about the sweeping course of history in the practical terms of those who currently found themselves at its sharp end. Early one Sunday morning at the end of October 1951, Dr. Shimes came from Sudak to see him, bearing a half-liter bottle of dilute surgical spirit, an extremely strange gift for a teetotaler to bring, and to Samuel's great surprise he asked Medea to leave them on their own.

Thereupon, rattling with false teeth which had not been very well fitted—not by Samuel, be it said—and drumming his fingers on the table's edge, he announced that the end had come. There had been a Party meeting at the sanatorium the previous day at which, with provincial intellectual obtuseness, he had been accused of cosmopolitanism because of the wretched Charcot shower which the doctor had been promoting for many years alongside other physiotherapeutic methods, all of which had been devised by foreign physiologists at the end of the nineteenth century.

"That moron who runs the sanatorium thought 'Sharko' was

a Ukrainian. Somebody enlightened him about that. I tell you though, Samuel, what I thought I might do. How would it be if I were to show him the certificate? We've got it safe at home," Shimes whispered.

"What certificate? That Charcot was a Ukrainian?" Samuel asked in surprise.

"That I've been christened. They think I'm a Jew, that's what it's all about, but my father was baptized and had the whole family christened back in 1904, just before the pogrom. What do you think I should do, eh? What should I do?" He dropped his bald head onto his hands.

He had nevertheless remained a real Jew, because at such a moment no Russian would ever have allowed himself to forget the bottle of spirits he had brought. Samuel scratched his little beard before answering in his usual manner: "Keep that certificate of yours for your funeral, so your priests can chant that Christian Kaddish of theirs over you. That's no solution. For Russians you are still a Jew, and for Jews you are worse than a goy. But as regards Charcot, you announce to those donkeys that Dr. Charcot stole his invention. From Botkin, say, or from Spasokukotsky. Or better still from Academician Pavlov. What are you looking at me like that for? Write up in your treatment room, 'Academician Pavlov Shower,' and they will all go back to sleep. And Pavlov won't mind: he died before the war." Samuel smiled waspishly and added, "And if you are as Orthodox as all that, you can even light a candle in church for him. My Medea will show you how, she knows all about that sort of thing."

Poor Shimes took offense and left, but after further thought he did hang up a notice in large red letters reading, "Academician Pavlov Shower." Alas, it was too late: he was fired from his job, although the notice hung on the door for more than two years. But at that time, after Shimes had gone off, Samuel felt his fear gradually being replaced by regret that there should be such rank stupidity all around. Or perhaps his illness was already beginning its secret work in Samuel's apparently still-healthy body.

It stayed warm for much longer than was usual in these parts, right through to the end of November. But then, from the first days of December, the cold rains began, quickly turning into snow and storms. Although the sea was quite far away and considerably lower, bad weather at sea affected the Village, especially at night. The wind bore masses of visible and invisible water, and the thick cushion of water vapor over the earth was so dense that it was impossible to imagine that a mere five kilometers or so above this cold porridge there shone the inexhaustible, infinite sun.

Samuel ceased going outside. Medea took his wicker chair back to the summer kitchen and put on the winter padlock. She was cooking now on a cooker in the house and in addition lit a small wood stove which had been installed by a Theodosia stove setter the year they moved here. Tatars did not put stoves in their houses, and left the floors earthen. Samuel and Medea had them covered over a year after they moved in.

Samuel asked her to hang heavy curtains in his room. He did not like the transition of twilight and would pull down the heavy blue blinds and light the table lamp. When they had a power cut, which was fairly often, he would light an older miner's lamp which gave a bright whitish light.

They kept the windows closed now, and Medea was forever burning oil infused with herbs in little homemade lamps, and the house was filled with a sweet oriental fragrance.

Samuel no longer read the newspapers; even the periodical fishing out of cosmopolitans in all areas of science and culture ceased to interest him.

By now he had read his way to the Book of Leviticus. This relatively less engrossing book, by comparison with the first two books of the Pentateuch, was addressed primarily to priests and contained almost half the 613 commandments which supported the Jewish way of life.

Samuel immersed himself in this strange book for a long time but still couldn't see why "of every winged crawling thing that goeth upon all four" you could eat only those which "have legs above their feet with which to leap upon the earth." But even of those the only ones pronounced fit for eating were the locust, and the hargol and harab which nobody had ever heard of, while all the rest were considered an abomination.

There was absolutely no logical explanation given for this. It was rough and inflexible, this law, and a lot of space was devoted to all manner of rituals connected with service in the Temple, which was complete nonsense given that there had long been no Temple and there was no prospect of its ever being restored. Then he noticed that the overall design of this ungainly law, sketched already in Exodus and fully developed in the Talmud, examined every imaginable and unimaginable situation in which a human being might find himself, and gave precise instructions on how to behave in these circumstances, and that all these chaotically imposed prohibitions were in pursuance of a single aim: the holiness of the life of the people of Israel and an associated total rejection of the laws of the Land of Canaan.

This path had been offered to him in the days of his youth, and he had rejected it. More than that, he had rejected even the laws of the Land of Canaan, which promised, if not holiness, then at least a certain relative orderliness founded on justice, and as a young man he had managed to work for the destruction of both of them.

Researching now the ancient Jewish legislation, he came to a realization of the profound lawlessness in which the people of his country were living, and he among them. This was no less than the universal rule of lawlessness which, worse than the laws of Canaan, overruled the distinction between innocence and brazenness, intelligence and stupidity. The only person, he now recognized, who was truly living in accordance with a law of her own was his wife Medea. The quiet stubbornness with which she had brought up the children, toiled and prayed and kept her fasts, could be seen now not to be an extension of her strange personality, but an obligation freely assumed, the observance of a law long since repealed everywhere by everyone else.

He did actually know other people of a similar disposition— his Uncle Ephraim, randomly killed by a drunken soldier who disappeared around the end of the street without looking back; and possibly Rais, the feebleminded cleaner, was someone of the same kind, a young Tatar who had just two rules in his little head: to smile at everyone; and to meticulously—idiotically meticulously—sweep the paths of the sanatorium park.

Samuel, who had been used to blurting out everything that came into his head to Medea, kept his present thoughts to himself, not from fear of not being understood, but rather from a feeling that he could not express them with total accuracy. From what he did say, Medea understood how much his inner life had changed and was glad about that, but she was too concerned about his physical condition to delve more deeply. He had begun to have back pain, and now she was giving him injections to enable him to sleep.

December passed, the storms abated, but it was as dismal and cold as ever. By the middle of January they were looking forward to the coming of spring. Medea, who had previously replied promptly to letters from her relatives, now responded only with brief postcards. "Received your letter, thank you, everything with us is as it was, Medea, Samuel."

She had no time for letter-writing. In all that winter she wrote only two real letters—to Elena and Alexandra.

February seemed to go on forever, and as luck would have it, this had to be a leap year. But then, in the third week of March the sun appeared, and from then on never missed an hour, and immediately everything started turning green. On the way home from work Medea climbed up a sun-warmed hill, picked a few violets and asphodels, and arranged them in a dish beside Samuel. He was hardly getting out of bed now and didn't even sit up because sitting seemed to make the pain worse. He was eating only once a day because the business of eating was too exhausting. His expression was continuing to change, and Medea found him full of spirituality and marvelous.

The last Sunday of March was a warm day with no wind, and Samuel asked her to take him outside. She washed the chair, dried it in the sun, and covered it with an old blanket. Then she dressed Samuel, and it seemed to her that his coat weighed more than he did himself. He walked the twenty steps from his bed out to the chair with immense difficulty.

On a nearby slope the tamarisks were doing their best, their branches laden with lilac color which they were still holding back within themselves. He looked toward the table mountains and they looked back at him in a friendly way, as equals regarding an equal.

"God, how wonderful, how beautiful," he said again and again, and tears flowed from the inner and outer corners of his eyes at the same time and were lost in the pointed beard he had grown.

Medea was sitting next to him on the bench and did not notice the moment when he ceased to breathe, because tears continued to flow for a few minutes more from his eyes.

He was buried on the fifth day. His withered body waited patiently for the relatives to come, showing no signs of decay. Alexandra came with Sergei, Fyodor with Georgii and Natasha, brother Dimitry with his son Gvidas from Lithuania, and all the men of the family from Tbilisi. The men bore him to the local graveyard and sat down afterward to a modest meal in his memory.

Medea did not allow any baking of pies or a big funeral party.

There was traditional kutiya with rice, raisins and honey, there was bread, cheese, a bowl of Central Asian greens, and hard-boiled eggs. When Natasha asked Medea why she had arranged it this way, she replied: "He was a Jew, Natasha, and Jews don't have funeral parties at all. They come back from the graveyard, sit on the floor, pray and fast for a set number of days. I have to say that seems to me a good custom. I don't like our parties where people always eat and drink too much. Let it be this way."

After the death of her husband, Medea put on widow's weeds and surprised everyone with her beauty and an expression of unusual gentleness which people had not noticed in her before. With this new expression she embarked upon her long widowhood.

All that year, as we have said, Medea read the Psalter and waited for news from beyond the grave from her husband as diligently as one might wait for the postman to bring an overdue letter. But nothing came. Several times it seemed to her that the long-awaited dream was beginning, that everything was full of her husband's presence, but her anticipation was dispelled by the unexpected arrival, in her dream, of some hostile stranger, or in reality by a strong gust of wind slamming the window and driving sleep away.

He first appeared to her in early March, shortly before the first anniversary of his death, but the dream was strange and brought her no comfort. Several days passed before its meaning became clear.

She dreamed of Samuel in a white doctor's coat. That was good. His hands were covered in plaster or chalk, and his face was very pale. He was sitting at his work table tapping with a little hammer at some unpleasant jagged metal object, but it was not a set of dentures. Then he turned to her and stood up, and he was holding a portrait of Stalin which for some reason was upside down. He took the hammer, tapped it on the edge of the glass, and removed him neatly; but while he was fiddling with the glass, Stalin disappeared, to be replaced by a large photograph of the young Alexandra.

That very day it was announced that Stalin was ill, and a few days later that he had died. Medea observed the spontaneous grief and sincere tears, and also the unutterable curses of those who could not share that grief, but she herself was completely unmoved by the event. She was much more concerned about the second half of the dream: why was Alexandra in it and what did her being there presage? Medea had a vague sense of alarm and even wondered about going to the post office to ring through to Moscow.

A further two weeks passed and the anniversary of Samuel's death came around. That day the weather was rainy, and Medea was completely soaked by the time she got back home from the graveyard. The following day she decided to go through her husband's belongings, give some of the things away, but mainly she wanted to find some instruments and a small German electric motor which she had promised to the son of a friend in Theodosia.

She made a pile of his folded shirts and set aside his good suit for Fyodor, who might have a use for it. There were also two sweaters which retained the living smell of her husband, and she held them for a while in her hands before deciding not to give them away to anyone but keep them for herself. In the very bottom of the cupboard she found a map case with various documents: one certifying completion of the course in dental prosthetics of the Commissariat of Health; one about graduating from the workers' faculty course; several deeds and official congratulatory letters.

"I'll put them away in the trunk," Medea thought, and opened an inconspicuous side section of the map case. A thin envelope lay in there, written in Alexandra's handwriting. The letter was addressed to S. Ya. Mendez, Sudak Post Office. That was odd.

She opened the envelope mechanically and was stopped short by the first line: "Dear Samsy," Alexandra had written. Nobody called him that. Older people called him Sam, the younger ones Samuel Yakovlevich. "You have turned out to be much better at arithmetic than I thought," Medea read.

You are absolutely right, but it doesn't mean anything at all, and it would be best if you forgot about your discovery straightaway and forever. I and my sister are complete opposites. She is a saint and I am a swine three times over, but I would rather die than that she should discover who the father of this child is. For this reason I beg you to destroy this letter straightaway. The girl is completely mine, only mine, and please do not think that you have a child—this is simply another of Medea's many relatives. She is a splendid little girl, redheaded and smiling, and looks as though she's going to be a bundle of fun, and I just hope she doesn't look like you—by which I mean so that this secret will remain between the two of us. Thank you for the money. It was not unwelcome but, to tell the truth, I do not know whether I want help from you. The main thing is that my sister shouldn't suspect anything. I'm suffering pangs of conscience enough as it is, and really where would I be if she ever found out?

And where would she be? Look after yourself and enjoy your life, Samsy.

Sandra

Medea read the letter standing up, very slowly, and then she read it again. Yes, of course. They had often gone down to the coves together that summer, Alexandra and Samuel. And it was that summer that Alexandra had lost her maiden's ring.

Medea sat down. A blackness the like of which she had never known engulfed her. Until late evening she sat there, not moving, then she got up and started packing her things. She didn't go to bed that night.

In the morning she was standing at the bus stop with her black shawl neatly tied, with a large rucksack on her back and carrying a carryall she had made herself. At the bottom of the carryall, in an old-fashioned carpetbag, lay her application for leave which she had decided to send when already on her way, her identity documents, some money, and the ill-starred letter. She caught the first morning bus to Theodosia.

CHAPTER 12

Standing at the bus stop with the rucksack on her shoulders, Medea felt herself a second Odysseus. Probably, indeed, even more heroic, since Odysseus standing on the shores of Troy, while he might have been unaware of the many years that would have to pass before his return, did at least have a fairly good idea of the distance separating him from home.

Medea, however, was accustomed to measuring distance in terms of hours of her brisk walking, and could not begin to imagine the length of the journey she had embarked on. Odysseus, moreover, was an adventurer and a mariner, and did not pass up any opportunity to delay his return, mostly just pretending that his ultimate destination was the crude habitation in Ithaca called the king's palace and the embraces of his aged and domesticated wife.

Up to that time Medea had spent her whole life in the Crimea, apart from that single journey to Moscow with Alexandra and her firstborn, Sergei, and this rooted life, which had itself been subject to violent and rapid change—revolutions, changes of government, the Reds, the Whites, the Germans, the Romanians; some neighbors being deported, new neighbors, outsiders with no ties, imported—had finally given Medea the stolidity of a tree which has put down its twining roots into the stony soil, living beneath the unchanging sun as it completes its daily and yearly rounds, and exposed to the same winds with their seasonal smells of seaweed drying on the shore, or fruit shriveling in the sun, or bitter wormwood.

For all that, she was a maritime person. From an early age the men of her family went to sea. Her father had died at sea, and Alexander Stepanyan had gone away forever over the sea, taking with him Anait and Arsik; a decrepit steamer had taken her aunt and two of her brothers from Batumi; and even her sister Anelya, who had married a Georgian from mountainous Tiflis, had left home long ago from the new dock at dear Theodosia.

Although there were no direct sea routes to the far-off city to which Medea had been intending to travel for decades, and for which she had now packed her bags and set out in a single night, she decided to go at least part of the way, the first part, by sea, from Kerch to Taganrog. The first two legs of the journey, from the Village to Theodosia, and from Theodosia to Kerch, were as familiar as crossing her own yard. Arriving that evening in Kerch, she found herself on the frontiers of her oikoumene, which had the ancient Pantikapeia as its easternmost point.

In the port Medea learned that passenger sailings began only in May, and that the few ships which were now sailing between Kerch and Taganrog carried only freight and no passengers. She was nonplussed, recognizing her first mistake: she should after all have gone directly via Dzhankoy, not allowing herself to be tempted by marine digressions.

Turning away with some aversion from the brackish, yellowy-grey maeotian waters, she went to see her old friend Tasha Lavinskaya, who had dedicated herself from the days of her youth to "bone-grubbing," as it was jocularly described by her husband, old Dr. Lavinsky, an intellectual and bibliophile who was almost as much of a local sight as the Vault of Diana. They lived at the back of the museum, and their apartment looked like an annex of it: fragments of crumbling Kerch stone, ancient dust, and dry paper filled the house.

Tasha did not immediately recognize Medea. They had not seen each other for several years, since Samuel had fallen ill, when her small number of friends, some from a feeling of tact, some for selfish reasons, had almost ceased to visit them in the Village. Having recognized her, however, Tasha fell upon Medea's neck, not giving her time even to take off her rucksack.

"Wait, wait, Tashenka, let me get these things off first," Medea said, fending her off. "Let me get washed. Samuel used to say Kerch was the world's pole for dust." It was a damp springtime and there was no dust in evidence at all, but such was Medea's confidence in what her late husband said that she felt covered in dust.

Sweeping piles of tattered books and sundry sheets of paper, covered with tiny drawings and infrequent illegible lines of writing, from the edge of the table with a practiced gesture, Tasha laid out the food on a newspaper, making no attempt to disguise its paucity and unprepossessing appearance. Sergei Illarionovich, the majestic old husband of a once-young beauty who magnanimously failed to notice how old and ugly she had become at an early age, the occasional coarse hairs sprouting from her chin, or her increasingly buck teeth, all his life viewed Tasha's extreme aversion to housework as a delightful foible. He had not lost an archaic ability to play the host, and plied Medea with dried and tinned fish, which was a complete absurdity in this fishing town.

But the wine was good. Someone had given it to them. Although long retired, Sergei was still practicing a little, and the intimates he treated would bring gifts of food to the house in addition to the customary fee, as they had in the past years of famine which had already almost faded from people's short memories. Hearing of the hitch in his guest's traveling plans, he immediately phoned the director of the port, who promised to see Medea on her way in the morning on the first available vessel, although he warned that he could give the traveler no guarantees regarding comfort.

They sat up until late into the night, the three of them at the table, drinking the good wine, then drinking bad tea, and Tasha, who showed no interest in why Medea might need to be going to Taganrog, launched into a long narrative about some kind of grid she had discovered from the Azov Mesolithic period. For a long while Medea couldn't grasp why she was so excited, until Tasha placed before her, on top of the remains of the fish, some very soiled little pictures drawn by an expert hand, depicting what looked like a grid for tic-tac-toe, and announced that this grid was one of the most persistent sacred symbols, found in the Paleolithic period and discovered in Egypt, on Crete, in pre-Columbian America, and now if you please here too, in the Azov region. Sergei Illarionovich, overcome by the drowsiness of old age and dozing in his armchair, was roused from time to time by his innate courtesy to nod a sleepy head in agreement and murmur some word of approbation before relapsing into slumber.

Not in the least interested in Tasha's scholarly researches, Medea waited patiently for the lecture to end, surprised that she had said not a word either about her daughter or granddaughter who were living in Leningrad. At each turning point in Tasha's speech Medea nodded in agreement and reflected on how stubborn human nature is, how persistent a passion can sometimes be, as unchanging as these grids of hers, these ovals and dots which, having once been imprinted, live on for millennia in every remotest corner of the world, in the cellars of museums, in rubbish dumps, scratched in the dry earth and on ramshackle fences by children at play.

In the morning a burly man in a maritime uniform without epaulettes came and collected Medea from the sleeping Lavinsky household, and an hour later she was being rocked in the middle of the Bay of Kerch on an ancient cargo steamer of a type so familiar that it might have belonged to the old armada of her grandfather Harlampy. Wheezing and straining powerlessly like an old man, the little steamship struggled into Taganrog only toward evening. By this time the drizzle had turned into a grey light rain and Medea, having sat twelve hours on a wooden bench on the deck with her back straight and her knees tightly together, walked down the gangplank feeling more like a part of the wooden bench from which she had just torn herself than a live human being.

On the landing stage she looked around her: apart from a single streetlamp and a boy who had traveled with her all the way from Kerch, who had been reading a thick tome during the hours of daylight, there was nobody and nothing around. The boy was in that final stage of childhood when being called "young man" still causes confusion.

"Can you tell me, young man, which the best way would be to get to Rostov-on-Don: train or bus?"

"Bus," he replied laconically.

Beside the boy stood a two-handled basket wrapped in old material with a pleasantly familiar pattern. Medea's eye lingered on it: faded, barely discernible daisies in round posies . . . The boy seemed to catch her gaze and said something that didn't make sense, pushing the basket with his foot: "If it fits in the boot, there'll be room for you too."

"What did you say?" Medea asked in surprise.

"My brother's coming from Rostov to pick me up. In his car. I think there'll be room in it for you."

"Really? Splendid."

The spiritual darkness which had enveloped her without relinquishing its grip for an instant since she had read that dreadful, hurried, offhand letter, did not stop her from rejoicing: "Lord, I thank you that you have not forsaken me in my travels, and that you send me your wayside angel as you did to Tobias."

The youth who, unknown to himself, was performing the office of wayside angel, moved the basket aside with the squared toe cap of his boot and explained to Medea, "He has a large car, a Victory, but he might already be transporting something in it."

The boy's speech was correct, and his intonation seemed familiar. He sounded as if he came from a good family. Evidently the thick volumes he read had done him some good.

Some fifteen minutes later a thickset young man came up, kissed the boy, and slapped him on the shoulder. "Well done, Leshenka! Why didn't you bring Auntie?"

"She said she'll come in the summer. Her legs are hurting her."

"Poor woman. How's she managing there on her own?" It wasn't an idle question: he was listening for the answer.

"It seemed to me she was getting by. She's renting one room. The lodger's a decent man, from Leningrad. He works at the meteorological station. He brought her some firewood in his car. Look, she's sent some presents." He nodded at the basket. "I didn't want to take them, but she insisted."

The man shrugged. "That's just how it has to be."

He went to pick up the basket. The boy stopped him. "Tolya, this lady's going to Rostov too. Have you got room for her?"

Tolya turned to Medea as if he had only just noticed her, although she had been standing alongside throughout the conversation. "I do have room. I can give you a lift. Where do you need to get to in Rostov?"

"The train station."

"Give me your rucksack," he stretched out a hand and slipped it onto his shoulder.

Medea was still murmuring to herself, "Lord, I thank you for all your goodness, for all that you send, and may I have room for it in my heart, rejecting nothing." This was her ongoing conversation with God, a mixture of prayers memorized long ago and her own voice, alive and grateful.

Medea, who had barely had time to straighten her old bones after sitting so long on the deck, now climbed into the car where it was warm and comfortable. Her damp clothing, if it didn't exactly dry out, was at least soon suffused with her own warmth. She nodded off and through her half-sleep heard scraps of the brothers' conversation: something about their sister's wedding; about the teacher training institute where the boy was a freshman; about Simferopol; about the aunt whom he had been visiting in Old Crimea.

"I really ought to visit Nina," Medea thought blearily through her sleep, remembering her former Theodosia neighbor who had moved to Old Crimea after a fire destroyed her house in their street. Through her drowsiness Medea remembered Nina, and her old mother who had gone out of her mind that very night, and her younger sister whose arm had been burned and to whom Medea had given first aid using a primitive but effective folk remedy.

They brought Medea to the train station in complete darkness in the middle of the night. The driver took Medea's rucksack and saw her to the ticket office. At one window there was a long, silent queue; the other two windows were shut so firmly it was difficult to believe they were ever open.

Medea stopped in front of one of these unpromising windows and thanked the driver. He took the rucksack off his shoulder, put it on the ground, and said uncertainly, "Would you perhaps like me to take you home for now and you can go on from here in the morning? Just look at this queue."

Before Medea could thank him, the window by her shoulder opened, and without having time to be taken aback, she asked for a ticket to Tashkent.

"Reserved seats only," the cashier warned her, "and you'll have to change twice, at Saratov and Salsk."

"Fine," Medea said.

The crowd immediately stampeded with much shrieking and yelling toward the window which had unexpectedly opened, and a furious argument broke out, with some people wanting to keep the old order of the queue, while those who had been at the back and now found themselves nearer the front didn't think that was at all a good idea.

A moment later, squeezing her way with difficulty through a seething crowd up in arms in pursuit of justice, her ticket in her hand, Medea took the rucksack from Tolya. He could only spread his arms wide in amazement: "Well, that really was a stroke of luck!"

They went out onto the platform and consequently didn't see that the window from which Medea's ticket had been issued was promptly closed again, and the crowd, now split in two, seethed in front of both of the closed windows, impatient fists drumming on unyielding plywood.

Medea's train arrived twelve minutes later, although it was five hours behind schedule. It was only when they were out of Rostov that she realized why the cloth with the daisy pattern had seemed so familiar: it was her own curtain, which she had given to Nina along with many other essentials after the fire thirty years ago. So the aunt in Old Crimea that they had been talking about was her own former neighbor Nina, and the young men were the children of the girl whose burn Medea had treated that night.

Medea smiled to herself and felt reassured. Despite being so much more crowded and having so much more hustle and bustle, the world still functioned in its old way, the way she understood, with small miracles happening, people coming together and parting, and all of it forming a wonderful pattern.

She got two rusks out of her rucksack and a large German thermos with a lid. The tea poured into it back in Kerch was hot and sweet. Medea sat for about four days by the carriage window, stretching out occasionally on the lower bunk and falling into a fitful and vibrating sleep on the bottom of which lay that black, insoluble precipitate of darkness.

The train rumbled slowly on, making countless little stops and standing for long senseless periods at the dual-track passing places. The entire timetable had been vitiated when the train was dispatched with a long delay to its point of departure. At every station and every halt it was met by a crowd wearied by their waiting. Not many people in the slow, dirty train were making as long a journey as Medea. Most of them got in with their baskets, sacks, and bundles for a few stops, crowding the corridors and, when they got out, leaving behind them pungent smells and the husks of sunflower seeds.

Although she had lived through many unsettled times in the Crimea, and remembered the typhoid-infected huts, the famine, and the cold, Medea had never been directly caught up in the huge migrations which have accompanied Russia's history, and knew only by hearsay about the goods vans, the cattle trucks full of people, and the queues for boiling water at the stations. Now, when she had passed fifty, she had for the first time torn herself away from her dear settled life of her own free will, and observed with astonishment what uncountable hordes were on the move over this vast, uncared-for land littered with rusting metal and broken stones. Down the railway embankments, just beneath the spare spring grass, lay the remains of a war which had ended eight years before, eroded shell craters full of stagnant water, ruins and bones embedded in the ground which filled the landscape from Rostov to Salsk and from Salsk to Stalingrad.

It seemed to Medea that the war was etched more deeply in the memory of the land than in that of all this multitude of people so loudly and uniformly lamenting the recent death of Stalin. Only a few weeks had passed since he died, and all her fellow travelers were constantly mentioning it as they talked among themselves.

She heard a lot of fantastic nonsense: an elderly railway worker, on the way back from his own mother's funeral, told in a whisper of the great slaughter which had occurred in Moscow on the day the nation was bidding farewell to Stalin, and about the Jewish conspiracies which had been at the root of it; another gloomy individual, with a wooden leg and a chest bright with medal ribbons, told of an underground city full of top-secret American weapons which had supposedly been dug up by chance in the middle of Moscow; two schoolmarms on their way to a regional meeting of some description endlessly debated in strained professional tones between themselves who there now was to lead the country to the Communist dream. In contrast, a tipsy traveler who had not taken off his cap with its earflaps all the way from Ilovinskaya to Saratov, and who had been listening the whole journey to their loud chatter without saying a word, as he was getting off the train suddenly pulled the hat from his head to reveal a patchy baldness, spat on the floor and said in a powerful voice, "You're two daft old biddies! It can't get worse than this under anybody."

Medea smiled out of the window. From her early years she had become used to treating political changes like changes in the weather—something you just had to put up with: in the winter you were cold, in the summer you sweated. She did, however, take care to prepare for each season in good time, getting in firewood for the winter; stockpiling sugar, if such a thing were anywhere to be found, for jam making in the summer. She never expected anything good from any authorities, kept her guard up, and stayed well away from people who were part of the power structure.

As for the Great Leader, the family had long had a bone to pick with him. Well before the Revolution, in Batumi, he had turned the head of her aunt's husband Iraklii, and landed him in a thoroughly unsavory episode involving a bank robbery from which he had to be extricated by his family putting together a very large sum of money.

In the Village on the day the Leader died, flags of mourning were put out and a meeting called. A party boss came from Sudak—not the top boss, someone fairly new. He gave his speech; they turned on some solemn music; two local women, Sonya from the food shop and Valentina Ivanovna the teacher, burst into tears; and everyone decided to send a telegram expressing their grief to "The Kremlin, Moscow." Medea, more appropriately dressed than any of them in her mourning clothes, stood at the meeting for as long as was necessary and then went to her vineyard and pruned it until evening.

For Medea all this was the distant echo of a life in which she had no part. Her present traveling companions, individuals who collectively constituted the Russian people, were now loud in their anxiety, fearful of their future as orphans, weeping; others, unspeaking, were quietly rejoicing at the tyrant's death; but all of them had now to resolve things in a new way, and to learn to live in a world which had changed overnight.

What was strange was that Medea too, in quite a different connection, was experiencing something similar. The letter lying deep in her bag was forcing her to see herself, her sister, and her late husband in a new light, and first and foremost to reconcile herself to a fact which seemed to her completely impossible.

An affair between her husband, who all the years of their marriage had deified her, extolling her merits, which he had partly invented himself, to excess, and her sister Alexandra, someone she could read like a book, was an impossibility not only on practical grounds. Some higher interdict, Medea felt, had been flouted, but judging by Alexandra's pert letter and its easy tone, she had not even noticed this incestuous and sacramental wrongdoing. All she was concerned about was ensuring that the secret did not inconveniently become public knowledge.

A special torment was that the present situation called for neither decisions nor action. All the previous misfortunes in her life—the death of her parents, her husband's illness—had called for physical and moral exertion: what had happened now was just the echo of something long past. Sam was no longer alive, his daughter Nike was, and there was no possibility of having a posthumous showdown with him.

She had been degraded by her husband, betrayed by her sister, abused by fate itself, which had denied her children while the child fathered by her husband, the child that by rights was hers, had been placed in her sister's relaxed and fun-loving body. The gloom in her soul was made deeper also by the fact that Medea, who had always been on the move herself, was being forced to sit for days at a time by this window where all the movement was outside, in the rolling by of the changing scenery through the window and, to some extent, in the restless movement of other people in the railway carriage.

Her journey lasted three and a half days, and as the route was quite whimsical, veering far up into the heart of the Continent, she appeared to overtake the spring in its northward progress: she left the Crimea where the leaves were coming out, and again saw snow lying in the ravines in the pre-Urals, the bare earth still gripped by frosts at night; and then, traveling to the east and the south, she came back to the spring with the hot steppes of Kazakhstan in full flower and dotted with vivid tulips.

The train arrived in Tashkent in early morning. She got out with her now-depleted rucksack and, knowing that her relatives lived not far from the station, asked which direction to take.

The street was called Twelve Poplars, but if poplars ever had grown here, they had meekly yielded to the flowering apricot trees planted along the irrigation ditch at the roadside. It was earliest, newborn morn, the time Medea loved best, and after her taxing days on the dirty train, she was particularly alive to this

God-given purity and the smells of the morning, in which familiar mingled with unfamiliar: the smoke from a different fuel, and the spicy smell of an unknown meat dish. Everything, however, was overpowered by the heady perfume of the lilac hanging out its trusses of blossom as blue and heavy as bunches of grapes above the clay walls and plank fences. Even the birds seemed to be singing in a foreign language, not so much singing as chirping.

As Medea walked down the interminably long road, enjoying the exercise, slightly swinging her shoulders, which were pulled back by the rucksack straps beneath which she had tucked her light coat in soldierly fashion, she was taking in, in addition to the numbers of the houses, all sorts of little details and surprises. On a fence a brown and pink turtledove was sitting as cool as could be: it was a bird she had been familiar with since she was a girl, only in the Crimea it was very wild and timid and never flew into the town.

The heavy mood of her journey, which she had seemed to be carrying on her shoulders, was washed away by the gentle waves of the morning breeze which, as she knew, always sprang up at sunrise. She heard a sudden shouting in the distance, carried over from the east on the breeze. It too seemed to roll in like a wave, and these were the piping voices of children.

"Water! The water's coming! *Suvgia!*"

Several little children immediately came dancing out of the gates, and other children's heads peeped over fences. A fat old woman in felt boots and a Ukrainian shirt which had worn through on her bosom waddled out to the ditch.

Medea stopped. She knew what was about to happen and had been waiting for just this moment. The bottom of the shallow ditch was covered over with a smooth, pale brown film of what looked like the skin skimmed from boiled milk, and, blown by the dawn breeze, pink petals of apricot blossom which had just fallen from the trees slowly settled on it; now there came the grumbling sound of water, and in front of its brown tongue there rose a pink cloud of apricot-blossom debris.

The shout passed down the street, the water was gurgling in the ditch. Young children and old men opened the ditch inlets to their yards. The time for the morning irrigation had begun.

Immediately outside Elena's house Medea collided with a little blond boy of about ten. He had just let the water into the yard and was washing his freckled face in the brown, rather suspicious-looking water.

"Hello, Shurik," Medea said to him.

He took a step backward in surprise and disappeared into the bushes with a shout: "*Mamunya!* Someone's here to see you."

Medea stopped in the yard and looked around: three small houses, one with a verandah and a high porch, and two more straightforward, whitewashed ones, formed a square in the center of which stood a platform for tea drinking, and from the summer kitchen with its side awning there came walking slowly toward her, greying, fat, wearing a white apron pinned up high in front, dear Elena. She did not recognize Medea at once, but when she did, she threw her arms open wide and ran toward her with a silly, joyful cry: "My own dear heart has come back to me!"

Doors and windows banged. The old sheepdog in its kennel finally woke up and started energetically barking, aware of having neglected its duty. The yard filled up with what seemed to Medea to be a huge crowd, but these were her own people: Elena's daughter Natasha with her seven-year-old son Pavlik; Georgii, Elena's younger son, who had grown over the past winter into a handsome young man; and a thin little old woman with a crutch.

"Old Nanny Galya," Medea guessed.

Up on the porch, inclining the arrogant face of an oriental beauty to one side, stood thirteen-year-old Shusha, Natasha's older daughter, wearing a white nightgown which her shining Asian hair almost entirely covered. Little blond Shurik peeped out from behind the trunk of a peach tree.

"Oh, Lord, Fyodor is away on a business trip. He left only yesterday!" Elena said, crestfallen, still not releasing Medea from her hug. "But why didn't you warn us? Georgii could have come to meet you."

Elena's family stood around, waiting their turn for a kiss from their aunt or great-aunt. Only Old Galya muttered something to herself and hobbled off to the forgotten stove where some domestic crisis had occurred: black smoke was rising from a frying pan.

"Oh, I'll get you some tea, some tea! Oh, what am I saying, coffee, coffee! Oh, my own dear heart has come back to me!" Elena clucked, repeating every word and flapping at the air around her head with a gesture totally unique to herself.

Seeing this movement of Elena's small hand, which had quite slipped her memory, Medea suddenly felt very happy.

Since 1920, when Medea saw her brother Fyodor off from the Theodosia station to his new job with his new wife, entrusted to him only the previous day after Medea's firm hand had matched the two of them, the friends had seen each other only twice: in 1932 soon after Medea and Samuel moved to the Village; and in 1940 when the entire Tashkent branch of the Sinoply family had come to visit.

That last summer before the war Medea had had a great family congress: Alexandra with Sergei and Lidia; her brother Constantine, who was killed a year later in the very first days of the war; Tasha Lavinskaya . . . There had been no room to move in the house. Everything was alive with children's voices, the July sun, and Crimean wine.

That year Fyodor won the State Prize and was expecting a new appointment, almost at ministerial level.

Medea had been unable to get off work and had had to go in every day and then come home and cook and cook and cook. Her sister and the young bride would have been glad to help, but Medea didn't like other people getting involved in her house-work, moving things from where they belonged and generally not doing things her way. Only with the passing years and the coming of old age had she resigned herself to letting young rela-tives busy themselves in her kitchen and never being able to find anything.

There had been so many people there and the kitchen had constantly been so busy that the friends hardly had a chance to talk. Medea remembered only their last conversation the night before they parted, when they were washing up in the kitchen after the farewell supper and Elena, drying a pile of plates with a long towel, had complained bitterly that Fyodor was putting his head straight in the lion's mouth. She was prudent enough to be fearful of his successful career and transformation from a modest surveyor into virtually the top official in charge of the irrigation system of Uzbekistan.

"How can he not understand?" Elena asked despairingly. "My father was a member of the Crimean government. He's never mentioned that in a single curriculum vitae. And the higher you rise, the more exposed you become."

Immediately after Elena and Fyodor left, Anelya had arrived from Tiflis with her family, then the younger Nastya with her young husband, and in a short interval between visitors Medea had written Elena a letter which concluded with the words "What a shame that we hardly saw each other. We're probably doomed to correspond for the rest of our lives."

Now in Tashkent, Medea was the only, and a profoundly welcome, guest. In the mornings after the children had been sent to school, Elena and Medea went to the Chorsinsky Bazaar not far from the house, bought mutton, early greens, sometimes chickens: two weren't quite enough for dinner, but three were too many.

Everyone in the family was used to eating a lot, to Medea's amazement. The end of March was a lean time and there was none of the summer lushness of an Asian bazaar, but they stuffed their bags full and went home in the tram.

The table was usually set for dinner late, at around eight when Fyodor got back from work. Before that the children nibbled, helping themselves to a piece of bread or whatever. Dinner, however, lasted a couple of hours, and in addition to the usual local food, sapsa dumplings and noodle soup, there was always an Armenian delicacy of some kind on the table—Elena was still a dab hand at making baklava.

Late in the evenings, when the house was quiet, they would sit together for a long time by the cleared table, laying out an intricate game of patience, which came out for Elena not more than once a year, going over early memories, beginning with their school days; they hooted with laughter, they sighed, they wept for those they had loved and who had been lost in the chaos of the past.

A heavy rock slowly shifted at the bottom of Medea's heart, but their conversation did not move in a direction which would have allowed her to mention the letter. Something stopped her, and the tragedy she had experienced so recently suddenly began to seem to her quite simply indecent.

In the heat of the day, added to by the heat from the summer stove, the hearth in the yard and the constantly boiling water for the laundry, whose blueness and crackly starchiness was Elena's special pride, Medea observed how Elena's life was structured and noted approvingly the customs of the old Stepanyan house, a mixture of generosity toward those around and a certain stinginess where cooking was concerned. Elena counted the eggplants and the walnuts, but money—never.

Fate had taken Elena's close family from her when she was very young, and her nineteen-year-old elder son in the war years, but at least it had never let her experience poverty. It was as if she had been destined from birth always to wear gold and eat from silver. Amazingly enough, in her first year of living in Tashkent she had been sought out, not without help from Medea, by Old Ashkhen, the servant of her Tiflis aunt, who had died a rich, childless widow. Ashkhen walked all the way from Tiflis, carrying a dirty traveling bag containing the family treasures bequeathed to Elena by her aunt.

Elena, who by then had lost everything that she had left from the old life, promptly put two rings on her fingers, one with a pearl, the second with a blue diamond; she put black agate discs with a small pearl in the center on her ears, and put the rest in the bottom of a basket in which she was laying down the dowry for her firstborn, whose appearance in the world seemed imminent. Old Ashkhen lived six more years in her house, right up until her death.

Elena set about arranging her house in Tashkent, this same house which Fyodor had been allocated immediately upon his arrival, in the manner customary in her family, with such modifications as their very modest means dictated. She named the best room the study and gave it to her husband; she returned to the bedroom two beds which had been taken from the house and put in a shed by the Uzbeks who had occupied the house after its previous owner, the deputy governor, shot himself in a fit of senile depression at the beginning of 1917.

In the same shed Elena discovered the remaining furniture which had not been consigned to the stove. She created the semblance of bedside cabinets from two stools she covered with bright scarves, bought a quantity of copper pots and pans at the bazaar, and their residence began in some elusive way to resemble the old house in Tiflis, the dacha at Sudak, and their apartment in Geneva. The tastes of the late Armik Tigranovna were everywhere in evidence.

They later bought the second house in their yard for Natasha, and were currently negotiating with their remaining neighbors to buy the third one, which stood to the right of the central house. Elena had plans to settle Georgii in it.

Medea knew all this from Elena's letters, in which she mentioned every remotely significant event, but in which for both of them the most important things were still the mode in which they communicated, girlish and confidential, and their writing style, their handwriting and, of course, the French language which they both easily slipped into. Each letter was a secret oath of loyalty, although three-quarters of them were devoted to dreams and presentiments, or descriptions of a wayside tree or of someone they had met.

Describing her daughter's wedding, Elena wrote in immense detail about the unusually heavy rain which fell in only one district of the city at just the moment when the newlyweds were coming out of the Registry Office, and of how the material of Natasha's white dress got wet and shrank, creeping up and exposing her plump knees, but for all that Elena did not mention that Natasha had married Victor Kim, a Korean communications engineer, who even then had gained a reputation throughout the city for his extraordinary linguistic abilities. Apart from the standard Russian, the Korean he spoke at home, and the German and optional Uzbek he had learned at school, he had somehow managed by the age of twenty-five to learn English as well and was studying Chinese, although he anticipated having to spend not less than five years on mastering it.

Only six months or so after the wedding, describing in one of the letters her trip to the suburb of Kuilyuk and the tiny paddy fields sprouting bright rows of narrow-leaved rice, Elena had mentioned the parents of Natasha's husband in passing, a wrinkled Korean couple whose outward appearance was so similar and so sexless that it was difficult to tell which of the two was the husband and which the wife. At all events, when another six months later Medea received the first photograph of newborn Shusha, she was not surprised by the pretty little round face with narrow slit eyes from which you would never have anticipated today's beauty.

Sometimes during the day Elena would put Medea on a tarpaulin folding bed under the awning, which was almost completely covered with young vine shoots, and thrust into her hands a French book from the library she had assembled here from the only antiquarian bookseller in town, and Medea, absentmindedly leafing through *Les Liaisons dangereuses* or *La Chartreuse de Parme*, for the first time in her life enjoyed being indolent, totally relaxed, as if the current which maintained tension in her muscles had suddenly been turned off and every fibril was smoothed out in bliss.

She read a little and dozed a little and watched the children a little. Shusha kept herself distant and aloof but had the appearance of someone immersed in her own thoughts. Her younger brother, Pavlik, played the violin for days at a time and, when he did appear in the yard, was just a bit too polite. Medea looked in vain for family traits in them: their Asian blood had totally overwhelmed the Greco-Armenian.

Oddly enough, it was the fair-skinned little blond Shurik, whom they had adopted, who gave every indication of being a Sinoply: although his light, downy hair had not the least tinge of the family's russet, his narrow, pale face was covered in deep ginger freckles. Even more significant—Medea did not immediately notice this, but when she did, she was amazed—his little finger was short, barely reaching the end of the first knuckle of his fourth finger. She did not, however, pass on her observations.

"What a good boy he is," Medea said quietly, glancing over

toward Shurik, who was whittling a seasoned lilac branch in order to replace the charred handle of the coffeepot.

"He's just like my own son to me," Elena responded. "Although nobody can ever replace Alexander in my heart. But Shurik—yes, he's a very good boy. His mother was a deported Volga German. She worked in Kokand at one of Fyodor's projects. She died of tuberculosis immediately after the war. He was sent to an orphanage at first and had a hard time there. Fyodor visited him once, and then a second time, and then brought him home. He has fitted into the family very well. Very well."

Medea listened, said nothing, and looked. When she had been there five days, she noticed Elena taking a bowl of soup after dinner into a side room by the entrance, where Galya lived.

Catching Medea's glance, she explained, "We have Musya living in there, Galya's younger sister."

"Musya?" Medea asked in surprise, never having heard the name.

"Well yes, Musya. She's paralyzed, poor thing. Her daughter rejected her and Galya took her in," Elena answered. Medea immediately remembered Armik Tigranovna's paralyzed wet nurse whom the Stepanyans took everywhere with them for ten years or so, whether to the Crimea or Switzerland, in a specially made German chair of tubular brass, and Armik Tigranovna fed the wordless, withered old woman herself because she would not accept food from anyone else.

How everything recurs.

"God will always send them riches," Medea reflected, although the family's current prosperity could hardly be called riches. "Nobody knows better than Elena how to put them to good use."

When Elena had fed Musya, whom Medea never did get to see, she immediately went to tell Galya off for throwing out half a jar of vine leaves prepared the previous year for making dolma.

New, fresh leaves were fluttering above Medea's head and she smiled.

At last Fyodor, having completed his official trip to the lower reaches of the Amu-Daria and the Aral Sea, called from Nukus to tell Elena he would be back home soon.

"Splendid, I'll just see him and then go back home. Yes, home again in time for Easter," Medea decided.

But Fyodor arrived only on Lazarus Saturday, the eve of Palm Sunday, in the middle of the day. A car snorted and Shurik rushed headlong to open the gate, but Fyodor was already walking through the yard. A fresh crimson tan shone out from beneath his provincial white hat. Shurik flew up to his chest and hugged him around the neck. Fyodor kissed the white top of his head and detached him from himself. Putting his hand on Shurik's head, he walked through the garden.

"Papa is back home!" Elena shouted from the window in a ringing voice, as if he had been away not two weeks but two years.

Medea quickly took her feet off the couch but hadn't time to get up before he caught her under the arms, lifted her up, and pressed her to himself like a child. "My kid sister, my clever girl, you've come to see me!"

Medea breathed in the smell of his hair and his body, and recognized the half-forgotten smell of her father's working sweaters, which few people would have found pleasant but which for Medea's retentive memory was a precious gift.

Everything began to revolve around Fyodor exactly as it had around Medea the morning she had arrived. The chauffeur who had driven him opened the gate and started unloading the car. He pulled out an assortment of parcels and sacks. These were valuable presents, and Elena immediately got to work on an enormous salted sturgeon. Shurik stood beside her, cautiously touching the fish's mean face with his finger. Although Elena had made the preparations for her husband's return, the sturgeon threw her, and telling Natasha and Galya to set the table, she got to work on the fish. She armed herself with a knife and poked her shortsighted face into its ripped open belly.

The chauffeur, another Fyodor, was a handsome man of around forty but with cheeks pocked by gunpowder. He pulled a case of anonymous unlabeled bottles out of the bottomless expeditionary vehicle.

At the meal Fyodor ate little, drank much, and without removing his heavy arm from around Medea's shoulder, told them all about his latest trip in the confident voice of a boss. And Fyodor's deputy came, a couple of elderly friends, and a pretty young Greek girl, Maria, a postwar political refugee, the first real Corinthian Medea had met in her life.

Shurik and Pavlik sat quietly on the children's side of the table, and Elena scurried into the summer kitchen or out to the brazier in the yard. The unlabeled bottles contained something strong and tangy along the lines of a cheap brandy, but Medea found it to her taste. Fyodor drank out of a large silver goblet, and his face, fiery with his fresh tan, gradually turned purple and heavy.

Then two of Georgii's classmates came in, and they too sat down at the table. Elena, true to her principles, took the hot dishes away as soon as they got cold and brought in new ones held up high in the air.

Medea, who had only recently completed an immensely long journey throughout which she had eaten only small grey rusks, rejoiced from the bottom of her heart at the abundance of the feast but, like Fyodor, barely touched the food. It was Lent, and Medea, taught from early childhood to observe the fasts, not only accepted them freely and joyfully, but managed somehow to grow stronger during them. Elena, on the contrary, had always found obligatory fasting hard to take and since moving to Central Asia had stopped even going to church, let alone observing the fasts.

Medea knew all this very well, but she also knew what fits of apparently groundless wretchedness overwhelmed Elena from time to time, and explained them by her having lapsed from the Church. This was another of the topics of their correspondence. They were both sufficiently enlightened women to understand that a person's spiritual life is not by any means confined to their relationship with the Church, but Medea saw life within the Church as the only way possible for her.

"For me, with my limited understanding and self-willed character," she wrote to Elena long before the war when the little Greek church whose dean was Harlampy's younger brother, Dionisy, was closed and she started going to the Russian one, "the discipline of the Church is as necessary as medicine for a chronically sick person. It has been a stroke of great good fortune in my life that my mother instructed me in the faith. She was a simple person of exceptional goodness who had no doubts, and in my life I have never had to rack my brains fruitlessly over philosophical questions which it is by no means essential for each individual to try to resolve. I am content with the traditional Christian resolution of the questions of life, death, good and evil. Thou shalt not steal, thou shalt not kill—and there are no circumstances which can turn evil into good. And the fact that the ways of error have become universally accepted has no significance for us whatsoever."

Elena was fairly immune to the temptations of killing or stealing. She knew only domestic and housekeeping trials which might have been too much for a less doughty woman but which she not only took in her stride but thrived on.

Her family expanded and so did her house, and Elena started taking an interest in the girls in Georgii's class, assessing which of them might make him a good wife. Future children were accordingly already peeping into her life, promising to add to her family, as it had been added to by the adoption of Shurik and by unseen Musya. Accepting these people into her home was her religion, as Medea fully understood.

By midnight the guests had departed, the table was bare, but Fyodor still hadn't taken his arm from Medea's shoulder. "Well, then, sister," he said in Greek. "Do you like my house?"

"Very much, Fyodor, very much," she said, lowering her head.

Elena was clearing the dishes away and had long ago sent Galya off to bed. Medea wanted to help, but Fyodor held her back.

"Sit here, she can manage by herself. What do you think about my youngest? Did you recognize our blood?"

He asked in Greek, and this shared blood of theirs, mingled in the boy with that of someone else, made Medea's face flush, and she lowered her head even more. "I did. Even the little finger."

"You recognized it all, but she is a holy fool like you and sees nothing," he said in an unexpectedly mean and harsh tone.

Medea stood up and, in order to terminate the conversation, replied to him in Russian: "It's late, brother. Sleep well. And you sleep well too, Elena."

She couldn't sleep for a long time between the hard starched sheets, her head resting on the plump pillows, and tried putting together words heard long ago, fleeting glances, words not said, and having put everything together realized that the secret of Alexandra's last child was no secret from anyone apart from herself, and that to judge by everything, even Elena knew, but for all her garrulousness had spared Medea the knowledge. But was Elena really as trusting as herself? Or did she perhaps know full well that she had taken into her house a half brother of her own children?

"Wise Elena, greathearted Elena," Medea thought. "She wants to know nothing about it."

Her unexpected discovery, which might have made the friends even closer if they had spoken about it, kept Medea from sleeping.

It got light outside the window, the birds began singing, and Medea started quietly getting ready to go to church. She had loved Palm Sunday ever since she was a child.

She got to the church on Hospital Street too early, an hour before the service began, before the doors were even open. The market, however, was already humming and she walked past the stalls, looking absently to either side.

There were almost no women among the traders: they were all Uzbek men in thick coats. The customers, however, were all women, and mainly Russians. In fact, Tashkent seemed to Medea to be a completely Russian city. She had seen Uzbeks only at the station on the day she arrived and at the bazaar. Living in the Russian center, she had not got as far as the old city with the Asian layout she was so familiar with from the old Tatar Crimea, and especially from Bakhchisarai.

"They've beaten everyone down," she thought. "It's turned into a huge provincial Russian town."

She made a circuit of the bazaar and approached the church again. It was open now. By the church box an old woman in a white head scarf who looked like a fat rabbit was scuffling about. On the box stood a tumbler in which there were several sprigs of sparrow-grey pussy willow.

"Ah, it grows here too," Medea thought with pleasure.

She took two scraps of paper, and writing on one "May they rest in peace," she wrote out the names in their customary order: Father Dionisy, Father Varfolomey, Harlampy, Antonida, Georgii, Magdalina . . . The other, still-living part of the family she listed on another piece of paper under the words "May they be well."

Every time in this place, writing out the names of her dear

ones in large copperplate letters, she had exactly the same feeling: as if she were sailing on a river and in front of her, like a spreading triangle, were her brothers and sisters, their young and infant children, and behind, fanning out in the same way but much longer, until they disappeared in a rippling of the water, were her dead parents, her grandparents, all the ancestors whose names she knew, and those whose names had been lost in time long past. She had no difficulty at all in containing all these many, many people within herself, the quick and the dead, and she wrote each name mindfully, recalling the face, the presence, even, if such a thing is possible, the taste of that person.

It was at this unhurried labor that Elena found her. She touched her shoulder. They kissed. Elena looked about her: the people in the church were pathetic looking, the old women so ugly.

Through the sweet smell of the incense came the unmistakable smell of dirty, worn-out clothing and old, unhealthy bodies. The old woman standing next to them smelled of cats.

"Can there really be this kind of poverty and squalor even in Tiflis, in the little Armenian church in Solulaki, which we went up to along that terraced street?" Elena wondered. How fine and solemn it had been when she was a child, when her grandmother in her lilac velvet hat with the silk ribbons tied under her soft chin, her mother elegant in a light-colored dress, and her sister Anait were standing at the front of the laypeople, opposite the sole icon of Hripsime and Gayane hanging on a whitewashed wall, and everything smelled of wax, incense, and flowers.

A voice rang out, "Blessed is the Kingdom . . ." The service began.

Elena looked at Medea, who was standing firmly with her eyes closed and her head bowed. She possessed the art of standing for a long time without changing her position, not shifting her weight from one foot to the other.

"She stands like a rock in the midst of the sea," Elena thought tenderly, and suddenly shed tears for Medea's fate, for the bitterness of her loneliness, for the curse of childlessness, for the wrongs of deception and betrayal. Medea, however, was thinking nothing of the sort. Three old women's rattly voices were chanting the Beatitudes, and new tears suddenly flowed from Elena's eyes, no longer for Medea but for all of life. It was an acute experience in which there merged a tenfold sense of the loss of her motherland, the living closeness of her dead parents and of her son killed in the war, and it was a happy moment of complete self-forgetfulness, a momentary filling of her heart not with her own, vain preoccupations, but with something from God, something light, and her heart ached so greatly from this overflowing that she said to herself, "Lord, take me like Sephora, here am I."

But nothing of the sort happened. Not only did she not fall down dead; on the contrary, the moment of acute happiness passed and she found that the service was already halfway through. The priest was whispering inaudible words which she had known by heart from childhood.

Elena suddenly felt bored. Her legs ached and her heart was weary. She felt like going out but couldn't leave Medea.

The priest came forward with the communion cup: "Come in the fear of God and in faith," but nobody came and he went off into the altar.

Barely waiting for Medea to kiss the cross, Elena came out of the church. They wished each other well on this festival day, and kissed solemnly and chastely.

Not one word did Medea say to Elena about her bitter hurt, and right up until death parted them, they would write tender letters to each other, full of dreams, memories, impressions, announcements of the birth of new children, and new recipes for jam.

Medea left three days later. Fyodor tried to persuade his sister to stay but, seeing the inexorable look in her eyes, bought her an air ticket and on Spy Wednesday took her to the airport.

It was the first time in Medea's life that she had flown in an airplane, but she proved completely unmoved by the event. She wanted to get back home as soon as possible. Elena, sensing her impatience, was even slightly hurt. Now the letter lying in the bottom of Medea's rucksack had entirely ceased to trouble her. The plane landed in Moscow, and Medea spent eight hours at Vnukovo Airport waiting for the connecting flight to Simferopol. She didn't telephone Alexandra. Then or ever.

CHAPTER 13

Medea had a partial changeover on the fifth of May. Nike, Katya, and Artyom left in the morning, and after dinner the Lithuanians arrived: Gvidas, the son of Medea's brother Dimitry, who had died three years previously from neglected heart disease, his wife Aldona, and their disabled son Vitalis.

The little boy was paralyzed, permanently seized in a painful convulsion. He moved awkwardly and could hardly speak. Gvidas and Aldona, crushed by their son's illness, were mesmerized by one agonizing and unanswerable question: why us?

They came here every year in early spring, lived with Medea for a couple of weeks until the beginning of the swimming season, and then Gvidas took them to Sudak, rented a convenient apartment in the former German colony beside the sea from Aunt Polly, a friend of Medea's, and left. He reappeared in mid-July to take them from the heat back to the cool of the Baltic coast.

Vitalis passionately loved the sea and felt happy only in water. He also loved Liza and Alik, the only children he was friends with. It was difficult to say whether he remembered them during the winter months, but the first time he met them again the following spring was a special day for him.

The adults prepared the children for Vitalis's arrival, and they were primed with good intentions. Liza selected the best animal to give him from her menagerie of dogs and bears. Alik built a palace in a heap of sand for Vitalis to demolish. They had a game which consisted of Alik building things and Vitalis knocking them down, and it made both of them happy.

Masha moved to Samuel's room, freeing the larger Blue Room for the Lithuanians. She had been in a state of chaotic inspiration since morning: words and lines of poetry were overwhelming her, barely giving her time to commit them to memory. There gradually formed, "Accept too that beyond all measure, like heaven's grace on heaven's grace, like rain, like snow, like faith to treasure, like that with which we can't keep pace . . ." That was all there was so far.

At the same time, and quite independently, Masha was comforting Liza, who was doing her best to be a big girl but soon after her mother's departure did nevertheless burst into tears; then she fed the children, put them to bed, and, abandoning the dirty dishes, lay down in Samuel's room with the blinds drawn, rolled herself up in a ball, and mentally reran the whole of yesterday evening from the barmaid's gold jacket to the movement with which Butonov had rotated the dial of the telephone. She recalled too the way her body had responded to that first chance touch from him on their outing, when her arm had burned and she had become feverish.

"It's a turning point in my destiny, another turning point," she thought. "The first was when my parents drove out that morning onto the Mozhaisk highway when I was seven; the second was when Alik came over to me at the studio when I was sixteen; and now again, at twenty-five. A change in my life. A watershed of my destiny. I was waiting for it, I had a presentiment. Dear Alik, the only person out of all of them who could understand. Poor Alik, he has a better understanding than anyone else of destiny, a feeling for destiny. There's nothing I can do. It can't be undone. I can't help it."

And neither could anybody do anything to help her: she had a feeling for destiny all right, but no experience in adultery.

"Love comes sometimes as a guest, a mistress, sometimes as a horse thief, or a horse, sometimes at midday comes as coolness, at midnight comes as fire and force . . ." She fell asleep.

In the evening it was party time as usual. Instead of Nike and her guitar, the proceedings were presided over by Gvidas the Hun with his red mustache and by his wife Aldona with her mannish face and undulating feminine locks manufactured at the hair salon.

Next to Georgii sat Nora. Stilted conversation, awkward pauses. They were missing Nike, whose mere presence rendered any social gathering smooth and relaxed. Medea was pleased. Gvidas had as usual brought presents from Lithuania and had, in addition, given Medea a decent sum of money to repair the house.

Now he and Georgii were discussing the water supply. There was a water main in the Lower Village, but it had never been extended to the Upper Village, although this had been promised for many years. There were not many houses here, and they all used imported water that was kept either in old reservoir wells or in tanks. Georgii didn't have too much faith in the pumping station and doubted whether the water would make it up to them.

Aldona often went out of the kitchen to listen at the door of the Blue Room and see whether Vitalis was asleep. Usually he woke up several times a night with a shriek, but now, after the exhausting journey, he was sleeping well.

Masha took no part in the conversation. It was past ten and she hadn't yet lost hope that Butonov might look in. Seeing Nora get up, she was pleased: "Shall I walk back with you?"

Georgii stopped talking in midsentence before regaining his presence of mind: "I'll see her back, Masha."

"I want a walk anyway," Masha said, getting up.

They walked in silence and in single file to the Kravchuks' house. They stopped at the back gate. It was dark and quiet in Nora's cottage. Tanya was asleep, and Nora regretted having left so early. Georgii had it on the tip of his tongue to say something to her, but wasn't quite sure what, and in any case Masha was crowding them.

Masha looked closely at the Kravchuks' profitable homestead with its sheds, annexes, and terraces, but could see light coming only from the owners' house.

"I'll go and see Aunt Ada."

She knocked at the Kravchuks' door and went in. Ada was reclining in front of the television with her pink bosom boiling over à la Madame Recamier.

"Oy, Mash, is that you? Come on in, dearie. Can't say we've seen much of you. Nike came to visit us, but you're too up in the air. Oy, you're so scraggy, look at you!" Ada commented disapprovingly.

"I've always been like that, forty-eight kilograms . . ."

". . . of skin and bones," Ada retorted.

Masha came to an agreement about renting a room for a Moscow friend from the first of June, and asked whether Mikhail Stepanovich could meet her in Simferopol.

"How should I know? He's got a chart. Ask him yourself. He's in the shed talking about something with the lodger. It's bedtime, but there they are . . ."

Like all the local people, Ada went to bed early.

Masha went over to the shed. The door was half-open and the light, hung on a long cord from a nail on the wall, threw an oval patch of light in which two heads were lowered: those of Mikhail Stepanovich and Butonov.

"Well, what is it?" Mikhail asked without turning around.

"Uncle Misha, I came to ask about a car."

"Oh, it's you," he said, surprised. "I thought it was Ada."

Butonov looked at her out of the light into the darkness, and Masha couldn't tell whether he had recognized her or not. She stepped into the light and smiled.

His mouth was clamped shut. Two braids of hair not held by the rubber band were hanging down, and he pushed them aside with the back of a hand which was gleaming with black oil. His eyes said nothing.

Masha was frightened: Was this him? Had she dreamed being scorched yesterday by the moon?

She forgot why she had come. Actually she did know why: to see him, to touch him, and obtain proof of something which by its nature can be neither proved nor disproved—something that has happened.

"What car is that?" Mikhail Stepanovich asked, and Masha came to herself.

"To collect my friend from Simferopol."

"When?"

"On the first of June. She's going to be living with you, in the guest room."

"Hey-ho!" Mikhail Stepanovich hemmed. "We might not live till then. Come back nearer the time."

Masha hesitated, waiting to see whether Butonov would say anything, or at least look in her direction; but he was frowning at the metal, shifted his shoulders inside a taut T-shirt, didn't look up but smiled wryly to himself: Kitty's little pussy was on fire!

"Right then," Masha whispered, and going outside, leaned against the wall of the shed.

"The engine's absolutely fine, Stepanovich," she heard Butonov's voice.

"What did I say?" he responded. "It's the spark plugs pinking, that's what I reckon."

"Didn't he recognize me? Or did he not want to recognize me?" Masha agonized, unwilling to reconcile herself to either possibility. No third possibility suggested itself. It was dark. Yesterday's mischievous moon was lighting up other hills and mounds; other lovers were disporting themselves in its theatrical light, its frozen magnesium flash.

Barely holding back her tears, she returned home not by the short path but over the Hub, to convince herself that at least the place was real where everything had happened yesterday. What was going on? Could it be that for one person something could signal a changing of their destiny, an abyss, a rending of the heavens, while the other simply had not noticed anything had happened?

She sat down cross-legged in the very middle of the Hub. Her left hand pressed down on the ground, and her right pressed into her own plaid handkerchief which had lain here for twenty-four hours and whose crumpled, starchy texture did indeed prove that yesterday's event had taken place. She finally began to cry, and, having cried a little, from the force of a habit of many years of translating her thoughts and feelings into more or less short, rhymed lines of poetry, she murmured: "I'll cancel all I cancel can—myself, and you, and cares and caring, intoxicated lover's daring, inveterately sober life."

It didn't quite work, but it had something . . . "I'll cancel all I cancel can, forgetfulness, forgetting self, myself . . ."

It didn't make anything clearer, but she felt a bit better. Shoving the handkerchief into her pocket, she went into the house. Everybody was asleep. She went into the children's room, which was all faint moving currents of light and darkness from the striped curtains. The children were sleeping. Alik asked clearly, without waking, "Masha?" and murmured something incomprehensible.

Masha went to bed in Samuel's room next door without washing her feet or switching on the light. She couldn't sleep, the lines of poetry wouldn't compose themselves. Regretting that Nike had left and there was no one to share her new experiences with, Masha lit the table lamp and took from her pile of books the most dog-eared one: it was consoling Dickens.

Soon she heard a quiet knock at the window. She moved the dark blind aside—the little window was blocked by Butonov. "Are you going to open the door or the window?"

"You won't get through the window," Masha replied.

"My head will, and the rest can follow," Butonov answered in a voice which sounded grumpy.

Masha pulled back the bolt. "Wait, I'll move the table away."

Butonov climbed in. He looked in a bad mood and said not a word, and she only gasped weakly when he pressed her to himself with both arms.

To the touch she really was like Rosa. The heavens were again rent for Masha, and the gate into them proved to be not at all in the place where she had diligently and consciously sought it, leafing through Pascal, Berdyaev, and the cinnamon-scented wisdom of the East.

Now Masha slipped easily, without the least effort, through to the place where time was absent and there was only an unearthly space, a high alpine space radiating a brilliant light, with movement free of the necessity of following the laws of physics, with flight and sailing and total forgetfulness of all that was beyond the bounds of the sole reality of the outer and inner surfaces of a body which had dissolved with happiness.

She was slowly sliding down from the last summit, a fold of skin on his arm firmly squeezed between her lips, when she heard the artlessly plebeian enquiry "I don't suppose you've got a cigarette, have you?"

"I have," she replied, her delicate foot coming down to earth on the boarded floor.

She felt around with her foot—the cigarette packet was somewhere on the floor. She found it, reached down, lit up the cigarette herself, and passed it to him.

"Actually, I don't usually smoke," he told her confidentially.

"I didn't think you would come. You didn't even look at me," she replied, lighting a second cigarette.

"You pissed me off. Why did you have to come bouncing in on me like that? I really hate it," he explained straightforwardly.

"I'm tired. I'll go."

He got up, pulled on his clothes, and she moved back the blind. It was getting light.

"Are you going to let me out the door, or do I have to climb through the window?" he asked.

"Through the window," she laughed. "It's closer for you."

Vitalis's amusements were wholly infantile: He threw everything that came into his hands down on the ground, so Aldona always had enameled rather than glass cups and plates for him. He enjoyed breaking toys, and would laugh in a reedy little voice while tearing up books. Sometimes he would have fits of aggressiveness, and then he would wave his little clenched fists and scream with rage.

By being born, the boy had brought a lot of dissension into the lives of those around him. Gvidas was still profoundly at odds with his mother Aushra, who had in any case been against his early marriage to Aldona, who was much older and who, on top of that, had a child from her first marriage. At his mother's insistence Gvidas delayed getting married for a long time; but he married immediately when Aldona came out of the maternity hospital with her incurably sick child, something that was established within minutes of his birth. Aushra hadn't even seen her grandson.

Aldona's elder son, Donatas, put up with the dubious advantages a healthy child has over a sick one for two years, but gradually progressed from secret jealousy to open hostility toward his brother, to whom he invariably referred as "the damned crab," and went to live with his father. Shortly afterward, unable to settle in his father's new family, he moved to his paternal grandmother's in Kaunas.

Poor Aldona had this to put up with too. Once a week, on Sundays, with bags she had packed with food and toys, she would set off for Kaunas on the first train of the day, returning on the last one. Her former mother-in-law, who had many sorrows of her own, as a Lithuanian smallholder, an exile, and a widow, accepted the food without thanks. Hiding the happy or greedy gleam in his eyes, handsome, broad-shouldered Donatas would take the expensive toys out of her hands and show her his neat notebooks, full of boring "Good's" combined with an equal quantity of "Average's." She helped him with his mathematics and Lithuanian, and then he saw her as far as the gate. Grandmother wouldn't let him go farther than that.

With a heavy heart Aldona left Vilnius in the morning, leaving the little one with Gvidas, and with a heavy heart she left Kaunas in the evening; but the bitterest thing was the feeling that she was a means to an end: everybody needed her care, her help, her efforts, but nobody needed herself or her love. For the younger one she was still a womb providing nourishment and warmth; the older one seemed only to put up with her for the sake of her presents.

Gvidas, who had married her after a major reversal in love here, in the Crimea, had a smooth, steady relationship with her, devoid of emotional attachment.

"It's just too Lithuanian," she had said to him in a rare moment of irritation.

"But how else, Aldona? It's the only way we can get through this. It's only possible by being Lithuanian," he confirmed, and she, a Lithuanian born and bred and with a strain of Teutonic blood, was suddenly seared by an unusual feeling: "If only I were a Georgian, or an Armenian, or even a Jewess."

But she did not receive the gift either of the joyous relief of wailing, or of the wringing of hands, or of liberating prayer—only of endurance, rocklike peasant endurance. Indeed, she was an agronomist. Before the birth of Vitalis she had managed a hothouse enterprise. In the first year of her child's life, deprived of her usual green solace, she suffered cruelly, painstakingly learning to be the mother of a chronic invalid, not letting her twisted babe out of her arms. When she did lower him into his cot, he emitted a faint rasping, wholly nonhuman sound.

The second year, in early spring, she made cardboard flower-pots, sowed seeds, and created a vegetable garden beside the window. She sank her fingers into the soil, and all the bad static electricity generated by her superhuman endurance and tension flowed away into the crumbly sandy-brown border planted with the arrows of spring onions and the rosettelike tops of radishes. The more acidic vegetables grew particularly well in her borders.

By then they had already moved to a half-built house in a suburb of Vilnius. Gvidas put up a high fence even before building began: neighbors' eyes focused on their little cripple were unendurable.

Gvidas put all his passion into the building. The house was a fine one, and life became a little easier in it. It was in this house that Vitalis got to his feet. It would be too much to say that he learned to walk: rather, he began to rise out of his sitting position and to get around.

Changes for the better were also to be seen in the boy after he had been living at the seaside, and Gvidas and Aldona did not cancel their annual pilgrimage to the Crimea after the building work was completed, although it was difficult for them to leave their house for the sake of something as frivolous as a holiday.

Dozens of small children had passed through Medea's hands, including Dimitry, the late grandfather of the little freak. Her arms knew the inconsistent feel of the weight of a child's body, from the eight-pound newborn baby, when the bundle of the little sleeping bag, the blanket, and diapers seems greater than what they contain, to the sturdy one-year-old who has not yet learned to walk and who stretches your arms in the course of the day like a sack weighing several stones. Then the little fatty grows up, learns to walk and run, and three years later, having added a few insignificant kilograms, now rushes to throw himself at your neck and again seems as light as a feather.

And at ten years of age, when a child became seriously ill and lay in a fever, unconscious, with a rash, he was so heavy you could hardly lift him when he needed to be moved over into another bed.

Medea had made another small discovery while looking after other people's children: up until the age of four all of them were engaging, bright, acute, and sensible, but between four and seven something elusive but important occurred, and in the last summer before school, when the parents invariably brought their future schoolchild to the Crimea, as if it had to be inspected by Medea, some proved to be indubitably clever now and for the rest of time, while others were simply not too bright.

Of Alexandra's children Medea put Sergei and Nike down as clever, while Masha was under a question mark; and of Elena's the clever one, who in addition had a captivating personality, was Alexander who was killed in the war. Neither Georgii nor Natasha, in Medea's view, were clever, but she valued kindness and good character no less. Medea had a saying, which Nike was fond of quoting: "Cleverness covers any failing."

In this season it was Vitalis who was particularly close to Medea's heart. He was the youngest Sinoply—the son of adopted Shurik was due to appear in the world two weeks later in the form of Athanasii Sinoply, so for the time being he did not count.

In the evenings Medea would often hold Vitalis on her knee, pressing his back to her bosom and stroking his little head and sluggish neck. He liked being stroked. Touching probably partly compensated him for the lack of interaction through speech.

"I'll let them go off to Yalta on Saturday and Sunday," Medea decided to herself. "Aldona can go for walks in the Botanical Gardens, and they can stay overnight with Kastello."

Medea had an old friend, Kastello, who for a good twenty years or so had been in charge of some interminable building program in the Nikitsky Botanical Gardens. Medea would also have liked Aldona to liberate herself from the eternal slavery of motherhood, and to sit late at night with her, drinking some of the rowanberry or apple vodka she had stored away, and sigh, "God knows, I'm completely worn out." And she would complain and perhaps cry, and then Medea, silently taking a few sips from the heavy liqueur glass, would explain to her that suffering and calamities are given to us so that the question "Why us?" should be replaced by the question "What is this for?" And then sterile attempts to find a culprit can end, and attempts at self-justification, gathering evidence of one's own guiltlessness; and then the law devised by cruel and unmerciful people that punishment is proportionate to sin would be seen to be invalid, because God does not have punishments he visits upon innocent little children.

Perhaps too Medea would have told her in quiet and simple words about various events in life which occur not because of unfairness but just because of the nature of life. She would have remembered the most wonderful of Elena's children, Alexander, killed at the front, and little Pavlik who had drowned, and the little newborn girl who had been taken together with her own mother, and possibly after a while everything inside Aldona would have shifted of its own accord, simply with the passing of time, in the right direction, and she would have been healed just by getting used to things, a cure which is as strong as a callus.

But Medea was never the first to start a conversation. She needed an invitation, a lead-in, and of course a ready willingness to listen.

A few days later, after the lunchtime nap which divided the children's day into two unequal halves, a perambulating brigade of three mothers, Masha, Nora, and Aldona, and four children, after various hesitancies over the route, reached the hospital. Vitalis was usually taken out in a wheelchair, his back to the road and facing his mother. On this occasion his wheelchair was being pushed by Liza and Alik. Medea saw them through the window and came out onto the porch.

Liza, squatting down in front of Vitalis, was prizing his little fingers open, singing, "Thieving magpie was baking some bread, thieving magpie's babies got fed . . ." And gently waggling his little finger, she squealed: "But she didn't give any to this one!"

He shrieked piercingly, and there was no telling whether he was laughing or crying.

"He likes it," Aldona explained, with her invariable awkward smile.

Medea looked over toward the children, adjusted the shawl wrapped around her head, looked at Liza again, and said to Aldona: "I'm so pleased, Aldona, that you bring Vitalis here. Our little Liza is a willful, spoiled child, but she plays with him so well. Let her spend lots of time with him. It will be good for everyone." Medea sighed and said, perhaps reflecting an old sorrow, perhaps in pity: "It's so sad: everybody wants to love the strong and the good-looking. Off you go home, girls, I'll be back soon."

They headed off back home. Masha picked a thick green blade of grass with a sweet stem and chewed it. What had Medea meant when she talked about the strong and good-looking? Was it a hint about her guest in the night? No, that wasn't like Medea. She didn't hint. She either said something straight out or kept her peace.

Butonov came to Masha every night, knocking on the window, squeezing each of his brawny shoulders through its narrow opening in turn, completely filling the space of the small room with himself, and all of Masha's body and soul, and departed at dawn, leaving her each time immersed in a tingling sensation of the newness of her whole being and of renewal of her life. She fell into a brief, potent sleep in which he was still present, to wake a couple of hours later and get up in a ghostlike state of infinite strength and equally infinite weakness. She woke the children, cooked, washed, and everything happened easily and by itself, only the glass tumblers got broken more often than usual, and the silver-plated spoons fell soundlessly onto the kitchen's earthen floor. Imperfect lines of poetry appeared in the bubble-like space, turned sideways and floated off, wagging their awkward tails behind them.

Butonov for his part used no words other than the most elementary: "Come here . . . move . . . wait . . . I need to smoke." He didn't even once say he would come the next day.

One evening he visited Medea in the kitchen. He drank tea and talked to Georgii, who had been putting off his departure from one day to the next but had finally packed his bags. Masha tried to catch Butonov's eye from the dark corner of the kitchen, but the air hung motionless around his beloved face and his motionless shoulders, and no indications of intimacy were forthcoming. Masha was in despair: could this be the same man who came to her in the night? She speculated briefly on the possibility of an incubus.

Saying goodbye to Georgii and not saying the least word to her, he left, but came again that night, secretly, and everything was as it had been, only when they were resting on the shore after their passion had receded, he said, "My first real lover was like you. She was a horse-rider."

Masha asked him to tell her about the horse-rider. He smiled. "What is there to tell? She was a good horsewoman, thin, bow-legged. Before I met her, I thought making babies was just so unbelievably boring. She disappeared, although my guess is that her husband killed her."

"Was she beautiful?" Masha asked, almost reverently.

"Of course she was." He put his hand on her face, touching the cheekbones and her chin, which narrowed lower down. "All my women are beautiful, Masha. Except my wife."

For a long time after he left, she pictured first the horse-woman, then his wife, then herself—as a horsewoman.

Three vast nights passed, as long as three lives, and three ghostly days, and on the fourth day Butonov arrived unexpectedly, while Aldona was washing the dinner dishes in the kitchen and Masha was hanging up the children's laundry by the well. He came down and sat silently on a flat rock.

"What's wrong?" Masha asked, frightened, and threw some pajamas she had just wrung out back into the bowl.

"I'm leaving, Masha. I've come to say goodbye," he said levelly.

She was horrified.

"Forever?"

He laughed.

"Will you never come to me again?"

"Well, perhaps you'll come to see me some time in Rastorguevo, eh?" He slowly got up, brushed off his white trousers, and kissed her tight-lipped mouth. "What is it? Are you upset?"

She was silent. He glanced at his watch and said, "Okay, let's go. I've got fifteen minutes to fill."

For the first time they went into Samuel's room by the light of day, successfully avoiding Aldona, who was intently scrubbing plates, and fifteen minutes later he left for real.

"The way gods depart. As if he had never existed," Masha thought, hugging the striped floor covering which had skidded right across the room with her. "I just hope Alik comes soon."

Now, when everything had ended just as suddenly as it had begun, and all she had left was a thin pile of coarse grey half-sheets of paper written all over with a blotchy ballpoint pen, she wanted to read Alik her new poems as soon as possible and tell him, just him, about how the roof had fallen in on her.

At this moment Alik was approaching Sudak, and Butonov, heading toward him, was being driven to Simferopol in Mikhail Stepanovich's old Moskvich in order to catch the same plane Alik had arrived on and return to Moscow that evening. Medea was on her way back from work and was the first to see Alik walking up from the Lower Village—wearing a navy-blue peaked cap and sunglasses on his town dweller's untanned face. Shortly afterward Alik was spotted also by Masha, who was walking with the children in the high grass of the Hub.

With shrieks of "Alik! Alik! Daddy's come!" they rushed down the road. He stopped, cast the small tightly packed ruck-sack from his shoulders, and threw his arms wide open for a communal hug. Masha got there first and threw her arms around his neck with the sincerest joy. Liza and Little Alik were jumping up and down with shrieks of delight.

By the time Medea came up to them, half the rucksack had been turned out. Masha had opened one of the letters he had brought her. Liza was pressing to her person a bag of toffees and a pale-looking doll the size of a mouse, a present from Nike, and little Alik was pulling open a box with a new game. Big Alik was trying to stuff everything that had been pulled out of the rucksack back into it.

He kissed Medea three times and immediately pressed a cardboard box into her hands, his usual professional contribution: "An aid package from our Red Cross to your Red Cross."

There were various medicines which were in short supply, a couple of packs of plasters, and some standard rubber gloves which it had been impossible to obtain in Sudak last year.

"Thank you, Alik. I'm glad you've come."

"Oh, Medea Georgievna, I've brought you such a wonderful book!" he interrupted her. "It's a surprise! You're looking really well." He put his hand on top of his son's head: "Alik, you've grown a whole head higher." He opened his fingers a thimble's breadth: "A mosquito's head."

Masha was shifting impatiently from one foot to the other and jumping up and down: "Let's go now, Alik. At last!"

Medea went on ahead. "How strange. Masha really is glad her husband has come. She's not embarrassed, she doesn't look guilty. Does marital fidelity mean nothing at all to them? As if this athlete didn't come to her every night. And I, old poker that I am," Medea smiled to herself. "Well, what business is it of mine? It's just I like Alik. He's like Sam: not his facial features, but the quickness of his dark eyes, his liveliness, and the same unhurtful quick wit. I must be susceptible to Jews, the way other people are susceptible to colds or constipation. Especially to the grasshopper kind, thin and agile. It is interesting, though: how is Masha going to get out of her romance now?"

Medea did not know that Butonov had already left, and supposed ruefully that she would again have to watch other people's comings and goings in the night, their love trysts and their lying.

"How lucky I am that I was completely blind to all this side of things when it involved me. And now thirty years have passed, thank God, since that summer. There now, they forgot to say it in the Beatitudes: Blessed are the idiots."

Medea looked around: Alik was carrying Liza on his back and the rucksack in his hand, his white teeth gleaming in a broad smile. He didn't look at all like an idiot.

Alik the Husband was called Big Alik to distinguish him from Alik the Son. Big, however, he wasn't. He and Masha, husband and wife, were the same height, and given that Masha was the smallest in her family, size was not one of Alik's strong points. He bought his clothes in the Children's World department store and in thirty years had never had a decent pair of shoes, because only very basic blunt-nosed boys' shoes came in his size.

For all his diminutiveness, however, he was well proportioned and good-looking. He was one of those Jewish boys who take off intellectually at an early age, magically becoming literate and amazing their parents with the fluency of their reading just as the latter are wondering whether to introduce their child to the alphabet.

At seven he was plowing his way through the weighty tomes of the World History series; at ten he was fascinated by astronomy, then mathematics. He was already setting his sights on big science. He went to the Mathematics Club at Moscow University's Faculty of Mechanics and Mathematics, and his brain revved at such high rates that the leader of the club could only groan at the thought of how difficult it would be for this young genius to break through the percentage quota for Jews at the university.

The unexpected death of his much loved father, which resulted from an absurd succession of medical mishaps in the course of a few days, deflected Alik to a different course. His father had been through the war and been wounded three times, but died from an incompetently performed appendectomy. While his father was dying of peritonitis, Alik gained insights into suffering and compassion which rarely figure in the curriculum of a child prodigy.

After his father's hurried funeral, with a military band and the wailing of his grief-crazed mother beneath the pestilential December drizzle, his father's former regimental friends and present-day colleagues returned from the slushy quagmire of the Vostryakovsky Cemetery to the large room on Myasnitsky Street, drank their way through a crate of vodka, and departed. That same evening the impressionable Alik underwent a conversion, turning his back on his ambitious plans and the biography he had planned for himself—a hybrid of the lives of his favorite heroes, Evariste Galois and René Descartes—in favor of medicine.

From that day on, his vigilant mind began to assimilate the disciplines in which he would have to pass examinations: physics, which after his mathematical vaccination struck him as an eclectic science lacking in rigor; and biology, which disconcerted him because of the weakness of its overall theoretical foundations, the multilayered nature of its processes, and its lack of a consistent terminology. In the secondhand bookshop next to his apartment block, he bought by good fortune a practical course on genetics by Thomas Morgan which had been published in the 1930s, and privately noted that genetics, currently being excoriated and crucified along with its practitioners, was the only area of biology in which it was possible to pose a clearly formulated question and receive an unambiguous answer.

Since he received not a gold but merely a silver medal on graduating from secondary school, getting into university meant going into battle against a five-headed dragon. The only top grade he gained without a fight was for an essay in which Alexander Pushkin gave him a helping hand: the topic of "Pushkin's early lyric" was a gift from heaven.

The other exam grades he had to appeal against: he knew full well that he deserved nothing less than a Five, while his teachers knew equally well who it was they weren't allowed to award Fives to. He first appealed against a Four for mathematics. The members of the commission were hirelings from the Faculty of Mechanics and Mathematics, since there was no separate mathematics department at the medical institute. The postgraduates were far from stupid and quickly recognized that this was a very clever boy. He also displayed exceptional stamina, answering their questions for four hours until, when they finally asked him one he couldn't answer, he laughed and said to the five-member commission: "The question is incorrectly formulated, but I beg to draw your attention also to the fact that none of the questions I have been asked falls within the school syllabus." He knew he had nothing to lose and decided to go for broke: "Something tells me that the next question is going to be on Fermat's Last Theorem."

The examiners exchanged glances, and one asked, "Well, can you formulate it?"

Alik wrote a simple equation and sighed. "Where n is greater than two, there are no whole positive solutions, but I will not attempt to give a general proof of that."

The chairman of the subject board, with a feeling of profound distaste for the boy, for himself, and for the situation in which they had been placed, entered a Five in the register.

The procedure for his chemistry and biology results was the same, but with less éclat. For English he also received a Four, but this was the last exam, and as it was clear that he had accumulated enough points to matriculate, he didn't bother appealing. He was worn-out.

The tale of his matriculation became a legend at the institute, and bore more than a passing resemblance to the tale of Cinderella. His school years had been poisoned by his physical insubstantiality: he was the smallest pupil in his class; the youngest too, as it happened. His intellectual distinction, if indeed anybody noticed it, did nothing to save him from the humiliations of physical education. In fact, his childhood was laden with humiliations: the maid who accompanied him and who tied the sheepskin earflaps of his girlish fur hat under his chin; the fear of going home alone, when he himself had insisted that the maid should no longer escort him; the main break as a major unpleasantness, with the impossibility of going to the school toilets. If he was desperate, he would go to the doctor complaining of a headache, be excused lessons, and, shoving the slip of paper with the letters "Exc." into the hands of his beloved teacher, rush home for a pee.

He was acutely aware of his pariah status, vaguely intuiting that it had more to do with his strengths than with his weaknesses. His father was an editor at the Military Publishing House and all his life had been embarrassed by his Jewish second-class status; he could do nothing to help his son, beyond giving him valuable guidance on what to read. Isaak Aaronovich was a well-educated philologist, but life had driven him into a corner where he was only too glad to edit memoirs of the late military campaign written by semiliterate marshals.

The merging of the boys' and girls' schools did oddly enough alleviate Alik's fate. His first friends were girls, and when he was a grown man, he would constantly declare his belief that women undoubtedly comprised the better part of humanity.

In the medical institute the better part of humanity was also numerically dominant. From the very first months of his studies, he was surrounded by an atmosphere of respectful admiration. Half his classmates were from other towns, had worked in medicine for two years already, and had a varied experience of life. They crowded into the big room on Myasnitsky Street. At the end of the year Alik's mother was allocated a two-room apartment in New Cheryomushki. It was in this new apartment, still unfurnished and heaped with bundles of as-yet-unpacked books, that two of Alik's fellow students, Vera Voronova from Sormovo and Olga Anikina from Kryukovo, skillful, agreeable nurses with distinctions on their diplomas, deprived Alik of his romantic illusions and simultaneously relieved him of his burdensome virginity.

From about his third year, when it was time for practical work and being on duty in the wards, quick, easy copulation in the laundry room, the house doctor's office, or the examining room was as casual as the cups of tea they drank at night, and even had a suggestion of medical practicality about it. Alik did not ascribe any great significance to coition performed on the state's laundry: he was much more interested in those years in science—natural science and philosophy.

His daily journey from New Cheryomushki to the Pirogov Institute was a real Göttingen for him. He started with the works of Comrade Lenin, compulsory reading for the course on the history of the Communist Party of the Soviet Union. Then he dipped into Marx, raided Hegel and Kant, reversed back to the sources—and took greatly to Plato.

He read quickly, in a special way of his own, snaking up and down so that several lines simultaneously comprised one larger line which was being read. Many years later he tried to explain to Masha that what mattered was the reaction time of the perceptual systems, and even drew her a diagram.

Giving his agile brain its rein, he constructed a syllabus for a universal man, and in addition to the medical institute, started attending the university, taking specialist courses in biochemistry in Belozersky's department and in biophysics with Tarusov. He was fascinated by the problem of biological aging. He was no madman in pursuit of immortality but calculated from certain biological parameters that 150 years was the natural limit for human life. In the fourth year of his course he published his first scientific article, coauthored with a respected scholar and another whiz kid like himself.

After a further year he came to the conclusion that research at the cellular level was too crude, but that he had insufficient knowledge for working at the molecular level. He gained what he needed from the foreign scientific literature. Many years later, occupying an extremely high position in American science, Alik said that intellectually the most intense period of his life had been precisely these years as an undergraduate, and that all his life he had been exploiting ideas which came to him in his final year of study.

It was in the same year that he met Masha. His former classmate Lyuda Linder, a lover of unofficial poetry, occasionally dragged him to apartments and literary clubs where samizdat flourished and where even Brodsky, when he was in Moscow, sometimes did not disdain to recite the poetry which in the fullness of time was to earn him the Nobel Prize.

On this occasion Lyuda had taken him to a party where several young authors would be reading their poetry, including one exceptionally promising young man who had discovered hard drugs earlier than the rest and died shortly afterward. Masha read first, as the youngest young author. There were not many people present; as people say of such occasions, just a few friends plus the KGB informer on duty that day, who was simultaneously responsible for maintaining public order.

The times were changing as never before. It was 1967. Bread cost nothing, but words, spoken and printed, acquired an unheard-of weight. Samizdat was already covertly undermining the System, Sinyavsky and Daniel had been found guilty of publishing their works abroad, "physicists" were distancing themselves from "lyricists," and the only areas which were off limits were to be found in the zoo. Alik was not drawn into this process: he always preferred theoretical problems to practical, philosophy to politics.

Masha, blue-eyed, with slender hands which lived a slightly absurd life of their own in the air beside her dark, cropped head, read her poems with quiet pathos. Alik did not take his eyes off her the whole thirty minutes allotted to her, and when she finished reading and went out into the corridor, he whispered in Lyuda's ear, "I'll be right back."

But he didn't reappear. He stopped Masha halfway to the toilet.

"Don't you recognize me?"

Masha looked at him closely but did not recognize him.

"It's not surprising. We don't know each other yet. My name is Alik Schwartz. I wish to propose to you."

Masha looked at him questioningly.

"My hand and my heart," he elaborated in all seriousness.

Masha laughed merrily. Something was beginning which she had heard so much about from Nike. An affair. She was more than ready for it.

" 'Maria Miller-Schwartz' sounds pretty awful, but let's think about it," she replied airily, terribly pleased by the inconsequential tone of their conversation.

A sense of triumph engulfed her. At last she would be the equal of Nike and say to her on the telephone this very evening, "Nike, darling, I've hitched up with this guy, he's so sweet, cute face, designer stubble, and you can tell at a glance that he's got all his marbles about him."

"Only bear in mind," he warned her, "I have absolutely no time for courtship. But I'm free this evening. Let's get away from here."

Masha had been intending to go back and listen to a bespectacled youth who had been crumpling his papers while waiting for his turn, but there and then thought better of it.

"Okay, wait for me here." She went into the lavatory, and he stood by the door.

Masha hurriedly put on her things. She had a feeling that there was absolutely no time to lose. Alik, without knowing it, had already infected her with his innate sense of urgency. He helped her on with the thin, elegant little coat that Alexandra had made.

Outside, it was dark and desolate, the worst kind of winter, with no snow but severely cold. Masha, as was the fashion in the preboot era, was wearing light shoes and no hat. Alik took hold of her cold, bony fingers.

"We're always going to be very short of time, and there's a lot to be said. To get the boring stuff over with: in weather like this it wouldn't be a bad idea to wear felt boots and your grandmother's shawl. I offer you that advice as a doctor. But as regards your poems," he unconsciously moved closer to her, "there are some you should throw out, but some of them are remarkable."

"Which ones should be thrown out?" Masha asked, flustered.

"No, it's better if I tell you which ones you should keep." And he recited to her one of the poems he had just heard and which he had memorized by ear and with total accuracy:

> *"We live like exiles in the busy Hades*
> *of this sad, homeless world our orphaned Earth;*
> *the autumn day is bright with light unfading*
> *And pangs of piercing cold attend a birth.*
> *Above the graveyard, cloudlike in the air,*
> *a silence hovers redolent with singing,*
> *a promise of relief through sculpted prayer,*
> *a promise of tumultuous torrents bringing.*
> *Though rustling maple leaves astound the gaze*

> *and unconsumed by flames the eye astonish,*
> *Though graves like martyrs' pyres accusing blaze,*
> *the calendar has yet to be abolished."*

"I think that is a very fine poem."

"It's in memory of my parents. They died in a car accident ten years ago," Masha said, amazed how easy it was for her to tell him something she had never spoken about to anyone else.

"They lived their lives happily together and died on the same day?" Alik looked at her seriously.

"There's nothing else left now but to believe that."

Some marriages are made in bed, while others burgeon in the kitchen to the metallic music of the kitchen knife and the egg whisk; some couples are nest builders, forever redecorating, snapping up bargain lots of timber for their dacha plot, nails, drying oil, and fiberglass wrap; other couples live for blazing, set-piece rows.

Masha and Alik's marriage was consummated in conversations. This was their ninth year together, but every evening when he came home from work, the soup would be left to get cold and the rissoles to burn while they told each other about the important events of the day.

Each of them lived life twice over: the first time directly, the second time in selective paraphrase. The paraphrase did slightly rearrange events, giving more prominence to something which had been less significant at the time and bringing a personal coloration to what had happened, but both of them were perfectly aware of that and took the other's interests into account when deciding what to offer.

"Here's something you'll like," Alik would say, stirring the hot soup in his bowl, "I've been saving it up for you all day."

There would follow a description of a ridiculous row in the Metro that morning, or of a tree in the yard, or a conversation with a colleague. Or Masha would lug an old volume into the kitchen with so many bookmarks in it they looked like noodles, or a samizdat brochure and slew it around at the right place and say, "Here's something I picked out specially for you."

In recent years they had partly exchanged roles: previously he had been the one who read more and dug deeper into cultural problems, but now his researches left him no time for intellectual distractions, especially since he couldn't yet move on from working in the ambulance service which, apart from being professionally interesting, left him with enough free time for research work in the laboratory. He had completed his postgraduate studies through extension courses, which had suited him fine.

Masha sat at home with her son, a unique little boy who could keep himself meaningfully occupied from morning till evening. She churned out entries for a journal of abstracts, read large numbers of books avidly, and wrote poetry and other less readily classifiable texts which seemed to have been plagiarized from a variety of other writers. She hadn't yet found her own voice and was pulled in different directions—sometimes toward Rozanov, sometimes to Kharms.

Her poems were also written in different voices, and although they had been published along with those of other poets in magazines, hers had seemed peripheral and unremarkable. On the page they hadn't looked like hers, the overall selection didn't seem to have been made very well, and to crown it all there had been two printing errors. Alik was terribly proud and bought up a whole stack of copies to give to all their friends, but Masha privately resolved not to allow any more ephemeral publications but to wait until she could bring out a proper volume of her own work.

Their closeness was so rare and so complete that it showed in shared tastes, in the structure of their speech, and in the tone of their humor. Over the years even their body language became similar, and it looked as though by the time they were old they would be like a couple of parrots. Sometimes, guessing an unspoken thought from the other's eyes, they would chorus their beloved Brodsky: "They had lived so long together that the second of January again fell on a Tuesday."

Masha found a German word in a linguistics textbook which expressed their special relatedness: *Geschwister*. It was a unique word meaning "brother and sister," but the German conjoining had some hidden additional meaning.

They had given each other no vows of fidelity. Indeed, on the eve of their wedding they had agreed that their union should be a union of two free people and that they would never stoop to jealousy and deceit because each would retain the right to independence. In the first year of marriage, feeling a slight disquiet that Alik should be the only man she had known, Masha undertook a few sexual experiments: with a former classmate, with a literary bureaucrat at a youth journal where she had once been published, and with some completely random individual, just to make sure she hadn't been missing out.

She didn't discuss it with her husband, but read him a poem written that year:

> "Despised fidelity that smacks of duty
> holds out the lure of casual affairs,
> for only love is constancy and dares
> bind not itself with vows and sophistry
> and asks no bargain for the gift it shares."

Alik guessed the meaning, said nothing, and gained a great deal thereby: Masha was completely reassured. Over the years of their marriage a few episodes came his way too. He did not go looking for them, but he didn't run away from them either.

With the years, however, they became ever more closely attached and found more and more advantages in their family life. Observing colleagues and friends who married, divorced, or lightly embarked on a life of bachelor debauchery, he, like the Pharisee of whom he knew nothing, said in his heart: "God, we thank Thee that we are not as others are. We live an orderly and worthy life and are therefore content."

His scientific work was going splendidly: so much so, indeed, that few of his colleagues were capable of appreciating the results he was obtaining. His elite status, which in childhood had been such a heavy burden, made heavier by the embarrassing, unasked-for, and highly inconvenient fact of his being a Jew, changed its complexion over the years, but a good upbringing and his inborn good nature masked an ever-growing awareness of his superiority over the mediocre brains of the majority of his colleagues.

When his first article appeared in a prestigious American science journal, he looked down the list of the editorial board on the cover and told Masha, "There are four Nobel Prize–winners there."

Masha glanced at his swarthy face, more Indian than Jewish, and knew that he was trying himself for size against the highest scientific honors. Reading his thoughts, she asked Nike, who still had a muffle left over from her dalliance with ceramics, to inscribe a poem on a china cup, which was Alik's birthday present from his wife that year and on which in thick blue letters was written: "These things shall be: your morning dress; my evening gown; the King, listening, in his crown; a banquet for his guests." The birthday guests greatly admired the cup, but no one apart from Alik caught the allusion.

Both of them enjoyed the fact that their wordless communication worked even in a crowd: they had only to exchange a glance to have shared their thoughts.

This time they had not seen each other for around two weeks, and Alik was bringing his wife sensational news. A famed American scientist who specialized in molecular biology had come to the Academy of Sciences to read a conference paper and give a lecture. He had duly visited the Bolshoi Ballet and the Tretyakov Gallery as prescribed by his social program, and had asked his interpreter to arrange a meeting for him with Mr. Schwartz. The interpreter contacted her superiors, passed on the intelligence, and received her instructions: the visitor was to be informed that Mr. Schwartz was unfortunately on holiday at the moment.

Mr. Schwartz was not, however, on holiday. Indeed, he came to the conference specifically to ask the American a particular specialized question. A five-minute conversation ensued during which the quick-witted American (not for nothing had his grandfather been born in Odessa) soon saw how the land lay, took Alik's home telephone number, and late that evening came to visit him, paying the taxi-driver, who was also quick-witted in his way, a sum equivalent to Alik's monthly salary.

All this had occurred in Masha's absence. Debora Lvovna, Alik's mother, was on holiday at a sanatorium. Mountains of unwashed dishes and piles of open books finally convinced the American that he was dealing with a genius, and he lost no time in making him an offer to come and work for him. In Boston, at the Massachusetts Institute of Technology. That raised one technical but not insignificant problem: emigration. This was the development that Alik was bringing to his wife. Both of them were bursting to tell the other their news.

The topic of emigration was one of the most contentious among the intelligentsia in those years: to be or not to be, to go or not to go. "Yes, but supposing . . ." "No, but what if . . . ?" Families were split, friendships sundered. Political motivations, economic, ideological, moral . . . And the actual business of getting out was so complex and agonizing, sometimes taking long years, demanding resoluteness, courage, or desperation. The official gap in the Iron Curtain was only open for Jews, although non-Jews used it too. This time it was the Black Sea that divided its waters to allow the Chosen People through, if not to the Promised Land then at least out of the latest Land of Egypt.

"It says in Exodus," exclaimed Lyova Gottlieb, a close friend whom Alik called "the Principal Jew of the Soviet Union," "that Moses led six hundred thousand men on foot out of Egypt, but nowhere is it said how many remained behind. Those who stayed simply ceased to exist. And those who didn't leave Germany in 1933? Where are they?"

Alik was completely uninterested in his own life from a Jewish viewpoint: for him what mattered most was the advancing of science. Needless to say, he heard all these conversations taking place, and even took part in them himself, introducing a theoretical and unemotional perspective, but all that really concerned him was cellular aging.

What the American offer meant to him was that he would be able to work more effectively. "By about three hundred percent," he estimated when telling Masha all about it. "The best equipment in the world, no problems with reagents, laboratory assistants to help me, and absolutely no material problems for you and me. And Alik can study at Harvard, eh? I am entirely ready for this. It's up to you, Masha. Well, and Mother too, of course, but I can talk her around."

"But when?" was all Masha could ask, entirely unready for events to take this turn.

"If there are no hitches, then in six months' time, if we submit our documents straightaway. But it could drag on for a long time: that's what I'm most worried about, because I'll have to leave work immediately in order not to land my boss in trouble." He had already thought everything through.

"Two weeks ago a proposal like this would have delighted me," Masha thought. "But today I can't bear to think about it."

Alik had been hoping in the depths of his heart that Masha would be gladdened by the prospects this opened up, and he was puzzled by her hesitancy now. He didn't yet know that their home life, so logical and well thought out, had cracked right from its crystal top down to its much despised bottom. Masha had not yet fully realized it herself.

Then Masha read Alik her recent poems, and he praised her and noted their new quality. He received Masha's ardent confession about the revelation she had received in a new and intense relationship, about a special kind of perfection she had found in a different person, about a new experience in her life, as if a dulling film had been lifted from the whole world: from landscapes, from faces, from ordinary feelings.

"I don't know what I should do with all this now," Masha complained to her husband. "Perhaps from the generally accepted point of view ['bourgeois' wasn't a word she ever used] it is terrible that it should be you I am telling this to, but I trust you so much. You are the person closest to me, and it only makes any sense at all to talk about this to you. You and I are one, as far as that is possible, but all the same I don't know how we are to go on living. You say we should emigrate. Perhaps we should."

She was slightly shivery, her face burning and her pupils dilated.

"Bad timing," Alik decided, and brought half a bottle of brandy out of the kitchen. He poured two glasses and concluded magnanimously: "Well, let's face it, this experience is indispensable for you. You are a poet, and in the last analysis, is this not the material that poetry is made from? Now you know there are higher forms of fidelity than sexual. I already knew that. You and I are both researchers, Masha. It's just we have different areas. At the moment you are making a discovery of your own, and I can understand that. And I won't stand in your way." He poured them each another glass.

Brandy was the right prescription. Masha soon buried her face in his shoulder and murmured: "Alik, you are the best person in the world. You are my fortress. If you want, let's go anywhere you like."

They comforted themselves in each other's arms, and reassured themselves of their eliteness, and confirmed to themselves their superiority over other family couples of their acquaintance who might indulge in all sorts of petty mischief, transient couplings in a locked bathroom, and have all sorts of piffling lies and baseness in their lives whereas they, Masha and Alik, were totally open and lived a life of purest truth.

Three days later Alik went back, leaving Masha with the children, the washing, and her poetry. She would be spending another month and a half in the Crimea, because Alik had brought her the money needed for that.

Two days after he left, Masha wrote her first letter. To Butonov. And followed it up with a second and a third. In the intervals between writing letters, she wrote short, desperate poems which she herself liked very much.

Butonov conscientiously collected her letters from the mailbox. He had given Masha his Rastorguevo address only because during the summer, when his wife and daughter went to stay at the university-owned dacha of Olga's friend, he usually stayed in Rastorguevo rather than in his wife's apartment in Khamovniki. Butonov never worried about keeping secrets from his wife: Olga wasn't nosy and would never have dreamed of opening someone else's letters.

Masha's letters surprised him greatly. They were written in tiny handwriting which sloped backward, and had drawings in the margins and stories from her childhood which had absolutely no bearing on anything; and for some reason they contained references to writers he'd never heard of, and a lot of hints that were quite unclear. In addition, the envelopes contained separate sheets of rough grey paper with poems. Butonov guessed she had written them herself. He showed one of the poems to Ivanov, who knew about that sort of thing. Ivanov read it aloud with a strange expression:

> *"Though love is of the soul, the body hale*
> *has at this feast its own allotted ration.*
> *You put your hand in his in joyous fashion:*
> *the warmth that makes your spirit quail,*
> *the blazing heat of carnal passion*
> *are measured on a single scale."*

"Where did you get this, Valerii?" Ivanov asked in astonishment.

"A girl sent it to me," Butonov said, shrugging. "Any good?"

"Yes. She probably lifted it from somewhere. Although I can't think where," Ivanov pronounced his highly professional judgment.

"Out of the question," Butonov retorted confidently. "She's not the kind to copy someone else's stuff. She wrote it herself, I'll swear she did."

He had already forgotten about his latest southern romance, but this sweet girl seemed to have given it some quite excessive significance. Butonov had never had anyone sending him letters, had never written any himself, and had no intention of replying to these; but still they came.

Masha kept walking to the post office in Sudak and was terribly upset when there was no reply. Unable to bear it any longer, she rang Nike in Moscow and asked her to go out to Rastorguevo and see whether anything had happened to Butonov or why he wasn't replying to her. Nike refused irritably, saying she was far too busy.

Masha was mortified: "Nike, what are you saying? Have you gone crazy? I've never asked you to do anything like this before! You have a new affair every season of the year, but I've never known anything like this!"

"Oh, to hell with it! I'll go tomorrow," Nike agreed.

"Nike, I beg you! Today! Go this evening!" Masha implored.

The next morning Masha again walked all the way to Sudak with the children. They romped around the town, went to a café, and had an ice cream. She didn't manage to get through to Nike, though. There was no one at home.

That evening Little Alik fell sick. His temperature went up and he started coughing. It was his chronic asthmatic bronchitis, which was the reason Masha stayed down here with him for two months at a time in the Crimea.

Masha was dancing attendance on him for a whole week and only on the eighth day did she get to Sudak. There was still no letter for her. Actually there was, but only from Alik. She phoned straight through to Nike who reported drily: "I went to Rastorguevo. I saw Butonov. He has received your letters, but he hasn't replied."

"But is he going to?" Masha asked stupidly.

"How should I know?" Nike responded testily.

By now she had actually been to Rastorguevo a number of times. On the first occasion Butonov had been surprised, but everything had been relaxed and fun. Nike really had only intended to run Masha's errand but ended up staying the night in his large, half-redecorated house.

He had started renovating the house two years before, after the death of his mother, but somehow things had come to a halt and the half which had been redone stood in striking contrast to the half-wrecked part which was cluttered with wooden trunks, rough peasant furniture left over from his great-grandfather's time, and lengths of handwoven cloth. There, in the wrecked half, Nike built their hurried little nest. Leaving in the morning, she did remember to ask him: "Why don't you reply to her letters? She's really upset."

Butonov was used to being informed on but didn't like being told off. "I'm a doctor, not a writer."

"Well, try very hard," Nike suggested.

The situation struck Nike as comical: Masha, as clever as clever could be, had fallen in love with this very basic stud. He suited Nike admirably: she was in the middle of getting divorced; her husband was being a complete bastard and making all sorts of demands, even to the point of wanting his share of the apartment; her fill-in lover had finished his film production course in Moscow and left; and her long-term Kostya was annoyingly eager to embark on a life of matrimonial bliss with her as soon as he heard about the divorce.

"If it's that important, write them yourself," Butonov muttered.

Nike laughed uproariously. The suggestion struck her as wild. How she and Masha would laugh together about all this nonsense once her sister got over being so hot for him.

CHAPTER 15

Medea retired from her job in the autumn, on the Revolution Day holiday in November. Her immediate plan for filling her new free time was to mend the quilts, which became tatty unbelievably quickly over a summer season. In readiness she got in satin material and a boxful of good bobbin thread, but discovered the first evening she laid a distressed quilt on the table that its flowers were detaching themselves from their faded background while others, three-dimensional and shifting, came floating in to replace them.

She was running a temperature, Medea guessed, and closed her eyes to shut off the stream of flowers. Happily, Nina had come from Tbilisi only the day before.

It seemed to be the same illness from which she had suffered just before her marriage, when Samuel had looked after her so zealously and with such tremulous love and tenderness that he had every reason to quip later, "Other people have a feverish honeymoon, but Medea and I had a honeymonth of fever." In the intervals between attacks of furious shivering and fuddled semiconsciousness, Medea lapsed into a state of serene tranquility in which it seemed to her that Samuel was in the next room and would come in to see her in a minute, awkwardly bearing a tumbler in both hands and with his eyes slightly bulging because the tumbler was hotter than he had expected.

Instead of Samuel, however, it was Nina who emerged from the semidarkness, enveloped in the fragrance of St.-John's-wort and dissolving honey, with a thick glass tumbler in her thin, flat hands and her matte-black eyes deep-set like Samuel's, and Medea realized something she seemed to have been waiting for for a very long time, and now it finally had come to her like a revelation: Nina was their daughter, Samuel's and hers, their little girl; she had always known that but for some reason had forgotten it for a long time, but now it had come back to her and it was such a joy. Nina helped her up from the pillow, gave her the fragrant drink, and said something, but the meaning didn't quite get through to Medea, as if she were speaking a foreign language: "Yes, yes, Georgian," Medea remembered.

But the intonation was so rich and clear that she could understand everything just from the expressions on Nina's face, the movements of her hand, and also from the taste of the drink. It was surprising too that Nina could anticipate her wishes, and even opened and closed the curtains a moment before Medea was going to ask her to do it.

Medea's relatives in Tbilisi were the descendants of her two sisters: Anelya, who was the elder, and Anastasia, whom Anelya had brought up after the death of their parents. Anastasia had left a son, Robert, who was unmarried and seemed to be slightly touched in the head. Medea had no contact with him.

Anelya had not had any children of her own. Nina and Timur were adopted, so the Tbilisi relatives were a grafted branch of the family. These children were blood relatives of Anelya's husband Lado, his nephew and niece. Lado's brother Grigol and his wife Susanna were an absurd and unhappy couple: he was a fervent champion of a fair deal for traditional craftsmen; she was the city's madwoman, with a penchant for Communist Party work.

Lado Alexandrovich was a musician and professor at the Tbilisi Conservatory. He taught cello and had nothing in common with his brother, whom he had hardly seen since the mid-1920s.

Lado and Anelya first saw their nephew and niece early one

morning in May 1937. They were brought to their house by a distant relative after the arrest of both parents in the night.

The law of pairs is only a particular instance of a more general law of recurrence of the same event, whose purpose seems sometimes to be character formation, sometimes the accomplishing of destiny. In Anelya's life it operated very precisely. Exactly ten years had passed since Anastasia married and left home, and now fate had again brought orphans into their house, but two this time.

Anelya was already past forty, and Lado was ten years or so older. Their bloom had faded, their skin withered, and they were preparing themselves for a peaceful old age, not the lifestyle of young parents. The old age they had anticipated never came to pass. It took time to bring the neglected children around, and then the war began. Lado did not survive the rigors of the times and died of pneumonia in 1943.

Anelya set the children on their feet by realizing the assets of a once-prosperous household. She died in 1957, shortly after the return from exile of Susanna, who was by now completely demented. Nina was a young woman by then, and had a much loved stepmother replaced by her natural mother, a one-eyed harpy full of spite and paranoid devotion to the Leader. Nina had been looking after her for twenty years now.

The three or four days Nina had been planning to spend with Medea stretched to eight, and as soon as she had Medea back on her feet, she returned to Tbilisi.

Medea's illness had not completely passed. It spread to her joints, and she had now to treat herself with her home remedies. She bound her knees with thick bandages of old wool over cabbage leaves, or beeswax, or large boiled onions, and having completely lost her usual agility, hobbled around the house, but sat most of the time repairing quilts. As she did so, she was thinking about Nina and her crazy mother, and about Nike, who had spent the whole of September in Tbilisi because the theater was on tour there and, to judge even by Nina's toned-down stories, had staged quite a few performances of her own.

"Idle thoughts," Medea decided, stopped herself there, and reverted to doing what old Dionisy had taught her in her youth: "If worldly thoughts are troubling you and you can't let go of them, don't struggle but think prayerfully, addressing them to God."

"Poor Susanna. Forgive her, Lord, for the dreadful and stupid things she has done. Soften her heart and let her see how Nina is suffering because of her. And help Nina. She is meek and patient. Give her strength, Lord. And protect Nike from all manner of evil. The girl is following a dangerous path. She's so kind, so lively. Show her the way, Lord."

She again recalled Nina's account of how Nike had turned the life of a famous actor's family upside down. She had embarked on a wild romance in full view of the citizens of Tbilisi, sparkling, dazzling, chortling, and the actor's poor wife, dressed in black and consumed by jealousy, had rushed around to her husband's friends at night, trying to force her way through closed doors in the hope of catching her faithless spouse in flagrante delicto. Which, in the end, she did. There was a smashing of crockery, and people leaping out of windows; there was screaming and passion and a total breakdown of all propriety.

Perhaps most surprising was that back in October Medea had received a short note from Nike describing her visit to Tbilisi, the great success the theater had enjoyed, and even congratulating herself that her costumes for the production had been written about separately. "It's ages since I enjoyed myself so much and had such fun," the letter concluded. "But in Moscow the weather is dreadful, the divorce is dragging on forever, and I would give anything just to live somewhere a bit sunnier."

As regards the weather, Nike was absolutely right. The summer had ended in August and late autumn set in immediately.

The trees had no time to turn properly yellow, and the leaves fell to the ground quite green, bludgeoned from the trees by strong, cold rain. Her merry September in Tbilisi was followed by an unendurable October in Moscow. The weather got no better in November, but at least Nike's mood improved as a lot of work came her way.

She had another production to complete in her theater. She was forever looking into the workshops where, without her beady eye, the seamstresses were far too slapdash; and on top of that she was earning money on the side from work she was doing for the Romany Theater.

She was seduced by the Gypsy ambience, but found working for the theater very difficult indeed. Those same free and easy Gypsy ways which looked so enchanting in city squares and trams and on the stage, were a complete nightmare at the workplace: meetings arranged by the producer had to be rescheduled half a dozen times, and all the actresses threw terrible tantrums to back their impossible demands. Then, on the very day when one of the most strident of them, a lady already past her prime, threw in Nike's face the burgundy-red costume she had been given instead of the lacy white one she had wanted, and Nike equally adroitly shot it straight back at her, lining it with solid theater swear words the way small weights used to be sewn into the hems of light dresses, something very unpleasant happened which Nike had been doing her best to avoid.

Shortly before midnight Masha came to see her. No sooner had she opened the door than Nike realized that the long-expected unpleasantness had occurred. Masha rushed to hug her. "Nike, say it isn't true! It can't be true, say it!"

Nike stroked her hair slippery with rain and said nothing.

"I know it can't be true," Masha insisted, crumpling in her hands a crepe de Chine head scarf with a lilac, grey, and black diamond pattern. "What was it doing there? Why was it there?"

"Shush, shush! You're all tensed up." Nike made a warning gesture in the direction of the children's room.

Nike had been expecting this inevitable storm for so long, ever since July, that now, if anything, she felt relieved. The whole ridiculous business had dragged on all summer. When she left the Village in May, Nike had genuinely intended to give a secret present to Masha by letting her have Butonov, but things hadn't worked out that way.

All the time Masha had been taking the children for walks in the Crimea, Nike had been seeing Butonov, saying to herself that time would tell. They had slipped into an amazingly relaxed relationship. Butonov was delighted by Nike's forthrightness, the way she could talk about absolutely anything, and her complete lack of possessiveness; but when he did one time try to express this in his halting way, she stopped him: "Butonchik, the head on your shoulders is not your greatest asset. I know what you are trying to say. You are quite right. The point is that I have a male psychology. Just like you, I'm afraid of getting stuck in a long affair, in obligations, in marriage, for heaven's sake. You might like to bear in mind that means I'm always the first to dump my men."

It wasn't quite true, but it sounded good.

"Okay, but I'll need two weeks' notice," Butonov joked.

"Valerii, if you are going to be so witty, I shall fall head over heels in love with you, and that would be dangerous." Nike burst into peals of laughter, throwing her head back and making her mane of hair and her breasts shake.

She was constantly laughing: in the tram, at meals, in the swimming pool they had gone to one time, and Butonov, who didn't usually laugh much himself, was infected by her laughter, guffawing till he sobbed, till his sides ached and he couldn't speak. They laughed themselves silly in bed too.

"You are a unique lover," Nike said admiringly. "Laughing usually deflates erections."

"I don't know, I don't know, perhaps you just haven't made me laugh hard enough."

As soon as Masha got home at the beginning of July, she dropped the children on Alexandra and immediately rushed off to Rastorguevo. She was doubly in luck: she found Butonov at home, and she didn't find Nike there, because she had left the day before.

Masha's arrival coincided with the height of the renovations abandoned two years previously. The day before, Butonov had cleaned out his grandmother's half, in which nobody had lived for twenty years, and now two men he had hired to help him had arrived. Nike persuaded him not to line the walls with paneling as he had planned, but rather to strip everything down to the logs, clean and recaulk them, and repair the rough-hewn furniture left from the distant past.

"Mark my words, Butonov, you are using this furniture as firewood today, but in twenty years' time these will be museum pieces."

Butonov was amazed, but he consented, and now he and the workmen were stripping off the many layers of wallpaper.

"Butonov!" a woman's voice shouted up from the street. "Valerii!"

He came out in a cloud of dust, wearing his old doctor's hat. Masha was standing at the gate, although he didn't recognize her immediately. She had a deep and very attractive Crimean tan, and a wide grin which filled her slender face. Pushing her hand through a space between the pickets, she drew back the latch and, while he was still slowly wondering what to do, rushed up the winding path and threw herself at him like a puppy, burying her face in his chest.

"It's been so terrible! So terrible! I was beginning to think I would never see you again!"

A strong smell of the sea came from the top of her head and

he again heard, like that time in the Crimea, the thunderous pounding of her heart. "What's going on?! I can hear your heart as if I were listening through a stethoscope."

She was radiating heat and light like the white-hot coil of a powerful lamp, and Butonov remembered all he had forgotten about the way she furiously, desperately struggled with him in the little room in Medea's house; and he forgot what he had re-membered: her long letters full of poetry and reflections on things which were not exactly beyond his understanding, but of no earthly use to anyone.

She pressed her lips to the dusty white doctor's coat and breathed out hot air. She raised her face. The smile had gone and she was so pale that he could clearly see the two inverted cres-cents of dark freckles running from her cheekbones to her nose.

"Here I am."

If Grandmother's half of the house was in a mess from the re-decorating, then the attic, which they climbed up to, was a com-plete dump. Neither his grandmother nor his mother ever threw anything out: old washing troughs with holes in them, boilers, the bric-a-brac of a hundred years. The house had been built by his great-grandfather at the end of the nineteenth century when Rastorguevo was still a trading village, and there was a good cen-tury's worth of dust in the attic. It was impossible to lie down, so Butonov sat Masha on a rickety cabinet; and she looked just like a pottery money-box cat, only thinner and without the slit on the top of her head.

It was all so powerful and over so quickly that Butonov couldn't tear himself away, so he carried her over to an armchair which was in tatters and again he was seared by the tightness of the chair and even more by the tightness of her childlike body. Tears flowed down her otherworldly face, and he licked them off and they tasted of seawater. God Almighty!

Masha soon left, and Butonov went back to stripping wallpaper with the workmen, who seemed not even to have noticed his absence. He was as empty as a stovepipe or, more precisely, as empty as a rotten nut, because his emptiness was enclosed and rounded and now had no outlet. He fancied he had given away more than he meant to.

"Well, those sisters"—he didn't know their exact relationship—"are a complete contrast. One laughs, the other cries. They go well together."

For three days Masha could not catch Nike at home, although she phoned constantly and Alexandra had told her Nike was in town. Finally she got through.

"Nike! Where on earth have you been?"

It never occurred to her that Nike had been avoiding her, feeling ill prepared for this meeting.

"Three guesses!" Nike snorted.

"A new romance!" Masha said, bursting into laughter, swallowing the bait without a moment's hesitation.

"Top marks and then some!" Nike rewarded her perspicacity.

"Your place or mine? Yours is better. I'm on my way," Masha exclaimed, burning with impatience.

"Let's meet at Uspensky Lane instead," Nike countered. "Mother must be at her wits' end after having them for three days."

Having taken the children to Alexandra on her first day back, Masha had quite forgotten about them. Alexandra and Ivan Isaevich were celebrating a festival of love with their grandchildren and were not in the least tired of them. Ivan Isaevich would, though, have liked to take them to the dacha: much better than having them cooped up in town.

"No, no. It's better if I come to your place. We couldn't talk there," Masha begged, and Nike surrendered. There was no escape, and she knew in advance that she would be receiving Masha's confession.

From that day Nike was cast in the role of confidante. Her

position was ambiguous to say the least, but it seemed too late now to admit to her own involvement in the affair. In her ardor, Masha was bursting to tell Nike about every meeting with Butonov. It was terribly important for her.

Over many years Masha had got used to sharing even her most insignificant experiences with her husband, but she could not talk to Alik about this, so she dumped everything on Nike, including the poetry which she was constantly writing. "Pushkin's Boldino Autumn, my Rastorguevo Autumn!" Masha joked.

If before she had been no stranger to insomnia, in these months Masha slept a ragged and fitful sleep full of sounds, lines of verse, and disturbing images. Unreal animals came to her in her dreams, animals with many legs, many eyes, half-birds, half-cats, with symbolic allusions. One, fearfully familiar, rubbed up against her, and its name was also familiar to her. It consisted of a series of numbers and letters. When she woke, she remembered its strange name: Zh4836. She burst out laughing. It was the number printed in thick black ink on the linen ribbon she sewed to the bed sheets before sending them to the laundry.

All this nonsense was imbued with significance. One time she dreamt a completely finished poem which she wrote down while half-asleep. She was amazed when she read it the following morning. "It isn't mine, it isn't mine. I could never have written this myself."

> *Through lust to love and into the abyss*
> *of destinations reached past our contriving:*
> *I give the words that tell of you and this,*
> *I serve as target too of all your striving;*
> *and in the brooding darkness of our blood*
> *the instant blazes like a blunderbuss,*
> *and all is swept away as in a flood*
> *and leaves no brim between the one of us.*

"It's exactly as if I had written it under dictation. Look, not a single correction," she crowed, showing Nike the record of her nighttime inspiration.

Nike did not like these poems. They frightened her. On the other hand, she found it hilarious that, with Masha informing her about every word Butonov uttered, about his every movement, she knew minute by minute how he had spent the previous day.

"Any fried potatoes left?" she would innocently ask, because Masha had told her she had been peeling potatoes for him the day before and had cut her finger.

Butonov did not speak to Nike about Masha and she never said a word about her rival, but Butonov had the impression they both knew perfectly well how things stood and were even sharing out the days of the week between them, with Masha coming on weekends and Nike on weekdays. There was no such deal, of course. It was just that during the week Nike went to the dachas to visit the children: either Liza, who was staying with Alexandra, or Katya, who was living with her other grandmother. Little Alik was staying with Alexandra too.

Big Alik was trying to arrange his duty roster so that emergency calls fell on the weekends, so that he would not lose laboratory time; and Masha, preferring not to lie but to keep a more honorable silence, left home when Alik wasn't there. Although of late he had had very little time to spend at home.

Alik was steady and good-humored, and didn't ask awkward questions. Their conversation centered on emigrating. They had already arranged for an invitation from Israel, but although Masha contributed to these conversations, their emigration seemed unreal to her.

When Nike went off to Tbilisi in September, Masha was devastated by her absence. She tried ringing through but found it impossible to catch her at the hotel. She wasn't able to contact her through Nina either.

In September, Butonov finished his renovating and went to stay with his wife in Khamovniki, but the redecorated house in Rastorguevo drew him back and he would sleep there two or three times a week. Sometimes he came to collect Masha, and they drove there together. One time they even went to gather mushrooms in Rastorguevo, found nothing, got soaked to the skin, then dried their belongings by the stove and one of Masha's stockings caught fire; and this too was a little event in their life, like the cut finger, or a scratch or a bruise Masha suffered in the course of their amorous endeavors. Whether Butonov's house was inimical to her or whether she brought out a tendency to sexual horseplay in Butonov himself, she had not a few of these little injuries, and was even rather proud of her souvenirs of passion spent.

When Nike finally came back from Tbilisi, Masha related all these trivia to her at great length, and finally mentioned in passing that their invitation from Israel had arrived. Nike was amazed at how Masha's head had been turned, when she couldn't see that receiving the invitation was what really mattered.

Emigrating meant parting from your family, perhaps forever, yet here was Masha showing off her bruises and reading her poems. This time Nike too had something to relate. She was getting very deeply involved in her new affair and had decided this would be a good moment to dot Butonov's *i*.

She waited a whole week, like Penelope, for her Vakhtang to come from Tbilisi to Mosfilm for his auditions, but his arrival kept being postponed, and in order not to get out of condition Nike took herself around to see Butonov. As Masha constantly reported on her own movements, there was no problem in finding a suitable moment.

Butonov was very pleased to see Nike. He wanted to show her the newly redecorated half of the house. Nike was, after all, his personal interior designer. He now loved the idea of the exposed beams, but Nike was horrified to see that the logs had been drenched with varnish. She comically berated him at length and ordered him to clean the varnish off with solvent. She moved the furniture around and pointed out to him what needed repairing and what was best left alone. She had lived many years with a stepfather who was a cabinetmaker and with her talents had rapidly understood the ins and outs of his profession. She promised to bring Butonov some colored glass to replace what was missing in the buffet and to sew curtains for him in the theater workshop.

At some point in the proceedings Nike's head scarf slipped off and insinuated itself snakelike between the sheet and the mattress. Nike couldn't find it, although she looked for it for a long time in the morning. The scarf was one she had made herself when she was learning batik at college.

When Masha, barely through the door, crumpling the scarf in her hands, fired the question straight at her as to whether it was true, Nike sternly cut her short: "Well, what did Butonov say?"

"That you and he have . . . for ages, since the Crimea. It can't be true, it can't. I told him it was impossible."

"And what did he say?" Nike asked, keeping up.

"He said, 'Accept it as fact.' " Masha was still screwing up Nike's scarf, the embodiment of the fact.

Nike drew the scarf out of her hands and threw it under the mirror. "Well, accept it!"

"I can't, I can't!" Masha wailed.

"Masha," Nike suddenly softened. "It's just how things turned out. What do you want me to do, hang myself? Don't let's make a tragedy out of it. God knows, it's *Les Liaisons dangereuses* all over again."

"But, Nike, my sunshine, what am I to do? You want me to

just get used to it? I don't understand myself why it hurts so. When I pulled this scarf out, I almost died." She became flustered again. "No, no. It's impossible."

"What do you mean? Why is it impossible?"

"I can't explain. It's as if anyone can do anything with anyone. Nothing matters. It doesn't matter who you choose. One person is just the same as another. But here, I just know, there is something unique and special, against which nothing else has any meaning. Unique."

"My angel," Nike stopped her. "Aren't you just imagining that? Every case is unique, believe me. Butonov is an excellent lover, but you measure that in centimeters, minutes, hours, the level of hormones in the blood. They're all just parameters. He has a good body, no more than that. Your Alik is a remarkable person, intelligent, talented. Butonov isn't worthy to lick his boots, but Alik just hasn't given you enough—"

"Shut up!" Masha screamed. "Shut up! Take your Butonov and all his centimeters. You're welcome to him!"

She rushed out, for some reason seizing the head scarf she had just returned to Nike from the pier table.

Nike did not stop her. Let her rage. If people have idiotic delusions, you have to leave them to get rid of them. When all was said and done, Butonov had put it quite correctly: "Accept it as fact." But then . . . to her annoyance Nike recollected Masha's poem: "Accept too that beyond all measure, like heaven's grace on heaven's grace . . ." Well, go ahead and accept it. Accept it as fact.

Dear Butonov! I know that correspondence is not your forte, that of all the forms of human interaction the most important for you is tactile. Even your profession is like that—everything in the fingertips, in touching, in delicate movements. And if one stays on the superficial, the surface level, in both a literal and a metaphorical sense, then everything that is happening is perfectly proper. Touches have neither faces nor eyes, it is only receptors at work. Nike tried to explain that to me too: everything is determined by centimeters, minutes, hormone levels.

But this is just a matter of faith. I evidently belong to a different confession; what is important for me is the expression on someone's face, their inner impulse, a turn of phrase, what they feel in their heart. And if that is not there, then we are only objects for each other to use. To tell the truth, that is what torments me most. Are there really no relationships other than those of the body? Is there really nothing between you and me other than embracing until the world disappears? Is there really no communion higher than the physical, when all sense of the distinctness of our two bodies is lost?

Nike, your lover, my more-than-sister, told me there is nothing more than centimeters, minutes, hormones. Say no. Tell me it isn't true! Was there really nothing in what took place between us that can't be described by parameters of one kind or another? If that is true, then you don't exist, neither do I, neither does anybody or anything at all and we are mechanical toys and not the children of the Lord God. Here is a little poem for you, dear Butonov, and I beg you: say it isn't true.

> *Play on, centaur, play on, chimera of two breeds,*
> *burn, fire, along the boundary dividing*
> *the human soul and its immortal needs,*
> *the stallion, his lusts unbridled riding.*
>
> *Your destiny it is to mediate, to ferry,*
> *to ply shores which forget how close they used to be,*

and heedlessly you plunge into those waters merry
which care no more than you if you remember me.

Masha Miller

Butonov read the letter and groaned. Knowing Masha's personality well enough, he was expecting major ructions when she
discovered her rival but had never imagined that her jealousy
would be expressed in such a complicated, elaborate manner. He
really had pissed her off.

Ten days or so later, having given things a chance to settle
down a bit, he rang Masha to ask whether she fancied a trip out
to Rastorguevo. After much hesitation, periodical yeses and nos
(Butonov could tell even over the telephone that it was exactly
what she wanted), she agreed.

At Rastorguevo everything was new. There had been a heavy
snowfall, so heavy that the path from the gate to the porch had
been buried, and in order to drive the car in Butonov had had to
scrape the snow up with a wooden shovel into a large snowdrift.

It was cold in the house: it seemed colder inside than out, but
Butonov promptly gave Masha such a workout that they both
started feeling too hot. She moaned through her tears, and kept
pleading, "Say no!"

"What do you want 'no' for, when it's all 'yes, yes, yes'!" Butonov laughed.

After that he lit the stove, opened a tin of sardines in tomato
sauce which had been around for ages, and ate it himself, Masha
barely touching it. There was nothing else in the house.

They decided not to go back to Moscow and walked to the
railway station. Masha rang home from the public telephone and
told Debora Lvovna that she wouldn't be home that night, as she
was visiting friends at their dacha and didn't want to come back
so late.

Her mother-in-law flared up: "Of course not! You don't care

two hoots about your husband and child! If you want to know what that's called—"

Masha hung up.

"That's all fixed. I told them I wouldn't be home."

They walked back to the house along a path of white snow. Butonov showed her the windows of the apartment block where Vitka Kravchuk lived.

"Want to drop in?" he enquired.

"God forbid," Masha laughed.

It was cool in Butonov's house. It did not hold the heat.

"Next on the list is a new stove. I'll put one in next year," Butonov resolved.

They settled themselves in the kitchen, where it was at least a bit warmer, and dragged mattresses in from all over the house. They had no sooner warmed up, however, than Butonov got pains in his stomach and went out to the toilet in the courtyard. He came back and lay down. Masha, running her finger over his face, began talking about the spirituality of sex, and the personality which expresses itself through touch.

The tinned sardines had Butonov running out to the courtyard all night. His stomach was churning, and the tender voice of unsleeping Masha cooed on in tones of neurotic enquiry.

To give him his due, he was polite and didn't ask her to shut up. Only sometimes, when the pain subsided a bit, he slumped into sleep. In the morning as they were driving back to Moscow, Butonov said, "One thing I really am grateful to you for at this moment is that when I was suffering from the runs you did me the favor of not reciting any poetry at me."

Masha looked at him in astonishment: "But I did, Valerii. I recited 'Poem Without a Hero' to you from start to finish."

Masha's relations with her husband did not come unstuck, but recently they had been seeing less of each other. The invitation they had received had not been submitted yet because Alik wanted to resign from his job before filing the application, and before that there was a series of experiments he needed to finish.

He disappeared into the laboratory until late at night and turned down any further emergency-duty work. He periodically carted a rucksack full of books to the secondhand bookshop, since he was going to have to say goodbye to his father's library. He could see Masha was disturbed and jumpy, and treated her solicitously, like a patient.

In December, Butonov went off to Sweden, for a couple of weeks, he said vaguely, although of course he knew perfectly well which day he would be back. He liked his freedom. Nike barely noticed his absence. She had a children's play to get ready in time for the school holidays, and in any case Vakhtang had finally arrived and she spent all her free time with him and his Moscow Georgian friends. Life was a busy whirl of restaurants, sometimes at the Cinema Club, sometimes at the Theater Society.

Masha pined. She kept trying to get through to Nike to talk to her about Butonov, but Nike was incommunicado. Masha had no wish to talk to other friends about him, and in any case it would have been impossible.

Insomnia, which until then had only been sharpening its claws, overwhelmed Masha in December. Alik brought her sedatives, but the artificial sleep was even worse than the insomnia. Her obsessive dream would start at any random place but led always to the same ending: she was trying to find Butonov, to catch up with him, but he kept slipping away, spilling like water, turning into different objects, as if in a fairy tale, dissolving, vanishing into smoke.

Twice Masha went to Rastorguevo just for the sake of making the journey from Paveletsky Station, taking the train to his stop and walking to his house, to stand for a time at the gate, see the house shrouded in snow, look at its dark windows, and go back home. In all, it took around three and a half hours, and the journey there was more enjoyable than the journey back.

Two weeks passed and still there was no sign of him. Masha rang his home in Khamovniki. An elderly woman told her in a weary voice that he would be back at around ten; but he wasn't there at ten, or at eleven, and the next morning the same voice replied, "Call again on Friday."

"But has he come back?" Masha asked timidly.

"I said ring on Friday," the woman replied rattily.

It was still only Monday.

"He's come back and hasn't phoned," Masha thought, hurt. She called Nike to ask whether she knew anything about Butonov's whereabouts, but Nike didn't.

Masha set off for Rastorguevo again, this time in the late afternoon. The snow had been cleared away from the gates of his house, and they were closed and locked. His car stood in the yard. In his grandmother's half a faint light was burning. Masha yanked the icy side gate. The path to the house was deep in snow, and as she walked along, she sank almost up to her knees in it. She rang the bell for a long time, but nobody opened the door.

She wanted to wake up, so much did all this feel like one of her dreams, just as vivid and hurtful; and Butonov gave some flickering sign of his presence in just the same way: his beige car parked there with a blanket of snow on the roof. And she couldn't get hold of Butonov himself.

Masha stood around for forty minutes or so and left.

"Nike must be in there," she concluded.

In the train she was thinking not of Butonov but of Nike. Nike had been part of her life from an early age. They were linked, quite apart from everything else, by a physical liking for each other. Since she was a child Masha had loved Nike's full, puckered lips, her endless supply of smiles, the creases of hidden laughter at the corners of her mouth, her rustling red hair; and in just the same way Nike had liked Masha's diminutiveness, her little feet, her gawkiness, the delicacy in every aspect of her being.

Masha for her part would unhesitatingly have preferred to be Nike than herself. Nike, of course, didn't lose time thinking about things like that. She had all she needed in herself.

And now Butonov had joined them together in some sacramental way, like Jacob marrying two sisters. They could have been called comrades-in-arms. Jacob entered the tents, took the sisters, took their handmaidens, and they were one family. And what after all is jealousy but another form of covetousness? You can't possess another person. Well then, let it be: everybody would be brothers and sisters, husbands and wives. She smiled to herself, thinking about utopian Chernyshevsky and the grand brothel in one or other of the dreams of his heroine in *What Is to Be Done?*

Nothing unique, nothing personal. All of it boring and bereft of talent. Are we free or not? Where does our awareness of shame and indecency come from? By the time she got back to Moscow, she had written Nike a poem:

> *A rift between the tree trunk and its shadow;*
> *a rift between the thirst and taking drink;*
> *across the abyss a poem's swaying ladder*
> *the only way to help us pass the brink.*
> *The shades of sleep, the corridors all gaping,*
> *my only light a captured German torch;*
> *and from contrition there is no escaping:*
> *we do not kill, no ironing we scorch,*
> *don't slop through puddles, try to hide our errors,*
> *don't sing forbidden songs, don't practice guile,*
> *but know, and live in superstitious terror:*
> *the two of us are doing something vile.*

She got home around midnight. Alik was waiting for her in the kitchen with a bottle of good Georgian wine. He had finished his experiments and could file their application to emigrate tomorrow if they liked. Only then did it finally sink in for Masha that she would soon be leaving forever.

"That's splendid. It will put an end to this whole shameful, grisly affair," she thought. She spent a long evening with Alik, which continued until four in the morning. They talked, made plans, and then Masha fell into a dreamless sleep holding Alik's hand.

She woke late. Debora Lvovna had not been home for several days. Recently she had often been away on lengthy visits to her ailing sister. The Aliks had already had breakfast and were playing chess. It was a picture of domestic tranquility and even included a cat lying on a cushion on the sofa.

"That's good! I seem to be recovering," Masha thought, turning the stiff handle of the coffee mill.

Later they took the sled, and the three of them went to the ice hill. They fell off into the snow, got wet, and were happy.

"Do they have snow in Boston?" Masha asked.

"No, they don't. But we will go to Utah and ski there, and that will be just as good," Alik promised.

He always delivered on his promises.

Butonov rang that same evening.

"Not missing me, by any chance?"

The day before, he had seen Masha stamping her feet by his gate but had not opened the door to her because he had a lady visitor, the nice, if fat, translator who had been on his trip with him. They had exchanged glances for the two weeks but no opportunity had presented itself. A soft, lazy woman, very similar as he subsequently realized to his wife Olga, she had writhed like a sleepy cat in Butonov's arms to the trilling of Masha on the doorbell. Butonov had felt acutely irritated by the translator, Masha, and himself. He needed angular, sharp Masha with her tears and her sighs, not this fatso.

He had been ringing Masha since morning, but first there was no reply because the telephone was unplugged, then Alik picked it up twice and Butonov hung up, and only toward evening did he get through to her. "Please don't ring anymore," Masha said.

"When? When can you come? Quickly now," Butonov said, not hearing what she had said.

"No, I'm not coming. Don't ring me anymore, Valerii." Then with a strained, tearful voice she added, "I can't take any more."

"Masha, I'm missing you terribly. Have you gone crazy? Are you hurt? It's a misunderstanding, Masha. I'll be at your house in twenty-five minutes. Come out then." He hung up.

Masha was in total confusion. She had decided so splendidly, so firmly, not to see him anymore and had felt a sense of, if not liberation then at least relief, and today had been such fun, with the ice hill and the sunshine. "I won't go," Masha decided.

But thirty-five minutes later she threw on a jacket, called to Alik, "I'll be back in ten minutes!" and rushed down the stairs without stopping to call the lift.

Butonov's car was waiting by the door. She wrenched the door open and sat down beside him.

"I have to tell you—"

He scooped her into his arms and shoved his hands under her jacket.

"We'll talk all about it, of course we will, little one."

The car moved off.

"No, no. I'm not going anywhere. I came out to say I wouldn't go with you."

"But we've already gone," Butonov laughed.

This time Alik was offended. "What an appalling way to behave! Can't you see that?" he berated her late that night when she returned. "Someone goes out for ten minutes and comes back five hours later! What am I supposed to think? That you've been run over? Been killed?"

"Please forgive me, for God's sake. You're absolutely right, it's a terrible way to behave." Masha felt profoundly guilty. And profoundly happy.

Next, Butonov disappeared for a month, and Masha tried with all her might just to accept his disappearance "as fact," but it was a fact that burned right through her. She ate almost nothing, drank sweet tea, and conducted an interminable inner monologue with her absent lover. Her insomnia was becoming ever more acute.

Alik was alarmed: it was obvious she was on the verge of a nervous breakdown. He started giving Masha tranquilizers and increased the dose of sedatives. Masha refused to take psychotropic drugs.

"I'm not a lunatic, Alik, I'm an idiot, and you can't treat that."

Alik didn't insist. He saw this as just one more reason why they needed to emigrate as soon as possible.

Nike came to see her twice. Masha talked only about Butonov. Nike cursed him, felt very penitent, and swore the last time she had seen him was in December before he went to Sweden. She also said that he was empty-headed and that the only good thing to come out of the whole saga was that Masha had written so much splendid poetry. Masha obediently read her poems and wondered whether Nike could be trying to deceive her now and whether it was Nike who had been with Butonov when she was ringing at the door.

Alik was doing the rounds of all manner of bureaucratic institutions, assembling a whole mountain of documents. He was in a hurry not only for Masha's sake: he wanted to get to Boston to carry on with his work, the lack of which was making him feel ill too. They were not emigrating in a straightforward manner:

first they would travel to Vienna under the provision for Jews, and then go on to America. It was possible that between Vienna and America they would have a spell in Rome. That depended on the speed with which documents were dealt with by, at that stage, foreign bureaucrats.

To all these complexities there was suddenly added a rebellion by Debora Lvovna. "I'm not emigrating anywhere. I have a sick sister, the only person close to me in the world, and I'll never leave her." There then followed the canonical text of a Yiddish mama: "I've devoted my whole life to you, you thankless boy, and now . . . that damned Israel: it's because of them we've had troubles all our lives. That damned America, may it come to a bad end."

In the face of such arguments Alik held his peace and took his mother by the shoulders: "Mother of mine! Can you play tennis? Can you ice-skate? Is there anything in the world you can't do? Could there maybe be something you don't know? Some little detail? Be quiet, I beg you. Nobody is going to abandon you. We are going together, and we will support your Fira from America. I will earn a lot of money there."

Debora Lvovna was quiet for a moment, but then worked herself up into even more of a lather: "What do I need your money for! To hell with your money! Your father and I always despised money. You will ruin the child with your money!"

Alik clutched his head and went out of the room.

When all the documents had been collected, Debora Lvovna categorically refused to go but did give permission for them to emigrate. The exit permits were finally issued, only for Butonov to announce himself again. It happened one morning. Masha got Little Alik ready, took him over to Alexandra, and went to Rastorguevo to say goodbye.

It was a good leave-taking. Masha told Butonov this was the

last time he would see her, that she would soon be leaving forever, and she wanted to take every last detail with her in memory. Butonov was agitated: "Forever? Well, of course, you're right, Masha, quite right. Life here is crap compared to the West, I've seen that. But forever . . ."

Masha walked through the house memorizing it all, because she wanted to retain the house in her memory too. Then the two of them went up to the attic. It was as dusty and cluttered as ever. Butonov tripped over the knocked-out seat of a bentwood chair, and picked it up: "Look."

The center of the seat was pierced through with knife throws, and marks from near misses were all around it. He hung the seat up on a nail.

"This was the main thing I did as a boy."

He took out a knife, went off to the far end of the attic, and threw it. The blade stuck in the wall right through the middle of the punched-out circle.

Masha pulled the knife out of the wall and went over to Butonov. He thought she wanted to throw it at the target too, but she only weighed it in her hand and gave it back to him.

"Now I know everything about you."

After that trip Masha began quietly preparing to emigrate. She took all her papers out of the writing-desk drawers and decided what to keep and what to throw away.

The customs officials did not allow manuscripts to be taken out of the country, but Alik knew someone in the embassy, and he promised to send Masha's papers out through the diplomatic bag. She sat on the floor surrounded by them, rereading every page, pondering each one, and feeling sad. She could suddenly see that everything she had written was only a draft for what she wanted to write, now or some time in the future.

"I'll compile a collection and call it *Insomnia.*"

The poems came out to her like wild animals coming out of the forest, complete but invariably with a defect of some kind, a limp in the foreleg, a limp in the first verse.

> *There is clairvoyance in the nighttime,*
> *all detail hidden by the dark;*
> *of stripes on walls it's only white ones*
> *that on the paper show their mark.*

> *The baggage that I bear at nighttime,*
> *the cares and trivia fall away:*
> *the brilliant genius of nighttime*
> *by far outshines the light of day.*

> *I have come to love insomnia,*
> *the crystal vistas of the deep:*
> *their gift, a delicate deposit,*
> *dispels all likelihood of sleep.*

Masha grew very thin, becoming even more fragile, and the daytime world, which seemed to her so dull in comparison with the world of night, became more fragile too. An angel appeared. At first she could not actually see him but sensed his presence, and sometimes turned around quickly because she thought she might glimpse him that way. When he came to her in a dream, his features were clearer, and the part of the dream in which he appeared was like a color sequence inserted in a black and white film.

He looked slightly different each time and could assume human form: one time he appeared to her in the form of a teacher dressed in white like a fencing instructor, and started teaching her to fly. They were standing on the slope of a living, softly breathing hill, which was also taking an ill-defined part in the lesson.

The teacher indicated a region of the spine to her, below the level of the shoulders and deeper, where a small organ or muscle was located, and Masha knew that she would fly just as soon as she learned the gentle, precise movement which controlled this organ. She concentrated, and it was as if she had pressed a button: her body began very slowly to break free from the mountain, and the mountain gently helped her with the movement. Masha flew clumsily and slowly, but it was already entirely clear to her what she had to do to control the speed and direction of her flight—to wherever she wanted to go and for as long as she wanted to fly.

She raised her head and saw that the translucent people flying above her were strong and free, and she understood that she too could fly in just the same way. Then she slowly came back down, without having tried out all the possible delights.

This flying was not at all like the flight of birds: there was no flapping of wings, no fluttering, no aerodynamics, just an effort of the spirit.

Another time the angel taught her the techniques of a special verbal intellectual wrestling which does not exist in our world. It was as if you had a word in your hand which was a weapon. He put it in her hand, smooth and comfortable in her palm. He turned her hand, and a sharp ray of meaning glinted out of it. Immediately two opponents appeared, one to the right and above her and the second to the left and slightly below her. Both of them were practiced and dangerous enemies, skilled in this martial art. One glinted at her, and she gave a riposte. The second came in close and directed a quick blow at her, but in some miraculous way she managed to deflect it.

There was a razor-sharp dialogue in these attacks, untranslatable but completely clear in its meaning. Both combatants were ridiculing her, pointing out to her how inferior she was and how hopeless her attempts were to compete with their mastery.

To her growing amazement, however, she deflected every blow and with each new movement discovered that the weapon she held was becoming more intelligent and accurate, and that this combat really did seem closest to the art of fencing. The opponent to the right was more vicious and sarcastic, but retreated. Then the second one backed off too. They were gone, and that meant she had won.

Sobbing openly, she threw herself on her teacher's breast. He said, "Don't be afraid. You have seen, nobody can harm us."

Masha cried even more bitterly because of the terrible weakness which was truly her own, because all the intellectual power with which she had prevailed had not been her own but lent to her by her teacher.

Masha experienced a superhuman freedom and an unearthly joy from this new experience, which came from regions and spaces the angel had revealed to her; but for all the novelty and unimaginableness of what was happening, she intuited that the extremes of pleasure she experienced when she was closest to Butonov derived from the same root and were of the same nature. She wanted to ask the angel about this but he did not let her; when he appeared, she subjected herself to his will eagerly and diligently.

When he disappeared, however, sometimes for several days, she felt very low, as if the joy of his presence had inescapably to be paid for by depression, gloom, emptiness, and miserable monologues addressed to the almost nonexistent Butonov: "So dazzling, the light of Tabor daunts us, but far harder to gaze upon the disk whose empty blackness taunts us through all the following days."

Masha hesitated over whether to tell Alik about this. She was afraid that, ever the rationalist, he would view the matter in a medical rather than a mystical light. In her case, however, the realm of poetry lay between medicine and mysticism, and there she was the ruler.

She decided to approach him from that direction. Late one evening when the whole house was asleep, she began reading him her latest poems:

> *"I noticed how, angelic guardian,*
> *your powers were looking after me,*
> *as to the rock of sun-warmed granite*
> *I pressed my head, still all at sea;*
>
> *When from the depths of Freud's dominions,*
> *from darkling realms where sleep is host,*
> *a wave propelled me to my kingdom,*
> *like flotsam cast up on a coast.*
>
> *And, as in concrete and in metal*
> *there nestle empty voids, a thing*
> *both void and strong had come to settle*
> *in my room, an angel's wing.*
>
> *I thought I saw my angel weeping:*
> *his heavenly eyes discerned with rue*
> *the gruesomeness of lovers' sleeping,*
> *and wept for me and wept for you."*

"I think, Masha, that is a very good poem." Alik was genuinely delighted. This was not one of those occasions when he felt obliged to express approval out of family solidarity.

"It's the truth, Alik. I mean the poem. It's not metaphor or imagination. His presence is real."

"Well, of course, Masha, otherwise creativity of any kind would be impossible. It's a metaphysical realm—" he began, but she interrupted him: "Oh, no! He comes to me, just like you. He's taught me to fly and much more that I can't tell you because it can't be put into words. But here, listen:

> *"Behold how strained the seagull's flight,*
> *ungainly wings' uncertain beating,*
> *the tensing of her neck a fight*
> *with wind and gravity, a cheating,*
> *not to founder in the waves*
> *while finding food beneath the surface.*

> *Yet, Lord, you promise all the homeless*
> *feathered wings and eyes that see,*
> *in place of rags and penny pieces,*
> *to soar and dance in heaven's breezes*
> *unrehearsed and faultlessly."*

"It's such a simple little poem, and you wouldn't really know from it that I was flying, that I was actually there, where flight is as natural . . . as everything . . ."

"You mean, hallucinations?" Alik asked anxiously.

"Oh no. They aren't hallucinations. It's like you, like this table, reality. Only slightly different. I can't explain. I am like Kitty here." She stroked the cat. "I know everything, I understand everything, but I can't express it. Only she doesn't suffer from that and I do."

"But Masha, I can tell you everything comes through splendidly in your writing. It really works."

He was speaking gently and calmly, but he was extremely disturbed. "Is it schizophrenia, manic-depressive psychosis? I'll phone Volobuev tomorrow and ask him to see what it is."

Volobuev, a consulting psychiatrist, was a friend of someone who had been in Alik's class at the university, and in those times the guildlike community of doctors, a legacy from better times and better traditions, had not yet fallen apart.

But Masha was still reciting, unable now to stop:

> "And on that day when free as birds,
> transformed by my six-winged translator
> beyond the wit of their creator,
> burst forth in power my random words,
> 'Let me depart' shall be my supplication,
> a coat of many colors consummation
> of all my sins, 'at last no more to roam,
> Into my Father's house, my heavenly home.' "

Still, Butonov would not leave Masha alone. She went to him in Rastorguevo three times more. It seemed that the note she had struck was so high that there was no going higher—her voice would break, everything would break. Only now, when every meeting felt as if it were the last one, did Butonov admit to himself that Masha had so far eclipsed her prototype, half-forgotten Rosa, that he could no longer even remember the face of his lost horsewoman; and now he no longer saw Masha as being in the likeness of Rosa, but that fleeting love affair seemed to have contained the promise of the present one. The inevitability of parting intensified his passion.

He had dropped the two or three other women who had been a simultaneous but less-than-crucial part of his life. One, whom he actually quite needed to keep sweet for his work, a secretary of the sports organizing committee, had given him to understand that she was offended by his neglect; the second was a client, a young ballerina for whom he had made an exception to his rule that the massage table was a work surface and not a suitable place for dalliance, who had fallen out of contention automatically when she moved to Riga. He really hadn't seen Nike since December. They had phoned each other a few times, expressed a polite desire to meet, but neither had made the least effort to do so.

Butonov had a major career decision looming. He was fed up with sports medicine, the unvarying impact injuries he was constantly dealing with, and the no-holds-barred politicking associated with trips abroad. A timely offer had materialized: a rehabilitation center was being set up for high-ranking Communist Party and government officials and their families, and Butonov was a likely candidate to manage it. This held out a number of interesting possibilities. At the age of thirty-five his wife Olga had reached her professional ceiling, as happens with mathematicians, and she was egging Valerii on: a new direction; state-of-the-art equipment; you can't spend your whole life running your fingers over the same old pressure points, etc.

Ivanov, by now wrinkled and yellow and with the passing years looking ever more like a Buddhist monk, warned him, "You don't have the brain for it, and you don't have the stomach for it." His remark contained both respectful appreciation and a subtle put-down.

Butonov rated Nike's judgment highly, especially since her very successful intervention in his interior decorating, and decided to consult her. He met her by the Maly theater and they went to a ghastly little restaurant on Taganskaya Square which, lying at the intersection of their routes, was at least convenient.

Nike was looking on top of the world, although everything about her was slightly *de trop*: the long fur coat, the short skirt, the large rings, and her flowing mane of hair. They chatted about this and that in an easy, cheerful way. Butonov explained his problem to her. She became unexpectedly severe, frowned, and told him abruptly: "Valerii, you know, in our family we have a very good tradition, which is to stay as far away from the authorities as possible. I had a close relative, a Jewish dentist, who put it splendidly: 'In my heart I love Soviet power so much, but my body just won't react to her.' If you take this job, you will have to spend all your time cuddling that body.'" Nike swore just within the bounds of acceptability, fluently and with great artistry.

Butonov felt a huge sense of relief. Her jocular swearing had answered his question. The Fourth Directorate's rehabilitation center was off, as he gratefully informed Nike there and then.

Their friendly feelings for each other reached a sufficient temperature for them to finish their shashlyks and get into Butonov's beige Moskvich and for Butonov, without needing to ask any further questions, to make a U-turn on Taganskaya Square and head for Rastorguevo.

Masha was suffering the most unbearable form of insomnia, when all possible sedatives have been taken and arms, legs, back, everything is asleep except for a small center in the brain which is transmitting the same signal over and over again: "I can't sleep . . . I can't sleep . . ."

She slipped out of bed, where Big Alik was sleeping with his knees drawn up to his chin, looking very small in this fetal position. She went to the kitchen, smoked a cigarette, put her hands under the cold tap, washed, and lay down to rest on the couch in the kitchen. She closed her eyes and again heard: "I can't sleep . . . I can't sleep . . ."

He was standing in the doorway, her usual angel, clad in somber dark red raiment. She couldn't see his face clearly, but his eyes were deep blue, as if he were looking through the slits of a theatrical mask. Masha noticed that the doorway was a false one: the real door was farther to the right. He stretched out his hands to her, placed them over her ears, and even squeezed a little.

"Now he's going to teach me clairvoyance." She understood

that she had to take off her dressing gown. She stood there now in her long nightgown.

He was behind her and pressing her ears and eyes closed, and with his middle fingers began to massage across her forehead and right down to the bridge of her nose. Delicate waves of color floated toward and away from her, rainbows extending to a great range of hues. He was waiting for her to stop him, and she said, "Enough."

The fingers stopped immediately. In a beam of pale yellow light with an unpleasant green tinge, she saw two people, a man and a woman. They were very young and slender. They came nearer as if she were watching through binoculars until she could recognize them. They were her parents. They were holding hands and aware only of each other. Her mother was wearing a familiar light blue dress with dark blue stripes, and she was younger than Masha herself. What a pity they could not see her.

"This can't go on," Masha understood. He began stroking across her forehead once more and pressing on some particular point.

"Butonov's art, pressure points," Masha thought. She stopped the beam of yellow light and saw the house in Rastorguevo, the closed side gate and herself beside it. The car was inside the main gate, and the small light was burning in Grandmother's half. She passed through the side gate without opening it and approached the lighted window, or rather the window approached her, and rising easily into the air, she flew up and dived smoothly inside.

They did not see her, although she was right beside them. Nike had thrown back her long neck, and she could have touched it. Nike was smiling, even perhaps laughing, but the sound was turned off. Masha ran her finger down Butonov's gleaming chest, but he did not notice. His lips trembled and parted, and revealed his front teeth, one of which was set slightly off true.

"Turn around, please, and go back," Nike said quietly to Butonov, looking out through the window at Ryazan highway.

"Is that what you want?" Butonov asked in some surprise, but did not argue, engaged reverse gear and turned the car.

He stopped in Usachevka. They parted warmly, with a good, live kiss, and Butonov was not in the least put out. He could take no for an answer. In these matters nobody owes anyone anything. It was still early evening, light snow was falling, and Katya and Liza were waiting up for their mother.

"So much for Rastorguevo," Nike thought, and lightly ran up the stairs to the third floor.

Masha was standing in the corridor between the kitchen and the living room in an icy draught and had a sudden revelation, as if she had been struck by lightning, that she had once before stood in her nightgown in this exact same freezing current of air. The door behind her would open in a minute and something dreadful would be behind it. She ran her fingers across her forehead to the bridge of her nose, rubbed the middle of her forehead: wait, stop . . .

But the horror behind the door kept growing. She forced herself to look around. The false door moved slightly.

Masha ran into the living room and pushed the door to the balcony. It flew open without creaking. The cold which blew in from outside was fresh and joyful, and the air behind her was icy and stifling.

Masha stepped out onto the balcony. The snow was falling gently and it was a choir with a thousand voices, as if every snowflake carried its own musical note, and this moment too was something she recognized. This had happened before. She turned; something dreadful was standing behind the living-room door and it was coming nearer.

"Oh, I know, I know." Masha climbed onto the box the television had come in, from there onto the long window box fixed to the side of the balcony, and made the inner movement which raises you into the air.

His legs drawn up to his stomach, her husband Alik slept on; in the next room, in exactly the same position, her son was sleeping. It was the start of the spring equinox, a glorious festival of the heavens.

CHAPTER 16

Medea received the telegram twenty-four hours later. Klava the postmistress delivered it in the morning. Telegrams were sent in three eventualities: Medea's birthday, the imminent arrival of relatives, and a death.

With the telegram in her hand she went through to her room and sat down in the armchair which now stood where she herself used to stand, facing the icons. She sat there for a considerable time, moving her lips, then got up, washed out her cup, and got ready for the journey. From her illness in the autumn she still had a disagreeable stiffness in her left knee, but she was used to it by now and just moved a little more slowly than usual. Then she locked the house up and took the key to the Kravchuks.

The bus stop was nearby. It was the same route her guests usually took, from the Village to Sudak, from Sudak to the bus station at Simferopol, and from there to the airport.

She was in time for the last flight and late that evening rang the doorbell of Alexandra's house in Uspensky Lane, which she had never visited before. Her sister opened the door to her. They had not seen each other since 1952, twenty-five years. They embraced and shed floods of tears. Lidia and Vera had just left. Her face swollen with tears, Nike came out into the lobby and clung to Medea.

Ivan Isaevich went to put on the kettle. He guessed this was his wife's elder sister come from the Crimea. He vaguely recollected some kind of long-standing feud between them. Medea took off the downy head scarf which made her look as if she had just come up from the country. Beneath it the black scarf was wound around her head and Ivan Isaevich was amazed by her iconic face. He saw a great resemblance between the sisters.

Medea sat down at the table, looked around the unfamiliar house, and gave it her approval. This was a good place.

Masha's death was a great sorrow, but it had also brought Alexandra Georgievna a great joy, and now she was puzzling over how one person could contain such different emotions at the same time.

Medea for her part, sitting to her left, simply couldn't imagine how it had come about that she had not seen the person dearest to her for a quarter of a century, and was horrified. There really seemed to be no good reason or explanation for it.

"It was an illness, Medea, a serious illness, and nobody understood it at all. Alik's friend, a psychiatrist, apparently examined her a week ago and said she needed to be taken into the hospital straightaway: she had an acute manic-depressive psychosis. He prescribed some drugs. They were waiting for permission to emigrate any day, you see. That was the problem. But I could see there was something wrong with her. I didn't hold her hand the way I did before. I'll never forgive myself," Alexandra blamed herself.

"Do stop, for God's sake, Mama! Don't blame yourself for this at all. It really is my . . . Medea, Medea, how am I to live with this? I can't believe it," Nike sobbed, while her lips, designed by nature herself for laughter, seemed still to be smiling.

The funeral took place not on the third day, as would have been usual, but on the fifth. There was a postmortem. Alik came with two friends and Georgii to the forensic-medicine mortuary somewhere near the Frunze Metro station.

Nike was already there. She had wound a piece of white crepe de Chine around Masha's shaven head and neck, on which the prosector's coarse stitches had been visible, and tied it with a firm knot at the temple in the way Medea did. Masha's face was untouched, pale and waxen, its beauty undefiled.

The priest from the Preobrazhenka church, which Masha had attended occasionally over the last few years, was deeply saddened but refused to conduct a funeral service for a suicide, so Medea asked to be taken to a Greek church. The most Greek of the Moscow churches was one affiliated to the Antioch congregation. There, in the church of Theodore Stratilatos, she asked to see the dean, but the serving woman subjected her to an interrogation. While she was explaining, with her lips pursed and her eyes lowered, that she was a Pontic Greek and had not been in a Greek church for many years, an old hieromonk came up and said in Greek, "I can recognize a Greek woman from a long way off. What is your name?"

"Medea Sinoply."

"Sinoply . . . Is your brother a monk?" he asked quickly.

"One of my brothers went to a monastery in the 1920s, in Bulgaria. I have had no news of him since."

"Agathon?"

"Athanasii."

"Praise be to the Lord," the hieromonk exclaimed. "He is a hermit on Mount Athos."

"Glory be to the Lord." Medea bowed.

They had some difficulty understanding each other. The old man proved to be not Greek but Syrian. His Greek and Medea's were very different. They talked for over an hour sitting on a bench beside the candle box. He told her to bring the girl and promised to conduct the service himself.

When the bus with the coffin arrived at the church, a crowd had already assembled. The Sinoply family had representatives of all its branches: Tashkent, Tbilisi, Vilnius, and Siberia. The various golds of the church's icon frames, candlesticks, and vestments were complemented by the different shades of copper on Sinoply heads.

Ivan Isaevich stood between Medea and Alexandra, a broad man with a floury pink face and an asymmetrical wrinkle running obliquely across his forehead. The elderly sisters standing before the coffin adorned with white and lilac-colored hyacinths both had the same thought: "It would be more fitting for me to be lying there among these flowers which Nike has arranged so beautifully, and not poor Masha."

In the course of a long life they had learned to live with death, to be at ease with it: they had learned to meet it at home, veiling the mirrors, living two strict, quiet days in the presence of the body to the murmuring of psalms and the flickering of candles. They had known peaceful departures, painless and dignified; they had known of death at the hands of roughnecks, and the lawless invasion of death when the young perished in the lifetime of their parents.

But suicide was more than anyone could bear. What reconciliation could there be to that fleeting moment when a young lively girl had leapt of her own volition out into the slow rumbling whirlpool of snowflakes and out of life.

The hieromonk came out to the coffin, and the choir began singing the most expressive words of all those composed in times of earthly leave-taking and separation. The service was in Greek and even Medea understood only certain words, but all those present could clearly feel that in this bitter, inaccessible singing there was more meaning than even the wisest sage can contain within himself.

Those who wept, wept silently. Aldona wiped away her tears with a man's checkered handkerchief. Gvidas the Hun nervously wiped a leather glove under his eye. Debora Lvovna, Masha's mother-in-law, was all for wailing in loud lamentation, but Alik gave his doctor friends the nod and they led her from the church.

Masha was buried in the Foreigners' Cemetery, in the same grave as her parents, and then everyone went back to Uspensky Lane: Alexandra Georgievna had insisted on having the funeral party there. There were a lot of people, and there was space at the table only for the older ones and relatives who had come a long way. The young people were all on their feet, with glasses and bottles.

Little Alik found a moment to ask his father in a whisper, "Daddy, do you think she has died for always?"

"Soon everything will change and then everything will be fine," his father answered diplomatically.

Little Alik gave him a long, cold look. "Well, I don't believe in God."

On the morning of that day, their permission to emigrate had arrived. They were given twenty days to pack their things, which was fairly generous. In the memory of their friends the farewell merged with the funeral party, although Alik arranged it in Cheryomushki.

Debora Lvovna duly stayed with her sister, and Alik left with his son and a checkered medium-sized Bulgarian suitcase. The customs officials took one sheet of paper from him—Masha's last poem, written shortly before her suicide. Needless to say, he knew it by heart.

> *Researching lures the intellectual sleuth*
> *to hurl himself into his sweet researches.*
> *He plots the ways of pigeons, or he lurches*
> *through dusty tavern vaults in search of truth;*
>
> *But even as he struggles to attain*
> *experience appearances belying—*

he will himself become the pigeon's wing,
the demon drink of all his mental prying;

And beavering to secure our daily bread,
removed from fears and cares and snares infernal,
we stand in awe and meekly bow our head
before a soul dissolved in fame eternal.

EPILOGUE

The last time my husband and I were in the Village was in the summer of 1995. Medea had passed on long before. A Tatar family was living in her house, and we didn't feel right about going in to trouble them. We went to see Georgii. He built his house even higher up than Medea's and drilled his artesian well. His wife Nora still looks like a child, although close up you can see that the skin under her eyes is dissected by fine wrinkles, which is how the most delicate blondes age.

She has given Georgii two daughters.

The house was very full. I had difficulty recognizing these young people as the grown-up children of the 1970s. A five-year-old girl with ginger curls who looked very like Liza was throwing a tantrum over some kind of little-girl nonsense.

Georgii was glad to see my husband, whom he hadn't seen for a long time. My husband is a Sinoply too, not from Harlampy's branch, but from that of his younger sister Polixena. They calculated the degree of their relatedness at great length before deciding they were third cousins.

Georgii took us to the graveyard. Medea's cross stands next to Samuel's obelisk, and modestly yields to it in height. Georgii told us on the way back how unpleasantly surprised Medea's relatives had been when a will was discovered after her death leaving the house to a Ravil Yusupov nobody knew anything about.

They made no attempt to trace this Yusupov, and Georgii moved into Medea's house with Nora, Tanya, and their little daughters. He got a job at the research station.

Ravil appeared a few years later, in just the same way as when he had come to see Medea, late on an early spring evening. Georgii produced the will out of the trunk and showed it to him. Several more years were to pass, however, before Ravil could take possession of his house. For two years there was an absurd lawsuit to change the registration of ownership of the house, and this was ultimately achieved purely through Georgii's doggedness in taking the case all the way to the republican level in order to have Medea's will proved. After that, everyone in the Village considered him completely mad.

He is past sixty now, but as strong and sturdy as ever. He was given a lot of help in building his own house by Ravil and his brother. When the house was completed, the people in the Village changed their minds and now say Georgii was fiendishly cunning: instead of getting Medea's ramshackle old house, he has a new one twice as big.

This was the house in which we spent the evening. The summer kitchen is very much like Medea's. There are the same copper jugs, the same crockery. Nora has learned to gather the local herbs, and bunches of drying herbs hang from the walls just as they used to.

There have been many changes over this period. The family has spread over the world even more widely. Nike has long been living in Italy, married to a fat rich man who is witty and charming. She looks matronly and simply loves it when relatives from Russia come to visit her in her luxurious house in Ravenna.

Liza lives in Italy too, but Katya didn't take to the country. As sometimes happens in children with dual nationality, she has become a raging Russophile. She came back to Moscow and lives in Usachevka, and the red-haired little girl who was making such a scene in the courtyard was her daughter.

Big Alik has become a member of the American Academy of Sciences, and before you know it may become a benefactor of humanity by discovering a drug against old age; but Little Alik after graduating from Harvard University reverted to Orthodox Judaism, learned Hebrew, put on a *kipa*, grew earlocks, and is currently studying all over again in a yeshiva in Bnei Brak, in Israel.

Little Alik published a collection of Masha's poetry a few years after the move to America. Georgii showed us this slim volume. It has a portrait of her on the first page taken from a snapshot of the last summer she spent in the Crimea. She has turned and is looking into the lens with delighted surprise. I won't attempt to assess her poems: they are a part of my life, because I too spent that last summer in the Village staying with my children at Medea's house.

Butonov really took to his house in Rastorguevo, and moved his wife and daughter there after a great deal of persuading. He has had a son of whom he is inordinately proud. He has not been working in sports medicine for a long time now: he changed direction and works with spinal patients, of whom he has had a regular supply first from the war in Afghanistan and then from the war in Chechnya.

All the older generation have passed on except for Alexandra Georgievna. She is a tough old lady, already nearing ninety. After Masha's death she came here every summer. She and Ivan Isaevich were here for Medea's last year, and Alexandra saw her sister to the grave.

The last two years she hasn't come to the Crimea. It has become too much for her.

Ivan Isaevich considers both sisters to be saints, but Alexandra smiles a smile which old age hasn't dimmed and corrects her husband: "Only one of us was a saint."

I am so glad that through my husband I became a member of this family, and that my children have a little Greek blood, Medea's blood, in them. To this day her children come to the Village: Russian, Lithuanian, Georgian, and Korean. My husband hopes that next year, if the money can be found, we will bring our little granddaughter here, the child of our older daughter-in-law, a black American born in Haiti.

It is a wonderful feeling, belonging to Medea's family, a family so large that you can't know all its members by sight, and they merge into a vista of things that happened, things that didn't, and things that are yet to come.

1996

Printed in the United States
by Baker & Taylor Publisher Services